TWILIGHT OF AVALON

A NOVEL OF TRYSTAN & ISOLDE

ANNA ELLIOTT

A TOUCHSTONE BOOK

PUBLISHED BY SIMON & SCHUSTER

NEW YORK LONDON TORONTO SYDNEY

Touchstone
A Division of Simon & Schuster, Inc.
1230 Avenue of the Americas
New York, NY 10020

First Touchstone trade paperback edition May 2009

TOUCHSTONE and colophon are registered trademarks
of Simon & Schuster, Inc.

For information about special discounts for bulk purchases,
please contact Simon & Schuster Special Sales at
1-800-456-6798 or business@simonandschuster.com.

The Simon & Schuster Speakers Bureau can bring authors to your live event.
For more information or to book an event contact the Simon & Schuster
Speakers Bureau at 866-248-3049 or visit our website at www.simonspeaker.com.

Designed by Carla Jayne Little

Manufactured in the United States of America

10   9   8   7   6   5   4   3   2   1

Library of Congress Cataloging-in-Publication Data
Elliott, Anna.
    Twilight of Avalon / by Anna Elliott.
        p. cm.
    1. Iseult (Legendary character)—Fiction. 2. Tristan (Legendary
character)—Fiction. I. Title
PS3605.L443T85 2009
813'.6—dc22   2008021830

ISBN-13: 978-1-4165-8989-1
ISBN-10:   1-4165-8989-9

To my Dad, who taught me to write

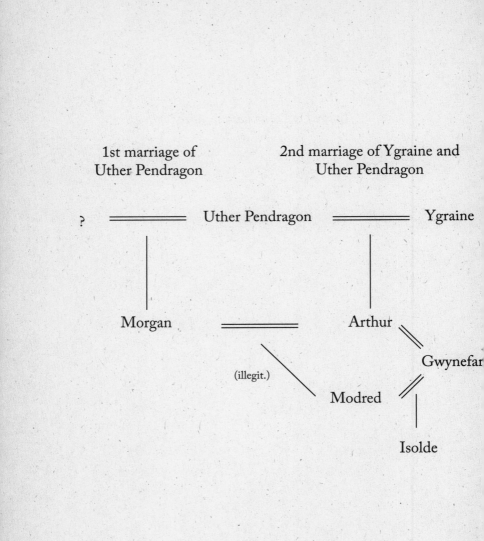

1st marriage of
    Ygraine

═══════   Gorlois of Cornwall ═══════   ?

                                       (mistress)

                             (illegit.)

                    Cador

═══════   Constantine
                  (mother unknown)

Dramatis Personae

Dead Before the Story Begins

Arthur, High King of Britain, father of Modred, brother of Morgan; killed in the battle of Camlann

Constantine, Arthur's heir as Britain's High King; husband to Isolde

Gwynefar, Arthur's wife; betrayed Arthur to become Modred's queen; mother to Isolde

Modred, Arthur's traitor son and Isolde's father; killed in fighting Arthur at Camlann

Morgan, mother to Modred; believed by many to be a sorceress

Uther Pendragon, father of Arthur

Rulers of Britain

Coel, King of Rhegged

Huel, eldest son of King Coel of Rhegged

Isolde, daughter of Modred and Gwynefar; Lady of Camelerd; Constantine's High Queen
Madoc, King of Gwynedd
Marche, King of Cornwall
Owain, King of Powys

Outside Tintagel's Walls

Bran, a young escaped slave
Brother Columba, a Christian hermit
Hereric, a Saxon and friend to Trystan
Kian, a former British soldier, now outlaw
Trystan, a Saxon mercenary and outlaw

Others

Cerdic, King of Wessex, a Saxon
Octa, King of Kent; a Saxon
Brychan, captain of Constantine's guard
Cyn, Saxon prisoner at Tintagel; comrade of Trystan
Dera, camp follower and prostitute
Ector, Constantine's armorer
Erbin, soldier of King Marche's guard
Hedda, Saxon slave and serving woman to Isolde
Hunno, soldier of King Marche's guard
Myrddin, a druid and Arthur's chief bard
Nest, cousin and chatelaine to King Marche
Marcia, Nest's serving maid

Isolde's Britain

Rhegged

Ynys Mon

Gwynedd

Mercia

Anglia

Powys

Dyfed

Gwent

LONDON

Camelerd

Kent

TINTAGEL

Dumnonia

Wessex

Cornwall

Prologue

I am a singer, I am steel.
I am a druid, I am a serpent.
I am love.

So I SAY TO CALL the visions into the scrying bowl.
Three drops of oil to sweeten the waters. Three drops of
blood as payment to lift the veil.

*In the name of earth and fire, water and air. By the silver Lady
and the golden Lord. Make this space a place of joining, a world between the worlds. Let the nine silver apples chime.*

Let Avalon be reborn here.

The bowl's pattern is as old as the words. Though the trac-
ings are worn smooth, I can follow them yet with the fingers of
one hand, for they are familiar as the lines on my palm. Serpents
of eternity, forever swallowing their tails.

And I wonder if it be true what they say, that time is an
endless curve. And in what form I'll be reborn when the wheel
makes another round. What body Arthur will fill.

And whether that turning will, at last, be a time for love.

My name is Morgan. "Sea-begotten," it means, in the old tongue. Morgan of Avalon. Water faerie of the sacred glass isle.

An exalted name indeed for the unwanted girl-child of Uther the Pendragon's murdered bride. But then, even in this world, we all rise and fall on the turnings of the serpent's wheel.

"Are you ready?" I say, and the girl at my side nods.

Isolde, her mother called her. Beautiful one.

"Then close your eyes."

I give her two twigs, one in each outstretched hand. "Now tell me which is the alder and which the beech."

She starts to rub the bark with her thumb, but I make her stop, twitching another twig hard against the back of her hand.

"Not with your fingers. With your mind. There is a voice to all living things. A thread that ties us to Dana, the Great Mother Earth. That echoes like the strings of an unseen harper's lyre, if only we can teach ourselves to hear. Reach into yourself for the space where the harp strings are tied, and you will hear the voice of the twigs. Or of the trees. Or of women and men and the threads that weave the pattern of our lives, joining future and past as one.

"And that is the Sight. A gift of the Old Ones, yours by birth and by blood."

WHEN AT LAST I ALLOW HER to look in the scrying bowl, the water shows only swirling oil and dispersing blood. Then, slowly, slowly, a newborn babe's face takes shape. Reddened with crying, the small mouth puckered in a silent O. And an old, grizzle-haired man in a tattered robe of the druid-born stoops over the child's cradle and lifts one hand.

Is this, I wonder, where the story begins? When the High King Uther, Pendragon of Britain—my father—made war on

Gorlois of Cornwall? When he swore his lies of adultery and witchcraft as excuse to see my mother burn? When he took Gorlois's lady Ygraine as his queen and got on her a son. And bribed his druids with gold to call it the gods' will and prophesy that only the child of Uther and Ygraine would save Britain from the invading Saxon hordes.

There was a king, once, King Arthur, son of the Pendragon and his queen Ygraine. Destined from birth to battle back the Saxon tide.

So run the harpers' songs.

Or does the tale begin earlier still? With the first Saxon who set foot on Britain's shore, the first drop of blood spilled when he seized land not his own? Or earlier yet, when the Romans sacked the holy places and groves of the Old Ones.

When Avalon, once the druids' holy isle, became in this world only a name in a tale.

The babe and the old man shimmer and dissolve. The water is clouded for an instant, then shapes begin to form once more.

A boy's face, now. He is almost a man. Flushed with drink, eyes both clouded and bright, face still smeared with a rusty streak of dried blood. He raises a drinking horn and throws the draft back, laughs and waves the cup, shouting for more.

So all men look, after a battle won.

His head weaves as he scans the room. Then his eyes fix on a girl. A year or two older than the girl at my side, but with the same black hair and milk-pale skin.

Isolde is very like me indeed. Or like what I was at fifteen.

The boy-man smiles. And I have to fight to keep from plunging my hands into the scrying bowl, from tipping it out onto the floor. But the waters are kind after all. The picture breaks and dissolves, and my granddaughter will not see how Modred, her father, was made.

All these years gone by, and the hurt is still there, an ember ready to blaze into flame, a taste in my mouth as bitter as bile.

Though, in fairness, Arthur was young as well. I suppose I may grant him that now. And far gone in drink, as the water showed. Too far gone to hear a girl crying "no" or recognize her for his own half sister? Or to care whether she was branded whore?

That I cannot say.

When the image in the water forms again, a woman wearing the habit of a Christian holy woman sits on the wooden pallet in a narrow cell. The cell is empty, save for a tallow candle and a jar of water on the floor. She stares at the wall, her eyes unseeing and blank and the same clear gray in color as those of the girl at my side.

And then she seizes the water jar and hurls it as hard as she can against the floor.

I suppose I should be sorry for Gwynefar, Arthur's bride. I, who knew best all what Arthur was. Knew that to expect her to grow a spine and fight would have been like asking a rabbit to stand against a pack of wolves.

A wonder, really, that she ever had the nerve to betray Arthur with my son. Though she fled to a convent rather than chance facing her husband's wrath.

At least she died soon after, and the child was left to my care. And she's nothing like her mother, praise be. For all she has Gwynefar's gray eyes.

With the breaking jar, the image in the scrying bowl breaks as well, then forms again. One last time.

Two men. Almost they might be brothers. Black hair and broad shoulders and deep-set dark eyes.

Modred pulls the tunic over his head and starts to bathe, splashing water over his chest. His skin is golden-tan.

The second man watches, and his face looks . . . hungry. He licks dry lips.

A warrior, this man, with the scars of battle on his face and the backs of his arms. And yet, in his eyes, I at least can See the shadow of a boy, one who aches all over with his father's blows and tries his hardest not to cry. Because you're only punished if you're weak. And maybe tomorrow his father will love him if only he can learn to be brave.

Maybe we all have a child like that buried deep inside. And it's only that Marche of Cornwall's buried child has never stopped crying in all these long years.

Sometimes I would give much to relinquish the gift of Sight. To look at Arthur and see only the king, not the boy who was given the throne and a sword too heavy for him to wield when Uther our father fell. Who walked the practice yard at night in fear that he'd fail to live up to the prophecies and fire-tales and tickled the stable cats for the warmth of their fur.

The Modred in the scrying bowl looks up. Catches Marche watching. Sees the look on the other man's face. Hunger—no, more than that. Desire. And for a moment my son is stunned. Then disgust blooms, naked and involuntary and unguarded, in his eyes.

And without a word, Marche turns and strides from the room, and the image is gone. The bowl holds nothing but water and blood and oil.

I look down at the child at my side. I suppose it is some compensation for being captured in a tale. If a soul lives with each mention of its name, I will be forever young and beautiful as the Morgan in the tales.

As this child is now.

She has the healer's hands, as well as the Sight. A wicked temper, too. That's also mine.

And she has now a glimpse, at least, of the blood and flesh and bone beneath the songs the bards sing.

There was a king, once, King Arthur, son of the Pendragon and his queen Ygraine. Destined from birth to battle back the Saxon tide.

Arthur's queen was Gwynefar, of the white hands and golden hair.
And under Arthur the Brave there was peace in Britain, and the
land without pillage and fear.

But Gwynefar the queen bore King Arthur no heir.

And so Arthur named Modred his heir. Modred, son of his sister
Morgan, whom some say was a wisewoman, some say a witch. But
of all the men who fought at Arthur's side, none was braver, or more
loved by the king, than Modred his heir.

But Modred it was who betrayed his king. Who seized the throne.
Coerced Gwynefar to betray Arthur, her lord. Who begot on Gwyne-
far a daughter, child of treason and sin.

So run the harpers' songs. Bright threads in the tapestry of
the land.

I wonder if the tales, as much as anything I or Modred or
Arthur has done, have led to this moment, this meeting at Camlann. And all at once I am cold, with a crawling feeling I am
deadly afraid is fear. And there is no place for fear now.

Marche, strongest of my son's allies, is gone. And tomorrow
two kings will meet in battle. Arthur and Modred. My brother
and his—my—son.

Stories I've told, countless numbers of them, of a time before
Britain, of worlds beyond our own. When I stitched a soldier's
wound or helped a mother bring her child into the world. But
this story—my own—could I have made it a tale of forgiveness
instead of vengeance? Blessing instead of bane?

Or were the threads of this story woven long ago, by a hand
other than mine, the ending fixed, unchangeable as one of the
old druid tales?

In an instant, I have caught up the knife, drawn it hard across
the palm of my hand, then across the girl's. My son's daughter.
And Arthur's grandchild, as well as the child his wife bore another man. That thought seems very strange.

She gasps, but does not cry.

The priests of the Christians preach fire and hell-fury against the old ways. But their God once demanded his blood sacrifice as well, in payment for men's souls.

I let the blood drip into the clouded waters of the bowl. If I have trapped the child beside me in the net of a tale, let this blood offering join us somewhere, beyond the veil. Let her be protected. Let me see her safe from harm.

BOOK 1

Chapter One

THE DEAD MAN'S EYES WERE weighted with gold. From the chapel doorway, Isolde saw the coins wink and gleam in the light of the candles that burned on the altar above. Payment for the holy women who would ferry him across the waters to the Isle of Glass. Or perhaps only a means to keep the sightless eyes closed; this was a church, consecrated to the Christ-God, after all. The old ways would have no place here.

Isolde stood still, her eyes adjusting to the dimness of the place. Even the chapel at Tintagel smelled of the sea; the stones even here thrummed like a bard's harp with the echo of all the fortress's walls had seen. Of Uther the Pendragon defeating Duke Gorlois and winning the duke's wife Ygraine for his queen. Of the birth of Arthur, Lord of Battles. Arthur, who had ridden out from these walls to drive the Saxons back with blow after crushing blow, and so won peace in Britain, for a time.

And all of that, Isolde thought, ended here, now, with the death of this king. Constantine, Arthur's heir.

She had seen fighting men with spear or sword wounds turned putrid, so far gone that the arm or leg had to be taken off if the soldier's life was to be saved. She'd made the cuts herself, had held the hot knives to cauterize the severed limbs and stop the bleeding. And seen how, for a brief, blessed moment after the glowing metal touched their skin, the men were numb, immune from pain, before they fainted or started to scream.

It was the same with her now.

The autumn dusk was drawing in, carrying with it the salt-laden mist that drifted up jagged cliffs from the ocean below, and the chapel felt dank and chill. And maybe, Isolde thought, the peace was ended long ago, when Arthur himself fell. And all these last seven years have only been part of that same long, crumbling fall.

A shield, likewise bearing the bloodred badge of the Pendragon, rested on the dead man's chest, and on the floor all about the coffin lay the great battle-axes, the knives, the helmet with its royal circlet of gold, and the jeweled and gilded sword that he had once carried into battle. Isolde drew her cloak more closely about her. Then she stepped out of the shadow of the arched lintel above.

Instantly, the armed and helmeted guard to the left of the altar stiffened to attention, his hand moving reflexively to the hilt of his sword. His fellow, the broader, taller man of the two, had been standing at the side of the coffin, his back to Isolde, but at the sound of Isolde's footsteps he whirled to face her, as well. Isolde looked from one man to the other. Neither guard was known to her, but she recognized the emblem of the wild boar blazoned on their shields.

Marche's men.

She let the hood of her cloak slip to her shoulders, and saw them relax slightly, as they caught sight of her face. She could remember one of the older serving women telling her, with venomous sweetness, that she was the very image of what her grandmother had been when young.

The harpers' tales spoke of Morgan's fairness. Of raven-black hair and milk-white skin and a beauty to entrap and ruin a man's soul. But it was not for beauty's sake that Isolde was thankful, at times like this, if she was like Morgan, the daughter of Avalon. The grandmother who, for seven years now, had been to her nothing but a name in those same tales.

The guards had dropped their heads in greeting, but now the man who had stood by the coffin straightened and spoke.

"You are alone, lady?"

He was the elder of the two, forty or forty-five, his face hard, scarred with the marks of battle, his hands large and powerful. "You should not have come out without a guard."

A thin prickle rose on the back of Isolde's neck, but she said only, "I wish to keep vigil a time. I require no guard here."

She saw the two men exchange a quick sidelong glance, and then the first man said flatly, "You have a moment to say what prayers you will—and then we will see you return safely to the women's hall. There is danger everywhere in such times as these."

Isolde stiffened, her brows lifting, and said, before she could stop herself, "Do you tell me so, indeed?" Then her gaze fell once more on the motionless figure beneath the dragon shield, and she drew a slow breath, willing herself to keep the flare of anger from her tone.

"May I know the names of those who keep such careful guard on my life?"

Again she saw the eyes of the two men slide sideways, the candlelight gleaming in the whites of their eyes. Then the elder said, "I am Hunno, lady, and this"—his head jerked toward his companion—"is Erbin."

"Very well, then, Hunno . . . Erbin." She looked from one man to the other. "I thank you—both of you—for your concern. But my lord husband and king has been dead but three days. And I would be alone with my sorrow. You are released from your duties here for the evening. You may go."

"Thank you, lady." Hunno's jaw was set, his voice still harsh. "But we have our orders from my lord Marche. We stay."

A chill ran through Isolde at the memory of what it had cost her to get away on her own, even for this brief time. And all for nothing, she thought, if I cannot force them to go.

"Orders?" she repeated. "My lord Marche may be king of Cornwall, but Tintagel is still the domain of the High King, as it has been since the Pendragon took the throne. It is not Marche who gives orders here."

"Is that so, lady?" A sly, ugly light appeared in Hunno's eyes. "Who is it who gives orders, then? As you say"—he jerked his head backwards toward the coffin and the gleaming weapons of war—"your husband King Constantine lies dead. Even a king's widow has small power on her own."

The second guard, a slight, dark youth with a thin, nervous face, stirred uneasily at Hunno's words and made to lay a restraining hand on his companion's arm, but Hunno shook him off with an impatient twist and took a step toward Isolde.

"Well, my lady?"

Isolde forced herself to stand without moving. "Have you forgotten, Hunno," she asked softly, "who I am?"

Hunno had started to take another step forward, but now he checked, and she saw a flicker of something that might have been fear stir at the back of his gaze.

Isolde's own eyes moved again to the still figure in the coffin, the hands lying limp against the folds of the crimson lining. Then she drew in her breath, looked up, and said, "Leave me. But before you go, return the ring you took from my husband's right hand."

She heard the younger man, Erbin, catch his breath in a sharp gasp, but Hunno didn't move. Fear pulled tight inside her, and she thought, as she always thought at such times, If, after all, I have guessed wrong . . .

There was time for her to count seven beats of her own heart while she forced herself to wait, hand extended, keeping her eyes on Hunno's.

And at last, with an angry mutter and a half-sullen, half-fearful look from under his brows, Hunno drew something out of his belt and dropped it into Isolde's outstretched hand.

For a moment, his gaze locked with Isolde's, and then he turned to Erbin. "Come on, then." His voice was angry, his tone gruff. "There'll be ale yet a while in the fire hall."

Hunno swung round on his heel, but before following, Erbin took a step toward Isolde and said, in a stammering rush, "Forgive us, lady. We did not mean—"

Isolde cut him off curtly, her hand tightening about the ring in her palm. "It's not for me to forgive. Make your peace with the king and go." She paused, looking again from one man to the other. Then she added, very quietly, "I will know if you disobey."

ISOLDE WAITED UNTIL THE SOUND OF their booted footsteps died away, then she pressed her eyes briefly closed, feeling a prickle of perspiration on her back, despite the cold. Then, slowly, she turned once more to the open casket. Seven years now, she thought. Seven years that I have fought this battle. But now I am left to fight it entirely alone.

She let out a shaking breath. *The stars will still shine tomorrow, whatever happens to me here.*

She'd repeated the words so often over the years that they held the same familiar echo as one of the old tales. And now, as always when she thought or spoke them, a vague memory stirred in the shadows of her mind, of someone speaking them to give her courage as she'd done countless times since.

But that was part of a lifetime—and a world—that had died

on the battlefield when Arthur fought her father, his traitor heir. Seven years ago. When she'd lost both Sight and memory of all that had gone before.

Isolde hadn't intended to move, but somehow she found herself at the edge of the coffin, looking down at the man who lay within and hearing the words she'd spoken seem to echo in the chapel's stillness. Alone with my sorrow, she thought. Alone with my sorrow, when I haven't even been able to cry for Con yet.

She had prepared the body for burial herself. Washed the blood and muck of the battlefield from his skin, anointed it with sweet oils. And seen in his side the blue-lipped, knife-thin wound where the dark heart's-blood had seeped out. But now, surrounded by the gleaming weapons, his head covered by the leather war helm, he seemed all at once frighteningly unreal. A figure from legend or song, remote as the great Arthur himself.

And yet, even now, Con's face looked scarcely older than that of the twelve-year-old boy he had been on the day of their crowning, his brow unlined beneath the wisps of straight, nut-brown hair, his skin smooth, with only a faint stubble of beard shadowing the rounded chin. Almost, she thought, he might be asleep.

Save for the folds of loosening flesh about the gold coins that covered his eyes.

A shudder twisted through her, and Isolde closed her own eyes, trying to summon up a memory of the living Constantine. The memory that came, though, was an older one. Not of the husband—or even of the man.

They had met only once before they were wedded and crowned. Only once—in the yard behind the stables of the great fortress of Caerleon, where the ceremonies had been held. Isolde had slipped away from her attendants and ladies to the only place she could be sure of finding a moment's solitude and peace. But instead, amid the muck and straw and broken-down wagons, she'd found Con, twelve years old to her thirteen, his leather tunic torn and streaked with horse dung, his chin blood-smeared, with a purpling bruise over his right eye.

He'd been kicking furiously and aimlessly at the broken spokes of a loose wagon wheel, his face flushed and angry, his jaw set. But there'd been something in his face—or maybe in the childish, oddly vulnerable curve of the back of his neck as he bent over the wheel—that had made Isolde speak to him instead of slipping quietly away to be alone as she'd meant.

"I can give you a salve for that, if you'd like."

He'd whirled, startled at the sound of her voice. His face, beneath strands of sweat-soaked brown hair, had still the full-cheeked, rounded look of childhood, though he'd been even then nearly full grown, taller than she herself by more than a foot, the broad planes of muscle along shoulders and back holding a man's strength—or the promise of it, at least. The look he gave her was guarded, his body tensed as though bracing to attack or to ward off a blow.

"What did you say?"

"Your eye." Isolde gestured toward his right eye, puffy and swollen nearly closed, and with a cut on the brow that had dripped a trail of blood onto temple and lid. "And your mouth, as well." His upper lip, too, was bruised and bloodied, shiny with spittle since it was too swollen to be comfortably closed, and crusted with drying fragments of what looked like mud.

"I don't—" he'd started to say, but Isolde had stopped him.

"Come up to my rooms. You'll feel better with something on those bruises." She paused, and, half against her will, a note of bitterness crept into her tone. "And we'd best get acquainted if we're to be married at the end of this week."

In the end he'd followed her without speaking, stood, rigid, in the center of Isolde's chambers while she drew out her box of medicines and salves. When she motioned him to sit on a low

wooden stool and started to swab his bruises with witch hazel,
though, he stiffened, and cast a quick, nervous glance around
the room.

"You won't—" he began. "I mean . . . they say your grandmother . . ."

"I know what they say."

A hot flush swept up under the clear, bright skin of his face.
"I'm sorry. I didn't mean . . ." He stammered to a halt again.

Isolde studied him, smearing all-heal salve over the cuts on
brow and eye. His hands were clenched tight at his sides, but
he'd made no sound, though Isolde knew she must be hurting
him a good deal, gentle as she tried to be.

She thought of Morgan—the grandmother Con had been
about to call sorceress or witch, if not something worse—and
an ache of grief rose in her throat. But she'd promised herself,
on the road to this place, that she'd not look back anymore. And
here, now, was this boy. Frightened and in pain and trying desperately to hide both.

"Do you know any stories?" Isolde asked.

Con looked up, startled, then swallowed heavily, gulping and
blinking away the tears that had risen to his eyes. "Stories? How
do you mean?"

Isolde turned to her medicine box and drew out needle and
thread. "The cut over your eye is deep—it should be stitched
if it's to heal properly. But I can tell you the story of Bran the
Blessed and his magical cauldron while I'm stitching it."

A press of tears burned behind her own eyes. No, she
thought. No more remembering. The past is a tale. Words.
Nothing more.

And already the memory of Morgan's face was fading.

Isolde frowned, deftly clipping off a length of thread and
passing it through the needle's eye. "It won't hurt as much if
you've something to think about besides the pain."

When at last she was done, Isolde returned the needle and thread to their case, then turned away to dispose of the dirtied linens and swabs.

"How did all this happen?" she asked.

Con had been gingerly touching mouth and eye, running a finger over the row of stitches now set over his brow, and at the question he hesitated. Then, "A horse kicked me," he muttered. "It was my fault. I—" He stopped. "I startled it. Made it buck and lash out."

Isolde's brows rose. "A bucking horse?" She shook her head. "If I couldn't tell lies better than that, I'd give up trying."

A flush—of anger, this time—spread up Con's neck to his face, his head snapping up. "Are you saying I'm a liar?"

Isolde eyes moved to the marks on Con's arm, visible beneath the sleeve of his tunic. The marks of fingers, clear and reddening angrily against the fair skin. "I'm saying, at any rate, that it's a rare horse with a hand to twist an arm behind your back and hold you down on the ground."

Abruptly, the flush faded from Con's cheeks. His shoulders sagged, and his head dropped again. He was silent so long Isolde thought for a moment he wasn't going to respond at all, but then at last he said, in a low, sullen tone, "It was Caw—he's one of Lord Marche's men."

Isolde nodded. She knew the man—or boy, rather, however much he might seem a man to Con. A heavyset, ugly boy of fifteen or sixteen, with a pasty, small-eyed face and powerful arms.

Con's eyes were still trained on the floor, and he said, in the same low tone, "We were practicing swordplay in the stable yard, and I got the better of him in the last match. And some of the others laughed and said hadn't he got any better skill than to be beat by"—his cheeks flushed again—"by a snot-nosed brat. And Caw got angry at that and said my—"

Con stopped abruptly, as though he'd recollected where

he was and to whom he spoke, and he glanced at Isolde, the flush on his cheeks darkening. "That is . . . I mean . . . he said I wouldn't . . ." He rubbed the back of his neck, seeming to grope for words, then gave up, his eyes falling again as he went on, his voice quick and almost toneless. "He said I'd have no better idea what to do with a wife in bed than a gelded horse would. And I said that I knew well enough—that I'd seen dogs hump a bitch in heat dozens of times, and breeding stallions serving mares. And he—"

Con stopped again, hands tight at his sides. "He laughed."

He almost spat the words, his eyes dark with remembered fury. Isolde herself had bitten her lip to hide a brief, unwilling smile of her own, but the smile faded almost at once. She could see the ugly little scene. Con shamed and humiliated in front of his fellows—the men and boys he would soon lead into battle as their crowned and anointed king.

And whether what Caw said was true or no, she thought, I'll belong to this boy soon enough. Body and spirit and mind, I'll be his, by the law of the land.

Con had gone on, the words coming in an angry rush. "I said at least I'd have a woman instead of fu— . . . of bedding goats and cows because I couldn't get anything else. And he said he'd make me eat horseshi— . . . dirt for that. We fought—but he got me in a wrestler's hold. One I didn't know. So—"

Con stopped, the flush on his cheekbones deepening again, his shoulders sagging once more. Isolde, watching him, understood, now, the streaks of filth about his mouth.

Con glanced sideways at her. "I suppose you'll not want to be wedded to me, now you know I lost a fight to a . . . a swine like him."

And small difference it would make, Isolde thought, if I did not. The flash of angry bitterness ebbed, though, as her eyes met Con's, dark and suddenly anxious, with a childish look of appeal overlaid only slightly by the struggle for indifferent calm. She thought briefly of giving him a soothing lie, then stopped herself. She owed him honesty, at least. And so she said, "I'd sooner wed you than anyone else, I suppose—if I've got to be wedded at all."

Con's brow furrowed, but then he let out his breath in a sigh and nodded, giving a slight, indifferent shrug. "I suppose that's the way I feel about it, as well." He stopped, then, the flash of anxiety visible once more at the back of his eyes, "You won't— you won't tell Marche, will you? About what happened today with Caw?" He stopped, then went on, awkwardly, "He . . . he doesn't know me much, yet. Only from the ride here with the rest of his men. But he's to be my regent. And if he found out, he'd be angry and say I wasn't fit to be king."

So, Isolde thought. You've already learned that much, at least, of Lord Marche. Marche, whose betrayal had cost her father the field of Camlann, and his life, as well. And her grandmother—

If not for Marche, Isolde thought, Morgan of Avalon would be alive still. And I'd not be here now, forced into marriage with this overgrown boy. But Con was watching her, his face still anxious and taut, and she said, "No. I won't tell. But Caw may, you know."

Con shook his head. "No, he won't."

"Why not?"

Con's jaw hardened, making his face appear strangely adult, childish no more. "Because after he'd made me eat the horseshit I gave him a couple of good fistings in the balls. It will be a while before he can say anything and not sound like a squeaking girl."

NOW, IN THE SILENT CHAPEL, ISOLDE opened her eyes and stared un- seeingly straight ahead, the twelve-year-old Con's face vivid in

her mind's eye, the rounded, childish planes of his face contrast-
ing so oddly with the slow, grim smile that had stretched his
mouth that long-ago day. Only a year younger than she'd been
herself, and yet, for all his strength and height, the difference in
their ages had seemed greater than that by far. As it always had,
even later on. And maybe, she thought, maybe that is why after
seven years of marriage, that boy Con seems, tonight, more real
to me than the man.

The soft footfall from behind made her whirl, heart jerking hard against her side. Then, as the spare, shadowed figure
stepped forward into the circle of candlelight, Isolde let out her
breath once more.

Myrddin. He had kept his promise, then, to come.

Myrddin Emrys, sometimes called the Enchanter or the
Prophet of Kings, was an ugly man. His face was narrow, with
a high, prominent forehead, a crooked nose, and a flowing
white beard that nearly covered a wide mouth and jaw. He
wore the white robe and bull's-hide cloak of the druid-born,
and beneath it his body was bent, gnarled with age, one leg
lame and twisted, the right shoulder a little higher than the
left.

Only his eyes were beautiful—his eyes, and his hands, as well.
His eyes were a deep, clear gray-blue, the color of the sea where
the lost land of Lyonesse was said to lie beneath the waves. And
his hands were slender, long-fingered and all but untouched by
age, save for the harper's calluses, worn with years of plucking
the instrument's strings.

He came toward her now, leaning heavily on the carved
oaken staff he carried, the lame leg dragging a little behind. The
hair that fell nearly to his shoulders was plaited with dozens of
tiny braids, and a raven feather had been bound on a leather
thong at the end of one braid, a streak of black against the snowy
white.

"Isa."

Isolde knew he'd not meant to hurt her, but all the same the old childhood name brought a sudden, fierce stab of longing, and for a moment Isolde wished, with all her heart, that she could go back. Back to the time before Camlann, before she had been wedded and crowned Britain's High Queen. Back to the time that, for seven years now, she'd not let herself remember at all.

"Thank you for coming, Myrddin."

She had seen him seldom in the years since she and Con had been crowned. He had left the court to wander the lands as a bard, to live in a cave, to journey to the western Isle of Glass, depending on which story you chose to believe. But always he would appear again at Tintagel, to meet with Con and the rest of the king's council before taking his leave once again. And he had arrived two days ago to pay final respects and join in the mourning for the High King.

"Did you doubt that I would?" His voice was slow and deep, with something of the cadence of the western lands where it was said he had been born—and something, as well, of the hum of a harp, lingering in the air a moment after the words themselves. A brief smile touched the corners of his thin-lipped mouth, just visible beneath the snowy beard. "I heard on the road coming here that I'd run mad and gone to live wild in the forest—taken to keeping pigs and enchanting them to speak back to me like men."

Then the smile faded as his gaze fell on the coffin. He touched something at his belt that at first glance looked like a strand of yellowed beads, but was, Isolde saw, the skeleton of a snake, strung on another thin leather thong. Myrddin's fingers caressed the yellowing bones, so that they moved almost with the semblance of life. Then, slowly, he raised one hand and made a brief gesture over Con's breast. His skin was papery with age, the hand blue-veined, but beautifully formed even still, the movement graceful and sure.

"There will be tales sung of him, now, in the fire halls," he said. "As well as of Arthur."

It was almost an echo of what Isolde had thought only a moment before. "Arthur, king that was," she said. "King that is. King that shall be. King who lies asleep in the mists of Avalon while his battle wounds heal—and will come again in the hour of Britain's greatest need."

Myrddin gave a short laugh, a breath of mirth, no more, eyes crinkling above the flowing beard. "I wonder," he said, "what Arthur himself would say if he could hear the tales told of him now. The harpers singing of how he bore a sword forged by the spirits of water and earth and triumphed at Badon by bearing the cross of Christ on his shoulders for three days and three nights."

He shook his head. "Probably the same as I do when I hear the poor fools babbling their tales of the Enchanter's magic and talking swine. Arthur, who bristled at all talk of magic like a dog facing wolves—and set foot inside a church only once, to my knowledge. And then it was to demand that the priests sell their silver and gold plate from the altar and pay taxes to fund the Saxon war as the common folk do."

Myrddin stopped, and then added in a different tone, "Few of the tales told of those times are true, child. No man—or woman, either—is entirely villain or hero, except perhaps in the memories of those who remain."

Isolde started to answer, but, outside, the wind must have shifted to blow from the west. For all at once she heard a voice in the blustering moan about the chapel walls. Soft and indistinct at first, as the voices always were. Then swelling until the sound blotted out all else.

She'd thought, at times like these, that perhaps the loss of the Sight had made her somehow a point of joining between present and past, truth and tale, like the hollow hills where the Otherworld and this one met.

Or maybe it was like the men in her care, who groaned aloud with ghost-pains in an arm or leg months, even years, gone. She'd felt the aching loss of Sight as much, these last seven years, as any amputated limb.

But though Sight was gone, every now and then—and only on a western wind—she would catch, briefly, the sound of a voice. The voice of someone who, like her grandmother, was nothing but a name to her now.

MY NAME IS MORGAN. BUT MEN have given me many names be-sides. Sorceress . . . witch . . . whore. And now I am dying.

A voice speaks beside me. The voice is sweet, clear, like the water I cannot swallow anymore, despite my cracked lips and swollen tongue. She is telling one of the old tales. As I taught her, long ago.

"Far away, in Avalon, the holy isle, nine silver apples chime on the tree bough."

I saw my face in the water jar yesterday. Raised myself up and looked when I was alone. I can feel the sores, but it is different to see. To see my face a ruin of blackened, running cankers. Once I might have mourned.

"And nine priestesses tend the Goddess flame," the voice goes on. "And time is a curve, without beginning or end."

I think, if I could feel anything at all, I would be afraid for her. But Arthur is dead. At last. And I am dust and ashes and nothing more.

I even begged Marche to let us leave this place. For her sake—not mine. I, Morgan, went down, pleading, on my knees. And even that roused in me no feeling. None at all.

Arthur is dead. And far away, on Avalon, the holy isle, nine sil-ver apples chime on the bough.

NOT THE SIGHT, FOR ALL THE voices seemed to echo in the hollow place inside her. The space where once she'd felt the voice of the earth, felt the ties that threaded together all life, and bound her up in the great pattern, as well.

These were only voices. Echoes. She Saw nothing at all.

As the voice now faded, Isolde drew in her breath. For a moment or two she knew—like a sleeper waking to the vague remembrance of a dream—that it was her grandmother's voice that the wind had carried this time. But a moment later, even that knowledge was gone. And, as always, the words she'd heard slid through her grasp like water through clenched hands.

Myrddin was watching her, eyes steady and grave, but he gave no sign that he, too, had heard the voice in the wind. Isolde moved her shoulder slightly, and said what she'd begun to say before.

"The tales are a comfort to those who tell them. And in times like these, there are many with cause to wish that Arthur might come again."

Myrddin nodded. "Arthur was a brave man. And a good one, at heart." He paused, then said quietly, looking down at Con's lifeless face and still hands, "As was the young king here."

Something in the old man's quiet tone pierced the numbness as nothing else in these long three days had, and brought the man, the husband Con, a step nearer. The man had struck her only once—and had cried after he'd done it like a child. Who'd loved her, in his way.

As I suppose, Isolde thought, I must have loved him. It had been so long since she'd let herself think of loving that she'd never allowed herself to put a name to what she'd felt for Con. *Friendship . . . respect . . . pity.* But love must have been there, as well, else she'd not now feel this raw, familiar ache of grief in her chest.

It was a moment before she could speak. Then, "Yes," she said softly, "Constantine was both brave and good. He would have made—did make—a fine king."

Myrddin nodded again, and Isolde saw in his high-browed face a look, not of weariness, exactly, or even of age, but of steady, clear-eyed sorrow.

"An evil day for Britain," he said at last. He paused, and when he went on, the Welsh lilt in his voice was stronger. "There is a story from the old times—the Old Way. A tale of the king of a wasted kingdom, who grew old and was slain that his blood might water the land. That with his death, he and the land he ruled might be healed and born again. But I can see only grief and bloodshed in the wake of this death now."

Isolde studied the lined, ugly face, the steady sea-blue eyes. Then she asked, "Myrddin, do you mind?"

Slowly, Myrddin looked from the coffin to the altar's gleaming cross, and from there round the high-roofed chapel hall. "You mean, do I mind that the old days are past?" he asked. "That doorways to Avalon are closed and Britain will one day be a Christian land?"

He paused, then shook his head slowly, one hand moving to lightly touch the serpent's skeleton once more. "To all under the sun there is an ebb and flow. And perhaps the old ways will not die after all, but only fade into the mists like Avalon itself and sleep with Arthur and his men."

The candlelight played across his face, deepening the shadows about his mouth and brow. His face was suddenly remote and ancient as a carving in stone, and Isolde saw, in that moment, what it was the common folk feared. But then he turned back to her, and the spell was abruptly broken, his face once more his own.

"No, child, I do not mind. The god of the Christ may not be mine, but I do not begrudge him the victory. Nor the priests who serve him in places like these."

His eyes, too, had cleared, and he studied her face a long moment without speaking. Isolde looked away. And how much, she thought, does he guess—or know?

It was Myrddin who broke the silence. "And now that I am here," he said, "what is it you would have me do?"

Isolde pushed aside the memory that had gathered, feeling as though she pried herself free of some great animal's jaws. "I would ask you to journey to Camelerd, the land I hold in my own right as last of my mother's line. A man called Drustan holds the kingdom for me. He has ruled there in my place since—"

She stopped. "Since my mother left the world behind. And since I was given in marriage to Con."

She looked up, and Myrddin nodded. "I have heard the name. A good man, so they say, and a strong fighter. Go on."

"I would ask you to carry the news of all that has occurred here to him. Tell him that my husband lies dead."

She broke off once more, her eyes instinctively sweeping the darkness beyond the pool of golden light in which she and Myrddin stood. All was silent and still, save for the distant throb of the sea far below, but still fear crawled over her at speaking the words aloud for the first time.

But if I cannot trust Myrddin, she thought, I can truly trust none.

"Tell Drustan," she went on, with an effort to steady her voice, "that whatever the rumors, Con died not by any blow from the Saxons, but by a traitor's hand."

Chapter Two

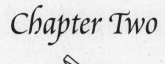

ONE OF THE ALTAR CANDLES guttered, sending a dancing play of shadow across the chapel's oaken benches and stone walls. Myrddin neither moved nor spoke, and the gray-blue eyes met Isolde's without a trace of surprise. Perhaps, she thought, the whispers about him are true. Or perhaps the Sight showed him, as well.

For a moment, the memory of Vision pressed against the backs of her eyes, and Isolde dug her nails hard into her palms with the effort of holding it at bay.

"Drustan has been hard pressed of late by Irish sea-raiders," she went on. "It was for that reason he could send no troops to aid in resisting this latest offensive of the Saxons against us in Cornwall—though Con summoned the kings from all parts of the realm to lend their aid. But Drustan will have heard that the battle was won. For the time, at least."

Isolde paused, looking down at her clenched hand. "With Constantine dead, though, another High King must be chosen —chosen from among those assembled at Tintagel now."

She stopped, and lifted from about her neck the gold chain that bore her own sealing ring, stamped with the image of the golden harp that had since ancient times been Camelerd's royal sign. She held the chain out to Myrddin.

"Here. Take this ring. Drustan will know, then, beyond question, that your message comes from me. Say . . . say that I ask him to come with all speed to my aid here, with as many men as his garrison can spare. For without him, I fear the throne of Britain will fall into a murderer's hands."

Her own hands had unconsciously knotted in the dark green folds of her gown, and she drew a breath, forcing her fingers to relax. Then she looked up at Myrddin once more. The old man held the sealing ring up to the light a moment, then nodded, securing it in the leather pouch tied at his belt.

"With luck and dry roads for travel, I shall return to you by Samhain."

His voice was still tranquil, his face calm, but all the same Isolde felt a sudden clutch of fear.

"Myrddin, are you sure? The journey to Camelerd will be a dangerous one, through lands firmly under Saxon control. I would not lay this on you against your will."

Myrddin shook his head. "Less danger for me than for any other you might send. I will have my harp, and those on the road, Briton and Saxon alike, will see only a poor old wandering bard, anxious to find a place at the fire of some lord before the winter snows." He turned once more to the coffined form, and his hand moved in a gesture Isolde recognized, this time, as one of blessing or farewell.

"I will go," he said, some of the cadence of a harper's song creeping again into his tone. "I will go for the sake of Constantine, nephew and heir to Arthur, the king I served as advisor and bard." He was still a moment, looking down at Con. Then he raised his head and added, more gently, "And for your sake, Isa." He paused. "I would that I might have spared you much of what you have borne these past years."

Isolde turned her head slightly away. "There are many far worse off than I have been."

Myrddin let out his breath in something like a sigh, and Isolde wondered, for the first time, how old he was now. He'd changed scarcely at all since her first sight of him, nearly ten years ago. But he'd been present when Arthur himself was crowned. And he'd been an old man even then.

"You'd not be wrong in blaming me, though," Myrddin said. "It was I who persuaded the king's council that you should be wedded to the young king. I thought it the best that could be done for you, but . . ."

He paused, a faint smile, slightly tinged with sadness, touching the corners of his mouth. "I could wish, sometimes, for half the powers credited to me by the harpers' songs. If I—"

Isolde stopped him. "You're not to blame. If I'd not been wedded to Con, I would only have been sent to join my mother in taking the veil—locked in a nun's cell for the rest of my days."

Myrddin didn't answer at once. Instead he watched her a moment, as though reading something more than she'd meant to reveal in her tone. "I don't suppose you remember her, do you?" he asked at last. "Your mother, Gwynefar."

Isolde was silent, listening to the bluster of the wind outside. "I don't remember her, no," she said after a moment. "She took the veil almost as soon as I was born, you know. And died soon after."

Myrddin nodded, and for a moment Isolde caught again that shadow of sorrow in his lined face. "She had her path to follow. As had Arthur. And Modred. And as I have mine."

He stopped, and then put a hand on her shoulder, his eyes

again steady and very clear on hers. "Remember that, Isa. That I have chosen this path. That you have laid nothing on me but what I choose to take up as mine."

The words were calmly spoken, but the sea-blue eyes had clouded, and Isolde felt another cold press of fear, stronger now, seeming to seep into her very bones.

She asked, "Myrddin, have you seen something of how this will end?"

But at that, the old man smiled again, shaking his head. "Would you tell me, then, that you believe the tales, as well? That Merlin"—he used the name given him by the common folk—"Merlin the Enchanter has lived time backwards? That he sees past and future as one?"

He paused. Then: "Whatever my end, it will not be on the road to Camelerd. That much I can promise you. But all the same—"

He stopped, smile lines gathering about the corners of his eyes. "All the same, if anything should happen to me, make up a story for me—one last tale to be sung at the hearths and the taverns and halls. Say"—the smile spread to the wide line of his mouth beneath the beard—"say that I was enchanted away by one of the fair-folk to dwell in the hollow hills. That would be a fitting end for the sorcerer's tale."

Isolde felt his hand tighten, briefly, on her shoulder, and then he turned, melting into the shadows with scarcely a sound, as though he were an enchanter indeed.

As she stood listening to the soft footfalls die away, Isolde felt, suddenly, as though he were already gone, vanished, as he had said, into the glass isles and hollow hills of the fairy world. And more than that.

To all things, he had said, there is an ebb and a flow. And if Arthur's death had been the end to a tale, it seemed to Isolde that she stood now at a twilight, the end of an age.

She closed her eyes, concentrating all of her will on the desperate hope that Myrddin would end his journey in safety, would return to Tintagel alive. And then she thought, with a bitter pang, That is all I can do, now.

It might have been those echoing snatches she'd heard on the wind—or the looming memory of what she had Seen three nights before—that made her close her eyes and try, one last time. She stood utterly still, listening to the beat of her own heart, forcing her breaths to quiet and slow, as though she could summon out of shadows dancing over the stone walls the shifting barrier that hung like the sea fog itself between this world and the Other, between the room about her and the realms beyond.

Seven years ago, the mists would have cleared for her without effort; now, even the attempt brought a sharp, lancing pain that pierced her from temples to brow. And still she met only silence and the blackness of her closed lids.

The place inside her was empty as it had always been, these last seven years, whenever she'd tried to call back the Sight.

It would seem, she thought, that whatever goddesses or gods or spirits of the earth bestowed such powers were as vindictive as the God of the Christ.

At last Isolde opened her eyes, looking down at the ring Hunno had returned to her, the metal warm, now, with the heat of her skin. A heavy gold band set with a stone of glowing red, the sides twined with rearing serpents far older than the Pendragon on Con's shield. And then her hand clenched on the serpent ring once more, so hard that the serpents' raised golden scales dug into her palm.

Seven years, she thought, without a flicker of the Sight. And then, whatever gods or fates rule the worlds beyond the veil grant a single flash of vision. When it can do no good at all.

And then snatch the Sight away as though it had never come
again.

Whatever lies I may make men like Hunno and Erbin believe.

"MY LADY."

The voice at her side made Isolde turn, heart pounding as
before, afraid that Hunno and his companion had returned
and heard what she and Myrddin had said. But the man who
stood beside her wore the dark robes of priesthood, and his
face was still flushed with outside cold, his eyes watering from
the wind.

Isolde caught the rich, sultry scent of incense and holy oil
that clung always about his robes, and, as always, the scent
clutched at the back of her throat. She swallowed, though, and
waited while Father Nenian hesitated, then, looking from the
coffin to Isolde's face, said, "I am sorry, lady, for your loss. Trust
and believe that my lord king your husband is safe in the arms
of Christ. He watches over you from Heaven."

Isolde's eyes moved to the altar, with its cross of gold. Sight
and memory she had lost seven years ago. Given them up of
her own free will. But faith—that she'd not lost until later. Four
years ago.

She'd heard many times the tales of the fort the Old Ones
had built in this place, long before Tintagel's walls had risen over
its remains. The story of how the gods they had worshipped—
the small gods vanished now into the mists and caves and hollow hills—had demanded the sacrifice of a child before they
would allow the fortress walls to stand.

And those gods, Isolde thought, those gods I might believe
in. Or at least understand.

But Father Nenian had meant to be kind. He was middle-aged, with a round, mild face and pale hazel eyes that looked always a little surprised, his crest of fine dark hair turning to gray at the temples and standing up on his tonsured head. A good man, with the simple, bright faith of a child.

And so Isolde only nodded and said gently, "I thank you, Father. I know my husband would be glad now to lie in your care."

"In God's care, lady."

Isolde's eyes moved again to the altar. Despite the voices, she'd never once felt any sense that the dead yet lived somewhere—much less that any were with her still. She shivered, unsure which was worse. To believe that the dead were swallowed by blackness, vanishing to nothing. Or that they were trapped somewhere like flies in amber, endlessly repeating their stories to the wind.

But she'd never want to shake Father Nenian's faith, and so she said only, "Did you wish to speak with me, Father?"

Father Nenian hesitated, lowering his pale, kind eyes. "I thought . . . I thought that it would be well, my lady, if you were not seen to be alone here for too long. There are rumors—"

He stopped.

"Rumors?" Isolde repeated.

Father Nenian fingered the rope belt of his robe. "Yes, rumors. Lies, of course," he added quickly. "Not worth repeating. But all the same, I—"

"You may as well tell me what the rumors are, Father. You do me no favors if you lie to spare me pain." Isolde paused. "And I will almost certainly have heard them before."

Father Nenian let out his breath slowly, then nodded, though the mild eyes were still troubled. "I suppose so, my lady. Very well. You know that when Arthur died, it was whispered that it was through sorcery—witchcraft—that he met his end. Well, now that the young king here has also been cut down, there are those who say . . ."

"That he died by sorcery, as well?"

"Lies, of course—all of it." The priest rubbed his nose. "One must have patience with the superstitions and beliefs that continue to abound here. It will take time to win the common folk over—the ones who pray at the altar here, but still light the sacred fires at Beltain for the Horned One and the Goddess." He sighed. "Or come to Mass, and then go to pour milk and wine over the standing stones on the moor. Or—"

Isolde scarcely heard him. Con meeting his death through sorcery, she thought. That might almost be funny.

With an effort she said, "Thank you, Father, for telling me. And for coming here to guard against further tales. That was kind."

Father Nenian bowed his head. "Of course, lady." He paused, then cleared his throat. "And if there's anything . . . any comfort I can offer you . . ."

He trailed off. Then: "I couldn't help but notice that you've not come to a confessional in some time."

"No," Isolde said quietly. "I have not."

Father Nenian seemed about to say more, then apparently changed his mind, and said, instead, "I was asked to bring a message to you, Lady Isolde, if I should find you here."

Isolde stiffened. "A message? From whom does this message come?"

"The message was from my lord Marche, lady. He asks an audience with you straightaway."

Isolde had known what the answer would be, and so she felt no surprise—nothing but a slow, cold chill. She said, in the same quiet voice, "Thank you, Father. At present I must re-

turn to my duties among the wounded. If Lord Marche wishes
speech with me, he may find me there."

WHEN THE PRIEST HAD GONE, ISOLDE found she was shaking with a
cold that had nothing to do with the damp, mist-filled air, and
she had to press her eyes shut to block the memory that threatened once again. The memory of a darkened war tent, partially
lighted by the orange glow of a fire outside the goatskin walls.
And a man lying on a narrow camp bed, his eyes closed, his
breathing even and deep.

At last, though, the shaking ceased, and Isolde opened her
eyes. Reaching out, she lifted Con's right hand. The stiffness of
death had come and gone, and the hand lay limp and cold in
hers, the flesh of the palm rough, callused by years of wielding
sword and spear and shield. Taking out the golden serpent ring,
she slipped it onto Con's third finger once more. I wonder, she
thought, whether I will now hear Con's voice, too, when the
wind blows from the west.

Very gently, she reached to smooth the strands of soft brown
hair away from Con's brow. "A blessing go with you on your
journey, Con. Wherever you are."

The hollow silence seemed to draw in around her, and her
whisper was scarcely more than a breath of sound in the vaulted
shadows. "And I won't let him seize the throne. That I promise
you, by whatever power I once had."

Chapter Three

THE ROOM THAT HAD ONCE been the king's ceremonial audience hall was hot and close, the sound of the sea blotted out by the thick, windowless walls and the groans from men who lay in rows of straw pallets on the floor. Isolde stood in the doorway a moment, consciously locking all thoughts of Myrddin—and of Con—away.

She had been in many rooms like this one these last seven years. Converted fire halls, stables, even chapels or leather-sewn tents pegged into bare ground, from the hill forts of the north to the grass marshes of the summer land. And everywhere, whatever the place, the smells and the sights were the same. The thick, iron-sweet tang of blood, the stench of wounds gone bad, and the pale, sweat-streaked faces of soldiers tossing and turning on beds of dirty straw.

Since the Roman Eagles had turned their backs on the British Isle, the Saxon armies had raided and burned, raped and ravaged the land, and pressed on ever farther in from the eastern shores. And through it all the Britons had fought. Led by Ambrosius, led by Uther, led by Arthur, and lately by Con. Britons had fought and died in battlefield mud—and carried the wounded away to be healed in places like these, or to die all the same.

This room was long and narrow, lit by torches held to the wall by iron brackets, the air faintly acrid with the smoke of a fire used to heat water and cauterizing knives. Two rows of pallets for the wounded stretched on either side of a central aisle. And I suppose we are lucky this time, Isolde thought. This time the battle was less than a day's ride away, so the wounded could be carried here, where the water at least is clean. And we have only one man to a bed instead of two or three.

As Isolde entered, a girl at the far end of the room straightened from where she was bending over one of the men. Isolde threaded her way through the pallets to her side.

"Hedda. You needn't have come in to help today," she said. "After riding in so late last night."

Hedda shook her head. She was a tall, broad-framed girl, her face heavy and plain-featured beneath the straight flaxen hair, with pale brows and pale blue eyes fringed by almost colorless lashes.

"It's . . . all right, lady. I come."

Isolde could vividly remember the time when Hedda had been brought to court by a band of Con's fighting men, manacled and chained by the neck to the other prisoners from a raid on the Saxon borderlands. Hedda had been the youngest, and the only girl among the boys and men. A tall, heavy-built, fair-haired girl of fourteen or so—almost the same age as Isolde herself had been. Her skirts had been torn and blood-stained, her mouth slack and half open, her eyes dull and without a shadow of interest in what went on all around.

Isolde had known it would be pointless to beg freedom, or even mercy, for the captured men. But she had asked that Hedda be given to her as serving maid, and Con had agreed. Isolde could guess, from the sly whispers among the fighting men who'd brought the prisoners in, what had happened on that raid and on the march to the fortress where Con had camped for the winter months. But she had never known Hedda to speak of it, any more than she had known her to cry in all the years she'd served her as maid—and ridden out with the army, too, like many of the women slaves, who served as cooks and washer-women to the soldiers on campaign.

Isolde had seen Hedda only briefly since she'd returned from this latest offensive at Dimilioc. There'd been just time to tell her of the meeting with Myrddin—though not the reason she'd summoned him—and so now Isolde lowered her voice and said, "It's all right, Hedda."

Hedda stared at Isolde a moment with something of the look Isolde remembered from years before, the blue eyes blank, her face showing nothing but stolid calm. The look had long since won her the reputation among the other serving women of being slow-witted and dull. That and her failure, even after all the years she'd served at court, to master fully the British tongue.

At last, though, Hedda bowed her head. Her voice, when she answered, was marked strongly with the Saxon accent, but the words were as quiet as Isolde's own. "I glad, my lady."

Isolde hesitated, but she couldn't risk saying any more here, in the open space of the hall, surrounded by men who had served Con and the rest of the chieftains and petty kings. With a nod, she turned away and moved toward a pallet near the end of the row, where an old man lay, one bandaged foot stiffly extended from the blanket that covered the rest of his thin frame.

Ector was a wiry, bandy-legged man, his limbs twisted by rheumatism, his shoulders bowed and his muscles stringy with age. He'd fought as a soldier under the Pendragon's banner, but now, unable any longer to wield a sword, he served—had served—as armorer under Con, riding out with the army to care for the men's weaponry, oiling and sharpening swords, refitting shafts of broken spears. He'd been wounded, not in battle but by chance when the sword he'd been sharpening had slipped from his grasp and sliced across the arch of his left foot. A slight injury, but amid the filth and muck of battle it had festered and turned bad.

He'd been carried into the infirmary two days ago, cursing and swearing loudly that he'd allow no damn fool of a woman to tend his wounds, queen or no. Now, as Isolde approached the pallet where he lay, he gave her a single, furious glance from under heavy, graying brows and then turned his face away, his lips set in an angry line.

Isolde knelt and unfastened the wrappings on the wounded foot. She'd bathed the wound morning and night with seawater, and had tried garlic and honey and hot poultices of goldenseal on it, as well, but even before the final layer of bandages fell away, she could smell the stench of rotting flesh, tainted by poison that none of her treatments could draw off. And when the injury was revealed, she saw that the skin around the cut was oozing wet and green, turning to black at the edges.

"The wound's still not healing."

She'd spoken more to herself than to Ector, but the old man's head snapped up and he gave her another fierce glare from under his brows.

"Suppose I can see that for myself, can't I? And smell it, too. God, what a stink."

He had a dour, wizened face, sunken cheeks and a narrow chin running into a wrinkled neck, his hair gray, greasy, and sparse with age. His eyes were small and dark and furious now, but Isolde saw, too, the shadow of anxiety in their depths. He'd have seen countless wounds like these end in the loss of the foot—or even the whole leg. And at the very least, she thought, seeing the lines that bracketed his thin mouth, the injury must be causing him a good deal of pain.

So she said only, her voice mild, "Yes, well, I'm a good deal closer to it than you are, you know."

Ector's heavy brows drew together. "And I've got to lie here and smell it day in and day out. Don't talk to me about whether it's healing or no. I'm here so you can do something about it, not stand there jawing at me."

Isolde nodded slowly. "All right. There's one thing I've not yet tried."

Ector lay in rigid silence, arms folded, while Isolde sorted through the jars and pots in her scrip, but when she drew out the glass jar she'd selected, he jerked out, "And what in hell's that, then?"

Through the walls of the jar a mass of wriggling white bodies could be seen.

"Maggots," Isolde said crisply.

Ector's brows shot up. "Maggots? Jesus bloody Christ! You think you're going to put maggots in my foot?" And then, before Isolde could reply: "Right, then, I'm off."

He sat up, swinging his legs out from under the blanket only to stop abruptly as he caught sight of his own naked, spindly lower limbs. The filthy leather breeches he'd been wearing when he'd come in had been cut away so that they could be drawn as painlessly as possible over the wound.

Isolde nodded. "Yes. You'll give the rest of the men in here quite a show if you get up and walk out that way."

Ector swore savagely under his breath, then set his lips together and hitched the blanket around his narrow hips, his jaw hardening to keep back a grunt of pain as he struggled to get his good foot under him.

"Breeches or no, I'm leaving." He spoke without looking at

Isolde. "Between infection and your treatment, I'll take the infection every time . . . my lady." He fairly spat the final words.

Isolde's brows lifted. "You know, I could just take you outside and slit your throat like a horse that's broken its leg, if you're so set on dying. It would be a cleaner death than having your body rot from the bottom up. And we could stop wasting food and drink on you a good bit sooner that way."

Ector's head came up once more, every muscle stiff with rage. Then, slowly, his shoulders relaxed, and a faint, unwilling twitch of a smile touched the corners of his mouth.

He grunted. "Have a devil of a mess to clean up afterwards if you do, lass. Man or horse, a cut throat makes for a wicked lot of blood." He was silent, studying her speculatively, then he shifted, seeking a more comfortable position on the bed of straw. "All right," he said at last. "Maybe I'll not go just yet. But just tell me why in blazing hell you'd put a lot of filthy crawling worms on my foot."

"To help it heal. I've used them before in cases like yours—though usually they're already in the wound, and all I've had to do is leave them in. They'll eat the rotting flesh away and stop the poison spreading any farther than it has."

For another long moment Ector stared at her in silence. Then, still without speaking, he turned and vomited, quietly and neatly, into the slop pot by his bed. But when his shoulders had stopped heaving, he raised his head, wiping his mouth with the back of his hand.

"All right," he said. "Let's get on with it if it's to be done."

"DOES THAT HURT?" ISOLDE ASKED, a short while later.

Ector lowered the cup of beer she'd given him to wash out his mouth and looked at her over the rim, brows raised. "Wasn't feeling exactly champion to begin with, now, was it?" But he sighed, then, and set the cup down. "Feels a bit twitchy-like," he said, shrugging his thin shoulders. "That's all. With the little buggers crawlin' around in there."

"Good." Isolde started to rewrap the linen bandages on the wounded foot, and Ector, after a moment's pause, turned to the boy on the pallet next to his.

"Your first battle, was it, lad?"

Isolde looked up, her hands going momentarily still. Ector's voice had been casual, but she doubted the question was as idly put as it sounded. She'd been watching the young man who lay beside Ector for several days; he was a slight foot soldier of fifteen or sixteen, with hair nearly as fair as a Saxon's. He'd been one of the youngest of Con's band of fighting men, and he'd taken an arrow in the upper arm during the battle most recently won. The shaft had penetrated deep into the muscle, and it had taken two of his fellow soldiers to pull the head free before he'd been brought in from the battlefield. Now, though, the wound was mending well, the flesh knitting together without infection, and he seemed in no great pain.

But where the other men in the infirmary—those who were able—talked and shouted to one another across the aisles, telling ribald jokes and reliving battles fought and won, this young man hardly spoke at all. Instead he lay with a white, strained face, his eyes fixed and staring at the raftered ceiling. Isolde had seldom seen him drift off to sleep on his own, and he took the poppy-drafts she offered him at night eagerly. But several times, now, he'd woken himself and the rest of the room with shrill, frantic screams, even dosed with the drug as he'd been.

Now, as the boy turned to look at Ector in response to the older man's question, he blinked a moment, as though returning from a long way off. Then he jerked his head in agreement. "That's right."

Ector nodded. "Thought so. Can always tell." He studied the boy's face, then asked, "What's your name, lad?"

The young man had looked away, his gaze fixed on the ceiling again, and now his throat contracted as he swallowed. When he answered, his voice was flat, barely audible. "Ralf."

Ector's eyes surveyed the boy's slender frame, fastening on the tightly bound upper arm. "Well, then, Ralf. Your first taste of war—and you've got the badge of honor to show for it. Get a good many more of those, I shouldn't wonder, before the Saxon devils are driven back where they belong."

Isolde saw—and she knew Ector saw, as well—the involuntary shudder that rippled through the boy's body, the flare of panic that widened his eyes. He didn't speak, though, and after a moment Ector said, "Made you feel a bit hollow, I expect. Takes some getting used to before you can stand on the business end of a Saxon war charge and not feel like your innards are gone liquid enough to leak out your arse."

The old man's words seemed to strike like blows aimed at the foot of a dam or like the lance of a knife on a festering wound. Another shudder rippled through the boy, and pent-up words spilled out of him in a voice low, hoarse, and almost toneless, while his eyes remained staring and fixed.

He'd been on the front lines, had faced the brunt of the Saxons' charge. He'd heard them coming, voices raised in battle cry, though at first they'd appeared only as a sort of moving wall. Then he'd seen them. Blond giants of men, swinging swords and great two-edged axes above their heads, the hooves of their horses churning the ground into mud.

And then the battle had been on him, and he could see nothing but the slash of weapons, the heave of bodies, men, and horses, all around, hear nothing but the screams of the horses, the shouts of the other men, though he knew by the raw pain in his throat that he was screaming, too. He'd seen the man beside him fall under a blow from one of the double-edged axes. He'd seen another man's stomach parted by a sword point, as one of the enemy took him from behind, and had seen others trampled, crumpled like broken rag dolls beneath the horses' hooves.

"Their wizards come first—howling curses. Like . . ." Ralf shuddered. "Like nothing you've ever heard. They've drums they beat on. Made of human skulls and the flayed skin of the dead. And horns they blow on—made of thigh bones. And the soldiers—they fight like . . . like animals," Ralf said hoarsely. "If their chief is killed, it's a shame to them to leave the field of battle alive. They'll come at you, seeking death. Wanting to die. Like demons. Like nothing that has a mortal soul. It's—"

He stopped. A fine sheen of sweat had broken out on his brow, and his eyes were dark with the memory, his hands white-knuckled at his sides.

"Well, they are heathens, lad." Ector's tone was matter-of-fact. "And like they say, if you talk to a pig and expect to hear anything back but an oink, you'll only be disappointed sore."

That brought a brief twist of a smile to Ralf's mouth, and he shivered convulsively again, some of the tension of his slender body starting to seep away.

Ector nodded as though satisfied and nudged the boy lightly on the good arm. "Never you mind it, lad. I remember once—in my young days, it was—during a raid on a Saxon war camp. I'd got one cornered, like, and we were fighting hand to hand. I drew first blood—struck him a blow on the thigh—and he came at me like Satan himself. I've got a mark of it still—just here, you see?"

He pushed back the sleeve of his tunic and held out a wiry arm, showing the puckered line of an old scar running up along the muscle from wrist nearly to elbow. Slowly, Ralf's eyes fixed on the mark, and he nodded, though he didn't speak.

"Well, this 'un," Ector went on. "This Saxon I was fighting

spoke a bit of the British tongue—enough that we could understand each other, he and I. We were fighting hard, blocking each other's blows, drawing apart and then charging at each other again."

The old man's voice was low, but all the same the words seemed somehow to echo the tension of that long-ago battle, to conjure up out of the air the ringing clash of swords, the thud of metal against leather shields. Isolde saw Ralf raise himself, his face quickening with interest as Ector went on: "Once, while we were circling each other, each looking for a place where a sword point could get in, he sort of hissed at me that he'd fight me till his lifeblood ran out of him in rivers, so long as he could take me with him. That if he died in killing me, he'd go to the warriors' hall and live on endless roast meat and mead from the udders of some kind of heathenish goat." Ector shrugged. "Or some such rubbish. Didn't catch it all."

Ector stopped. Ralf was watching the older man, and the remaining tension had by now ebbed out of the boy's frame. The fixed, glazed look had gone from his eyes, leaving them for the first time interested and alert.

"And what did you say to him?"

"Say?" Ector gave an explosive snort. "Told him he was in for one bloody great surprise when I'd killed him and he found himself in hell."

Isolde found herself laughing. She doubted the existence of Ector's Saxon, British-speaking or otherwise, and she'd seen wounds enough to know that Ector's scar had been made by a dagger or knife, not a sword. But beside her, Ralf was laughing, too, the taut, desperate strain lifted from his face for the first time since he'd come in, so that he looked—almost—like the same boy who'd ridden out to battle the month before. Or as much the same, Isolde thought, as he ever will.

"One bloody great surprise," Ralf repeated, still laughing and shaking his head. "One bloody great surprise. That's good, that is. That's really good."

Isolde had tied the last of the bandages on Ector's foot, and now she picked up her leather medicine scrip and turned away. Again and again and again, she thought, these men break my heart.

ONE OF THE MEN LYING AGAINST the opposite wall—a foot soldier with a crushed arm—had woken and begun to scream, and Isolde worked her way quickly across the room to kneel by his side. He was older, she thought, somewhere just short of thirty summers, with a dark, blunt-featured face; a thick, powerful neck; and a swordsman's heavily muscled frame. His body was unmarred, save for the right arm that lay useless at his side. It had been crushed by an ax blow into a mass of torn flesh and splintered bone, and now Isolde saw that it was still oozing blood through the linen wrappings she had applied last night.

He was still screaming as Isolde reached him, though his eyes were closed—harsh, rasping screams that made the muscles of his throat stand out like cords. Isolde put one hand on his forehead to quiet him, reaching with the other for the poppy-laced cup of wine that stood by his side. And all I can do, she thought, is try to drug away as much of the pain as may be until it is clear whether his body will heal itself or yield.

Though it would be miracle if he survived such a wound. In the two days he'd lain on the pallet here, he'd only brought up whatever drafts she tried to coax him to take, and already she could see the deadly red streaks spreading upward from the shoulder, despite the hot poultices and salves she'd applied.

The man's face looked pinched, the skin a muddy yellow-gray

and drawn tight over the bones of the skull. He was unknown to her, though the dark coloring and strong, compact build marked him for one of the Welshmen, and Isolde saw that about his throat he wore a roughly carved cross on a leather thong. One of Madoc of Gwynedd's infantrymen, maybe. Gwynedd was largely a Christian land, and Madoc a Christian king.

Isolde cradled the soldier's head in the crook of one arm, raising him enough so that she could hold the cup to his mouth. The first swallow he only retched up into the already vomit-soaked straw, but the second sip he kept down, and as Isolde eased him back against the pallet, he let out an exhausted sigh. Then his brow contorted as his pain-clouded eyes fixed blearily on her face.

"Mother . . . Mother . . . help me . . . hurts."

Usually, Isolde thought, it is a mother they call for. Some-times God, sometimes Jesus the Christ, but most often Mother these men want when they wake.

"Hush, now." Isolde closed her fingers around his. "You're safe. I won't leave you."

She started to unwrap the bandages with her free hand, keeping up the low murmur of words. "This is the tale of Pwyll, Lord of Dyfed, and Arawn, King of Annwn."

For as long as she'd cared for the men wounded in Con's campaigns, she had told one or another of the old bards' tales as she worked over the injured or ill, so that she scarcely thought of it as anything other than second nature now. She wondered, sometimes, where she had learned the stories that seemed sus-pended in an ever-ready wellspring inside her, rising effortlessly to her lips.

But it had also become second nature never to let herself dwell on questions like that for long. The answers were part of the time forgotten, for seven years now locked away behind a black wall.

For the men conscious enough to follow the story, the tales took their minds off the pain. And if she told one of the tales of the old heroes, of long-ago battles fought and won, the story sometimes seemed to give them courage as well. But even the ones too far gone to listen—like this man here—were usually soothed, quieted by the sound of her voice and the rhythm of the words.

Isolde went on with the tale of how, for one year, Pwyll had taken Arawn's place as king of the Otherworld. And, slowly, the soldier's pain-dulled eyes slid closed and his clutching fingers relaxed. As gently as she could, then, Isolde eased her hand away from the soldier's limp grasp, and, still speaking, drew a pot of salve from the leather scrip at her side.

The stories were so familiar she scarcely had to think about the words anymore; they came automatically, leaving her mind free. Still, the rhythm of the story helped to steady her hands and keep her from thinking too much about the pain she inevitably inflicted even as she worked to heal.

The last of the soldier's bandages fell away, leaving the shattered arm open to view. Useless, she thought, to wish the world can be other than it is. Useless even to be angry at the bloody, wretched waste of constant war.

But before she could begin salving the wound, the man's eyes flickered open again, and this time they widened in horrified awareness as his gaze fell on her face. Instantly, he threw himself sideways across the pallet, trying to wrench away, and his good hand flashed out in a gesture far older than the wooden cross he wore. Second and third fingers bent, first and smallest finger raised like horns. The ancient sign against evil or witchcraft.

Isolde rose to her feet and turned away without even trying to quiet him. There was no more good she could do here. Experience had taught her that much.

"Hedda."

Hedda had turned at the man's frightened cry, and now at the summons she crossed quickly to Isolde's side.

"He'll not let me finish—not now." Isolde spoke in a low voice and kept her face carefully averted from the wounded man. "And I'll only make things worse if I try. But his wound needs to be treated with this"—Isolde held out the pot of salve—"and then wrapped up again. You know the way."

This time, there was no pause, no blank-eyed stare before Hedda's nod. "I know. I see to it, my lady."

It was at moments like these, moments when she and Isolde were alone, that Isolde caught brief flashes of what she thought might lie behind Hedda's dull-eyed stolidity. Moments like these when she knew for certain that Hedda's dullness was a way of winning freedom, at least of a kind.

Hedda had been carrying a tray that held brown bread and cheese and an earthenware water jar. She shifted the burden to her hip to reach for the pot of salve.

"Here, I'll take it, Hedda." Isolde took the tray and handed her the salve pot in return. "Who was it for?"

The other girl was silent a moment, her pale gaze, fixed on the floor.

"For Saxon prisoners, Lady."

And at moments like these, Isolde thought, you could sometimes catch a flash of anger beneath Hedda's calm. Hedda's voice had been almost toneless, but all the same Isolde touched her lightly on the arm.

"I'm sorry, Hedda."

A brief spasm, as of pain, passed across the Saxon girl's broad brow. When she spoke it was almost an echo of what Isolde had thought only a moment before.

"Waste of tears to cry."

There was nothing that Isolde could say in reply, and so she only took the tray and said, "I'll take the prisoners' food tonight, if you can finish with this man here. How many prisoners this time?"

"Only two." Hedda had turned away, moving to kneel where Isolde had done, and spoke over her shoulder, her broad face stolid once more. "In cells. Under the north tower."

Chapter Four

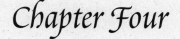

*H*E SAT AT THE SKIFF'S *steering oar, watching her as she trailed one hand in the water, the curling black hair fanned out over her shoulders in a windblown cloud. As though feeling his gaze, she rolled over onto her back to look up at him. "Did I ever tell you the story about Trevelyan? The only man to escape when Lyonesse sank beneath the sea?"*

He shook his head. "I knew you couldn't do it."

"Do what?"

He gestured to the fishing line, baited with a fish head from the leather bucket at his feet. "Stay quiet long enough for me to actually catch anything."

She scooped up a handful of water and flicked it at him, spattering his tunic and boots. "Do you want to hear the story or no?"

She had a sweet voice, musical and very clear. He'd always thought so. Even when she'd been an infuriating little ten-year-old shadow, trailing after him, dogging his every move.

"All right, tell me about this Trevelyan. What did he do?"

He'd heard her tell the tale at least a dozen times before, but he listened without interrupting all the same. As long as she talked, he could almost block out the memory of that morning. Of going into his mother's rooms and finding her, her eye puffed and blackened, the color of rotting fruit, her mouth bloodied and torn, with another tooth knocked free. His father was coming more often, now that he was home from the summer campaigns.

ISOLDE STOOD AT THE ENTRANCE TO the north tower as the echoes died away, leaving only the sound of the wind wuthering about Tintagel's walls. The words had gone, like all the others before. This one, though . . .

Not Morgan's voice. Of that much she was sure. She frowned. And this voice had seemed—what?

Closer, somehow, she thought. As though it called directly to whatever was behind the black wall in her mind. The part of herself and of the past she'd forgotten by force of will.

She shivered, suddenly, and stepped into the tower's torchlit door. *Put it away. Away with everything else.*

THE SMELL OF THE PRISON CELL was worse, even, than the stench of the infirmary hall. Filth and moldering straw, urine and sweat and unwashed skin, as there was in the room above. But here the smell was overlaid by the acrid reek of fear.

The prison block was unlighted, so that it was a moment before Isolde could make out, by the light of the torch in the passage outside, the two men crouched against the stones of the far wall. When she could see enough to pick her way through the piles of blackening straw, Isolde moved to the nearer of the two men and held out the tray. It was too dark to see his face clearly, but she could see his eyes, pale blue like Hedda's, staring at her with a stunned, dull gaze. He made no move to take the food, only sat slumped against the wall, his legs drawn up, arms limp and dangling between his knees.

"He'll not be able to take it." It was the other man who spoke, his voice harsh, though whether with thirst or anger or simply long disuse she couldn't tell. "He's got two broken wrists. Not much good for feeding himself."

Isolde had seen him straighten as she entered, then sink back as though he'd expected someone else. His face, though, was even more shadowed than that of the man before her, and she could see nothing of him save a blur of pale skin against the moisture-slick wall at his back.

Isolde turned back to the first man, and saw what she had not noticed before, that beneath the ragged sleeves of his tunic, both his wrists were swollen, blackened with bruises and tilted at a stomach-turning angle, like the splayed limbs of a child's doll. She could see, too, here and there, jagged edges of bone distending the skin.

Sharply, Isolde turned and called over her shoulder to the soldiers outside.

"Guard—bring the light in here."

Silently, one of the men obeyed, moving to set a lighted lantern beside her on the floor, and Isolde nodded.

"Thank you. You can go now. And shut the door."

The soldier hesitated at that, but he was a young man, with a thin face and a nervous, shifting gaze, and after a moment he bowed. "As you like, my lady."

Isolde waited until the heavy door had swung closed, then turned back to the first Saxon man. He was tall, with the long-limbed strength of his race, and a warrior's broad-shouldered build. His eyes, though, held the pitiful, bewildered look of an animal in pain. And he was young. Fifteen, at most, Isolde thought. As young as Ralf—and in a similar case.

His face, like his wrists, was covered with bruises, one eye swollen shut, his mouth bloodied and torn. But even so, his features still had the soft, unformed look of youth and his cheeks had only the faintest golden stubble of beard. His hair was probably fair, though it was so matted with sweat and dried mud that now it looked almost brown, and his clothes, too, looked stiff and gritty with sweat and filth.

"Here." Isolde knelt beside him and held the water jar to his swollen mouth.

The boy swallowed automatically, gasped with shock as the water reached his throat, and then, all at once, began to cry, great choking, racking sobs that shook his whole frame and smeared the dirt and dried blood on his face with tears.

Isolde started to reach a hand out to him, then stopped. Bad enough, she thought, for him to cry before one of his captors—and a woman, at that—without his being offered the insult of a comforting touch.

Before she could decide whether to speak or turn away, she saw the other prisoner stir in his shadowed corner. It was still too dark for her to see clearly, but she had the impression that he hesitated briefly, as though unwilling to move. At last, though, he rose to his feet and came forward into the circle of light. He was uninjured as far as Isolde could see, but he moved stiffly, as though guarding against jarring some inner hurt. Silently, he laid one hand on the boy's heaving shoulder.

The touch seemed to quiet the boy somewhat, for his sobs slowed. Beneath the bruises and the sheen of sweat and tears, his skin was dead white, but he drew a ragged breath and looked up at the other man with red-rimmed eyes.

"I'm sorry."

He spoke the Saxon language, but Isolde had learned enough from Hedda to understand that much—even low and broken as the boy's voice was.

The second prisoner gave Isolde a quick glance out of the corner of his eye. He was older than the boy by several years; she had time to see that much before he turned away. Twenty-four or twenty-five, maybe—as tall and broadly built as his companion, his face less battered and his hair a shade darker, somewhere between gold and brown. He seemed to hesitate again, but then dropped to sit in the filthy straw beside the boy.

"No call to be sorry, Cyn." He, too, spoke in the Saxon tongue, so that Isolde had to work to understand, guessing at the meaning of the words she didn't know. "Here—you see this?" He stretched out his left hand and turned it this way and that, letting the lantern light play across the spread fingers. The hand was strong and well formed, with a swordsman's muscled wrist, but Isolde saw that at least two of the fingers were twisted, as though the bones had been crushed and never properly set, and that the first joints on the middle and index fingers were gone.

He was silent a moment, and then he added something Isolde thought meant, *It was the same for me* or *I was just the same when this was done.*

His right hand tightened, briefly, on the boy's shoulder, then fell away, and he sat in silence, arms locked about his raised knees, letting the boy's choking sobs gradually fade and die. At last Cyn sat in huddled exhaustion, shuddering slightly, his head bowed.

Isolde said gently, "Cyn? Is that your name?"

The boy's head came up with a jerk, his pale eyes flaring wide, as though he'd forgotten she was there.

"I can set your wrists for you, if you'll let me. And give you something to ease the pain."

Though she could understand some of the Saxon tongue, she spoke only a few words, and so she used Latin to address the boy. She wondered, for a moment, whether he would understand, but his brow furrowed, as though he were trying laboriously to translate the words into his own tongue. Then comprehension dawned in the watery eyes, and beneath the mask of dirt and tears and blood, Isolde saw a warring of hope and disbelief, wariness and fear. He turned to his companion and asked something in his own tongue, his voice quickening into almost eagerness for the first time so that the words came too fast for Isolde to understand. *Do you trust her?* maybe. Or, *Can she be believed?*

His companion didn't answer at once. Isolde could see his face more clearly now, though his chin and jaw were hidden by several days' growth of beard. Above the beard, his cheekbones were sharply defined, his eyes deep-set and startlingly blue under oddly slanted gold-brown brows. He was studying her with a look that might have been hostility, or perhaps only appraisal, as though he was trying to decide for himself how far she could be trusted with Cyn.

As their eyes met, though, Isolde felt a stir of something at the back of her mind—a quicksilver flash, like the tug of a fish on a line, gone almost before she was sure it was there at all. Almost it felt like the flashes of Sight that had come to her long ago—a sudden feeling of sameness, of familiarity, like the returning memory of a dream. The certain knowledge that the words she spoke or the sight she saw she had already spoken or seen before. And years ago, following the abrupt feeling of sameness, there would have come a quick, bright vision of what the future would bring.

But nothing now followed that first quicksilver tug. No vision of the past, nor even any hint of what was to come, though the faintly dizzying quiver remained at the back of her mind, just beyond reach.

Isolde shivered. "I'll need help if I'm to set the bones," she told the bearded man. "Will you give it—if Cyn agrees he wants it done?"

The man's gaze still held the look of wary appraisal, but he only stared at her, his face blank, until Isolde realized that unconsciously she'd lapsed into her own tongue. She repeated the question in Latin and saw a flash of anger cross the man's face, the slanted brown brows draw together in a frown. The man started to speak, and Isolde waited for a curt refusal. But then he seemed to check himself and, still frowning, turned instead to Cyn, studying the young man's face. Whatever he saw there seemed to make up his mind, for at last, his eyes still on Cyn, he gave a brief jerk of a nod.

Cyn himself swallowed hard, then looked up at Isolde and spoke in stammering Latin, awkward and heavily accented. "I thank you, lady."

Isolde carried, still, the leather scrip of distillations and salves. She set it down on the floor and drew out the vial of poppy-laced medicine she had used before. There was a flicker of fear in Cyn's face as she held it to his mouth, and he looked at his companion as though in panic.

"It's all right," Isolde said quietly. "It won't hurt you. It will make you go to sleep while I set the broken bones, nothing more."

The boy hesitated an instant longer, but then he let out his breath and swallowed the draft in a single gulp.

"Good."

Cyn's brow was still beaded with sweat, his skin the sickly yellow of raw dough, but some of the tension was gone from his frame. He wiped his mouth and rested his head against the stone wall.

"The herb-craft . . . how . . . you learn?"

Isolde went still, her eyes on the dancing lantern flame. That was another question she never allowed herself to ask. The healer's craft, like the tales, was simply part of her, as she had been since she let herself remember. There was war, and her place was with the wounded. That was all.

There were sometimes moments—moments like this—when she thought that she might have begun healing the wounded at first as a kind of atonement. Payment for a life she'd failed to save.

But that, too, she never let herself consider for long.

"I learned as a child, I think," she said at last. She turned away, blinking to clear the imprint of the flame from her eyes. "That was a long time ago."

Cyn nodded. Already the poppy was beginning to take effect. His movements were slow, his eyes beginning to lose their focus, his head sinking onto the breast of his tunic. Then, abruptly, his head jerked upright, and Isolde saw his eyes widen and a dull, hot flush spread upward from the heavily muscled neck. For a moment she thought it was only the pain of his injuries, but then she caught the pungent smell and saw the wet stain spreading across his breeches, the puddle growing beneath him in the filthy straw.

It often happened. As a sleeping draft took effect, the body lost control—of bowels or bladder, or both. But that would make no difference to Cyn. There had been shame in his look before, mixed with the bewilderment and pain, but now the utter, helpless humiliation that filled the dull eyes and broad young face was almost unendurable. And there was nothing Isolde could do. Nothing but turn away even more swiftly than she had from his tears and spare him, at least, the indignity of her seeing his shame.

She bent her head, starting to unwind the strips of clean linen she carried in the scrip, and feeling a flash of blinding anger for the war—and the men—that had brought this boy here. Out of the corner of her eye, she saw the second prisoner touch Cyn lightly on the shoulder and say something in their own tongue.

The words—and what she thought they meant—made Isolde look up sharply, but they seemed to work, for Cyn gave a small, gasping laugh, the lines of fear and strain in his face easing a bit, his mouth relaxing into a watery smile.

"But you—" Watching out of the corner of her eye, Isolde saw Cyn gesture at the other man's shoulders, or maybe his back; she couldn't be sure. "It's my fault. If you hadn't—"

He stopped as his companion took hold of his arms, easing him down to lie on the straw-littered floor. "Never mind that. You think they wouldn't have given me a turn in any case?"

Cyn let out a shuddering sigh, his eyes half closed already with the effects of the drug. Then, abruptly, his lids snapped open and he struggled to rise, speaking with desperate urgency, though his voice was starting to blur and this time the words were once more too quick—and too low—for Isolde to catch the sense of them.

A question, though, Isolde thought, or maybe an admission of fear, for the bearded man put a hand once again on Cyn's shoulder and spoke quietly in what seemed like reassurance.

A tremor passed through the boy's frame, but he swiped clumsily at his eyes, then nodded, letting the other man lower him back onto the straw. A moment later, his lids had slid shut. When his breathing was even and slow, Isolde came to kneel beside him, turning to the bearded man.

"Can you hold him still while I work? He won't feel the pain as he would awake, but he may still move or try to break away."

The man's blue eyes met her own once again, the same shadow of hostility at the back of his gaze, and he seemed about to speak. But instead he silently bent to take hold of Cyn's shoulders, pinning him fast against the straw.

Isolde had set bones before, in rooms as filthy and stench-filled as this one. But these breaks were already more than a day old and had begun to knit themselves at stomach-twisting angles, wrenched out of alignment by the pull of muscle and sinew. She had to break them free before she could set them into place, and once, when the pulpy, jagged ends grated apart, Cyn half woke and gave an agonized, rasping scream that echoed long after in the stone walls.

And at the sound, the sick anger Isolde had felt before broke suddenly free, this time nearly choking her. It had happened to her before—though not as often, now, as when she had first started caring for the battle-wounded men who fought with Con. But sometimes she would be suturing a sword cut, or lancing an infected wound, thinking only of the task at hand—and then all at once a wave of blinding, dry-mouthed anger would sweep over her. And she would be unable, for the moment, to remember that it was useless to hate the world of men and battle and war.

And she had learned that at such moments she could scream, or cry, or curse the gods. Or she could call the men who'd inflicted the wounds every vile name she knew and get on with the job in hand.

She had a formula of curses worked out, the words as familiar, by now, as those of the old bards' tales. She could repeat it, too, almost as much without thinking, as she could the stories, until the anger retreated and she was once more able to look only at the wounds, and not at the men themselves, see only what could be done, and not the pain that doing it would cause.

She'd learned, too, long ago, that she couldn't stop the war. But she could sometimes, at least, stitch this one wound, set this one bone.

She'd begun, muttering the words under her breath as she bent over Cyn's right arm, when something made her glance up to find the older prisoner's eyes on her. His face was still guarded, but Isolde thought that now there was a gleam of something that might have been amusement at the back of the clear blue eyes, and that his mouth was twitching slightly beneath the beard. With the taut control lifted, his face looked younger, closer to her own age than Isolde had thought before.

"So," she said. "You do understand the Briton language after all."

The man hesitated a moment. Then: "Some." He spoke in Latin, as before, face unreadable, though there was still a flicker of amusement in his gaze. "Though 'filthy, crawling whoreson bastard' sounds about the same in any tongue."

The anger was only partially gone, and Isolde pushed the hair from her brow and sat back a moment on her heels.

"Yes, well. I've not yet threatened to cut off the guards' privates and hang them round their noses and ears. That was what you said before?"

For a moment, the hard, wary look returned to the man's gaze as though he was casting his mind back, trying to think what else she might have overheard. Then: "Cheered the boy, anyway. Made him forget he'd just pissed himself in front of a strange woman." One corner of his mouth tipped up in a brief, half-unwilling smile and he jerked a shoulder. "When a man's got your balls frozen in fear, insult his."

He stopped. The blue gaze turned at once distant and inward, and the smile died.

Isolde watched him a moment, then nodded. "Yes. I've no doubt both of you have seen it actually done. That and worse, besides."

But when she bent once more to Cyn, she found, oddly, that though she felt again a twist of wrenching pity at the sight of the shattered wrists, the anger had faded at least enough that she could go on.

The lantern cast only the poorest of light, forcing her to rely almost entirely on touch to draw the bones into alignment. By the time she'd finished the right wrist and moved on to the left, her back and ribs were sticky beneath the wool of her gown and she had to blink sweat out of her eyes.

The bearded man hadn't spoken again, and had kept all but motionless throughout. He must, though, have been at sick-beds and operations like this before, for he kept up a steady, even pressure on the boy's shoulders or arms, moving only when Isolde asked him to shift position or turn Cyn so that she could better feel the bones. And when she'd tied the final wrappings of linen about the left wrist, she found him watching her once again.

Isolde sat back on her heels, smoothing the damp hair away from her brow. He'd been kind to Cyn, whatever else he might be. And he had already endured at least three days in this foul place, just as much as the boy. She gestured toward the forgotten tray of bread and cheese.

"Eat. I can bring more for Cyn to have when he wakes. He likely won't want much, but you should see he drinks something, at least."

The man gave another short nod, stretching his muscles as though to relieve the stiffness of kneeling over Cyn, then reached for the water jug, took a long draft, and sat back, lean-ing one shoulder against the wall. He moved still, Isolde saw, with that slight, wary stiffness, as though tensing his muscles in expectation of pain. Not until he reached for the slab of coarse brown bread on the tray, though, did she see the marks on his shoulders, just visible above the neckline of his tunic. Angry, evenly spaced red welts. The marks of a whip.

"I can give you a salve for that," she said quietly.

The bearded man had torn off a hunk of the bread, chew-ing and swallowing quickly, as though the bite was the first food he'd taken in some time, but at that he looked up at her sharply, eyes wary, his body instantly stiffening. Then he shook his head. "No. Besides"—he laughed shortly—"not much point. Only give the guards the fun of opening it up for me again if it starts to heal."

He paused, his eyes meething hers, and Isolde caught another flash of anger at the back of the hard blue gaze. "Like Cyn's wrists."

"Like Cyn's—"

Isolde's eyes went to Cyn, lying where they'd left him amid the filthy straw. She could understand, now, the man's hesitation when she'd offered to set the broken bones. Though in the end he'd said nothing to Cyn.

The bearded man answered as though she'd spoken the words aloud, his voice turning harsh, though whether the anger was for her or the men who'd done it, Isolde couldn't tell. "I didn't tell him, no. Though I'm not sure whether it's not crueler this way. The guards will just come in tomorrow and break them again."

Isolde drew in a sharp breath, and the man, watching her, said, "You didn't know?"

"No," Isolde said. She was seeing again the badge of Cornwall's blue boar on the tunics of the guardsman now outside the cell. More of Marche's men. *I should have known, though,* she thought, turning to look down at Cyn's now neatly bandaged arms. *I know what men—even good men—are like in times of war.*

Some of the anger in the man's look seemed to seep away, and he rubbed a hand along the line of his jaw. "No, you wouldn't, I suppose." He shot her a quick, unreadable look from under the slanted brows. Then he said, letting out his breath, "Never mind. You meant well. And you've given the boy a night's ease, at least."

Isolde frowned. "Who did this? Marche himself? Or only his men?"

Instead of answering, he said in a voice that was a shade too calmly controlled, "Marche? Marche is here, then, at Tintagel?"

Isolde nodded, and he was silent for a moment, face still, his gaze once more turned inward, as though he followed some private train of thought. Then abruptly he looked up. "No. It wasn't him. We've seen no one beyond the guards outside the door. They share duty with two others."

He looked away, shifting as though trying to find a comfortable position without letting his back touch the wall. Isolde's eyes went again to the angry hatches on his shoulders, their edges crusted with blackening blood.

"What did Cyn mean when he said it was his fault?" she asked. "That you'd been hurt because of him?"

The bearded man gave her another unreadable glance. "Why should you want to know?"

"I might be able to help."

"Help?" The man gave another brief, mirthless laugh. "And just what help do you think you can offer? Cyn and I were dead men from the moment we set foot inside these walls. You going to see it's a nice sharp knife they use to cut our throats?"

Isolde only kept silent, her eyes on his, waiting. And after a moment, the man let out a sigh, half weary, half impatient. He sat full in the circle of lantern light now, and the flickering glow picked out the taut lines of strain and fatigue about his mouth and eyes.

"All right," he said. He raised a hand, rubbing the line of his jaw beneath the beard. "The guards had got to work on Cyn. And I . . ." He paused, the grim smile twisting his mouth. "I said the same thing to them you heard me tell Cyn. Made them angry enough that they got started on me instead."

"But why?" Isolde asked.

"Why?" He shrugged. "For one thing, if I'm going to be

beaten, I'd rather it was in anger than in cold blood—just for the sheer joy of the thing. And for another—"

He stopped, his jaw hardening, his gaze turning angry once more.

"For another?"

The bearded prisoner looked down at Cyn again and was silent so long that Isolde thought he wasn't going to respond. At last he said, expressionlessly, "The guard wanted Cyn to lick his cock and pray to him as God Almighty. And in another moment he'd have done it."

He paused, then looked up. "Hurt me a lot less to be horse-whipped than it would have Cyn to realize he's not as brave as he thought." He sighed, rubbing his brow with the back of one hand. "Though he's beginning to suspect it, all the same."

Cyn's face, peaceful now, looked even younger in sleep, the pale lashes golden against the bruised skin above his cheek-bones. Isolde felt slightly sick. She looked away. Then, her eyes falling on the mutilated fingers of the bearded man's left hand, she asked, "And did you really cry when that was done?"

He was silent again for a moment, watching her, as though debating how much to say. Then he shrugged and gave another of those quick, humorless smiles. He lifted the water jar to his mouth and swallowed another draft before saying, "Cry? No. I was too busy wanting to tear the liver out of the man that did it to cry."

He looked down, turning the hand this way and that, his eyes on the twisted fingers and white scars, then moved his shoulders—impatiently, this time, as though shaking off what-ever memory the sight recalled.

"Does no harm to let Cyn think so, though." He paused to take another swallow from the jar, then added, half to himself, "Mind you, Cyn faced his first battle without turning a hair—

and I puked my guts out and blubbered like a babe after the fighting was done. So I suppose it evens out, in the end."

Isolde studied his face curiously. "How old were you then?"

The man came back to himself with a start. He eyed her, then jerked one shoulder and picked up the bread again. "Thirteen—maybe a few months more." He raked a hand through his beard, then swore under his breath.

Isolde, watching him, said, "You're probably crawling with lice, the both of you. There's not much I can give you for a cure. But I could probably arrange for you to at least shave your beard. It would—"

"No!" The man spoke sharply, almost violently. He finished the bread in a few quick, savage bites, then looked up, the edge of hostility back in his eyes.

"You've done enough. And I can't imagine you've any wish to stay in this stinking hole. So go—get back to where you belong."

Isolde nodded. "All right. I'll be back in the morning to check on Cyn."

The man swore under his breath. "Haven't you meddled enough?" He stopped and eyed her, a muscle jerking in his jaw. "Just what makes the queen herself care so much about Saxon gutterscum?"

Isolde watched him a moment. She'd seen too many injured men snap like wounded dogs at the offer of sympathy or aid to blame him for his rage. And they'd not even had the gall of captivity to contend with—or the certainty of worse to come. In their place, she thought, let alone this man's, I'd likely feel the same. Being angry was better—easier—by far than crying for mercy or admitting to fear.

"Question for question," she said evenly, her eyes on his. "How does a Briton-born come to be fighting on the side of that same gutterscum?"

Utter stillness descended over the bearded man's frame, though, oddly, the anger died out of his eyes, leaving them only flat and wary once more.

"What do you mean?"

"You look Saxon enough to pass for one, and you speak the language well. But it's not your native tongue. And your accent in Latin isn't Saxon, either. I'd guess you're maybe half of Saxon blood. A Saxon mother, maybe, and a father Briton-born."

He was silent a moment, and when he spoke his voice was flat as his gaze. "Anything else?"

She was about to reply, when she saw for the first time a mark on the man's neck, half hidden by the strands of matted golden-brown hair. A circular patch of whitened skin that she recognized at once as the brand of a Saxon thrall ring. A slave, then—or at least he had been at one time. Captured, like so many others, by raiders as part of the fortunes of war and sold into the enemy's service.

Her eyes met those of the bearded prisoner, and for a moment she saw, not just hostility, but fury, tightly controlled, flare at the back of his blue gaze, and knew that he'd seen her notice—and understand—the scar.

And so she said only, "No. I'll go now. If you won't take a salve for your back, do you at least want me to leave you something for the pain?"

The man started to shake his head, but then he stopped, his gaze falling on Cyn. An expression Isolde couldn't read passed like a shadow across his face, and he nodded slowly, turning back to her.

"Yes," he said. "Give me a draft of whatever sleeping potion you gave Cyn, if you've any left. And can you leave some for me to give the boy later on?"

Isolde drew the drafts out of her scrip and handed them across. She followed his gaze to look again at Cyn's sleeping face. "What did he say to you?" she asked. "Just before the poppy-draft started to work?"

The man didn't turn, and for a moment she thought again that he wasn't going to answer. Then he said, still in the same flat tone, "He said he was afraid—not of dying, but that they'd break him if they started in on him again. That he was afraid of what they'd make him do or say if he had to suffer any more pain."

Isolde was silent a moment. Very gently, she reached out and brushed the mud-caked hair from the boy's brow, as she had done from the brow of her husband, just a short while since. Cyn stirred and gave a soft, indistinct murmur, but his eyes remained closed.

"And what did you tell him?"

The bearded man's gaze barely touched her, no more, before returning to his companion's face.

"I said I'd see him through. But that he'd manage fine."

Chapter Five

ISOLDE SHUT THE DOOR TO her workroom behind her, then paused a moment, leaning back against the closed door, her hands moving to rub the base of her neck as she felt the full weight of exhaustion settle over her like stone. Her neck and shoulders were stiff and sore from crouching on the floor over Cyn, and her wrists ached with the effort of holding the bones she'd set steady so that they might be bandaged and bound.

The workroom lay on the ground floor of Tintagel's southern wing, a square, windowless room, the low ceilings hung with drying bunches of herbs that sifted a light, fragrant dust over the whole. Along one wall ran the wooden countertop, its surface worn smooth and nearly black, that she used to hold the clay dishes and jars for sorting seeds, the stone mortars and pestles for grinding the dried stems and leaves. A great copper brazier stood in the center of the floor for melting the sheep's tallow used in ointments and salves, while set against the room's outer wall were the cupboards where she stored the salves and ointments themselves so that the cool of the outside air on the stones might keep them from turning rancid before their time. There was peace, here. Peace and silence.

It cost her a sleepless night every month, when, under a full moon, she gathered herbs from Tintagel's kitchen gardens, made sure the servants and guardsmen heard her murmuring under her breath in the ancient tongue. But the effect was worth the price she paid in whispers and crossings and surreptitious signs against the evil eye; here, if nowhere else within Tintagel's walls, she could be alone.

Isolde closed her eyes, and some of the room's cool, herb-scented calm crept over her. *Alder bark and barley seeds for burns, chamomile for fever, yellow nettle ointment for wounds.* She might not allow herself memory of where or how she'd learned the words, but they were comforting as a tale—or a prayer—all the same.

It was a sound in the doorway that made her turn, muscles just beginning to relax tightening instinctively once again, even before she saw who stood there.

Isolde forced herself to incline her head in formal greeting. "Good evening, Lord Marche. Father Nenian told me you wished private speech?"

Marche, King of Cornwall, stepped into the room, followed by a pair of armed guardsman, who stationed themselves on either side of the door. He made Isolde a brief answering bow. "Lady Isolde."

He must, Isolde thought, have once been a handsome man, broad-chested and powerfully built, with a square-jawed face, thick black hair, and strong, solid bones. But the years had coarsened him, leaving his skin weathered and scored with broken veins, and his eyes were puffy and tired-looking.

He watched her a moment before saying, "I wished to speak with you about your safety, Lady Isolde. The battle here was temporarily won. But the enemy will no doubt return. And a fortress under siege is no place for a woman. There is a house of holy women nearby. An abbey, standing on lands I granted to the Church some years ago. Not large, but all the same an establishment of some wealth. I would offer you escort there—from my men, or myself, if you prefer. At a house of holy women you would be secure from the fighting that will surely begin again."

It might even, Isolde thought, be true. Marche's voice was respectful, his face grave. Only his position, a little closer than courtesy would permit and blocking her path to the door, made her chillingly aware of his strength and the brute physical power that seemed to emanate from him in waves. That and the presence of the two armed men at his back.

Isolde was silent, selecting several more pots of salve to put in her scrip. Then: "I hadn't heard that the Saxons had taken to respecting the sanctity of either abbey or church. We've both heard the stories of chapels looted. Nuns raped and slaughtered like sheep on the altar steps. Surely I am safer here, surrounded by fighting men, than alone among a group of unprotected women, holy or no."

Marche shifted position, his mouth tightening in a grimace of pain, and Isolde remembered the wound he'd taken in the battle just fought and won. She'd not seen the wound herself—Marche had his own physicians to tend his hurts—but it was said to have been a sword cut to the thigh, laying the leg open nearly to the bone. And he'd been lucky, Isolde thought, to come through the battle with that his only wound.

The stories were already flying about the fire halls and campfires of how Marche had led the charge that won the day. A charge uphill, into almost certain death, past the Saxon wizards with their skull-and-skin drums to face the Saxon shield wall. And yet, so the story went, Marche had ridden first of all and showed not a flicker of fear. And likely true, Isolde thought. Marche, son of Meirchion, King of Cornwall, was a brave man.

Now he said, "I could offer you conduct to one of my own

holdings, my lady, if that be your wish. Castle Dore is farther removed from the fighting—on the southern coast. You have my assurance that my men there would see you kept safe."

Isolde began to fill her scrip, placing the vials and pots in one by one. "Yes, I've no doubt I would be kept safe at Castle Dore. As safe as the Saxon prisoners in their cell."

Save that she had survived by pretended witchcraft for seven long years, Isolde might have missed the brief flare of frustration that showed in Marche's eyes, the hardening of a muscle in his jaw. As it was, the look was gone almost at once, and he said, "My lord King Constantine would not have wished you to put yourself in danger, my lady. Can you imagine what the Saxons would do to the wife of the High King—the man who'd slaughtered so many of their own—should you fall into their hands?"

A battle, Isolde thought again, that I have fought these seven years.

"I can imagine," she said. "Quite well. But nor would my lord Constantine have wished me to abandon my duties here. The next High King has still to be chosen by the council. And so long as the council meets, I will sit in my husband's place."

Marche had regained control, and seemed not even to notice the shortness of tone. Instead his gaze, dark and suddenly weary, met hers, and he said quietly, "Do you think I don't grieve for the young king? I served as regent to Constantine—taught him the arts of war as was my duty. But he was like my own son, as well."

Words were easy. But the grief in his eyes was genuine. Isolde was sure of it, and the knowledge struck her more coldly than anything else had done. She turned abruptly away, gathering up the last of the jars and glass vials. Then: "I have nothing more to say. My decision is made. But there is another matter I would speak to you about. The men you have appointed guard over the Saxon prisoners are grossly mistreating their charges." Isolde paused, then turned back and gave Marche a level look. "I know you will be as shocked to hear this as I was."

Behind Marche, she saw the men-at-arms shift and stir, and Marche shot them a quick, lance-sharp glance that might have been either a warning or an order for silence. Then: "These men are spies, Lady Isolde. Sent to penetrate Britain's lines and carry back word of our defenses."

"And that justifies torture?"

The flare of frustration was nearer the surface this time, the anger less readily contained. But when Marche answered, his voice was grave, with only a faint metallic edge, though he did draw a step or two nearer.

"If you had seen the sights my men and I have, my lady—the villages burned by Saxon raiders, every girl and woman in the place above five years old raped and the men with their eyes gouged out, left to wander and starve—you might change your opinion of what Saxon prisoners deserve."

Isolde pushed aside the cold prickles that rose along her spine in response to Marche's slow advance. "I have seen the villages, Lord Marche, and every one of the horrors you describe. And I have just come from an infirmary filled with men maimed and broken and screaming with Saxon wounds. But I have also seen British soldiers driving nails into the road from a Saxon settlement to keep the ghosts from following behind—and thought that they had good reason to fear revenge from the dead."

Marche inclined his head, so that his face was momentarily hidden. "You have a tender heart, Lady Isolde. As befits a lady so young. But I assure you—"

Isolde's temper snapped. She was remembering the look of dumb, bewildered suffering in Cyn's eyes, the utter humiliation and shame in his face, and all at once she was too angry to play the verbal game of parry and thrust even a moment more.

"That was an order, Lord Marche, not an invitation to debate. Tintagel is still my domain, as Constantine's queen, and I will tolerate no torture in any place I rule. And so long as you are a guest within my walls, you will control your men. Is that understood?"

Before Marche could reply, she turned away, passing swiftly through the workroom's door. When she had reached the flight of stairs leading to her own rooms, though, she stopped and leaned back against the rough stone wall. She thought, Whatever I may say, I wonder whether I have any more real power here than the Saxon prisoners in their cell.

Slowly, she pushed back the sleeve of her gown and looked down at the rose-colored patch of skin on her inner wrist—the heart-shaped mark she'd had from birth. It was visible in the glow cast by the torches mounted at intervals along the wall. The sign of a witch, the devil's teat, so the stories went, given to suckle the spawn born when he came at night to her bed.

I must be growing used to it, Isolde thought. It hardly even hurts now. She raised a hand and pushed a strand of windblown hair beneath the hood of her cloak. Now . . . Now I only wish that even a part of what the men fear were still true.

THE COUNCIL CHAMBER WAS HOT, ACRID with smoke from the fire in the great central hearth, and the rows of benches were crowded with men. Isolde paused a moment in the doorway, listening to the buzz of voices as the men ate of the platters of roast mutton and drank ale from the cupfuls the serving women poured. Night had fallen, and from the courtyard outside came the raucous shouts of guardsman, some playing at dice, others calling out wagers on a fight between two snarling, yelping war-dogs.

And before these council sessions could end, one of those

here tonight must swear blood-oath to the land of Britain as the country's High King.

At the head of the room, set high in the wall, was a grinning skull, yellowed with age, the last remains of a warrior whose name had years since been lost to the mists of time. Tintagel might now be a Christian domain, but the skull had protected the hall longer still.

A harper was singing. He was a traveling minstrel with a thin, ugly face and a slender frame, who had only weeks ago won a place for the season at Tintagel's hearth. His fingers plucked deftly at the strings of his instrument and his voice, thin and reedy, rose over the low rumbling babble of the men.

> *"Men went to Dimilioc with a war cry,*
> *Led by Constantine the Brave.*
> *Speedy steeds and dark armor and shields,*
> *Spear shafts held high and spear points sharp-edged,*
> *And glittering coats of mail and swords.*
> *He led the way, he thrust through armies,*
> *The Saxons fell before his blades,*
> *Their fighting turned wives into widows;*
> *Many a mother with tear-filled eyes . . ."*

It was beginning, just as Myrddin had said. Soon, Isolde thought, maybe Con, too, will have a sword forged by the gods or a magic scabbard that stops blood spilling from a wound. She turned her gaze away.

There were thirty or more men in all here tonight, the dukes and petty kings of Britain, accompanied sometimes by their sons or chief men-at-arms. Their shields, emblazoned with the devices of their lands, hung on the timber walls, while their swords and spears lay close by on the floor at their feet. In such times as these, arms were kept within reach.

One of the guardsmen bearing Con's Pendragon badge had detached himself from the rest and now came to meet her, threading a path through the assembled men.

"My lady Isolde."

The leaping torchlight showed Isolde a taut, shuttered face, with sharply cut cheekbones; a proud, high brow; and heavy-lidded dark eyes that spoke of a bloodline stretching back to Rome. A face more suited to a monk or priest than a fighting man, despite the narrow scar of a Saxon sword cut along the jaw.

Brychan had been captain of Constantine's guard, and was only a year or two older than Con himself—twenty-two, now, or twenty-three. First among the king's fighting men—and Con's friend, as well, though he'd always been stiffly formal with Isolde.

Like the rest of Con's men, Isolde thought. Like all the men in this room. They might have willingly sworn the death oath to their king, but at best they'd pay just as much respect as was owed by duty to his queen.

Brychan's voice now was as cool as ever, and he kept his eyes trained on a point past Isolde's head.

"The troops of the king's councilmen, my lady. I have given them leave to make camp on the headland, save for the honor guards. Them I have housed in the barracks here, to be nearest their lords."

Isolde nodded. "Thank you, Brychan. That is well."

Brychan half turned, offering his arm. His look hadn't changed, but Isolde thought that his tone was altered very slightly when he spoke again. "King Marche has volunteered his men to garrison the fort at the base of the causeway, my lady."

As though of their own accord, Isolde's eyes went to the place along the opposite wall where Marche sat in the seat next in honor to the High King's, as was his right as king of Cornwall. He, too, now wore formal garb: a tunic of dark red, heavily embroidered with gold; a fur-lined cloak held in place with a heavy brooch, likewise worked in gold and bearing the crest of the Cornwall boar. As though feeling Isolde's gaze on him, he turned, and for a brief instant his gaze met hers.

"And you have accepted?" Isolde asked Brychan.

There was another brief pause. Then: "I knew of no reason to refuse, my lady."

Isolde realized her hands were clenched at her sides. Slowly, she forced her fingers to relax, forced herself to take Brychan's arm and move with him toward her own place on the benches. "No," she said. "No reason, as you say."

She was seeing in her mind's eye Tintagel's towering walls, built on the rocky promontory that was almost an island amid the vicious sea. On three sides of the fortress walls the jagged cliffs dropped almost sheer to the beaches and coves below. And on the fourth stretched the narrow causeway, passable only at low tide, that was the sole way back to the mainland and the road.

And now, she thought, King Marche has positioned his forces so that he may stop anyone who wishes to leave. And Brychan, Con's captain, has approved.

Isolde took her own place, opposite the great central hearth, drawing the skirts of her gown close about her. She had changed her stained and crumpled working dress for a formal one of scarlet-dyed wool with an embroidered overtunic of blue. With Hedda's help, she had rebraided and pinned her hair into a heavy knot at the nape of her neck, adding a gold fillet to hold the fine linen coif about her brow.

Now, looking up, she saw that Hedda, too, was here, one of the serving women who moved among the great oaken tables to offer platters of roasted boar and pitchers of ale. As Isolde watched, she leaned forward to fill a drinking horn for one of the men—brother to one of the petty kings from the north, Isolde thought. The man's face was flushed already with drink, and as Hedda poured the ale, he reached for her, one hand fastening on the curve of her breast beneath the shapeless gown.

Hedda, though, made no response, not even by look, to the man's touch. Her broad, heavy face was stolidly set, her mouth slack, her eyes slightly dull. The man's bleared gaze focused briefly on her, and Isolde saw him frown, then give a shrug and turn away, dropping his hold.

Isolde forced herself to sit still, telling herself that she would jeopardize the fragile alliance of the council by speaking out. And more than that, Hedda would not thank her for making a scene, for drawing all eyes to the way she was forced to bear such attentions, to how, as a slave, she was unable to defend herself. Still, even watching, Isolde had clenched her hands and gritted her teeth. But Hedda, without pausing, without hurrying, moved away to pour ale for one of the other men.

The harper's song came to an end, and there was a ripple of applause from the men, a few fists beating approval on the table, a few cries of "Well sung." But the shouts and applause soon died away, and an expectant silence fell, as the purpose of the gathering returned to every mind.

"My friends. Dukes and kings."

Coel of Rhegged had risen to face the room. Coel was an old man now, the only one of the king's council old enough to have fought not only under Arthur, but under the Pendragon, as well. The hair that fell to the shoulders of his tunic was silver-gray, and his face, strong-featured and handsome as it must once have been, was hollowed-cheeked, the skin yellow as parchment with age. Still, he carried the remnants of what must have been a warrior's strength. His shoulders were bowed, but very broad, and his frame was powerful even yet, though the flesh had begun to shrink and tighten over the bones.

Now Coel's eyes, deep-set and almost golden as those of a falcon or hawk, swept the room.

"My friends," he said again, "I have kept largely silent during these last days and nights in the council hall, by reason of my years, and because I could not take the field in the battle you have just fought. But I would ask you to hear me now.

"My friends, the High King whose bravery we have tonight heard sung gave his life in Britain's defense, and as we begin this session of council, I would beg that you hold the life he gave for us in mind. Every night and every day we spend arguing and debating here among ourselves is another day wasted, a day that could be better spent in planning Britain's defense, that the deaths of Constantine and all who fell with him may not be in vain."

They were the sort of words, Isolde thought, spoken at all councils of this kind, the kind that always followed a war leader's death, whatever the man he might have been alive. But Coel's voice had wavered slightly in speaking Con's name, and as Coel finished with a bow, first to Isolde, then to Marche, she thought she saw a glimmer of moisture in the old man's eyes.

Isolde blinked quickly and looked away. These meetings of the council had been the hardest hours of the past days to get through. When she sat in Con's place among the men and tried to hold the muffling numbness about her a little longer. When she tried not to think of Con, who had loathed all sessions like this one of endless talk and debate. Who would have been counting the hours until he could escape to drill at sword practice with his fighting men. Though he'd have sat grimly through until the end, however much the hours of talk and debate tried his temper.

Isolde was almost grateful to find that Madoc of Gwynedd had risen in response to Coel's words. Madoc of Gwynedd was thirty at most, a dark, barrel-chested man with a heavy-jawed face heavily shadowed by a stubble of beard and small, piercing dark eyes. And he had, Isolde thought, disliked her always—even more than the rest of the king's councilmen.

An odd, silent, brooding man, who spoke seldom and fraternized little with his fellow kings—though he was respected among them as a fierce fighter and a skilled man with a sword. He was known also for a quick, fiery temper, and he carried out more floggings among his troops than any of the other leaders by far. But he was reputed to be a devout Christian, and she knew he rose at dawn every day to hear Mass with Father Nenian. And despite the taunts of the other men, rumor held him to be faithful to the memory of the wife who had died in childbed two years before, leaving him an infant son as heir.

He'd lost his father at the battle of Camlann, which explained, perhaps, why he'd distrusted Isolde from the moment she'd been crowned Con's queen. They'd met for the first time looking across the bloodied head of a stable boy he'd been beating for mistreating one of the horses. Isolde had lost her temper and told him in scathing terms what she thought of a man who beat a child not even half his size—whatever the boy's crime.

"Is that what the Christ teaches you in your Masses and your church?" she'd demanded as she stanched the flow of blood from the stable boy's nose.

Madoc's face had been dark with fury, and he'd said, still breathing hard, "They teach at any rate that women should keep still in the presence of men. It's written so in the Holy Bible. Now get out—and don't meddle with what's none of your concern."

Isolde had refused to leave the boy, though, and eventually it had been Madoc who'd stormed out of the stable yard, leaving her to salve the lad's bruised ribs and broken nose. She'd never bothered to look up whether what Madoc had said of the Christ-God's teachings was written so in the Bible or not—though it wouldn't have surprised her to find he'd told the truth.

The Christ and His God, she thought, have a good deal to answer for.

Now Madoc's manner was stiff, as though he spoke respectfully with an effort, but he made Coel a brief bow. "My lord Rhegged, I mean you no insult. We all know you have seen much in your time, and fought nobly, as well. But it's we who rule and fight for Britain as she stands now who have to be heard in this hall."

Coel's face was impassive, but he gave the younger man a brief inclination of his silvery head, and Madoc swung round to face the rest of the room.

"My fellow kings. I wouldn't question the bravery of King Constantine. As a brother in arms, I loved the king well. But still I say the time for a High King ruling over all Britain has come and gone. In Gwynedd we fight not the Saxons but the wild raiders from Ireland. Of what use is the High King to me? And while I and my fighting men are called away to do service to the High King, my land is left ripe for their plunder."

Madoc paused, and Isolde saw the men on the benches shift uneasily under his gaze, and a few mutter to their neighbors. But some were nodding slow agreement.

Madoc raised his voice to be heard over the crowd. "I say we are better off each among us ruling our own kingdoms and seeing to the defense of our own."

"This is folly!" The speaker was Huel, Coel of Rhegged's son, his face angry, his voice ringing out across the hall. Huel's face was narrow and almost a younger mirror of Coel's own, with the same sharp brow and nose, the same strong chin, though his eyes were muddy brown instead of fiery gold.

Isolde didn't know Huel well—had never even spoken to him directly that she could recall. Still, as Huel rose from his place by his father's side and faced Madoc, she tried to remember all she knew of Coel's eldest son and heir.

She could remember Con returning from campaign and speaking of Huel. And for all she'd been trying to suppress any thought of Con, she found she was thankful that he'd known the men around her and had taken their measure in leading them into war.

A plodder, Con had called Huel, and Isolde herself had already judged him in these last days a less intelligent man by far than his father. Though a good commander and man-at-arms, for all that, according to Con. *A good fighter, chiefly because once he gets an idea into that thick head of his, he won't let up. Whether it's a sword fight or a battle or an argument at dice, Huel of Rhegged plows on until he's won.*

Con, Isolde thought, had not been a man to seek overmuch insight into the thoughts and minds of his fellow men. If a man was honest and could be trusted to seat his horse and wield his sword well, it was enough. But all the same, Isolde would have taken his word on any soldier's character, and she thought she might trust his judgment of the man before her now.

Con had said, too, that Huel would not make half the king his father had done. He'd neither Coel's keenness nor his gift at winning the hearts and allegiance of his men. Coel himself, Isolde thought, might fill the place of High King well. But he cannot live many years more—perhaps not even many more months.

And Huel would never hold the factions together. The kings of Britain might have united under Arthur—and even, though less willingly, under Con. But Huel would never be the man to unite them again.

Though that, Isolde thought, may be beyond the skills of all the rest of the men here as well. A wave of defeat swept through her as she remembered what she'd felt in the chapel. That the hope of Britain had already died with Arthur on the fields of Camlann.

Huel had drawn a breath and now went on, turning to in-

clude the room at large in what he said. "For seven years we
have watched lands—good lands—vanish into the gullets of the
Saxon armies. Watched our settlements pillaged and burned
and been able to do nothing but slink farther and farther west
like curs with our tails between our legs. Now we have made
a stand—done battle with the Saxon dogs and won. And you
would throw that away?"

"My friends, peace, I beg you."

Owain of Powys, too, was a young man, not yet thirty, Isolde
judged, and lean, almost slightly built, though with a slim, graceful strength about his frame. "Peace—and pray be seated."

Coel's son seemed about to argue, but Coel placed a restraining hand on his arm, and after a moment's hesitation the younger
man subsided onto the bench. Madoc, too, seemed to hesitate,
but then, with a grudging nod, yielded Owain the floor.

Owain turned to face the room at large.

He was a handsome man, his features refined nearly to deli-
cacy, with high cheekbones and a narrow, pointed chin; eyes of
greenish hazel set under straight dark brows; and a soft, almost
feminine mouth. He had a ready laugh and a quick smile, and
Isolde had seen the serving maids tonight vying to be the one to
refill his drinking horn or offer him platters of food—and seen
Owain, laughing, circle their waists with his arm and pull the
fairest down onto his knee.

The Popinjay, Con had always called him, for his liking of
rich fabrics and fine jewels and clothes. Con had said, too, that
he would sooner fight with the Saxon army ahead of him than
with Owain of Powys guarding his back. *When the fighting's at its
worst, you'll find him right squarely in the rear. Guarding that pretty
face of his from being damaged.*

Isolde was inclined to believe Con's valuation of Owain, as
well. She had never liked Owain. Not since she'd sat beside a
young serving maid, holding the girl's hand while she writhed

and hemorrhaged and bled to an agonized death. The girl had taken a dirty kitchen knife and tried to abort herself of Owain's child.

In fairness, though, Isolde was not sure that Owain had known anything of the baby—or the girl's death. And certainly none of those who lined the benches of the hall tonight would count the incident the slightest bit in Owain's disfavor.

These were, she thought, the same men who would have been utterly disbelieving—or angry—had she spoken out earlier on Hedda's behalf.

And all at once a hatred—an almost physical revulsion—swept through Isolde for everything about the council hall. The smoke-filled room, the smell of closely packed bodies, and sweat, and ale from the drinking horns. Everything about this world of men and killing and war that devoured and destroyed men like Con. Or gulped and spat them out, she thought, her mouth twisting, like the fair-haired boy Ralf in the infirmary, so that they were never whole either in mind or in body again.

With an effort, Isolde forced her attention back to Owain. The king of Powys had an easy, good-humored charm that had won him a following among the council's dukes and petty kings. And his holdings were among the largest—and the richest—of them all. He wore tonight a saffron-dyed tunic, edged with fur at the hem and throat, and over it a cloak of silvery wolf's-pelt, held in place by a jewel-studded brooch, the green of the stones echoing the flecks of greenish gold in his eyes.

"For myself, I agree with my lord Huel. A kingdom without a king is like a gelding who takes a wench to bed. Not much chance either one is going to get on with the job at hand."

A ripple of laughter went round the room at that, and Owain's mouth tipped up into an easy, self-deprecating smile as he paused. It was, Isolde thought with another flicker of disgust, the kind of speech she would have expected from him. Pleasant, humorous—and calculated to jolly the listeners into a mood where their allegiances could be easily won.

But as Owain stood, head thrown back as he waited for the laughter to die down, Isolde saw Coel lift his head alertly, his eyes, watchful and suddenly keen, going to the younger man's face.

"But if we cannot yet agree on the problem of choosing a High King," Owain went on, "perhaps we may at least agree on who shall take up the ruling of the High King's domain, since tragically my lord King Constantine died without heir."

Isolde stiffened, but forced herself not to react. She'd seen many of the councilmen turn hostile, searching looks in her direction at Owain's words, and she could see herself and their thoughts reflected in their gaze as clearly as if they'd spoken aloud. The traitor's bastard girl had failed to give their king an heir, and so now they would fight for the High King's lands like dogs over a bone.

And I wonder, Isolde thought, how long it will be before they begin to argue over who will win possession of Con's widow, as well.

Letting her gaze travel round the room, she happened to see Coel's face. The old man was looking not at her, but at Owain, and his mouth was thin, his gaze chill. Before Owain could go on, Coel raised a hand again. He was growing weary, Isolde saw. The earlier effort had tired him, and the arm he held aloft shook a little within the flowing sleeve. But he spoke in a clear, carrying voice, his eyes still on Owain.

"My lord of Powys. I would ask you to remember the presence of Lady Isolde."

His eyes moved briefly to Isolde's face, and she thought there was a flash of pity or compassion in their gaze, for all Coel had been entirely Modred's enemy and Arthur's man. If I were to trust any of them, she thought, it would be Coel. He was honest, a man of honor, whatever he thought of Isolde herself.

There was Huel, though. Isolde's gaze moved to the younger man, still seated at his father's side, his narrow face both shadowed and gilded by the flame of the torch at his back.

Another cold ripple slid through Isolde as the memory of a fire-lit war tent filled her mind's eye. Huel, she thought, who will rule Rhegged after his father is gone. And who was among those camped on the battlefield three nights ago with Con.

"Of course." In a moment, Owain had turned to face Isolde. "Forgive me, Lady Isolde."

Isolde let him take her hand and make a low bow over it. His skin felt dry to the touch, smooth and a little cool. Like the scales of a snake.

Owain of Powys raised his head. "You may trust me—and all of us assembled here—to serve you as we did your husband, Lady Isolde."

The chill was deepening, spreading to grip her bones and choke her throat. Slowly, Isolde nodded, telling herself it would be fatal danger to betray fear. "Yes, Lord Owain." Her voice sounded hard and flat in her own ears. "I know that I may trust you that much."

She watched Owain return to his place, then looked again over the assembled men, feeling a sudden bleak certainty that there was no use in her speaking out. That in the eyes of all those here anything she said was already damned.

Still, she rose, pitching her voice to address the room at large. "My lords. I would speak to you on behalf of my husband, King Constantine, whom so many of you have honored tonight."

Isolde felt a stir of uneasiness run round the room, but she continued.

"Three times in the last two hundred years, Britain has faced peril. First when the legions marched back to Rome and left Britain to the mercy of raiding Saxons and Irish tribes. King Vortigern was betrayed by his Saxon allies, and it was only because Ambrosius Aurelianus rode with his armies out of the Welsh hills that we were not broken and overwhelmed."

Isolde paused, then went on. "But Ambrosius died without an heir. And the Pendragon had to battle for the throne. The very fortress of Tintagel here he won when he met and slew Duke Gorlois, who had rebelled against his claim. And then again, when Uther died, there was no apparent heir to take the throne. And even when Arthur was named High King, many refused to follow a child gotten outside of wedlock, son of the Pendragon though he might be. And then . . . then Arthur fell at the battle of Camlann, and for the third time there was no king to take his place on the throne."

She paused again. "Three times Britain's High King has fallen without an heir to carry on the war against the Saxons and the defense of the land. Three times, the kingdom has been torn by Briton fighting Briton. And each time, we have lost ground to the Saxons. Now we hold only these lands of Cornwall, the western Welsh lands, and in the north the Orkneys and Strathclyde."

Isolde drew breath, letting her gaze travel the length of the room.

"And now we face again a king dead without an heir, and a fresh threat from the Saxon hordes. Can any of you doubt what the end will be if what few kingdoms remain in British hands are splintered by yet another struggle for power among their kings?"

For a long moment after Isolde had resumed her seat, there was silence in the timbered hall. In the flickering torchlight, the men's faces were grave, but none spoke. And none rose. Then Madoc of Gwynedd's voice rang out again.

"Pretty words—from the great traitor's bastard."

Chapter Six

B EFORE TURNING TO FACE THE room, Madoc sent Isolde a look as black and hostile as he had that long-ago day in the stable yard. Then went on, speaking with an effort to control his temper, though his voice turned rasping and tight.

"My lords, she speaks of times when lands have been lost to the Saxons because Briton has fought Briton and not the common foe. She, whose father Modred made alliance with the Saxons against Arthur the King. Modred, whose treason cost us all the lands east of the Severn and south of Ambrosius's wall. Have you all gone mad, to listen to her? Let her bespell you with that honey-sweet witch's voice of hers?"

Madoc's voice rose, his face darkening as he went on. "The granddaughter of Morgan, who caught Arthur by the balls and bewitched him into getting her bastard son. Whose arts set that bastard son on the throne—so that she could snatch the power she'd stolen from Arthur when she bespelled him and his cock. How do we know the queen here is not another such? She's reigned at Constantine's side for seven years—had him bewitched to jump and crawl at a flick of her hand. And now she'd set another man up in our king's place before he's cold in his grave. And as like as not in her bed, as—"

"My Lord, you forget yourself!"

Coel had risen as well, his carved face set with anger, his back erect, his golden hawk's eyes blazing beneath the heavy brows. He was nearing the end of his strength, though. His face had a waxen pallor, and Isolde saw the hand that grasped his son's shoulder tremble.

Isolde let out her breath. There was a strange kind of relief— a satisfaction, almost—in the confrontation, in feeling the suppressed tensions and hostilities of the council hall come to a head and spill into the open like poison from a festering wound. She found it far easier to keep hold of her temper than when she'd watched Hedda manhandled by the other petty king. Though that, she thought, might only be because she'd heard Madoc's words—or variations on them—so many times before.

"My lord Coel," she said, "I thank you for your defense." The eyes of every man in the hall were upon her, and she looked slowly up and down the benches, meeting the gaze of each one. Then she fixed her eyes on Madoc and said, her voice even and very quiet, "My lord Madoc forgets himself indeed."

She heard several breaths sharply indrawn, and saw a hint of fear come to light in Madoc of Gwynedd's dark eyes. The same fear she'd seen in Hunno and Erbin. Before she could speak again, though, another voice, loud and harsh, rang out across the hall.

"My lord Madoc, be seated." Marche had risen from his place opposite her own, and now strode forward to confront the other man. "Our king lies dead. To snap and snarl among ourselves now—like the very savages we fight—dishonors his memory. And I will not even speak aloud my opinion of offering insult to his queen."

He paused, making a brief bow to Isolde. Isolde, sitting

rigid in her place, felt the warming anger fade and a tendril of fear uncurl deep inside. Marche's face was grave, his expression showing nothing but cold, stern disapproval of Madoc's words. But there was something—something in his eyes—that made her wonder whether she'd not played directly into his hands in speaking out as she had.

Isolde's head had begun to pound with the heat and the noise, and she felt all at once as small and as powerless as though she stood alone under a leaden sky and tried to hold off one of the summer storms that sent the soil of the headlands plummeting into the sea. Sightless, unable to see clearly whom among the council she might trust, had she any chance of holding off Britain's ruin?

Have I even, she thought, the right to try?

Marche held her gaze a moment, then turned to face Madoc.

Marche had taken another step toward the younger man, and now went on, weary dark eyes intent on Madoc's. "And so I say again, Madoc of Gwynedd, take your seat once more—or leave the hall. The choice is yours."

Isolde saw Madoc's jaw harden, and a vein in the base of his neck begin to throb. His hand went, as though reflexively, to the knife he wore at his belt, and Isolde saw the knuckles whitening as he gripped the hilt. She saw, too, his dark gaze move to the pair of Marche's men-at-arms who had risen and moved to take their place at their lord's back, their hands, likewise, on the hilts of their swords.

From along the benches on either side came the clink and rustle of cloth as other men shifted and poised themselves to reach for daggers or swords. Isolde's every muscle tightened, waiting for the first blow to be struck and the violence that had rippled beneath the surface of every word spoken that night to erupt. She felt the same tense expectation from the rest of the crowd. But something else, as well.

Hunger, she thought. For a fight—for blood. She wondered bleakly whether warfare always changed men this way—made them lust after a fight, no matter who with, even after the battle with the enemy was done. A shiver twisted through her. Maybe Con, too, would have ended up this way if he'd stayed on the throne many years more.

Marche went on, lowering his voice and dropping one hand on the other man's shoulder.

"Madoc of Gwynedd, you say you loved the young king well, and I know you fought bravely at his side these many years since he took the throne. I know you, too, to be a man of honor. I cannot believe you will let the evening end with a spilling of blood in King Constantine's very hall."

It was, Isolde thought, masterfully done, and she felt the chill of fear curl and settle in the pit of her stomach. Easy to see why Marche had won a following for himself among those assembled here.

She saw the anger on Madoc's face quiver and then break, and then tension ebb away out of his frame. The hand on his knife hilt relaxed, moving instead to meet Marche's with a firm clasp.

"My lord Marche, son of Méirchion, I yield you the floor." Madoc bowed, then turned to Isolde and said stiffly, "My lady, forgive me." Then, before she could respond, he turned aside.

Marche waited a beat, drawing once more the eyes of all in the room. Then: "My lords. Our king will be buried tomorrow, but tonight—and for the last night since he fell—he will lie in the chapel here. I would ask you, all of you, to keep a vigil with me there. A vigil of fasting and prayer."

A low murmur ran round the room at that, but Marche spoke over it, spreading out one hand and gesturing toward Isolde.

"My lady Isolde spoke tonight of the Pendragon, and of King Arthur the Great. And you have all heard of the scarlet dragon that appeared in the sky as sign that Uther was to be king. Of how, as a boy of but fourteen, Arthur drew the sword of kingship from solid stone—another sign from God, proof that Arthur was the one chosen to take the throne when his father fell."

Marche paused, letting his gaze again play over the room, then went on lowering his voice once more. "My friends, I ask that you keep vigil over the body of King Constantine tonight and pray for another such sign. For another sign from God, showing His will as to who will rule now that our king is gone."

THE MOON WAS HIDDEN BY THICK cloud as Isolde crossed toward the queen's chambers, the great courtyard dark and still, lit only by the occasional flare of a burning torch. Her eyes still stung with the smoke of the council hall's fire, and her headache had grown worse, so that when a man's shadowed form stepped out of the stairwell that led to her rooms, she drew up sharply, biting back an exclamation of surprise.

"Lord Marche. I had thought you would be keeping your chapel vigil with the rest."

The flare of the torch that burned beside the door patched his face with shadow, picked out the gilding on the hem and collar of his tunic, and making the jeweled eyes of the boar on his shoulder brooch glow red.

"I came, Lady Isolde, to ask whether you have given thought to what your own position is now."

Isolde stepped through the doorway into the passage, and Marche followed, hitching the injured left leg a little awkwardly over the stone step.

"The hour is late, my lord. And I would ask that you speak plainly. What is it you mean?"

"I mean that you are without father—and now without a husband as well." Marche paused, then went on, without looking at her. "There is word going around the council that Owain of Powys intends to offer for your hand."

Isolde pushed back the hood of her cloak, remembering Owain's refined, handsome face, his smiling hazel eyes. History repeats itself, she thought, time and again. Ygraine, wife of Gorlois. And Gwynefar, my own mother. Even pretended witchcraft won't win power enough to escape the fate of a woman left alone.

"Then," she said evenly, "I would make to him the same reply I would make to any other man. My lord husband and king has been dead but three days. To think of taking another in his place would be dishonor to his memory."

Marche lifted a hand and let it fall. "Perhaps, Lady Isolde. But all the same, you will have need of a man's name—for your own protection, and for the sake of the lands you yourself hold." He stopped. "And as you are on Cornish lands, I feel it my duty to offer you mine."

Isolde found she wasn't even surprised. "So, for duty's sake, you will offer to marry me yourself? Is that the same duty that called you from my father's side at Camlann?"

Marche's eyes narrowed. "I have accounted for that before the king's council. I was imprisoned by your father. Forced into lending him aid. Drugged and ensorcelled by Morgan the witch. Then at Camlann I was at last able to break free and join Arthur, my rightful lord. I have nothing more to say."

And if, Isolde thought, the king's council doubted Marche's tale, they would—will still—have found it convenient to hold their tongues and believe. Those left to piece together a kingdom from the wreckage of Arthur and Modred's battles had had need of every man. And Marche commanded too rich a territory, too great a force of fighting men to be rejected. Especially when his swing of allegiance had been the final blow that had lost Modred the war.

Marche lowered his voice and added, "And I would be careful, Lady Isolde. In your current place, an enemy is a thing you can ill afford to make. Do you understand?"

Isolde put one hand on the stair's guardrail, then turned to face Marche again.

"What I understand, Lord Marche—and understand well—is that you would stand a far better chance of being named High King if you could claim sovereignty over Camelerd in addition to Cornwall. But I will make no man ruler over my own lands unless I believe he will both govern and defend the country well. And you, who betrayed my father, schemed and clawed for your own power all the time you ruled for Constantine, are the last man in Britain I would choose."

Marche was not a man who easily lost control. Now, though, in a flash, his hand shot out, dragging her toward him, so that Isolde saw just how tightly stretched he was, the ragged nerves pulsing beneath the veneer of civil calm.

"So you say, my lady." They were only a handsbreadth apart, and Isolde caught the reek of sour wine on his breath, felt the heavy rise and fall of his chest against hers. She flinched.

Marche smiled, his thumb tracing the line of her jaw. "I could force you, you know. Marriage by rape is still valid in the eyes of the law."

In the silence of the stone-built passage, the sound of Isolde's own breath, the beating of her heart in her ears, was very loud. Marche's grip hardened, his fingers tightening on her throat. I could scream, she thought. But who would come? One of Marche's men? One of the men who took the death-oath to guard Con?

She fought down a leeching wave of panic and lifted her head to meet Marche's gaze.

"Try it," she said, between her teeth. "I swear on my husband's soul I'll put a knife through my heart before I wed you or any other man."

THE FLIGHT OF STEPS SEEMED TO stretch on and on. Isolde forced herself to climb slowly, to keep her head utterly straight and her eyes on the gray stone wall ahead, though she could feel Marche's furious gaze still on her from where she'd left him at the foot of the stairs. But when she opened the door to her rooms and saw the woman who sat on the carved wooden settle beside the fire, she froze.

Nest.

Her control was beginning to feel as brittle as hot glass, but Isolde responded to the other woman's curtsy with a brief nod, then crossed to the tapestried chair that stood to one side of the hearth and gestured for Nest to be seated, as well. The room was the one used by her ladies and serving women for weaving and spinning, though the looms were now covered, the spindles and balls of wool piled in baskets on the floor.

"I must apologize," Isolde said. "If I had known I would be receiving visitors tonight, I would have had refreshment on hand."

A spark of irritation at the implied rebuke flared in Nest's eyes, but she shook her head. She was a big woman, a year or two past thirty, with a flat, almost masculine face crowned by straight, thick hair the color of coal, and a frame rawboned and heavy beneath an expensive saffron-dyed gown that was embroidered with gold and silver thread at the hem and sleeves.

"I want nothing." Her deep-toned voice, too, was almost masculine and her eyes were small and dark. She was a kinswoman of Marche's, a cousin on his mother's side, and

had served as chatelaine of his castle since her husband had
died.

Chatelaine and more besides, so rumor would have it. Certainly,
Isolde thought, she sees to the speedy dismissal or sale of whatever serving woman or slave Marche takes to his bed. Before the
woman could bear him a child that might challenge her own claims.

And these last three years, since the war had been concen-
trated in the south, she had served at Tintagel as mistress of
Isolde's ladies. Marche had offered, and Con had not, in courtesy, been able to refuse, as the battles were being waged over
much of Marche's land.

Now Nest was silent a moment. Then, abruptly, she said, "I
hear, Majesty, that you have dismissed your serving women."

"For a few days only," Isolde said. She used the same formula
she had used with Hunno and Erbin in the chapel, though this
time as she spoke the words she felt a twist of the panic she'd felt
with Marche in the stairwell below. "I would be alone with my
grief for the present time."

Nest bowed her head. "I understand, my lady. But it is hardly
fitting that the dowager queen should be served by a single slave.
My Lord Marche quite agrees with me, as do the members of
the council."

She paused, her eyes locking on Isolde's. "I have selected a
girl whom I deem worthy of the honor of serving you. She will
begin tomorrow."

So, Isolde thought. The rest of the men on the king's council
trust me as little as I trust Marche—or Nest. I wonder whether
Marche had even to work to persuade the councilmen that the
Witch Queen must have a spy to keep watch on her at all times.

Her skin still felt clammy from her encounter with Marche,
and all at once she wanted nothing—nothing—so much as to
snatch off the jeweled necklace and golden diadem she wore and
fling them, with all her strength, against the gray stone wall.

Yes, she thought, and what then? Nest's women would come in and curtsy and quietly sweep up the broken pieces. The jewels would be taken to Tintagel's metalworkers to be repaired. And Nest would have yet one more tale to carry back to Marche and the rest of the council. One more reason that the dowager queen must be forced to accept the protection of another man.

Isolde drew in a slow breath. *The stars will still shine tomorrow, whatever happens to me here.*

"I might have expected nothing less of you, Lady Nest." She rose. "And now I must beg you would excuse me. The hour is late."

Nest, though, didn't move. "There was another matter, my lady." The older woman lowered her lids, veiling her eyes. "I am sorry to bring you more ill news at such a time, my lady. But it's about Branwen."

Isolde looked up, startled. "Branwen?" Whatever she had expected, it was not this. The girl was one of the youngest of her serving women, the daughter of Con's steward. A thick-limbed, plump girl of maybe fifteen or sixteen with curling nut-brown hair and a round, pretty, gap-toothed face. Isolde could see her, laughing when Con pulled her onto his knee in the banquet hall—and preening herself because for nearly two months, now, the High King had called her almost nightly to his bed.

"What of her?"

Nest's eyes were still on the large, square-knuckled hands folded in her lap, and she said, with no change of voice, "She is dead, my lady."

Isolde stiffened. "Dead? How?"

"A sudden illness, my lady. She died last night."

Nest's dark eyes lifted to meet Isolde's, and Isolde worked to draw another breath.

Of course, she thought. Nest would not leave a girl alive who might be carrying Con's child. Such a child could be used as a pawn all too easily by one who would challenge Marche's claim on the throne.

It might have hurt her, once, to think of Branwen bearing Con a daughter or son, though since the girl had caught Con's eye, Isolde had felt nothing but simple pity for Branwen herself. Pity, because she knew the girl would keep Con's favor no longer than any of the rest. Though he'd have seen her as generously rewarded with jewels as the others—and probably married to one of his men-at-arms, as well.

And now Nest had killed her. As carelessly as she might have drowned a stray kitten.

Abruptly, Isolde rose to her feet, signaling an end to the visit.

"Very well," she said shortly. "I will speak to Father Nenian about the burial. And I will tell her father and mother myself."

Chapter Seven

ONLY WHEN NEST WAS GONE, the door closed behind her, did Isolde allow herself to let out a long, shuddering breath. For a long moment she stood in the center of the room, eyes closed. Then she turned and crossed to the curtained doorway that led to the bedchamber.

Someone—it must have been Hedda—had banked the bedroom fire so that it still glowed red and warm. A lamp had been lighted as well, showing walls hung with tapestries and, in the center of the room, a massive carved bed. The bed was made of wood nearly black with age and was hung with fur-lined scarlet curtains against the autumn chill, and the rest of the furnishings were of the same solid, carved wood.

Isolde paused in the doorway, her eyes drawn by a bowl that stood to one side of the hearth, the bronze sides thin with age and etched with serpents of eternity, tails in their mouths, the eyes picked out with bloodred stones. Then, with an effort, she turned away, crossing to the room's deep circular recess, part of the turret that here, on Tintagel's westernmost side, perched on the very brink of the sea.

The space held a single narrow window, as yet uncovered by the scraped and oiled hide that would be tacked over it in winter, so that now the ocean's salt tang and cooling mist came freely through. Isolde sank down on a chair, staring unseeingly out at the night and listening to the steady crash of waves against the rocks below.

It must have been easy enough, she thought, for Nest. A brew of something—nightshade or another poison—dropped into Branwen's cup of beer. She remembered the rumors still whispered about Nest, even now. Rumors of Marche's wife, dead these seven years.

She, too, belonged to the time Isolde had blotted out completely, but Isolde had heard Nest's women speak of her in sly, frightened whispers, when Nest was not there to hear. Marche's wife had been a Saxon princess, sold by her father, King Cerdic of Wessex, into marriage as part of Modred's alliance with the Saxon king. A slight, fair-haired girl, so the stories went, who crept about Marche's castle with a bruised face and terrified eyes.

And then, conveniently for Marche, she had died after the battle of Camlann, when alliance with the Saxons was spoken of as treason and shame, and a Saxon wife could cost a man his place on the newly reformed king's council, made up almost wholly of Arthur's surviving men.

Isolde had thought herself alone, but now a touch against her hand made her start and turn, then let out her breath as she saw the big white-and-brown hunting dog that had come to lay a massive paw across her knee and thrust his nose against her palm. Isolde stroked his head, and he answered her with an anxious whine.

"Good dog, Cabal. Good fellow."

As she spoke, the curtain lifted and Hedda slipped in, her fair hair laden with droplets of the mist from outside. She looked from Cabal to Isolde and shook her head.

"I not understand. That dog not come near you before. And now he not leave your side."

"He knows something is wrong, poor fellow."

Isolde stroked the big dog's head again. Cabal had been Con's hunting dog, and his war-hound, as well. Isolde's fingers traced the raised scar—left by a Saxon sword—that ran along the animal's shoulder beneath the creamy brindled fur, and all at once a memory rose before her, vivid as a scene tapestried in colored wool. Con riding out at the head of the army—nearly a half-moon's time ago, now—the red Pendragon banner flying in the wind above, and Cabal, running alongside Con's horse, keeping pace with the galloping hooves in a series of great, effortless leaps.

One of the king's council—Isolde thought it might have been Coel—had brought Cabal home to Tintagel three days ago, alongside the body of his king. And ever since, the big dog had stayed in Isolde's rooms, setting up a pitiful howl when one of the serving women tried to take him away. He'd refused to eat and had lain all but unmoving, head pillowed on his paws, liquid eyes dark with a look of almost human grief.

Now he whimpered again, and Isolde ran a hand along his back. "It's all right, Cabal. That's a good fellow."

The dog subsided onto the floor at her feet, and Isolde looked up to find Hedda watching her.

"What has happened, my lady?"

Isolde was suddenly unable to check herself, unable to stop from answering Hedda's look of concern. One hand still on Cabal's head, she said, "Lord Marche has offered me an alliance of marriage. And there is word that Owain of Powys means to offer for me, as well."

For all that Hedda was less guarded with her than with anyone else at the fortress, it was seldom they spoke together like this. Isolde waited for the blank, dull look to return to Hedda's eyes, the expression of stolid calm to settle over her face once more. Instead, though, Hedda said, "You expected that?"

"Yes, I expected it." Isolde paused, then added bitterly, "Camelerd is too rich a prize for any man of ambition to risk losing his chance by waiting until the king is cold in his grave."

Hedda nodded slowly. "And you think one of them—Owain or Marche—will be chosen the next High King?"

"I think them the most likely. Madoc of Gwynedd might have had a chance at the throne as well, but that he spoke as he did against the kingship in the council hall tonight. And Coel is too old."

Hedda turned away to stoke the fire with fresh logs from the pile. Then, when the glowing red embers had kindled to a blaze, she rose, moved to a carved wooden chest, and drew out Isolde's bed gown.

"You believe Marche's talk of sign tomorrow night?" Hedda asked.

Isolde sat down on the edge of the bed and began to untie the laces of her overtunic, though her eyes went, almost involuntarily, to the bronze bowl, tracing the threads of light that ran along its serpent-twined sides.

"I think," she said at last, "that maybe there was once a place in Britain for magic and signs. That once, before the Christ-God came, there were gods in the hills and pools and sacred groves. And a time when druid-men could walk untouched over beds of burning hazel boughs and read the future in the flight of the birds above." She looked up at Hedda, lifting one hand and letting it fall. "Maybe the God of the Christ isn't a god of magic. I don't know. But I think that time is now gone."

Hedda seemed to hesitate. Then: "You think Marche lied?"

Isolde was silent, ice settling in the pit of her stomach at the memory of Marche's grip on her throat. She was remembering, too, the anger that had simmered in him, the impression she'd had of desperation and ragged nerves. Something more was at stake for him than simply winning the wealth her own lands would yield. But what, she thought, I don't know.

"Lied?" she repeated. "I can't be sure. I mistrust him and his talk of a miraculous sign. But I have no father, no brother—and now no husband. And there are none among the king's council I would trust—"

Isolde stopped. Hedda had been helping her off with the embroidered overtunic of her gown. The Saxon girl didn't pause in her movements, but Isolde caught the brief stiffening of her frame and saw one of those quick, tight spasms flash across the broad planes of her face. "I'm sorry, Hedda," she said quietly. "You lost your family as well."

Hedda was still a moment longer, and then she turned, kneeling before the carved chest to fold the overtunic and gown away. When she spoke, her voice was once more flat and dull, the Saxon accent strong as it had ever been.

"True. Though in different way." She let the lid of the trunk fall with a heavy thud. "I go where the gods send—take what I can."

Her face was still turned away, but Isolde saw the blunt fingers clench and tighten on the edge of the wood.

"I'm sorry, Hedda," she said again.

Hedda drew in a long breath, and when she rose to her feet and turned, Isolde saw the weariness in her broad, heavy face, the shadows about her eyes. She looked pale, too, her mouth tight and drawn.

Isolde hesitated a moment. Then: "Hedda, are you well? You look as though you've been ill."

As though unconsciously, Hedda's hands went to her middle, grasping the rope girdle of her gown. And, watching, Isolde remembered the men in the council hall, with their drunken shouts and roving hands. She wondered for a moment whether she should speak. But before she could decide, Hedda had pushed the heavy braid of hair back over her shoulder and said, her voice flat, "I'm well, lady. And if not for you, I would have been sold into far worse life than what I have here."

She turned and began to sponge the dirt from the hem of Isolde's workday gown. "You spoke of the king's council. Is there . . . ?" Hedda seemed to hesitate again, then looked up. Her eyes, pale and unaccustomedly keen, searched Isolde's face, and then she said softly, "You think my lord King not die of battle wounds?"

Isolde hadn't meant to burden—or endanger—the girl with the knowledge she had carried these last three days. She'd not have suspected, though, that Hedda would guess so much, and something inside her seemed to crack at the unexpected question.

She'd taken up the bone and silver comb from her dressing table, but stopped. "I don't *think*," she heard herself say. "I know. I saw him killed. I watched him die."

Isolde was distantly aware of Hedda's sharp gasp, but the remnants of the vision were gathering and forming before her once more, and the sound seemed to come from a long way off.

"It was three nights ago," she said, "the night the king's messengers came to tell us the battle was won, the Saxon army in retreat, and that Con had taken a wound in the final skirmish. An injury—but by no means a grave one."

Her own voice, too, sounded distant to her, the words coming like something she had learned by heart. "I was sitting here, in this room, alone. I was watching the fire, and thinking of Con, wondering whether he would soon send me a message of his own. And then . . ."

And then, slowly, a scene had taken shape at the glowing heart of the flames. A circle of men, crouched about another fire, but this one open, built on a field under a star-studded

night sky. The air was thick with smoke, but Isolde could see
them vividly. The streaks of mud and sweat on their faces, the
stubble of several days' growth of beard on their chins. Their
stiff leather war tunics, emblazoned with the king's crest, and
the battle-hardened weariness in their eyes. They were passing
a skin of ale around the circle, and one man was speaking, the
words rhythmic and low. A tale of Arthur, it had been—of how
the king had slain nine hundred Saxons with his own sword at
Badon Hill.

After seven years of empty gray, without even a flicker of
Vision or Sight, the suddenness—and the clarity of the image—
had made Isolde gasp with shock. And then, even as she felt,
still, the heat of her fire on her hands and face, the hard wood of
the chair at her back, she was also there—able to feel the damp,
chill bite of the wind, hear the distant nickerings of the warhorses tied a few yards away, even feel the pull of the mud beneath her feet as she moved about the circle—though the men
one and all looked through her as though at empty air.

A strange burning, like cold fire, rippled through her veins,
and she felt herself move as though she stood apart from herself,
as though compelled by a will other than her own. A tent, larger
than any of the others and flying the dragon banner, stood beyond, and she turned toward it, walking with her heart beating
hard in her ears, though she could not have said why. The tent
flaps were drawn and tightly tied, but she had no need of an
opening or door. One moment she stood before the tent, surrounded by the smoke of campfires and the stench of battlefield
rot. And the next she was inside, looking down at Con's sleeping
form.

He slept on his back, his hands folded over his chest. His
face, in the orange glow from the fire without, looked peaceful
and frighteningly young beneath a scattering of bruises and a
smear of dried mud. His tunic hung open, and she could see the

wound he had taken in the side, covered by bandages held in place with a bronze pin. And all was silent, utterly deserted and still, the only movement the soft rise and fall of Con's breast. But it should not have been. There should have been guards here. Men-at-arms who slept at the feet of their king.

Isolde had time to see it, to see that the guards were gone, and that Con was alone save for Cabal, likewise asleep, in the tent's corner. And then with a soft rustling of leather, the tent flaps were drawn aside, and a figure, a man's dim form, slipped into the room. The man wore an ordinary soldier's garb, and a hood of some dark material had been drawn over his head, concealing his face. Isolde stood frozen, watching as he approached the bed, her veins still burning with those strange, cold flames that seemed to compel her to keep still, and only to look. And, slowly, she saw the figure draw out from his belt a dagger, a tiny thing, almost a child's toy, but for the narrow blade that gleamed in the fire's light.

Isolde stopped speaking. Her throat had gone dry as she told the story, and she swallowed, turning at last to meet Hedda's gaze. Hedda hadn't moved. There was something new in her eyes, though, as her pale blue gaze met Isolde's. A look almost of wonder, or fear. For whatever Isolde had pretended to others, she had never tried to make Hedda believe she had any of the old power left.

At last Hedda looked away. "What did you do, my lady?"

Isolde realized that her hands were clenched so tightly about the bone comb that the teeth had left marks in her palms, and when she relaxed her grip a few drops of blood rose to the surface of her skin. She looked down at the tiny beads of crimson, a shudder twisting through her.

"I screamed," she said at last. "And ran to Con—I could move, then. And speak. But he didn't hear. And when I tried to rouse him, to shake him awake, my hands only passed through his skin as though I—or he—were nothing. No more solid than mist or the smoke outside. And then—"

Isolde stopped, waiting until her voice was steady enough to go on. "And then the man struck," she said in a whisper. "A thrust to the heart. It's an easy enough blow to find on a sleeping man. And it kills almost at once. Con didn't even cry out. Just a little gasp—almost a sigh. And then he was gone. The physicians"— Isolde's mouth twisted—"the physicians said when they found his body in the morning that the battle wound must have been graver than anyone believed. It had opened during the night and bled until he died."

Hedda's eyes met Isolde's, and again there was a look of un- guarded understanding in their pale gaze. "Lord Marche's phy- sicians?"

Hedda, Isolde thought, knows far more than anyone suspects. Even I would not have thought she would guess so quickly at the truth.

She nodded. "As you say."

The vision had faded, then, as suddenly as it had come. The fire-lit tent, the smell of mud, the sight of Con—all had van- ished, leaving her sitting once more before her own hearth, her whole body icy cold, her head throbbing with the familiar sick- ening pain that marked always a return from Sight. The hearth held only common fire once more, nothing but the comfortable hiss and crackle of the flames.

But she'd had no doubt, either then or since, that the vision had been true. And she'd seen for herself the narrow, blue-lipped wound in Con's side when his body was brought home.

Isolde looked toward the window to clear her eyes of the memory, then went on. "I never saw the man's face . . . the man who struck the blow. But it wasn't Marche himself. This man was younger—not as heavily built. And he walked without any of the limp Marche has."

She paused. "He might have been one of Marche's men. But someone—someone close to Con—must have arranged for Con's guards to be away." Isolde looked down at the war-hound, still curled at her feet, his head resting on his paws. "And someone drugged Cabal, too, so he'd not raise an alarm."

Hedda didn't reply at once. She rose, the workday gown over her arm, and moved to fold it away, as well, in the clothes chest. Then: "You suspect treason from king's own men?"

Isolde remembered Brychan's dark, passionate face. The suppressed grief—or had it been triumph?—in his eyes. Slowly, she shook her head. "I don't know. But in any army—or at any court—there are men whose consciences can be bought for a high enough price."

A swell of desperate helplessness washed through her, and she had to wait a moment before going on. "And now you have the whole of the reason I have sent Myrddin to Camelerd," she said at last. "He—and Drustan—are my only hope to save the throne. And to keep from being forced into marriage with a man who may have killed Con."

Again Hedda was silent a moment before she spoke. Then she turned back to Isolde. "You could speak out to council. Tell them of what you saw."

"And expect them to take the word of the Witch Queen about a vision she conjured in the flames?" Isolde shook her head. "Some of them believe already that I have indeed a gift of Sight—and fear me the more. And some scoff at their fear. But if I spoke, none would take my word as true beyond doubt. Those who scoff would say it was nothing but women's superstition and charms. And those who believe would say a woman of magic may also lie for her own ends."

Another silence fell, in which Isolde could hear the steady whine of the wind outside the turret walls and the throb of the sea below. At her feet, Cabal stirred and whimpered again.

"Then we hope Myrddin returns in time," Hedda said quietly at last.

Isolde nodded. By Samhain, Myrddin had said. And even that might be too late. Still, she reached out and touched Hedda lightly on the arm.

"Thank you for letting me talk of it, Hedda. I'm glad that there is at least one in Tintagel to whom I can speak the truth."

Gestures of affection between them were rare, and even now Isolde felt the girl stiffen at her touch. But then Hedda covered Isolde's hand briefly with her own.

"I'm glad you . . . tell me, lady. I be on guard, now, as well."

WHEN HEDDA HAD GONE, ISOLDE SAT beside the banked and flickering fire and took up the bronze bowl, tracing with one fingertip the etched serpents, eternally swallowing their own tails. An ancient thing, part of the old ways and the time before time, before the Romans, before even Britain itself. And once the scrying bowl of Morgan of Avalon.

Abruptly, Isolde blew out the single remaining candle, leaving the room in darkness save for the fire's orange glow. One of the logs broke and fell, sending up a shower of sparks. Isolde watched them dance and then die against the hearthstones, wondering again at the capricious power that should send a vision to her, not in the ancient scrying bowl, but in ordinary flame, and without a single one of the summoning charms that still echoed, now and again, through her mind. *That should carry me to Con's side as he died, but leave me there to watch helpless, with no power to save his life or even ease his dying alone.*

Slowly, Isolde went to the ewer of water that stood in the washbasin and carried it to fill the bowl to the line made by the serpents' tails. She added a drop of sweet lavender oil from a tiny vial that stood by the bowl, then took a brooch from the jewel casket on her dressing table, pricked her finger, and let three drops of blood fall into the water. She stared into the bowl, breathed in and out, let her thoughts and breath and even her heartbeat slow.

By the power of the raven. The wisdom of the serpent. By Earth and Fire, Water and Wind.

Isolde had heard a tale, once, of a harp made from a murdered man's bones, strung with strands of his hair. It had sung the name of his killer until justice was done.

But the scrying bowl showed her nothing. Nothing save the glistening sheen of the oil, the spreading mists of red blood, and her own face, shifting and moving with the flicker of firelight. The room was utterly still, the only sounds the moan of the wind outside and Cabal's soft breathing from his rug on the floor.

Isolde turned away, shutting her eyes. The Sight was like the healing. Like the tales. Something from before Camlann. Something she could not let herself ask how she knew. Could not remember how she had learned.

Though maybe that, she thought, is why it will not return now.

Chapter Eight

T HE AIR OF THE PRISON cell was as fetid as it had been the previous day, chill and dank and heavy with the prison-reek of
fear, and by the light of the lantern she carried, Isolde saw that
the men, too, were positioned almost exactly as they had been
when she'd left the day before. The boy Cyn lay asleep on the
straw, while the bearded man sat propped against the wall, his
knees drawn up, head resting on his folded arms. He looked up
sharply, though, as the door swung open.

"I thought I told you not to come again." He sounded more
tired, though, than angry, Isolde thought, his voice still rough
either with sleeplessness or with thirst.

"And I thought if it was a choice between starving and seeing
me again, you'd maybe decide my coming wasn't so bad. Besides,
I wanted to look at Cyn's wrists."

Isolde set down the bread and water she'd brought with her
and knelt at the boy's side, touching him lightly on one shoulder,
but Cyn didn't move, didn't even stir. He must, Isolde supposed,
have taken the draft she'd given him for pain.

Isolde reached to touch him again, then stopped abruptly. His face was that of a sleeping child. But there was no rise and fall of his chest, and when she put a hand to his neck to feel for a pulse, she found his skin icy cold.

For a moment, she thought he must simply have died in his sleep—or that the draft had been too strong. But then she saw the faint, purpling bruises about his nose and mouth, just visible in the lantern's unsteady light, and the threads of cloth that clung to the slack lips.

Slowly, she turned to the other man. "He's dead."

"Yes."

Their eyes met, and an echo woke in Isolde's mind.

I told him I'd see him through.

Isolde looked again at Cyn. Dead, she thought, these many hours, to judge by the chill of his skin. Dosed with both the drafts I left behind and then smothered with a fold of his cloak by his companion and friend.

She looked up. "Because he'd have broken in the end?"

The bearded man said nothing. His eyes, startlingly blue amid the cell's squalor, were hard and flat as they watched her, but he sat just beyond the circle of light cast by the lantern, so that the rest of his face was in shadow. Isolde looked down at Cyn and felt a brief flicker of anger that he should have died this way. Without a choice of his own.

She remembered, though, something Con had once said, exhausted by battle only a few hours ended, his face bleak. *Men may live with honor. Few manage to die with it.* And the gods know, she thought, I've seen that true enough in the men who die of their wounds in my care. Some—a few—die the way a warrior would wish. The rest . . .

She thought of Cyn's eyes the day before, hollow with the dumb, hopeless suffering of an animal in pain. Gently, she lifted the Saxon boy's arms, one after the other, and crossed them over his chest. Then she looked up again at Cyn's companion, still motionless against the wall.

"You've seen Cyn out of this," she said. "As you promised. But what about you?"

He jerked one shoulder dismissively. "What you have to face, you can."

And then he looked up and watched her a moment, his face expressionless above the ragged tunic and dirt-streaked beard. "And now are you going to have me brought before the king's council on charge of murder?"

Isolde looked from the dead boy's face to that of the bearded man. "Do you think I would?" When he made no answer, she said, her eyes still meeting his gaze, "They may guess—as I did. But they won't know it from me. And I'll send the commander of the king's guard and some of his men to collect the . . . to collect him. In name, at least, Tintagel is still my domain."

The bearded man was silent, and then his head tipped in the briefest fraction of a nod, whether of simple acknowledgment or of thanks, Isolde couldn't have said. She rose to her feet and was about to turn for the door when another question made her stop.

"Your husband the king," the man said. "He was killed— wounded in the fighting, so the word went?"

Isolde, frowning, studied the man. She had the strange impression that he'd spoken almost against his will. As though he sneered at himself, even as he spoke, for the weakness of asking, but hadn't been able to keep the words back. Though what about the question had been urgent enough to force him into speech, she couldn't see.

Slowly, she said, "I see the news reaches even to these cells."

There was another silence, longer this time, and then abruptly the bearded man asked, "Will you answer me something?"

"That depends on what question you ask."

He laughed shortly. "Fair enough. All right, my question is, What are you going to do now—with King Constantine gone?"

Isolde stared at him, feeling . . . she supposed surprise was uppermost. Though just for a moment, she felt again the grasp of Marche's fingers on her throat, his breath hot and close enough to mingle with her own. She shook her head to clear the memory away and said, still frowning, "Why should you—?"

"Care?" Another brief, grim smile touched the prisoner's mouth. "Humor me. At any rate, there's not much I'm likely to do with anything you tell me down here, is there."

Isolde studied him, trying to guess at his thoughts or the reason behind the question, but his face was impassive as before, the blue eyes giving nothing away. At last she let out her breath. "All right. I don't know what I'll do now—I'm not sure I even know how to look beyond the next few days."

She heard the bleakness in her tone and stopped before she could say anymore, instead bending to pick up the lantern she'd brought. Then she straightened, looking across at the bearded prisoner once more. "But as you say, what you have to face, you can."

ISOLDE STEPPED OUT INTO TINTAGEL'S CENTRAL courtyard, drawing her cloak closed against the chill. She could still see Cyn's lifeless face, the marks of tears from the day before visible in the dirt on his cheeks. Tonight she would have to inform the king's council that one of the Saxon prisoners had died in his cell. She doubted any of them would think to ask more than that—or care. Likely they would assume Marche's guardsmen had gone a step too far in their interrogation and sport.

For now, though, she'd left the bearded man alone with his dead, though whether that was kindness or cruelty she'd not been able to tell.

The day was raw and damp, and beneath gray, sullen clouds a steady trickle of people flowed in through the gates that opened onto the wagon road. The unending stream of fugitives and refugees, fleeing from the scorched and blasted land—or returning to homes they'd fled from before the Saxon advance, in the hope of finding something still there.

Their faces held the stunned, exhausted look of those who have forgotten all else but the simple will to survive. Whole families in ragged, mud-spattered clothes, pushing handcarts piled with what possessions they had salvaged from home. Carpenters and smiths with their tools bundled on their backs. Filthy, hollow-eyed children clinging to their mothers' skirts, their faces gaunt, their bellies swollen with hunger.

Isolde approached one such mother, a woman dressed in ragged, threadbare wool, strands of dark, curling hair slipping out of a blue head-cloth. A child clung to her hand, a little boy of two, maybe, or three, his face dirty, his mouth crusted with dark sores. As Isolde reached her side, the woman turned, and Isolde saw that though her frame was slight, her belly was swollen with another child. Isolde hesitated, remembering the terrified scream of the Christian soldier in the infirmary the day before. But the woman's dark eyes, though weary, held nothing of fear.

Isolde thought of Marcia, the serving maid who, on Nest's orders, had attended her that morning. A thin, sharp-featured girl, her cheeks pitted with the marks of a childhood pox. Marcia had given the scrying bowl one swift, sharp glance as she'd entered Isolde's chambers, had watched Isolde, all the while she attended her, with wary, narrowed eyes. But she'd not been afraid.

Marcia and the rest of Nest's women might look askance

and whisper at the birthmark on Isolde's wrist. Might watch
with flint-eyed satisfaction when one of the girls Con favored
took ill, or a man in Isolde's care died, or a child she delivered
was born breech and strangled on the cord. But it's men, Isolde
thought, who believe in witches. And a rare woman who'll be
truly afraid of one of her own kind.

The woman before Isolde now had made a quick, awkward
curtsy, her movements clumsy with the weight of the child,
and Isolde put out a hand to steady her. She was still young—
twenty-five or twenty-six, at a guess—with a handsome, vivid
face, broad across the brow and tapering to a firm, squared-off
chin. But what might have been beauty was marred by a birthmark, a great, wine-colored stain that began at her temple and
covered nearly to her mouth, extending full to the corner of
the eye.

"What help can we give you?" Isolde asked her.

The woman ducked her head, the dark curls bobbing. "Thank
'ee, my lady. Just food enough to see us on our way, if it please
'ee, my lady."

Her head was still bowed, so that her face was hidden from
Isolde's gaze, and her voice had slipped into a beggar's whine.
But there was a perfunctory, almost bored note in her tone, as
well, as though both words and manner were an act so familiar
they could by now be assumed with a bare minimum of effort
or even thought.

And she probably has had training enough in pleading and
begging for aid, Isolde thought. On the road from wherever she
has come.

She gestured toward where Father Nenian stood at the far
end of the courtyard, distributing loaves of bread and sacks of
meal to men and women who stood in a mute, straggling line.
The priest's face was puckered with distress at the misery before
him, but he spoke a kind word to each as he handed out the

provisions, pressing bony hands and making the sign of blessing over the heads of the children. Sometimes one of those waiting would try to push ahead past some of the others, and an argument would break out, but he saw to it that such argument were quickly resolved, his manner as calm as before, his voice mild.

"Father Nenian will give you what provisions we can spare," Isolde said. "Where are you bound?"

The question seemed to surprise the woman, for her head came up and her eyes, long-lashed and dark, studied Isolde with a flicker of appraisal. Then: "Glevum, my lady, if we can get so far. I've kin there. And there's nothing to hold us here now, my poor boy and me."

The beggar's whine had crept into her voice again, and she darted another quick look from under her lashes at Isolde. Then, seeing Isolde had made no move to go, she said, "Come to that, lady, there is something more you could do for me—if you could find it in your heart to show a bit o' kindness to me and my boy, here. We'd a farm, you see. Lived in Perenporth, my man and me. But when the call came out to fight the filthy Saxon dogs— beg pardon, my lady, but that's what they are and I'll not say different—when the call for arms came out, nothing would do my man but that he must join your good lord's army and fight to drive the dirty devils back where they came. And my boy and me, we followed right along, for I'd not send my man off to the fighting to maybe die all on his own, without me there to care for him."

She looked up again, a sheen of tears glistening in the dark eyes. "And he was killed. In this here fighting up Dimilioc way. Died in my arms, he did, saying he was only thankful he could give his life in service to your good lord our king and making me swear on his spilled blood I'd bring up our boy, here, to fight the filthy Saxon devils, as well. And—"

She stopped, putting an arm about the child beside her. The

boy's nose was running, and she wiped it with a fold of her skirt before going on.

"Well, at any rate, my lady, if there was anything you could give us. Anything that might buy us a night or two of shelter on our way . . ."

She trailed off. The boy squirmed impatiently in his mother's grasp, but she didn't move. Her head was once more bowed, but her free hand came out suggestively, palm up.

"Yes, of course." Isolde reached into the embroidered purse she wore tied at her girdle and counted out a handful of coppers.

The woman's fingers curled tight around the coins, and then she dropped another quick curtsy, made awkward by the bulk of her swollen belly.

"God bless you, my lady. God and the Holy Mother and all His saints above. And I'll say a prayer for you at every church and chapel we come to, I swear it on my poor man's grave."

Isolde was retying the purse at her girdle. "What? Oh, thank you," she said absently. "That's very kind." She finished fastening the purse, then looked up. "Perenporth is a fishing village, though. If you use the same story again, you'd better make your husband a fisherman instead of a farmer—especially if you're telling it around here. Anyone in this area will know Perenporth, as well."

The woman's head lifted with a jerk, her eyes flaring wide in alarm. Then the wide mouth started to twitch, and at last she broke into a throaty, surprisingly musical laugh, her dark eyes crinkling to slits of amusement.

"All right, got me fair and square. A fishing village, is it?" She shook her head. "Ah, well. Can't be helped. Heard the name on the road and took a chance."

She'd dropped the Cornish accent, and without it her voice was low and slightly husky, with a lilting tone a little like Myrddin's. She grinned, showing a row of brown-stained teeth. "Not nearly the easy mark I'd have thought a fine lady would be, you're not. Was that all that gave me away?"

"That and your gown. It's cut too low to be the dress of a farmer's wife. And you'd better try and wash your face a bit more thoroughly, as well," Isolde added, "before you stop to beg aid again. You've still a bit of paint on your mouth."

The other woman glanced down at her half-bared breasts, the skin gray with dirt and streaked by the ash of cook-fires beneath her woolen shawl, then wiped her lips with the back of her hand, frowning at the smear of red ochre that came away on her skin.

She shrugged. "Well, there was no water to be had on the road this morning, so I had to do the best I could with the dew gathered on the grass and leaves." She sighed, rubbing the small of her back with one hand, then looked from the coins in the other palm to Isolde. "You'll be wanting the coins back, then, I suppose?"

Isolde studied the woman's face, weary beneath the wine-colored stain, despite the laughter and the wide-mouthed grin. The child beside her looked tired, as well, the bones of his small face prominent and sharp.

"What are your names?" she asked.

The woman looked startled. Then: "Mine's Dera, my lady. And this here"—she put an arm about the boy's shoulder, pulling him close—"this is Jory."

"Keep the coins, then, Dera—they're yours. And come and sit down, both of you. You look as though you'd be glad to be off your feet for a time."

DERA LET OUT SIGH AS SHE sank down onto one of the wooden benches that stood against the courtyard's southern wall, outside the entrance to the stables. She took the bread and cheese Isolde had brought over from Father Nenian's stores, then hefted her son onto the bench beside her.

"Ah, that's better." She stretched out her legs, showing ankles that were puffed above the worn leather of her shoes, then followed Isolde's gaze to the tightly stretched front of her gown and rested a hand on the mound of the unborn child.

"A nuisance, that's what it is. Makes it hard to keep up wi' the army when they're marchin' to a new town. And hard to earn a living, besides. Men—even soldiers—bein' not so eager to take their pleasure from a woman that's swollen up like a cow wi' the wind in her belly, you understand."

Her touch on her belly was gentle, though, and her face had softened, a brief, distant smile curving her mouth.

"Where do you come from, if not Perenporth?" Isolde asked. She held out another chunk of bread to the boy Jory. Half sullen, half wary, he watched her, then, as though fearing the offer might be withdrawn, shot out a hand and snatched the bread, cramming it into his mouth nearly whole, then flinching as his mother cuffed him lightly on the ear.

"Young lout! Have you no better manners than that? Anyone would think you'd been raised in a cow byre." Dera shook her head, but then, with a sigh, settled the child comfortably against her side, her hand moving from her belly to rest lightly on Jory's matted dark hair, smoothing it back from his brow. She looked up at Isolde.

"We're from Gwynedd, my lady. Near Deva. That's where this young heathen"—her fingers curled lightly around the small head resting against her shoulder—"was born."

She took a mouthful of bread herself, winced as though her teeth gave her pain, then leaned back and went on. "I had a husband there—that much was true enough. And a filthy, drunken brute of a man he was—like the devil himself when the drink was on him, which was most of the time. The boy's his." Dera stroked the dark hair again. "About the only good he ever did in all his born days—and the only good I ever had of him, that's certain sure."

She paused, then went on. "It was Irish raiders that killed him, though, not the Saxons—a year ago, come Imbolc time. Spilled his guts on his own hearth because he was too stubborn—or too drunk—to give up on the fight. And the best day's work the Irish scum ever did, I'd have said, except that it meant my boy, here, and I were put out to starve—seeing as they burned the house down and took all the crop we'd stored. And my people were all long since dead and gone."

Dera stopped to take another bite of bread, swallowed, then continued. "Anyway, I didn't see much hope of getting another man to wed. Not without he was an apple off the same tree as the first one. There's not many would want to wake up to this"—she touched the mark on her cheek—"every morning in bed beside 'em—unless they were the sort o' man no woman in her right mind would take to wed. Besides"— she gave Isolde another flash of the brown-toothed grin— "thought if I was going to have to play servant to a man's codpiece, I might as well get paid for the job. Your good lord's army was passing nearby at the time—on the way south to where the fighting was then—and I thought I'd never have a better chance than that. So young Jory, here, and me, we followed along." She shrugged. "Not been a bad sort of life, take it for all and all."

Dera cocked an eyebrow. "Soldiers don't wash so often as most, maybe, but they'll pay well for a woman once a battle's done, and without bein' too particular whether she's a mark on her skin so long as she's willing and doesn't smell too bad and has a pulse in her veins." She paused to brush bread crumbs from her lap. "Not a bad way of getting by. Though it's harder, now that the weather's turned cold an' the child's so close to bein' born."

"Is the father—?" Isolde began.

Dera gave a dismissive shrug. "Might've been any man—well, not any man in Britain, maybe, but any one in Britain's army, for sure." She drew the shawl more tightly about her shoulders and sighed. "I'd a purge I take regular, like, o' course. But it doesn't always work. And what with the war and the travel, I wasn't paying my bleeding no mind. So by the time I got to know this 'un was on the way I was feeling it move a bit and, well . . ."

She lifted her shoulders again. "Couldn't get rid of it then. Not when I was starting to get to know it, like. But no, I've nothing to hope for from any man in the way of help wi' the poor mite." She shifted, as though seeking to ease the strain on her back, and her hand moved again to rest lightly atop her swollen belly.

"It's quiet today at least, praise be. Been kicking me night and day these last few weeks, but now it's given me a bit o' peace. No kicks at all I've felt since yesterday supper time—first decent night's rest I can remember."

But she gave the mound of the child another caressing pat, and Isolde saw the same soft, distant smile touch her mouth. "Must be a little maid—no boy ever treated 'is mother so well, eh?"

She looked up, waiting for agreement or response, but Isolde didn't speak. She felt, all at once, as though she couldn't breathe, as though her chest were suddenly crushed by an iron hand. She swallowed, then rose abruptly to her feet. "I've . . . left orders that those who wish to shelter here for a time are to be given what room we can spare—in the stables, mostly, and the barns." Her voice sounded strange in her own ears, and she stopped, her eyes going from Dera to the boy beside her and back again.

Then: "I must go now. But you're welcome to stay as long as you choose."

Dera gave her a faintly puzzled frown, but then nodded. "That's good of you, lady. We thank you—and for the bread and the coins, as well."

"LADY ISOLDE."

Startled, Isolde turned to find that Coel of Rhegged had come unnoticed to stand at her side. In all the years she had known Coel, in all the years he had attended Con's council and led his men to fight at the king's side, she could remember no time when Coel, first and most loyal of Arthur's men, had spoken to her directly or addressed her by name. With an effort, she pushed aside all thoughts of the woman she had left—and all other memories—and acknowledged his bow.

"My lord Rhegged. Good day. You are well?"

Coel was dressed, this morning, in the blue tunic and fur-lined cloak he had worn the night before, but his face looked bloodless in the courtyard's cold, gray light, the skin almost translucent and stretched like parchment across the bones of chin and brow. He held himself as though he fought against some inner pain, and she saw that he pressed a hand tightly against his side. But he nodded.

"Very well, I thank you, Lady Isolde. But I would ask a word with you, if I may." His voice sounded weaker than it had last night, with a thready note of age she had never heard in it before.

"Of course. But please, come indoors. You should not be standing out here in the damp and the cold."

Coel gave her a brief, rueful smile that for an instant warmed the grim set of his face. "Do I look so old and infirm as that, then?" He shook his head, drawing the folds of his cloak more closely about his shoulders with one hand. "No, thank you, lady. I'm well enough. It's only that these old bones don't take to keeping vigil in a fireless chapel so well as they did years ago."

"So you kept the vigil? You and the rest of the men?"

Coel nodded. "We did. Midnight to dawn on our knees before the altar—offering prayers for a miraculous sign." There was a current of irony in Coel's voice that made Isolde glance up sharply, but then he added, more quietly, "Not that I would have begrudged my lord Constantine a vigil for his last night among us here." He paused. "The young king is to be buried at sundown, I understand."

The corners of his mouth were tightly folded, and his golden eyes were weary, the hooded lids papery. Watching him, Isolde felt a flicker of that same chill she had felt with Brychan the night before, that here was another man, likely an honorable one, that she could not let herself believe spoke true. She nodded. "He will."

Coel was silent a moment, his eyes on the door of the chapel at the far end of the courtyard. Beyond it, outside Tintagel's walls, lay the churchyard where Con would be buried at the end of the day. Then, abruptly, Coel seemed to rouse himself, for he turned back to Isolde and spoke with something of his usual decision, quick and strong.

"Will you come with me, Lady Isolde, out onto the headland? We ought to be able to speak privately there."

Chapter Nine

IN THE YEARS SHE HAD lived at Tintagel, Isolde had seen the sea in many moods. Had seen it still and smooth, the sunlight dancing on the waves. Today, though, under the gray and heavy skies, the sea below the headland boiled, the waves pounding, slashing at the rocky shore. Here, out in the open, the wind was stronger, tearing at her hair and whipping the folds of her cloak around her with a force that made it hard at times to keep her footing. But she and Coel were alone. Only the gulls that circled and screamed above might hear what they said.

Coel stood beside her, his eyes, too, on the pounding waves and on the jetty of clawlike black rocks that stretched out toward the horizon. The walk had tired him; he breathed with difficulty, his hand white-knuckled on a fold of his cloak, and his lips were blue-tinged and tight, as though some inner pain had gripped him again.

"The edge of Britain—and the edge of the world itself, it sometimes seems to me," he said at last. He turned, slowly, back toward land. "And a perilous time for us here, where the Saxons have pushed us nearly into the sea."

Isolde turned as well, so that the wind was now at her back, and looked out across the windswept, grassy plain of the headland to where the walls of Tintagel rose gray against the sky. On a jut of land to the east stood the great circle of stones built by the ancient ones for a reason long since swept away by time, and below them, past Tintagel itself, stretched the farmlands and villages of Cornwall.

"A perilous time, as you say."

Coel was silent for a moment. Isolde had the impression that he was gathering strength, battling back whatever hurt or weakness he had suffered with the climb, and when he turned to face her again, his voice was stronger, his manner more his own.

"You will be wondering, Lady Isolde, why I asked you to come here. But I wished to speak to you, and what I would say, I would have none among those now at Tintagel hear."

He paused, frowning, as though searching for words. Isolde waited, and at last he said, "Kings live by knowledge—knowledge of the lands they rule, of the lands bordering their own, of the men who rule them. Knowledge brought in by whatever means we can make serve—it's the only way to survive."

He stopped again, and Isolde said, "You are speaking of informers—spies."

Coel gave her a sharp glance from under his brows. "You are not surprised?"

Isolde moved her shoulder slightly. "I have lived my entire life at a royal court, Lord Coel. There are few things that would shock or surprise me about the means those in power use to keep order in their lands."

Instead of answering, Coel studied her face a long moment, and she caught in his gaze a flash of the same pity or compassion she had seen the night before. "You are full young," he said at last, "for the burdens you carry, Lady Isolde."

His tone was unaccustomedly gentle, and Isolde felt the hard knot of loneliness she'd carried these days since Con's death split open—a sudden, overwhelming wish that she might tell Coel everything flooding through her.

She could tell him now, lay the whole burden of Con's death, her suspicions of Marche, her own fears, upon the shoulders of the man at her side. She stopped herself, though, before she could speak.

By the look of him, she thought, Coel of Rhegged has cares enough already. Unfair to add further cause for worry. Besides, only a fool or a child trusts entirely on so slight an acquaintance as his and mine.

"Perhaps," she said at last, her eyes on one of the circling gulls. "But what I have I can bear." She turned back to Coel. "Go on, please. What is it you wish to tell me?"

Coel seemed to hesitate, then nodded and looked out again across the white-crested waves, so that all she could see of his face was the curve of one hollow cheek and the line of his mouth, still set and stern.

"Very well. I have made it my business to know what dealings my fellow kings and rulers have among themselves. Where their messengers are sent and, if possible, what intelligence they carry. And I would wager my sword and my shield that they do the same—for me and for the rest of their fellows on the king's council."

He paused, then went on. "In any army, among any king's force of fighting men, there are those whose loyalty can be bought. And the Saxon kings are no exception—not when they use Pictish raiders and Irish mercenaries to swell their ranks in battle.

"I received word yesterday from one such—one of those who will sell information about those he serves if the price is worth his while—that messengers from one of the men on the council have been received at the royal court of the Saxon king Octa of Kent."

Isolde stiffened. "Which man?"

She saw Coel's jaw harden. "Marche."

Then, when Isolde made no reply, he gave her another keen, appraising look. "This news seems to surprise you no more than my talk of spies."

One of the gulls circling overhead banked and then dived, plunging toward the sea. Isolde followed it with her eyes. "Lord Marche, too, I have known all my life." She paused. Then she turned back to Coel. "You spoke, though, of your informer as a mercenary—one who would betray his king to the highest bidder. Do you trust his word on this to be true?"

Coel was silent, and when he spoke the weariness was back in his eyes, the weight of age in his voice. "Trust him? No. I can only say that I've always found the man's information reliable in the past." He paused. "My informer also claimed that Marche was planning something. Massing troops secretly at his garrison at Castle Dore. Now, the message was brought me by a man I've used before as private messenger. A traveling goldsmith. Ulfin, his name is. His craft—and a rare fine metalworker he is, too—offers him an excuse to journey widely. And to call on the keeps and castles of the most powerful in the land to peddle his wares."

Coel paused again. "I've sent him to Castle Dore—to find whether Marche is indeed assembling troops in secret. Whether that part, at least, of what my informer claimed is true."

Isolde nodded slowly. "But you do believe, then, that Lord Marche is seeking an alliance with the Saxons? With Octa of Kent?"

"Marche would not be the first man to decide that an alliance with the enemy would win him greater power than continuing the war." Coel stopped, then added, his voice a careful blank, "Vortigern, to name but one such man."

Isolde went still, but then nodded and said quietly, "True."

But it is not Vortigern, she thought, whom Coel is thinking of. Vortigern, who betrayed his king to league with the Saxons and was betrayed by them in his turn so long ago that scarcely anyone living remembers him now. For if Vortigern sought alliance with the Saxons, my own father did just the same.

Aloud she asked, still looking out toward the sea, "Does anyone else on the council know of what you have learned?"

Coel shook his head. "None." His brows drew together. "The days following a High King's death are dangerous ones in any land, let alone one as besieged as Britain now. There's a gap in power that brings out the worst in the men left behind—as you saw last night in the council hall."

He hunched his shoulders against a gust of wind. "The lines of authority must be redrawn, new alliances formed. And there are none on the council I would absolve absolutely of the wish to seize power for themselves—or of being a part of whatever Marche plans."

Isolde turned to face him. "And yet you trust me?"

Their eyes met for a long moment. At last Coel said, unexpectedly, "I knew your father, you know. Few knew him better, though I say so."

Isolde didn't reply, and after a moment Coel turned and gestured to a place where a rise in the land and a jut of boulders formed a place of slight shelter.

"Come, we can sit down there and be out of the wind. If you will hear what I have to say?"

His speech was still nearly as quick and decisive as it had been, his chiseled face as proud. But Isolde saw the thready beat of a pulse in his temple and the dents of weariness about his mouth—and read, too, in the golden hawk's eyes something that in another man might almost have been a flicker of appeal. She nodded.

"Yes. If you wish it, of course I will hear."

When they had reached the sheltered spot, Coel sank down onto one of the stones and let out his breath in a long sigh, his hand pressed tight under his ribs.

Isolde started to speak, but he held up a hand. "No, no. It's all right. I'm well enough." He drew from his belt a soldier's horn drinking flask and flicked open the cap, then lifted the flask to his lips and took a long pull. He swallowed and grimaced. "Some concoction or other of my physician; it's mixed with wine."

Isolde nodded and took the place beside him on the rocks, smoothing the skirts of her gown and drawing her cloak about her. As Coel had said, they were sheltered from the wind here, and the quiet, after the high constant buffet and scream, was almost startling. "Stinging nettle, most likely. Or maybe vervain."

Coel glanced at her. "Is it? I wouldn't know." He swallowed and grimaced again. "Tastes vile, but it seems to help when the cold settles into my bones on days like today."

He recapped the flask, then shook his head so that the silvery mane of hair fell back from his brow. "Time was, I could have made a march over twenty leagues of country as rough as this—and still faced battle in the morning."

He leaned back, as though easing tightness in his spine. Then: "But if I am old, I also have a longer memory that the rest of the king's councilmen. I am old enough to remember what is only a tale to them. To have taken part in what they have heard only in song—or at best as boys at a father's knee."

He was silent a moment, his face growing remote, his gaze distant. Then he went on, "I knew your father well, as I say. I had the training of him from a boy."

Isolde brushed a tuft of dry grass from the skirt of her gown. "I never knew that."

"No." Coel looked at her sideways. "I don't suppose you did." His eyes were still on her, and he said, "I don't suppose anyone has spoken to you much of him—or of what happened during those times."

His look made it a question, and Isolde, after a moment's pause, said, steadily, "No. As you know, his name is spoken scarcely at all."

Coel nodded, his face turned once more to the sea, the golden eyes softened by the gray reflected light. "It was ill for Britain that so many fell at Camlann. Not only because we lost Arthur and so many more of our finest fighting men, but because it also left the reins of the country in the hands of the young—men who were not yet old enough to fight when your father and Arthur met in battle that final time."

After a pause he went on, "The men on the council are such men—young enough that it's easier for them to hate than try to understand. Not that I'm saying what Modred did was right. There are some crimes nothing can justify—treason the most filthy of them all. I fought at Camlann—saw my fellows slaughtered, my army hacked down to a shadow of what it had been. And I've done enough hating myself, in my time. But"—he raised one blue-veined hand and let it fall—"they say you outlive everything, in time. Hate and love alike. And maybe that's true."

He fell silent again, his face still remote, his mouth stern, then glanced down at Isolde once more. "You must have memories yourself of the man your father was. You weren't so young as that when he died."

For an instant, the darkness in her mind stirred, shivered. Isolde's hands tightened. "I was thirteen."

After seven years she was practiced in locking the doors of memory tight, quelling all such ripples that threatened to bring anything back. There was herself before, and herself after Camlann, the two separated by a high, dark wall.

But now there'd been the voice. And the feeling in the prison cell. And now this, today.

Maybe there's something in the past, she thought, that will not be forgotten. Something I've locked away that's battering at the door from the inside.

For a moment, her whole body was taut with the urge to spring up and get away, as far away as she could. To run and run until she could remember nothing but the ground beneath her and the open sky above and never hear what more Coel had to say.

One foot in front of the other. Look forward, not back.

Coel watched her a moment more, then turned away, nodding slowly. Isolde saw the fingers of his right hand absently tracing the lines of the flask still held in his left, his gaze growing remote once more, as though he looked past her across the years to the time that had gone before. Then he began, his voice making a counterpoint to the crash of the waves below.

"It was a time of peace, then—at least comparative peace. Arthur had won the day at Badon. Few among us thought the Saxons would ever rise again. And so when the Roman emperor sought help against the barbarians, Arthur answered—agreed to lead a force of men across the channel."

Coel lifted one shoulder. "Maybe he was wrong. I don't know. There was a great deal of confusion as to where the power in the land lay. Some saw Britain as a Roman province still, and hoped the legions might come to our defense as they had before. Some wanted no part of a united Britain. Wanted—as Madoc wants—to be left in peace to rule their own lands."

Coel stopped, brow furrowed, and flexed his gnarled fingers, rubbing the back of one hand. Some of the formality of his manner had dropped away, and Isolde could see the man of action, the soldier and commander of troops he must once have been—and still was, she thought, beneath the mantle of councilman and king.

"At any rate," he went on, "Arthur led his troops to the defense of Rome, and left Modred, your father, to rule as deputy in his stead while he was gone."

This was the part of the tale Isolde had heard before, many times, but she kept silent, letting Coel's words wash past her.

"There are leaders men follow because they win victories for those in their command. And there are leaders men follow out of love. Modred was one of those. I saw battle with him time and again in the years before Arthur left for Rome—saw him live in the mud and the cold with his troops, refuse to eat if they went hungry. Head the most dangerous charges—the ones that seemed like certain slaughter and death—himself, with only those men who would volunteer to be at his side."

Coel rubbed a hand along his jaw. "His men would have cut their throats for him if he'd asked it—marched into hell and back if he was at their head."

This time, nothing stirred, no rolling boulder of memory loomed in Isolde's mind. The man Coel spoke of was remote, a stranger in a tale and nothing more. And yet she found herself wondering, all at once, whether it would be comfort as well as pain to remember the time before Camlann. If there was anything in the past she'd forgotten that would give her courage to face whatever the future held.

For there had been happiness. That much she knew. Laughter, even. And she'd loved some at least among the voices that now came to her in the wind.

And that, she thought, is exactly why I can't let myself remember. Because if I start crying again for what's lost I'll want nothing but to lie down on my bed and never rise. Never set another bone or bind another wound. Or for that matter attend to Coel now and learn what I may to save Con's throne.

She looked out toward the white-capped sea. There was herself before Camlann, and she'd locked that girl and all her memories away. "Lord Marche might be called a fine leader of men as well."

Coel's face looked suddenly weary. "As you say. Though, mind you, there was reason—maybe even good reason—for what Modred did. At least at first." He rubbed a hand through his hair. "Soon after Arthur led his troops into Gaul, the Saxons formed an alliance with the Picts of the north. And the Irish raiders began to strike not only along the coasts, as they had before, but farther inland. It was a desperate time—the dragon of Britain under siege, and no hope of Arthur's returning for three years, maybe more. Modred believed Britain had need of a true leader—not a deputy king, but a king outright, who could rally the petty kings and nobles as Arthur had done and drive off the barbarian hordes. And maybe he was right, at that."

Coel lifted one hand wearily and then let it fall. "I doubt Modred thought of it as treason—not then, at least. Arthur had left Britain to fight for Rome, and Modred was Arthur's heir. The kingship was his right. That was the claim he made in the council hall, and I've no doubt he believed it true."

Isolde looked down at her hands, lying still across the folds of her cloak. "No man is evil to himself," she said. "He will always find reason enough to justify his acts, at least in his own mind."

Coel glanced down at her, then sighed. "True enough. At any rate, Modred claimed the High Kingship for himself. And there were those on the council who agreed to follow—swore oaths of allegiance to him."

"Marche, for one."

Isolde saw Coel's lips thin and tighten, but he nodded. "As you say," he said again. "Though there were others—other men I would give a better character to than I would Lord Marche." He paused. "But the rest of the council refused to accept Modred as High King." He looked down at her again. "You will have heard, perhaps, what was said of Modred's birth?"

"Heard?" Isolde looked toward the edge of the cliffs, her lips twisting in a brief, bitter smile. "The story is sung by every harper in the land—whispered everywhere, from the king's council chamber to the servants' hall."

Coel nodded again. "An ugly story, but no uglier than what was said at the time. The whispers began as soon as he was born. Morgan would not name the father of her child, and so there were those who claimed he was demon-born. Or that Arthur himself was the father, and Modred the bastard-gotten child of incest."

Coel shook his head. "At any rate, the truth died with those three—Arthur, Morgan, and Modred. I doubt any of us will ever know for sure. But there were those who objected, on the strength of the tales, to Modred's being named Arthur's heir. And maybe it was on that account that Modred did what he did—I won't even pretend to say for certain. But I do know that from the time I had the fostering of him as a boy, Modred had a grudge against the world. He kept it hidden away, as a rule, but it was there, just the same."

The wind lifted the hair away from Isolde's face, all but drowning out Coel's voice.

COLD. SO COLD. I CAN'T FEEL my legs anymore. And now my hands have gone numb. There's a bright light somewhere. A bright light. And a throbbing center of pain. But I can't tell where they are. I can feel the blood seeping out of me, though. And when I cough, I taste blood.

If I'd known it would end this way, would I have done the same? I suppose so. I'd no choice, if the prophesies of Myrddin are to be believed. Modred, boy from the sea. Born to be his father's bane.

War is for heroes, in the harpers' songs. And the dying are lifted *away by beautiful maidens. Ferried across the water to the Western Isles.*

I'm lying in mud. I can't lift my cheek. Can't spit the filthy grit from my mouth.

COEL HAD CONTINUED SPEAKING, EYES STILL distant, so that Isolde was able to blink the tears away without his seeing. Plainly the wind had brought him nothing save his own memories of the story he now told. No voice she knew distantly had been her father's, though as always the words he'd spoken were gone.

"The council was split," Coel was saying, "and Modred declared war on those who opposed his rule. Arthur heard of what had happened and turned his troops toward home." He broke off and took another swallow from his flask. Then: "There are plenty of tales about Arthur these days. But I doubt any of us who knew the man himself would find much to recognize in the stories you hear told and retold."

Isolde was silent. Then: "Myrddin said much the same."

"Myrddin?" For the first time since they'd reached the headland, Coel's face relaxed, and a smile of genuine warmth touched his thin mouth. "That's a name I'd all but forgotten. He must be as old as the hills by now. I should like to see him again, though. Is he at Tintagel now?"

Isolde looked away, and made her voice a careful blank as she replied. "No. He has already gone." She waited for Coel to ask her where he had gone, but although she could feel his gaze still on her, he only took another swallow from the flask before beginning again.

"Arthur was my king," he said, "and I loved him well. But I knew him also for a hard man—and a proud one. He would not brook opposition. Or forgive easily when he considered a wrong had been done. And Modred—Modred was another cast in the same mold. I don't wonder some took them for father and son. And when the two met as enemies—" He shook his head. "You will know what happened."

"A nine-years' civil war," Isolde said after a moment. "Nine years of war, in which my father tried to make alliance with Cerdic, the Saxon king, but ended by losing much of Britain's eastern lands. And then the year of the plague and Camlann."

"Yes, the plague year. The sign of God's wrath at the great traitor-king." Grim amusement flickered briefly about the corners of Coel's eyes. "Though I confess I've my doubts when anyone—priest or commoner—starts putting words in the Almighty's mouth. I don't know whether God made man in His image, but it's certain man has returned the favor."

There was a silence, broken only by the scream of a gull above. Isolde folded her hands together in her lap, and was distantly surprised, when she spoke, to find her voice as steady as before.

"Perhaps," she said. "But what has all this to do with you and me now?"

Coel studied her, his eyes keen on hers. Then he said, "I'm an old man. Too old to have a hand in ruling the kingdom, many would claim. I don't believe it—but then no soldier wants to feel he's outlived his usefulness to his land. But it does mean that few on the king's council would accept my word against Marche's that he's had dealings with the Saxon king. They would demand proof, and I've none. Not yet. And so I've told no one what I learned."

"Not even your son?"

"No. Not even Huel." Coel's face looked pallid, the dents of weariness plain about his mouth. "A king soon learns to trust no one absolutely—not even his own blood son. Not when his death will set a crown on that son's head." He recapped the horn flask and slipped it back into his belt. "I believe my son loyal, but belief isn't knowing beyond all possible doubt. And there is the matter of how young Constantine died."

Isolde's head came up sharply, and her whole body went still. Before she could speak, though, Coel held up his hand. "No. I'm not asking what you yourself know, or how. But if I was Arthur's man, I was also a friend to your father, years ago. And if anything should happen to me—" Coel broke off, though the hawk's eyes remained steady on hers.

"If I know that a king cannot afford to trust even close kin, I also know that no king is absolutely safe from those who may wish him harm. And if anything should happen to me before I can prove the accusation before the council, I would not carry what I have learned with me to the grave."

Chapter Ten

ISOLDE WATCHED THE PROCESSION OF councilmen—dukes and petty kings—as one by one they stepped silently forward to drop a handful of earth into the open grave.

Coel had taken his leave of her on the headland, returning to Tintagel alone. "Safer for you—and for me—if we are not seen to have had private conference." He had taken her hand, bowed, then looked up, eyes golden on hers. "I will see you again at the burial of my lord the king."

Now, standing in the mist-filled churchyard, Isolde let Father Nenian's voice wash past her, resonant and sure.

"I am the resurrection and the life, sayeth the Lord. Whosoever believeth in me, though he were dead, yet shall he live. And whosoever liveth and believeth in me shall never die. . . ."

Isolde's eyes moved to the curls of smoke rising from the army encampments on the headland, smudges of paler gray against a sky dark with low-hanging clouds.

She had tried, both in the chill of the stone-built chapel and in the graveyard here, to feel something of Con—some hint that he yet lived, as the words in Father Nenian's holy script promised. She'd sensed nothing, though, nothing of Con's presence amid either the candle-lighted stillness or the mist. Though she wondered whether Con's voice would come to her now, like all the others, when the wind blew from the west.

The scents of holy oil and incense from the chapel still clung about her clothes, and she shut her eyes as the smell carried her momentarily back. Back to lying in a bright, fever-soaked haze, her breasts hot and sore and weeping milk beneath the bindings the midwives had applied, as Father Nenian brushed the holy oil on her forehead, her feet, the palms of her hands.

And Con stumbling in, his eyes bleared, his breath reeking of drink, and striking her across the face for the first—the only—time.

The churchyard was enclosed by a low wall, built of the same gray stone as Tintagel itself, and Isolde turned to the south, where beyond the wall and a grove of slim white birch trees, an unmarked grave lay, grassed over and all but invisible now. Sight and memory she'd lost seven years ago. But faith . . .

Beneath her cloak, Isolde's hands moved to settle over her stomach, tracing the girdle laces tied by the serving girl Marcia back in her own rooms. Isolde had seen Marcia's eyes, hard and sharp, studying her as she stepped out of her workday gown. Had seen, as well, the calculations reeling off in the other girl's eyes. The number of days since Con had last shared her bed. The days that yet remained until her courses should come, if they were to come on this moon.

And maybe, Isolde thought, her eyes still on the southern wall, it's good thing I could feel nothing of Con—no sense that he was with me still. If he were, he might know what I have done. And that I doubt he could forgive—whatever Father Nenian and the Christ-God say of the world beyond.

The procession of men moved slowly on. Owain of Powys. Madoc of Gwynedd. Owain's face was composed and grave.

Madoc's eyes were reddened, as though he had indeed wept for his king. The king of Gwynedd's dark, ugly face looked more angry than sorrowful, though. Madoc, she thought, is not a man to submit easily to feeling, even grief.

Huel. Marche, moving slowly as though the old wound pained him, dark head bowed. And then Isolde's blood ran suddenly cold. She looked quickly up and down the line of petty kings and nobles, then scanned the group again, but the figure she sought was not there.

Coel of Rhegged had not after all come to bury his king.

Even as the realization struck, a touch on Isolde's arm made her turn. She noted automatically the blue boar on the man's tunic, but his first words banished every other thought.

"My lady, will you come to Lord Coel? He's been taken badly ill."

COEL HAD BEEN HOUSED IN AN upper floor of Tintagel's guest lodgings, a long, narrow room, the walls hung with tapestries, the air thick, now, with a fug of sickness and the heat of the fire blazing in the hearth. Isolde had gone first to her workroom for her medicine scrip, and now, as she stood in the doorway, she had an impression of many people crowded round the great carved bed in the room's dim light.

Father Nenian was one, his tonsured head bowed, his lips moving as though in silent prayer, while at the foot of the bed Coel's son Huel stood rigid, his narrow face a twisted mask of worry. And— Isolde stiffened. And Marche was there as well, standing beside Huel, one hand on the younger man's arm.

Isolde saw Huel look up sharply as she entered the room, and Marche's hand tighten its grip on the other man, but her gaze was fixed on the figure that lay on the bed amid a tangle of sweat-soaked sheets. Coel looked smaller, Isolde thought, the strong frame suddenly fragile. His eyes were clenched shut and his face was chalky white. He was curled tight on his side, and his hands gripped the edge of the sheet so tightly that the bones showed white beneath the stretched skin. His teeth were gritted and bared, and Isolde knew he was trying to fight back a scream or groan.

Almost before Isolde realized she had moved, she was beside the bed and taking one of the clenched hands. Coel's fingers felt clammy, the beating of blood through the wrist a fever-fast, unsteady thread, and his head was twisting violently on the pillow, as though he was trying to break free of the pain. At her touch, his eyes flew open and stared at her, though without a trace of recognition in their gaze.

Instinctively, she put a hand on his forehead.

"Be easy. It's all right. You're safe, my lord Coel."

The words were almost meaningless in this place of certain death, but they seemed to bring Coel a moment's peace, for his body relaxed a little. Keeping her hand on his brow, Isolde went on, speaking in a low, soothing murmur as she'd done countless times while sitting at other sickbeds. Then, slowly, Coel's gaze cleared, his eyes fixing with a kind of desperate urgency on Isolde's face. Isolde broke off, and for a long moment, the golden hawk's eyes held hers. Coel's lips moved, and Isolde swiftly bent her head to his. But she—or he—was too late. Before he could gather strength enough to speak, a spasm shook him and his face twisted, his eyes sliding closed.

For a moment he lay still, the breath coming in little puffs through the gray, flaccid lips, his every muscle gone suddenly limp, mercifully freed, now, from pain. But Isolde had seen death too often to doubt what would follow. She sat still, Coel's cold hand still in hers, until she heard a harsh rattle deep in the sick man's throat, followed by a small, soft sigh.

Coel of Rhegged was gone.

For a long moment after Coel's breathing stopped, the room was utterly silent. Then, in a low, shaken voice, Father Nenian began the prayer for the dead.

"Have mercy upon him; pardon all his transgressions. Shelter his soul in the shadow of Thy wings. Make—"

And like shattering glass, the stillness broke, the room coming to life in a flurry of movement and sound. Isolde was only peripherally aware of Huel, flinging himself toward his father with an anguished cry; of Marche, stopping him with a restraining hand; of Father Nenian, making the sign of the cross above Coel's forehead as he continued his prayer. She found she was shaking, the blood drumming in her ears as she stared at Coel's death-smoothed face, the lined cheeks pathetically fallen in on what she could see now were nearly toothless gums.

A warrior, she thought. A king. A man of honor and pride. And he was brought here, to die like this.

She had still the memory of Coel's last look, etched bright in her mind in that moment when sheer strength of will had forced open his eyes and allowed him momentary awareness in spite of both fever and pain. And she knew, as clearly as though Coel had spoken aloud, that he had been willing her to remember his last words as they'd stood together on the headland.

If anything should happen to me before I can prove the accusation before the council, I would not carry what I have learned with me to the grave.

The memory steadied her, clearing the boiling mist from before her gaze, and she became aware that a man she'd not noticed before—a plump, black-bearded man with soft white hands—was speaking in a hushed tone, edged slightly by fear, to Marche and Huel.

"All his food was tasted, my lords, before ever it touched his lips. The death must have been caused by exposure to the rain this morning. I saw my Lord Coel was ill, and I much feared . . ."

He must, Isolde thought, be Coel's physician. Though the words prove nothing but that the man either is ignorant or has been bribed by Marche to hold his tongue.

She had seen the ring of white flesh, like burn marks, about Coel's mouth, and she was certain—as certain as she'd been when Nest told her of Branwen's death—that Coel had been poisoned by Marche's will, if not actually by his hand.

Isolde stared down at the dead man's face, the burned, gaping lips open, as though still struggling for air. She was remembering Coel, raising the medicine flask to his lips while they'd talked on the headland, grimacing as he swallowed the draft down. Add poison to his medicine, she thought, and Coel would never have known—the herbs' bitterness would have masked the taste.

Slowly, she turned away and rose. She had no proof that could be brought before the king's council. Any more than Coel himself had possessed proof of Marche's alliance with Octa of Kent.

Huel still stood between the physician and Marche. The physician was still speaking, though Isolde doubted whether Huel understood or even heard the words. His brown eyes were dazed; his face was a taut white mask.

"My lord Huel," she said quietly, "I am more grieved than I can say for your loss. I wish that I could have done more."

Slowly, still as though he scarcely heard, Huel's ravaged face turned to her, his look for a moment utterly blank. "Done more," he repeated. He moistened dry lips. "Done more." And then, suddenly, something like rage kindled in the dull brown eyes. "You can say that, when—"

But Marche stopped him with a hand on the younger man's arm, the grasp hard enough to make Huel draw in a sharp breath.

"I must beg you to excuse us, Lady Isolde." Marche's voice

was quiet, the tone calm. "We must prepare for tonight's meeting of the council. Grieve though we do for Coel, we have still to choose a king."

Isolde felt suddenly sick, and she had to clench her hands hard to keep from striking out at the coarse, handsome face before her. She nodded. "I assure you, Lord Marche, I have not forgotten. I will be there."

ISOLDE DUCKED HER HEAD AND STEPPED through the low doorway and into the prison cell. Cyn still lay amid the filthy straw like a sleeping child. But she thought that this time the bearded prisoner must have expected her, for though his head lifted at her entrance, he remained seated, arms crossed on his chest, his legs stretched out before him.

The blue eyes flicked over her in a look that ended at her hands, empty save for the burning lantern. "No food this time."

"No."

Isolde waited, but he said nothing more, only watched her in silence, until she said abruptly, "Is there a name I can call you by?"

The prisoner shifted position, eyes still on her face. "Any reason I should tell you?"

Isolde set the lantern on the floor and took a step more into the room. "No," she said. "None at all. But then there's no reason, either, why you shouldn't."

He gave a harsh cough, wiping his mouth with the back of his hand, then said, "Nifaran. That will do."

"Nifaran." Isolde knew enough of the Saxon tongue to recognize the word. "Stranger," she thought, or maybe "traveler." But not a name. She judged, though, that it was as much of an answer as she was likely to get. "I asked because I've a bargain to put to you, and I'd rather treat with someone whose name I know."

"A bargain?" He shifted position again, mouth tightening as the movement stretched the lash marks on his back. "I thought we'd had all that before. Just what do you think you can offer me? Thinking of letting me go free?" Then, as Isolde made no reply, he said, "No. You might feed us, might even set Cyn's wrists. But you'd not risk that."

"And you think I'd expect better if I fell into Saxon hands? Or if our places here and now were changed?"

The man opposite didn't respond. His face and voice were almost expressionless, but all the same Isolde was abruptly aware of how alone they were. Of the thickness of the walls, and the strength of the hands that rested on the man's knees.

Despite his anger, she'd liked him for the way he'd spoken to Cyn the day before, and she'd not, until now, been afraid. But it came to her suddenly that she knew nothing whatever of him, save that he bore the brand of slavery on his neck. That he had every reason to hate her as one of those who kept him prisoned here. And that he'd killed the boy who lay now at their feet.

She pushed the flicker of uneasiness aside. If she was to win his help, she'd have to believe that her inclination to trust him was justified. There'd at least been honest grief in his face when he'd looked down at Cyn. And she supposed there was honor, of a kind, in the way he'd dealt with the boy.

She drew a breath and said, more quietly, "Risk has nothing to do with letting you free. You and Cyn were spies, sent to carry back word of our defenses to the Saxon command. I may—I do—grieve for Cyn. But we stand on opposite sides of a war. And letting you go would leave Britain's forces open to a death blow from the side you serve."

The man Nifaran studied her, the anger fading, to be replaced by the look of something like appraisal she'd seen the day before.

"And if I told you," he said finally, "that you were right in what you guessed before? That I was Briton-born and had no loyalty to the Saxon side save services bought and paid?"

Isolde's eyes went first to the scar on Nifaran's neck, then to the mutilated fingers of his left hand. "You could tell me that," she said. "And is there any reason I should believe you spoke true?"

He gave another short, humorless laugh, the sound more bitter than angry. He turned away.

"None. As you're probably about to point out, even a slave can decide where his loyalties lie." He paused. Then: "All right, what is it you want to offer me?"

Isolde wondered, for an instant, whether she was correct in her assessment of his character. She could think of other offers she might make an imprisoned man: food, blankets, warmer clothes. Even the shriving of a priest, if he was a believer in Christ. She had simply to hope that the bargaining piece she'd decided on for this man would be right. "A decent soldier's burial," she said, "for Cyn."

Instantly, the anger was back, cold, now, and iron-hard. "So you're going to ask me to bargain for burial of the friend I've just killed?"

"No." Isolde met his gaze and said, her voice quiet, "No, I'm not asking that. I would do my best to ensure a decent burial for Cyn in any case—and whatever you decide. But knowing that, I would ask from you—" She stopped, lifting one shoulder. "You can call it a favor, if you wish."

"A favor." Absently, he picked up a strand of straw from the floor, twisting it into a quick knot and rolling it idly between his fingers. "Of what kind?"

"The answer to a question. Nothing more."

There was another pause while the silence stretched between them like strands of hot glass. Then Nifaran jerked his head in a curt nod. Whether he was still angry, Isolde couldn't tell, but at last he said, "Ask."

Isolde let out a breath she hadn't realized she'd been holding. "All right. My question is about Lord Marche. He—"

What stopped her was not movement on the man Nifaran's part, but rather that utter stillness, of breath and body both, that she'd seen before. Nifaran didn't speak, though, and after a moment she went on.

"I've heard a report that Marche was seeking alliance with the Saxons. That he was in the process of exchanging messengers with Octa of Kent."

As she spoke, Isolde had the impression first of surprise, then of a faint slackening of tension in her companion's frame, as though he'd expected something else altogether. Then he frowned.

"And you want to know . . . ?"

"I want to know whether you've any knowledge that could prove the report either false or true."

Nifaran was silent, frowning. Then, slowly, he shook his head. "No. I've heard nothing—not even a whisper."

"Would you have heard?"

He shrugged. "Maybe. Or maybe not. Depends on how skilled the messengers were at avoiding being seen."

Isolde nodded, pushing away a wave of black defeat. It was never more than a chance, she thought. A slight chance, at best.

"There's nothing more, then, you can tell me?"

She thought Nifaran was about to refuse. But then his gaze fell on Cyn's body, lying in the straw at their feet. A shadow of something passed across his face, and he frowned again, picking up a handful of straw and jerking the strands apart with quick, thoughtless twists.

"It could be," he said at last. "Octa has faced and fought down war with Cerdic of Wessex—and a few of the petty kings who turned their coats and came to Cerdic's aid when he took up arms. It's left Octa in a weaker position than he'd like. And now this latest loss at Dimilioc—he may well feel it wiser to seek peace rather than war."

Nifaran stopped, still staring at Cyn, but the slanted brows were drawn—as though, Isolde thought, his thoughts followed some inward track of their own. Then he tossed the straw impatiently away and looked up. "There's nothing else I can tell you." His voice was flat. "And you can believe me or not, as you choose. But I know nothing of what Lord Marche may plan."

"MY LORDS." MARCHE ROSE FROM HIS place and turned to face the council hall. He was dressed in the embroidered tunic and fur-lined cloak he had worn on the previous night, but now he wore a heavy gold torque about his neck and the thick gold fillet about his brow that marked him for Cornwall's king. He paused, drawing the room's attention to himself, waiting for the babble of men's voices to die away. Isolde, watching, felt cold crawl the length of her spine.

Coel may not have carried his knowledge to the grave, she thought. But he might as well have done. I doubt there is one man present here who would not take Marche's word over mine.

In the courtyard outside, the men-at-arms were sparring with staffs and calling out wagers on another dogfight; she could hear the snarls and baying of the hounds, punctuated by an occasional high yelp of pain. Isolde turned, her gaze sweeping over the council hall, and wondered whether she only imagined a change in the group's mood tonight.

She had sat throughout the feasting, forcing herself to eat of the roasted meat, to sip at the cup of hot spiced wine one of the serving women poured. But she had seen, throughout, several of the men turn toward her, faces watchful and taut, then look from her to the empty place beside Huel of Rhegged, where Coel had sat until today.

"My lords," Marche went on, "as we gather tonight to mourn our lord King Constantine, we cannot help but mourn the loss of another of our number as well, and honor his memory and his name. As you will already know, King Coel lies dead."

Again Isolde caught a stir of sullen, half-angry mutters from the men on both sides of the hall, and again she saw several faces turn toward her.

"But those of us who knew Coel—who fought at his side and knew his devotion to Britain and his king—will know that he would not want grief for him to blunt our purpose here. He spoke to us last night of the need to draw together, to let the victory won at Dimilioc be only the first of the heights to which the dragon of Britain may rise."

The words were spoken in a resonant battlefield cry that echoed to the rafters of the long, narrow hall. Shrewdly done, she thought, on Marche's part. Without seeming to, he had called into every mind the battle so recently won—reminded all those who lined the benches of who had led the charge that had made Dimilioc a victory for Britain.

Isolde's eyes moved from the rows of painted shields that hung on the wall to the men about her, their faces shadowed, beards gleaming in the light from the torches above. The air was thick with the smell of them—oiled leather and ale and un-washed bodies and sweat—and the hall felt suddenly heavy, the timbered walls thrumming with a tale as old as Tintagel's stones. A memory of countless battles fought and countless men who had once lined the benches here falling and dying on the points of Saxon swords.

And I wonder, she thought, whether the day at Dimilioc would have ended the same if Marche had not been the man he is. If Marche had not been the kind of man who can watch his own murder victim die in agony—and then speak, a few hours later, of honoring his name—would he have led that final charge that won us the field?

Marche had gone on, lowering his voice slightly, his dark eyes sweeping the room. "Last night we heard two viewpoints raised, arguments—valid claims—made on both sides. My lord Madoc of Gwynedd spoke out against Britain's need of a High King."

Marche nodded to where Madoc sat on the opposite side of the hall, and the rest of the councilmen turned, almost as one man, toward Madoc, as well. Isolde had seen Madoc as she entered, his eyes glassy, his rugged, heavy-boned face flushed as though with wine, and she had seen, too, that though the food before him remained almost untouched, he drained the drinking horn at his place several times. Now he seemed to stare a moment as though struggling to take in what Marche had said, before acknowledging Marche's words with a single brief, jerky nod.

"My lords—" Marche stopped, and another taut, expectant silence fell over the room. Isolde stiffened in her place as, her eyes on Marche's face, she tried to anticipate what he planned.

"What I propose," he went on at last, "is a trial by arms. I believe in Britain's need for a High King. That you know. I tell you now that I am willing to put my belief to test by the sword." He turned once more to where Madoc sat on the opposite side of the glowing hearth and spoke in a low voice that nonetheless carried to every corner of the hall. "Madoc of Gwynedd, are you willing to do the same?"

The eyes of the two men met and, for a long moment, held, and then Isolde saw Madoc's gaze flicker to either side. Then, slowly, he raised his head once more to look at Marche and answered with another single nod of assent. Marche turned back to address the rest of the room, but Isolde, at least, caught the brief flare of something like triumph or, more than that, of pleasure at the back of his eyes and felt a prickle of cold premonition run down her neck.

"My lords, will you agree to the trial I propose? My lord Madoc and I will each of us defend his own position, and let God be the judge of whose claims yield the victor's blade."

There was a pause, and then, like the rumbling of thunder, came a slowly building roar of assent from the rows of men, shouts of agreement and hammering on the tables with the butt ends of drinking horns. Slowly, Marche's gaze traveled the length of the room. "Are there any who stand opposed to the trial? Let him speak now, if such a man is here."

But the hall was silent, once more utterly still. Marche let out his breath and turned back to Madoc. "Then, my lord Madoc, let us begin."

Madoc rose to his feet—rose somewhat unsteadily, Isolde thought, as though feeling the effects of the wine. But he crossed the hall with a firm, even gait and stood beside Marche, waiting as some of the other men—Huel and Owain of Powys among them—lifted benches and tables aside, clearing a square open space at the head of the room. When the space was made, Madoc and Marche stood facing each other, one on either side, their faces grim in the orange glow of the torches that lined the walls. Both men had stripped off the cloaks they had worn, and Isolde saw the rapid rise and fall of breath beneath their tunics.

Marche nodded to one of his own men, and the guardsman stepped forward, carrying the tusk of a wild boar, grown into a nearly perfect ring, the ends capped with gold. All talking ceased as the guardsman held the tusk up, and in the silence one of the fighting dogs outside let out a long, mournful howl. A ripple of unease went round the room, and Isolde saw a few men make the sign of the horns and spit to avert evil, heard several more muttering of ill omens. But Marche and Madoc clasped hands firmly through the gleaming ivory circle of the boar's tusk, looking up and bowing to the ancient warrior's skull at the room's head.

"I swear to abide by the outcome of the fight. May my oath be unbroken as the tusk of the boar."

And then they began.

Marche was, perhaps, the more skilled swordsman. But in a fight off the battlefield, on foot rather than mounted, the lameness in his right leg made him slower, more awkward in his movements than the other man. And Madoc was, too, the younger by ten years and more.

But Madoc, Isolde saw, was tiring fast. Tiring even before the initial ringing exchange of blows was over and the combatants had drawn apart to circle one another like wary dogs in the flickering shadows cast by the hearth fire. The younger man's face was still flushed, and his eyes had a fixed, staring look as he and Marche edged slowly round in a close circle, then, in a ringing flash of blade on blade, drew together again.

Isolde had never seen Marche fight before. She would have expected him to be savage, filled with the joy of battle she'd heard Con describe, but instead his face was almost expressionless, his mouth drawn and his eyes almost weary as the clash of parry and stroke went on.

Madoc was panting now, on the defensive as he sought to drive off the biting serpent-strikes of Marche's blade. And Marche was driving him slowly backward, back to where the space in which they fought was bounded by the hearth's leaping flames. Once more their swords met, locked, strained, as each man fought savagely to wrench the blade from the other's grasp. And then, with a splintering crack of metal that echoed through the room, Madoc's sword broke and fell to the ground, leaving him with only a jagged end of the blade and the jeweled hilt still clenched in his hand.

Isolde heard a ripple of movement, a hiss of sharply indrawn breath go round the room, and the moment seemed to drag on and on. The two men stood facing each other, Madoc frozen, his eyes moving from Marche to the broken blade he still held. From outside the hall came another low, baying howl from one of the war-hounds, echoed a moment later by fresh shouts from the watching men-at-arms.

Marche's face was as expressionless as before, though his chest heaved and the neck and shoulders of his tunic were dark with sweat. As though reflexively, Madoc took another step backward, his movements unsteady, a flash of something like panic at the back of his eyes. And then he lurched, seemingly off-balance, stumbled, half turned, and fell headlong into the fire's blaze.

Madoc screamed, and then the sound died in a hiss and crackle from the blaze as the stench of charred cloth and burning flesh filled the air. For an instant the room seemed to be held paralyzed, frozen as Madoc had been. And then Marche leapt forward, dragging the other man out of the fire, beating at the licking flames that burned in his tunic and ran like orange ribbons through his hair.

The rest of the room remained shocked into immobility, until all along the benches Isolde saw the men begin to stir, heard the murmurs and whispers begin: "It's a sign." "A sign." "The sign has come."

In that stunned hush, the crash of the hall door against the wall sounded like a thunderclap, loud enough that Isolde's heart jerked. A man stood in the doorway, his body outlined by torchlight against the night outside. He wore battle armor—leather tunic, helmet—and a traveler's cloak, and as he stepped forward into the hall, Isolde recognized Rhys, one of the men from the battalion of Con's army sent out to pursue the remnants of the Saxon forces from the battlefield.

His face and clothes were spattered with mud. He was breathing hard, so that it was a moment before he spoke. Then: "My lords. I come to warn you. Our spies have learned that the Saxon forces are rallying—the retreat was only a ploy. Octa of Kent has joined forces with Cerdic of Wessex. They plan to attack Cornwall within a fortnight's time."

Chapter Eleven

ISOLDE SAT MOTIONLESS ON HER hard wooden bench, watching the men file past her out of the hall. The night's council meeting was ended. It hadn't taken long. Madoc, unconscious, had been carried from the room by three of his men-at-arms. Unconscious, not dead—though Isolde, catching a glimpse of the blackened skin and the charred, bloody ruin of his face, thought that Madoc might well wish, if ever he woke, that he had indeed been killed.

And then a vote had been taken. And Marche was Britain's High King.

"Lady Isolde."

Isolde looked up. Marche's hair was still damp with the sweat of the recent fight, and she saw that he had a reddening burn on his left arm from where he had pulled Madoc from the fire. But his voice was cool, if grating.

"A word with you—if I may request that you remain?"

She had expected he would look exultant, or triumphant at least, but his face was expressionless as it had been in the heat of the fight. And his eyes—Isolde felt suddenly chilled—his eyes were black, and empty as twin pits dug over a grave. Two of his men-at-arms stood behind him, their faces as blank as their lord's. Pointless, she thought, to refuse. His men will be simply march me at knifepoint to the place of Marche's choosing.

She waited in silence while the councilmen passed out of the hall. Marche was High King. Though not, she thought, through his skill at arms or even through lucky chance. Drug, she thought, remembering Madoc's flushed face and glassy eyes. Just enough to unbalance him in the fight. And his sword would have been weakened, as well, before ever he took it up. Easy enough for one of Marche's men when all arms had been left behind for the vigil last night.

She doubted, though, that even Marche could have foreseen that final, headlong pitch into the fire's blaze. Almost, she thought, I could believe in the men's talk of a miraculous sign.

When the door had closed behind the last of the councilmen, Isolde looked up. "Well?"

With the benches empty and the fire dying to nothing but glowing embers, the room seemed unnaturally large, and her voice echoed eerily in the vast, shadowy space.

"I wish," Marche said, "to repeat the offer I made you yesterday. Marriage and the protection of my name." He paused, then added, "It's an offer you would do well to consider, Lady Isolde."

Against her will, Isolde was remembering their encounter in the stairwell the night before, and the clench of Marche's fingers on her bare skin. And now, once more, they were alone, out of reach of anyone she might call for aid.

She forced the tightening clutch of unease aside and said, "And why is that, Lord Marche?"

"Because as wife of the High King, you would be safe. Otherwise . . ." Marche paused, raising his shoulders, the heavy muscles pulling tight beneath the sweat-stained shirt. "You were at Coel's deathbed, Lady Isolde. Seen to murmur spells over him

by both his physician and his son. And during last night's council meeting, you were heard to threaten Madoc, as well. Few, I
think, would fail to believe that both Coel's death and Madoc's
fall tonight lie at your door."

Isolde sat without moving. She understood, now, the message that had summoned her to Coel—and the hostile, wary
looks from the men in the hall tonight. And she had no doubt
that any of the king's council would fail to believe such claims.

"I am sorry," Marche added after a moment, his voice still
soft, "to trouble you with such matters, Lady Isolde."

Isolde had caught her breath by now. "Are you indeed?
Since, unlike you, I do not tell lies, I will offer no thanks for
your concern." She paused. "To be quite clear, then," she said,
"you mean that if I refuse to marry you, you will have me ac-
cused of witchery?"

Marche made no reply, but his eyes met hers in a long, level
look.

Those condemned by trial as witches were drowned. Or
burned alive.

Isolde thought, suddenly, of standing in the churchyard and
looking down into the cool, silent darkness of Con's grave. And
I wish, she thought, I could tell Marche how little that threat
touches me now.

She had made Con a promise, though, as she stood beside
his coffin, that she would fight to protect his throne. And for the
sake of that promise, she thought, I have instead to hope that
Myrddin will return in time.

It was almost as though Marche had read the thought. He
said, voice still harsh and cool, "You can dismiss, Lady Isolde,
the thought of rescue from your man in Camelerd. Your messenger was intercepted. I hold him as we speak."

Isolde hadn't been afraid—really afraid—until now. But at
that, her heart froze in her chest.

She swallowed, then said with an effort, "You lie."

Marche's mouth tightened in a faint, brief smile. "I lie, do I?" He turned to the guards who stood by the door—Hunno and Erbin, Isolde now saw. "Bring the prisoner here."

HE STOOD BETWEEN HUNNO AND ERBIN, his gray-blue eyes as utterly calm as ever, without even a hint of acknowledgment, much less fear, of the knife blade pressed to his throat.

Myrddin. Isolde's lips shaped the word, but no sound emerged.

Myrddin's face was unmarked, his white druid's robe not even torn. Even Marche's men would be wary of mistreating the Merlin, whether they believed him enchanter or no. And even so, the guardsmen looked uneasy, Isolde thought. Erbin's face was tight and beaded with sweat. Hunno looked more defiant than frightened, but it was he who held the knife to Myrddin's throat, and she saw that his hand gripped the hilt so hard that the knuckles stood out.

Isolde's heart was hammering in her chest, and she felt as though she moved through a swamp of vile, sucking mud. Her every movement seemed impossibly slow, her body refusing to obey the orders of her mind as she worked to tear her gaze from Myrddin and turn to Marche.

"Let him go." She knew her voice shook, but she couldn't stop it or, for the moment, even care. "Please. He's an old man. He can do you no harm."

"No harm?" Marche's eyes rested on Myrddin a moment, then moved to meet Isolde's. He smiled thinly. "What would you do, Lady Isolde, to win him his life?"

Isolde started to speak, but before she could, some slight movement on Myrddin's part made her stop, the words freezing in her throat. Hunno and Erbin had come to a halt before Marche, close enough, now, for her to meet Myrddin's gaze. He stood quite still, the only movement the ripple of his robes in the breeze from the open door. And then, though he didn't speak aloud, Isolde heard the words, echoing in the hollow space inside her as clearly as any that had come to her on the wind.

Don't grieve for me, Isa. Then, the hint of a smile creeping into his tone: *Make the one of the fair-folk who enchants me away a beautiful maid.*

And then—he moved so quickly that it was over almost before Isolde realized what he had done—Myrddin made a quick, twisting movement. Hunno's knife flashed out, as if by reflex. A thin red line appeared at Myrddin's throat, beneath the beard. And then the old man swayed and crumpled to the floor.

When the pounding darkness cleared from Isolde's eyes, she was beside Myrddin, kneeling in the pool of blood that spread out from his cut throat. Her throat burned as though she were breathing in fire instead of air, and she found she was saying silently, over and over again, *Let this not be real. Let him not be dead. Let me go back just a few moments in time and think of a way I could have saved his life. Tell Marche I'll do whatever he asks if only he'll let Myrddin go free.*

Myrddin's face was peaceful, smoothed by death of even the lines of age, though the gray-blue eyes now stared sightlessly, and his beard and robe were soaked scarlet. Hunno stood to one side, looking dazedly—as though scarcely realizing what he had done—from the blood-smeared blade of his knife to the man who lay at his feet.

Another tale, Isolde thought numbly, of Merlin's magic to go the rounds of the fire halls. Hunno would say he'd been ensorceled, bespelled into the killing. As maybe he had. Or maybe Myrddin had only known what a warrior's reflexes would be.

Isolde looked from Myrddin's lifeless face to her own hands, wet and stained, as well, with his blood. And then finally, swallowing the aching lump in her throat, she raised her head and met Marche's eyes, hard and empty as twin chilled steel balls.

For a moment, the room spun around her again, and she dug her nails hard into the palms of her hands. No, she thought savagely. You're not going to faint. Not now. Not before Marche. Not here.

She focused on drawing first one breath, then another, telling herself that whatever she'd said or done, Marche would never have let Myrddin live. Willing herself to turn the guilt and the grief to anger, at least for now. Then, slowly, she rose to face Marche once more.

"You called me a witch, Lord Marche," she said. "And as such a one, I curse you now." Her chest felt as though it were on fire, painfully constricted and tight, but her voice was low and steady as she went on, her eyes on Marche's face.

"I curse you for Coel, for Branwen, for Constantine, and for all the other deaths that lie at your door. I curse you by water, by fire, by wood, by stone. I curse you by sea, by land, by sun, by moon."

She paused, raised her still scarlet-stained hand, the fingers outspread and pointing toward Marche's heart. Then: "And I curse you, Lord Marche, by the blood of the man murdered here tonight—the blood that now stains my hand."

Isolde stopped, hand still upraised, and saw the flash of fear in Marche's eyes. It was gone almost at once, leaving the heavy, brutal face frozen in an immobility of rage she had seen only once or twice before. She knew that he would make her pay, sooner or later, for what she had seen—and done. But it had been worth it, to see him momentarily afraid.

With a muttered oath, Marche turned away and rounded on Hunno. "Street-filth! Bastard whoreson! Get out—and bring the man Brychan to me."

Brychan. The name struck like another blow, but Isolde forced the shock of it back. Forced herself not to look again at Myrddin's still, crumpled form while Hunno moved to obey. ·

She hadn't even considered whether Brychan would be brought as an ally to Marche, or a foe, but when Hunno and Erbin returned, she saw that the captain of Con's guard was held as a prisoner, as Myrddin had been, his arms pinned at his sides. And Marche's guards had not been afraid of Brychan as of the older man. A purpling bruise showed on one of his high cheekbones, and a thin trail of blood ran from his mouth. His steps were stumbling, too, his body hunched over what Isolde thought must be bruised or broken ribs.

So, she thought, Brychan was loyal to Con after all. And if I had trusted him before, would—?

Isolde stopped herself before she could go on with questions that were pointless now. *As pointless as tears.*

She felt a swelling ache in her throat all the same, and she had to swallow again, hard, before she could ask, "What does this mean?"

Marche's face was still dark with anger, but though Isolde could see the pulse of blood hard and fast beneath his jaw, he had brought himself under control.

"I regret to have to tell you, Lady Isolde, that the captain of your husband's guard has been found guilty of treason against the High King." Their eyes met, and he added, "You understand?"

Isolde looked from Brychan's bruised face back to Marche.

"Yes," she said, "I understand very well, Lord Marche. Without Brychan, the men of Constantine's army will never dare rebel against your rule. Although with Constantine's forces divided as they are, half pursuing the Saxons and only a skeleton force left behind at Tintagel now, it would already be suicide for them— and easy slaughter for your own troops—if they were to try."

She stopped. "You must want Camelerd very badly, to tie yourself in marriage to a woman known as the traitor's daughter and a witch besides. Why? Is it part of your agreement with Octa of Kent?"

She had never really doubted the truth of what Coel had claimed, but the flicker of shock that narrowed Marche's eyes and tightened his jaw would in any case have proven the claim true. Out of the corner of her gaze, she saw Brychan, in the grasp of his two guards, react as well, his head coming up with a jerk.

"So," Marche said at last. "You know of that."

"Yes, I know." Isolde paused. Anger had come to life now, temporarily driving back grief and even fear. "You weren't able to murder Coel quite in time."

This time, though, Marche didn't react. He only watched her for a moment, then settled his shoulders in a brief, dismissive shrug. "So I see. Not that it matters. You've no proof."

A wave of loathing nearly choked her, and Isolde fairly spat the next words. "I might have known. You've broken three blood-oaths of loyalty. Betrayed three kings—first Arthur, then my father, and then Constantine. I might have expected you would betray your land—your people—as well. And in return for what? A place as a puppet ruler? A tame dog, begging at the Saxon table for what scraps of power they fling your way?"

"Enough!" Marche's hand shot out, catching hold of her wrist and twisting to pin her arm between them. His jaw hardened, mouth tightening to a thin line. "Year after year, we've fought the Saxons. Sent out our best men to watch them slaughtered and cut down. I saw countless of my fellows die—saw my own father die at the warrior Hengist's hand."

Marche's mouth twisted, and his eyes turned dark with memory—and, Isolde thought, with something more besides that she didn't quite understand. The look was instantly gone, though, and he went on. "As brave a warrior as ever held a sword, and he had his guts spilled at the Saxon dog's feet. I was at his side. Swore an oath to see him avenged. But how many lives must we pour into the Saxon maw before we admit we fight a losing war?"

"So you plan one final slaughter? A sacrifice of all Britain's remaining forces here?"

"Sacrifice? How many lives will be saved if I can negotiate peace? How many men will be spared if we admit the Saxons are in Britain to stay? That Arthur will never come again, and that we now fight a losing war?"

Marche stopped. No man, Isolde thought, is a villain to himself. Though I doubt even Marche believes entirely in his own words.

Marche's voice had been fiercely assured, but she'd seen something flicker at the back of his eyes. Something trapped and at bay, as though he'd set events in motion that now spiraled beyond his control. Octa of Kent, from all she'd heard of the man, would make for as dangerous an ally as a foe.

Almost, she might have felt pity. But not with Myrddin lying at her feet in a pool of his own blood.

Her lip curled. "I can believe, at any rate, that you know how to cut yourself free from a cause you believe will no longer profit you. My father—"

Even braced for anger as Isolde had been, the depth of Marche's response took her by surprise. Rage flared in his dark eyes, and he raised a hand and struck her, hard across the mouth, snapping her head back. "Quiet! You will not speak of him again! I gave all for your father. Betrayed a blood-oath to Arthur, my king. And did it gladly. Modred was weak. That was why he was punished."

Marche's face was still flushed, twisted with fury. "If you mislike what I am now, you can thank your father for making me so.

But I learned one thing from him. And learned it well. No oath is inviolable. Loyalties are as easily broken as made."

With an angry twist, Isolde jerked free of his grasp and said, her voice still biting, "And is that why you had Constantine murdered? Had he learned you were still playing the traitor?"

"I said be silent!" Marche struck her again across the face, harder this time, so that bright sparks of fire danced before her eyes. "You've no need to know more." He stopped, chest heaving, and then, regaining control, he grated out, "I made you a proposal, Lady Isolde. You can either accept it or die. The choice is yours."

All about them, the silence thickened. And Isolde, watching the massive, brutal face before her, the heavy body and powerful hands, felt sudden sickness roll through the pit of her stomach as she realized what she would have to do.

She drew in a steadying breath, willed her voice to be as cold and hard as his. "Very well. I will agree to marry you. Provided you grant me two conditions."

Marche's eyes narrowed. "And those conditions are?"

"One of the Saxon prisoners you hold in the north tower has . . . died," Isolde finished, after a brief hesitation. "You will see him given the rites of funeral of a Saxon warrior. His body sent by fire to his gods."

Marche was silent, frowning, and then he gave a short nod. "Very well. And the other?"

Isolde glanced at Brychan, still held fast between Hunno and Erbin, then back at Marche. "You will give me your word—your sworn oath—that Brychan's life will be spared. And you will leave me here now to speak with him alone."

Out of the corner of her eye, Isolde saw Brychan give a convulsive start and open his mouth as though to speak, but she kept her eyes on Marche's face. His expression was almost blank, but his eyes drilled into hers so long that Isolde felt cold sweat prickling on her neck beneath the heavy coil of hair, and she had to will herself not to break away from the gaze. Then, at last, Marche gave another curt nod.

"Very well. You have my word he will not die at my hand." He stopped, and then a slow smile curved his mouth. With another twist of sickness, Isolde knew that he was remembering that brief moment when she'd made him afraid. "The marriage will take place tomorrow. I will trust you to be prepared."

Chapter Twelve

HUNNO AND ERBIN HEFTED MYRDDIN'S limp body between them and were gone, and Isolde let out her breath in a shuddering sigh, pressing her hands tightly against her eyes. Her mouth throbbed where Marche's hand had struck, and her skin still crawled with the memory of the bargain she'd just made.

With every part of her will, she forced back all thought of Marche. All thought of Con, too, and what he would say about what she was about to do. Whether she ought to hope he saw and understood the choice she'd made—or to hope he was indeed gone to nothing, with neither care nor thought for this world.

Whether, even for the sake of saving his country and his throne, he would forgive her giving herself to the man who'd caused his death.

There was still a smeared, crimson pool of Myrddin's blood on the floor.

For a moment, Isolde thought she would be sick, but Brychan cleared his throat, starting to speak, and she managed to steady herself enough to look up at him. Brychan's olive skin was muddy, and she could see the effort it cost him to speak at all, but he said, with something of the old stiff formality, "My lady, I can't let you—"

Isolde shook her head, stopping him before he could go on. "No, Brychan. There's no other way. You heard what Marche said. I can either be wedded to him or die. And if I'm dead, there will be no one at all left to stand in his way or to keep him from betraying Britain to the Saxons."

She forced her voice not to waver, forced herself to sound certain and firm, with no trace of the doubts that were crowding in on every side. She paused, then added, her eyes steady on Brychan's, "You have never liked or even entirely trusted me, Brychan. I know that well. But you must trust me now. For I don't suppose Marche's men will leave us alone for long."

Brychan's mouth tightened briefly, and then he said, with an effort, and still stiffly, "I'm sorry, my lady. I know my lord king would have trusted you with his life. That should be—that is— enough to win my allegiance."

Isolde's throat ached with another of those quick stabs of grief, but she pushed that, too, away. *Later you can weep for Con. Bid him goodbye in case what you're about to do cuts you off from him for all time. But not now.*

"The night after the fighting at Dimilioc. There were no guards on duty in my husband's tent. Why?"

Instead of answering directly, Brychan asked, "It was true, then, my lady, what you said of Lord Marche? That he was responsible for the death of my lord king?"

"It was true."

Brychan was silent, his eyes black with fury, and a spasm of anger twisted the taut, shuttered face. "Would I had known. I'd have seen him dead for what he's done."

He stopped to draw breath, and Isolde saw him flinch as the movement jarred his ribs, but he went on almost without pause, the flare of anger dying to a cold, hard blaze. "The night after

Dimilioc, I should have been on guard at the tent of my lord king." His face twisted again. "And I would have been there. But that Constantine himself ordered me—and the rest of his guardsmen, as well—to stay away."

"Con told you to keep away?" Isolde repeated. "But why?"

Even as she spoke, though, she could guess what the reason would have been. And Brychan's face gave her answer enough to be sure. He looked down, avoiding her gaze, a dull flush of red creeping up under his skin.

"It's all right, Brychan," she said quietly. "I knew Con."

Brychan looked up at that. "They none of them meant anything, my lady. It's only that . . . after battle . . . a man needs—"

"A woman," Isolde said. She raised a hand and brushed tiredly at her cheek. "Any woman. I know." She paused, remembering Con's own words, a half shame-faced *I'm sorry.* And then: *It stops you from thinking about what you've just done. For a time.*

Brychan's face was working. "I should have stayed, though, all the same, my lady. I should—"

Isolde blinked a press of tears away. "You can't blame yourself for obeying his orders. You had no reason to expect danger that night, any more than Con did himself. And now . . . now we had better speak of what's to be done. I don't suppose Marche will leave us alone very long, whatever he promised."

Brychan's face still looked pinched beneath the bruising, but he nodded. "You indeed mean, my lady, to be wedded tomorrow to Marche?"

"I can think of no other way. Until we are wedded by law, Marche will have me under guard at all times. But after—"

Isolde stopped, swallowed, started over. "After the marriage, after he is sure he has won, he will relax his guard. And it's then I may find a chance to get away."

She paused. Then: "That is why, Brychan, I made speaking with you alone one of the conditions for agreeing to what

Marche proposed. You heard the message that Rhys brought tonight, and—"

She stopped, drawing in her breath sharply, as a memory of the picture Rhys had made, standing before the council hall, returned, sharp and clear. His face and clothes spattered with mud from a desperate ride, his chest heaving as he fought for air. His cloak—

"It was dry."

"My lady?"

Isolde turned her gaze back to Brychan. "His cloak—Rhys's cloak was dry. It was raining outside, but his cloak was dry. His entrance was planned."

"Then Rhys—"

Isolde nodded, her mouth tightening as she repeated what Coel had said only hours before he died. "In any army—among any king's band of fighting men—there are those whose loyalty can be bought. The story Rhys told may be true, or it may be false. But nearly all the fighting forces of Britain are now at Tintagel, gathered in one place together. And if Marche plans to betray them—offer them up to the Saxons—he would be a fool to give up the element of surprise."

Brychan nodded. "You mean that we can't count on the two weeks Rhys claimed it would take the Saxon forces to march here."

"No." Isolde stopped as another realization struck. "Coel told me, as well, that he'd received word that Marche was massing troops in secret at Castle Dore. And I would wager against any odds that those troops are Saxon, sent by Octa to wait at Castle Dore until the invasion begins. And then to strike at our troops from behind while the rest of the Saxon army attacks from the fore."

Drawing in her breath, she tried to steady herself. "Before he died, Coel told me that he had sent his informer—a traveling goldsmith, or at least so he appears—to Castle Dore to find whether the rumors of troops gathering there were true. If I can find this man—and if he has found what he sought—I can bring him before the council and give them warning of what Marche plans. They'd not take the word of the Witch Queen, not when they've just elected Marche High King. But they'd have to listen to a servant of Coel—at least learn for themselves whether what he claimed was true."

Brychan opened his mouth as though to object, but she stopped him. "It's a thin chance—scarcely any chance at all. I know that. And I may not even succeed in escaping from Marche's watch here. I know that, as well. I think I must try. But"—Isolde stopped again, and said, meeting Brychan's gaze one more—"I will not make the attempt without your consent and agreement that I should go."

Isolde saw comprehension dawn in Brychan's dark eyes. He said, unflinchingly, "You mean, my lady—?"

"I mean that at the best of times, Marche's oaths have all the value of a treaty scratched in blowing sand. I can't think the promise he made me tonight will be worth any more."

A faint smile touched the corners of Brychan's mouth at that, then faded, his lips tightening grimly. "True. And if you do manage to break free—"

Isolde nodded. "Especially then." She stopped. Then, quietly: "The choice is yours, Brychan. I would not leave you—"

But Brychan broke in, his voice steady. "As you say, my lady, there is no choice to be made. You must go—there is no other way if Britain is not to fall entirely into Saxon hands." He paused, then added in a different tone, "Is there anything . . . anything I can do for you, my lady? Any help I can give?"

The marriage, Isolde thought, will take place tomorrow. She saw again the exultation—and something more—in Marche's dark eyes, his slow smile.

She shook her head, as though it might clear the memory from her eyes. "No. Just try to stay alive. And I'll do the same."

AS ISOLDE HAD EXPECTED, HUNNO AND Erbin were waiting at the door of the hall when she and Brychan emerged. Without speaking or even exchanging a glance, the two guards separated, Erbin falling in beside Isolde, Hunno reaching to tie Brychan's wrists before him with a leather thong. Marche had given his orders, so much was plain.

Isolde saw, too, that Erbin took up a position beside the door to her own chambers, hands behind him, feet spread apart, his dagger drawn. I was right, she thought. The guard will not be relaxed before tomorrow night—if at all.

The girl Marcia was waiting within, slumped and dozing on a stool by the lighted hearth, though she started awake as Isolde entered.

"I have no need of you tonight," Isolde said shortly. "You may go to your own bed."

Marcia shook her head, her mouth curving in a small, satisfied smile. "My lady Nest has given orders that I stay. I'm to sleep at the foot of your bed until you're wedded to my lord king."

Isolde's lip was throbbing, still; her eyes were gritty with fatigue. "So that they can be sure I take no one else to my bed whose child I might pass off as Marche's—or even King Constantine's? The guard at my door should be enough to assure even Lord Marche I won't run—or receive anyone here. Unless you believe me witch enough to vanish and appear at will or bed with the demons of the air?"

A sullen look settled over Marcia's thin, pockmarked face, and she said, dropping all pretense at deference or servitude, "Serve you right if you were got with a demon child—like your grandmother before you—and bore a son like your father, God curse his name. I'd tell them—I'd give them an earful in the council hall if you tried to pass it off as my lord king's."

"You'd tell them what?"

Marcia gave Isolde another of those sly, sharp looks, then shook back her dark hair. "I'd tell them my lord King Constantine hadn't warmed your bed in months—he'd been too busy in mine."

"In yours?" Only a moment earlier, Isolde had felt almost nothing but dislike for the other girl. Dislike—and distaste, as well. Now, though, she couldn't find it in her to dislike Marcia. Or even to be angry. There was something pitiful in the girl's dark eyes as she made the claim. A kind of hollow, savage hopefulness that she might be believed. Not just that Con had shared her bed, but that she'd been wanted by a man—any man.

"That's a lie," Isolde said wearily. "Constantine would never have so much as looked at you. And you can be thankful Nest knows that as well as I do."

A flush of anger had spread across the other girl's face, and she said, eyes narrowed, "What do you mean?"

Isolde unfastened the brooch that held her cloak in place, then slipped the cloak from her shoulders. "You remember Branwen?" she asked. "You think she died of ordinary illness? Or maybe old age?"

She let the cloak drop onto the storage chest by the bed, then turned back to find Marcia watching her, fear for the first time shadowing her gaze. Isolde nodded. "Yes. You may be a favorite of Nest's now. But she's a dangerous ally to have, if she ever decides you're more threat to her than friend."

She saw Marcia's gaze waver—her look uncertain, then hardening once again.

"You'd say that, of course."

Isolde looked at the girl, standing with her chin slightly lifted, her shoulders set. Far, far harder, she thought again, to convince a woman that one of her own sex could have the power to harm. But pity or no, she thought, I can't have her stay the night.

"Very well," she said curtly. "Stay, if you wish."

She crossed to where the scrying bowl stood, knelt to light a candle by the embers of the fire, then set the candle in the center of the water.

"Here—what are you doing?"

There was uneasiness, now, in Marcia's tone, but Isolde didn't answer, nor did she turn from where she stood. Instead she bent down, eyes fixed on the candle that burned in the center of the bowl, the flame's reflection dancing and flickering on the surface of the water. "I, mistress of Satan, summon my lord. Powers and demons and spirits of the air," she whispered, "come to me now."

Behind her, she heard Marcia suck in a sharp breath. It was all she could do to keep from looking round, but she kept her eyes on the water, made her breathing slow, even, and deep. Slowly, she lifted the ewer of moon-blessed water to her lips, drew in a sip, then spat it deliberately on the floor.

"I curse the Father," she whispered. Then she sipped and spat again. "I curse the Son." She spat a third time. "I curse the Holy Ghost."

She heard Marcia let out another frightened gasp, then heard the patter of hurried footsteps, and finally the door of her chambers opening and closing. Isolde shut her eyes briefly, then cupped her hands and blew out the candle, tipped the water from the bowl into the basin, and set the bowl back where it belonged. Instantly, Cabal, who had remained curled in his corner until now, came to snuffle at her skirts.

Isolde laid a hand on his neck. A sin, probably, in the eyes of the Christ-God. And Goddess-blessed silly, she thought, as well. Myrddin would have bent double laughing at the performance she'd just given. The thought of Myrddin, though, brought back a cold press of grief—and guilt—that tightened her throat, and she rested her cheek against Cabal's head.

"My lady?"

Isolde looked up to see Hedda in the doorway, her face as impassive as ever, though Isolde thought there was a faint note of anxiety in her tone. "What has happened? Marcia said—"

"Marcia spoke true, Hedda. I have agreed to marry Marche. The services will be held tomorrow."

Hedda's eyes widened, a flash of surprise in their pale depths. "You have agreed?"

"It's the only way. Sit down." Isolde gestured toward a place beside her on the bed and drew a long, shuddering breath. "I'll tell you all that's happened tonight."

The worst was recounting Myrddin's death. A vision of the old man's still, gray face rose before her, and Isolde had to stop, struggling to remember the words he had spoken only the day before instead of his sightless, staring sea-blue eyes and blood-soaked beard.

Remember that, Isa. That I have chosen this path. That you have laid nothing on me but what I choose to take up as mine.

At last Isolde stopped, her hand still on Cabal's neck. She was grateful for the big dog's warmth and the bristle of fur beneath her fingers. The fire in the hearth was dying, the light just enough to gild Hedda's fair hair and lashes and pale skin. Hedda had listened without speaking, and now she remained silent a long moment, perched on the edge of the bed, the broad, capable hands folded at the girdle of her undyed gown. Then, as before, she reached out and clasped her fingers briefly round Isolde's.

Isolde gave the Saxon girl's hand a brief, answering clasp, then let Hedda withdraw from the touch. "Thank you, Hedda," she said softly. Then: "I will need your help if I am to get free.

I'll need a serving woman's gown and shoes. Can you get them for me—and have them here, ready, tomorrow night?"

Hedda was silent a moment more, then nodded. "Yes, my lady. I bring them to you before morning."

"Thank you, Hedda," Isolde said again. Then she stopped. Since she had parted with Marche in the council hall, she had been holding a cold, crawling sickness at bay, but now it swept over her, strong enough that she had to wait a moment before going on. At last she said, "There's one thing more. Something I'll need before tomorrow. A paste . . . made of mandrake and cedar oil."

Hedda had risen to stir the dying fire into life, but at Isolde's words she froze, then turned, her movements for once quick, her voice sharp. "But that's—"

"I know." Isolde shut her eyes a moment. "It will be in my stillroom, along with the other simples and herbs. I would get it myself, but that I doubt Marche will give me the chance to go to my workroom alone."

Slowly, Hedda nodded. Her expression was stolid as before, but there was something the girl's look that made Isolde's half-formed guess of the night before turn to certainty. Her eye's went to Hedda's stomach. Con's? she thought. No, surely not. Not when there were so many others far prettier—and far more willing—than Hedda to be had.

Hedda's eyes were still on Isolde's face, their pale gaze steady and for once bright and clear. "I understand, lady," she said quietly. "I do as you ask."

WHEN HEDDA HAD GONE, ISOLDE SAT down on a stool by the fire, letting Cabal creep forward to rest his head across her knees. The bronze scrying bowl was still in its place by the hearth;

mechanically, her eyes traced the swirling patterns in the bright metal sides—serpents of eternity, swallowing their tails. No use, though, to try once more to See in its depths. She might have heard Myrddin's unspoken words as he died, but that had been Myrddin's power, not her own. Even her witch's curse for Marche had been only empty show.

And I wonder, she thought, how I can hope to defeat Marche, when I cannot even bear my own past? When I can't make myself remember, even if it might bring back the Sight?

The storm that had threatened all day had broken at last, and Isolde sat listening to the pounding of rain against the walls outside, her fingers twined in Cabal's fur.

The stars will still shine tomorrow, whatever happens to me here.

Still, her mind went back to a tale she remembered hearing long ago. The story of a queen, forced to wed the man who had conquered her husband's army and taken his throne. She had married him, but offered him at the wedding ceremony a poisoned cup. And allayed all suspicion by drinking first, choosing death herself so that she might take her husband's killer with her to the grave.

Black rebellion broke over Isolde in a wave. And I haven't even that choice left, she thought. She stopped, was still a moment, then abruptly rose, throwing off her shawl and reaching for the gown Hedda had brushed and folded away. I was wrong. There is yet something more to be done.

"WAIT HERE FOR ME. I WON'T be long."

Erbin had insisted on accompanying her to the north tower, but at Isolde's curt dismissal he hesitated. He was nervous of her, even yet; all the way from her rooms, he'd been careful not to meet her gaze and to stay at enough distance that not even a fold of her cloak brushed his arm. Now he swallowed once, then gave a short nod and took up a place beside the other guards.

The man Nifaran was asleep—or seemed to be asleep—when Isolde entered the cell. His head was bowed, resting on his raised knees, his body still and his breathing even. As the door swung closed behind Isolde, though, his head came up with a jerk and he sprang to his feet, hands clenched, with pupils so dilated his eyes looked almost black. The movement was so sudden that Isolde drew in a sharp breath and took an involuntarily step backward, so that her shoulders rested against the wooden door, but Nifaran neither moved nor turned to look at where she stood.

His eyes were fixed, his head thrown back, and he breathed as though he'd been running, his face and tunic wet with sweat. With sweat, and with blood as well. Isolde had brought only a candle with her this time, but its light was enough to see the stains—some dried to rusty brown, others still wet and red—that patched the back and shoulders of his shirt. She thought, I should have known. I should have guessed that by winning burial for Cyn I'd also win another beating for this man. The guards sent to take Cyn's body away would have been angry at the task they were forced to perform.

She must have made some slight movement or sound, for Nifaran's head turned, though his eyes looked at her as though she'd not been there, and his muscles remained rigid as stone. Then, slowly, his gaze cleared and he blinked, the blue eyes focusing on her face. He drew a shuddering breath, and some of the tension seemed to ebb out of his frame. He didn't speak, either, but stood, his eyes still fixed on her face.

At last Isolde said, with a gesture toward the flattened patch of straw where Cyn's body had lain, "He's had his soldier's burial. You have my word."

Nifaran remained silent, his breathing gradually slowing, the pulse still pounding in his neck. But he acknowledged the words with a brief jerk of his head and dropped, moving stiffly, to the ground once more, his legs drawn up, his back held away from the wall behind.

"Is that why you've come now? To tell me that?"

He broke off with another of the dry, harsh coughs she'd heard before, and Isolde saw him flinch, then stiffen in resistance, as the movement jarred whatever other injuries he might have. She shook her head. "No." She reached through the side-slit in her cloak for the narrow bronze knife she'd slipped into her medicine scrip back in her rooms. A flicker of surprise showed in Nifaran's blue eyes as she drew the weapon out, but he didn't move.

Not taking her eyes from Nifaran's, Isolde bent and laid the knife between them on the floor. "I'm leaving this here," she said. "You understand?"

For a long moment, Nifaran held her gaze. Then, at last: "Why?"

"Why should I do this, you mean?" Isolde felt, suddenly, very tired, weary to the core of her bones. She straightened, steadying herself against the stone wall. "Because you won a way out of here for Cyn. And because I would not see anyone, Saxon or Briton, left without at least a choice to take the same way of getting free."

Chapter Thirteen

ISOLDE KNELT BY THE WASHBASIN, retching. She was crying, too, but when she realized it she dug her nails fiercely into the palms of her hands and forced herself to stop. It was over.

Over. Over. And at least I didn't let him make me cry out.

The tears hadn't started until later, after Marche had at last gone.

Her fingers found the woolen ball, smeared with the cedar-and-mandrake paste Hedda had brought her the night before, and she bit her lip to stifle a gasp at the pain inside her as she drew it out. The wool was wet and sticky. Her stomach twisted and she gagged again, dropped the ball as though it had burned her, and then plunged her hands again and again into the pottery jar of water. *Over. Over.*

And she was safe. Marche hadn't suspected, any more than Con had ever done. Still, though, her breath was quick and ragged, and she felt soiled, slimy all over, inside and out, where Marche's body had touched her own, as though she could never be clean again.

She caught her breath. *I can't,* she thought furiously. *I can't let myself feel that.*

If she did, the pain that had begun to throb deep within her would rise up and swallow her whole and there would be nothing left of her but shame.

Isolde shut her eyes a moment. And then she took up the water pitcher and began to wash, flinching in spite of herself when her fingers found the reddening bruises. There was blood, too. With shaking hands, she scrubbed until it was gone, then poured water over herself again. The fire had gone out, and she was soon shivering in the room's chill night air, but the very cold seemed to help, a little, to take away the imprint of Marche's body from her own.

Slowly, painfully, Isolde rose to her feet and pulled on first the rough linen shift, then the gown of plain undyed wool that Hedda had brought with the paste. Isolde's fingers were clumsy, fumbling at first with the ties, and when something hard butted against her side, she flinched and jerked round, her heart beating fast and hard. It was only Cabal, though, escaped somehow from wherever he'd been penned by Nest and the other women and come to slip, now, into her rooms.

Isolde dropped again to her knees, and the big dog whined and licked her face, raising one paw to claw at her skirts. She drew a long, shivering breath, resting her cheek against the rough fur of his neck. Put it away, she thought. Away with everything else.

She'd done it before. Slowly, deliberately, she took out each memory of the day, then locked it away behind a wall. Marcia, coming to her room that morning to see her dressed and robed. And Father Nenian coming, as well, his round eyes anxious, his baby-fine hair ruffled by the wind.

"I know well that a woman left without a husband's protection has small choice in whether she marries again," he had said. "But I would not bless this marriage if you do not truly enter into this union of your own will."

Isolde had wondered, briefly, whether she dared confide in him. But that would only have put him in danger, as well. He could be of no possible aid.

Like folding away a gown, Isolde set the memory of Father Nenian's kind, worried face aside, then went on. On with all the rest of the day, drawing the memories out and then pushing them back, into a room at the back of her mind with a door she could close. The exchange of vows in the chapel, which echoed with the clash of arms and the beat of hooves from outside—the sounds of the men-at-arms making ready for war . . . The banquet in Tintagel's great hall, brief and with only the bare minimum of food, so that the bustle of readying for attack might go on . . . Being undressed and put to bed by Nest and the others, just as she had been after being wedded to Con . . .

Isolde's hands started to shake, but she forced herself to go on. Lying under the canopy of the great, carved bed . . . hearing the chamber door open . . . Marche's mouth, reeking of beer and the vomit of drunkenness, pressed against hers.

Over, she thought, her cheek still resting against Cabal's fur. Put it away.

Finally, she rose unsteadily to her feet, found her traveling cloak where Hedda had hung it, and pulled it on over the gown. She had knelt to lace the rough leather shoes Hedda had given her with the gown when the door opened, and Hedda herself slipped in.

Isolde's throat still felt raw, her head stuffy with the aftermath of crying, but she rose and said, "Hedda—you ought not to be here. There could be trouble for you afterwards, if anyone saw you come. They'll know you helped me get away."

Hedda's eyes traveled slowly over Isolde, and Isolde knew the Saxon girl had taken in her swollen eyes, the reddening bruises on her wrists that the sleeves of the gown didn't quite conceal.

Hedda said nothing, though, only shook her head and then held out a parcel, wrapped in clean linen rags.

"Food, lady. I brought for you. To take with you when you go."

The tears Isolde had fought threatened again, but she took the parcel and choked them furiously back.

"Thank you, Hedda. That was good of you. Very good."

Instead of answering, Hedda shook her head once more, this time lifting one shoulder in a faint, dismissive shrug. She seemed to hesitate a moment, then asked, turning her gaze away, so that her face was slightly averted from Isolde's, "Where . . . you go, lady?"

One of the threads on the edge of the parcel had frayed, and Isolde smoothed it mechanically, twisting it between her fingers. She might have locked the day—and the night—away, but the ache inside her had settled into a kind of rhythm, a burning pulse of pain, and at the question she felt the room, the walls around her, her very self beginning to tilt and slide away.

"The northern road," she said at last. "It will be less heavily guarded than the way that runs along the coast. And Coel's goldsmith will almost certainly have chosen that route to and from Castle Dore. It's the faster—and drier—way at this time of year." She stopped. "Such a man—traveling with the tools and goods of his trade—will stand out among the rest of what travelers there are. I should be able to intercept him on the road."

Even to her own ears, though, the words sounded as impossible as the most fantastic of tales, and the thought even of leaving her own rooms was enough to make panic pull tight in her chest once again. With an effort, Isolde turned to her dressing table, where her jewelry lay: a necklace of coral beads, given her as a child, as well as other, heavier ornaments of silver and

gold. And a glass-inlaid brooch. Con gave me that, she thought.
When—

She stopped herself and quickly gathered up the simplest
pieces: a silver comb, a few bronze bracelets, a glass-inlaid ring.
Anything more valuable would only attract attention if she tried
to barter it for food or shelter. She knotted the items together in
one of the veils that lay folded beside the jewels, then added the
small purse of copper coins she kept to give the travelers who
came to beg.

"There'll be other travelers, as well, after the battle at Dimilioc—refugees, like the ones who come here. I should be safe
enough if I can join one of the bands already on the road."

Hedda didn't answer at once. She was moving round the
room, picking up scattered clothing, straightening cushions
and rugs, but Isolde thought her movements were unnaturally
abrupt, as though she were abstracted, or frightened. At last she
straightened and said, in a low voice Isolde had never heard from
her before, "May the gods guide your journey, my lady."

Isolde opened her mouth. But there was nothing she could
offer the Saxon girl in return. An offer to take Hedda with her—
to help her escape to whatever freedom she could find—would
only risk the girl's life, and likely to no good end. She would
have to leave Hedda here, a slave, to bear an unknown man's
child into the same slavery.

Isolde drew the hood of her cloak over her hair, dropped the
bundle of jewelry into her scrip and fastened the scrip about the
girdle of her gown, then took up the parcel of food once more.
"Thank you, Hedda," she said again. "My sister."

Isolde saw a spasm, as of pain, pass over the other girl's
broad face, but before Hedda could reply, a quick, urgent knock
sounded at the door. Isolde's heart stopped, her whole body
turned suddenly cold, and she saw Hedda freeze, too, her pale

eyes turning blank, her face rigid as a wooden doll's. Then the girl turned a questioning look to Isolde.

Isolde pressed her eyes briefly shut. "Open it—please." She kept her voice low. "If it's Marche, or one of his men, any delay will only make them suspect something amiss."

Isolde had just time to jerk the traveling cloak from her shoulders and fling it in a crumpled pile beside the bed before the door opened. It was not Marche, though, nor even one of his guards, who stood outside, but Marcia, her thin, sharp-featured face resentful and sullen.

"Well?" Hedda demanded fiercely. "What you want? You were told not to come here."

With the part of her mind not still paralyzed, Isolde thought that Hedda must have been more frightened than she'd shown, for her voice was unwontedly sharp, quicker and harder than her usual tones. Marcia flinched, then flushed angrily and turned to Isolde.

"Forgive me, lady." Her voice, already shrill with spite, added a sharp, ironic twist to the final words. "I'd not have troubled you tonight. Though I did see that my lord King Marche was already back in the great hall, so I thought—"

She stopped, her face brightening with malice, the close-set eyes lingering, as Hedda's had done, over Isolde's face.

So Marche had gone from her back to his drunken revels with his men-at-arms. And likely with the castle women, as well. A memory quivered behind the freshly constructed wall in Isolde's mind, and the bile rose once more in her throat. She found that her fingers had snapped the fraying thread from the parcel she still held.

"All right, Marcia," she said with an effort. "What do you want?"

The sullen look of resentment settled over Marcia's face once more. "I don't want anything. It's one of the beggars who came for help yesterday. Your orders were whoever wanted to stay a night or two could bed down in the stables."

Isolde nodded. "Yes, that's right."

"Well, one of the women—one of the breeding ones—says the babe's on its way. It'll come tonight, she says, for sure. She was asking for you. The guard on duty in the stables came to fetch me." She stopped, her tone as resentful as her face. "Ordered me to go and give you the message that she begged you'd come. So here I am. Though maybe you'd rather wait for my lord Marche—"

Marcia broke off. Isolde hadn't spoken, but her eyes locked with Marcia's, and the girl took an involuntary step back, looking suddenly frightened. With a bitter twist of something almost like amusement, Isolde saw the memory of her performance with the scrying bowl the night before pass across the other girl's face. And then Marcia's eyes fell. "I . . . I'm sorry. I'll tell her you can't come," she muttered.

But Isolde stopped Marcia before she could turn away. "No, wait. This woman. Is her name Dera?"

"How would I know?" Marcia said. "Didn't ask her name."

"Has she a mark on her cheek? Like a stain of wine?"

Marcia looked surprised, then gave a grudging nod. "That's her. All down one side of her face, it be. But what—?"

"Then go back to her, now." Isolde drew a steadying breath. "And tell her I'll come."

DERA'S FACE LOOKED FLUSHED AND MOTTLED in the light of the lantern Isolde had brought, and her eyes were screwed tight shut as she lay in the grip of a pain. The refugees had been bedded in the open loft above the stalls, used for storing straw and hay, and big as the area was, the floor was still crowded for room, the air thick with the smell of the horses below, of hay, and of unwashed bodies packed close together in too tight a space. Dera's hands were clasped tight over the swollen mound of her belly, and she breathed hard through her nose as the contraction tightened, reached its peak, and then finally eased.

Watching, Isolde wondered whether she ought to have had her moved to one of the rooms in Tintagel's guest hall. But that would need help—two strong men, at the least, to carry the laboring woman. And there was no one she could ask. The guards on duty tonight would be Marche's men. The best she'd been able to do was hang sheets from the loft's rafters, screening off this corner of the room.

She could hear distant shouts and occasional bursts of laughter from the great hall across the courtyard, but the loft itself was quiet and still, the only sound the shiftings and mutterings of the sleepers around her, and sometimes a soft whicker from one of the animals in the stalls below. So far, Dera had not spoken nor even opened her eyes, but now, as the contraction passed, her eyelids flickered and lifted, and she licked her lips.

"Here—drink this, if you can." Isolde held one of the vials she'd brought with her to Dera's lips—a distillation of skullcap and vervain to help the labor along.

With Isolde supporting her shoulders, Dera swallowed the draft, then looked vaguely round. Instantly, she stiffened, dark eyes widening in alarm as she found the space beside her empty.

"Jory?" she whispered. "My boy. Where—?"

"He's safe," Isolde said quickly. "With Hedda, my serving maid."

Hedda and Isolde had found the boy crouched at his mother's side, one filthy thumb thrust in his mouth, his face sullen but his eyes frightened and wide, uncertain whether the situation called for defiance or tears. Hedda had offered to stay, to help with the birth, but her face, as she looked down at the laboring woman, had held a look of taut, white fear that Isolde had never seen in her before. It might have been well for her to learn what she might about the birth of a child. But Isolde couldn't have brought herself to make her stay.

"Hedda's taken him to the kitchens for some honey cakes."

Dera started to reply, but then bit her lip as another pain gripped her. When the pain had passed, Isolde wiped the sweat from the woman's brow with a fold of her cloak.

"How long since the pains came on?"

Dera swallowed. "Since sunset. Not so strong as they are now, though. At first I thought maybe they'd stop. But now—"

She broke off with a gasp, and Isolde saw the muscles of her stomach bunch and tighten as another contraction struck. This time, Dera drew her legs up, so that Isolde saw the smears of blood on her thighs, though her gown and the straw were both as yet dry. Her waters hadn't yet gone, then.

Isolde waited until the contraction had passed. Then she asked, "Will you let me see how far you are along?"

ISOLDE SMOOTHED DERA'S GOWN, THEN TURNED away to wash her hands in the basin of water Marcia had brought. She'd felt the opening of the womb, thinned and softened, now, and open about half the area it must spread for the child's head to be born. And she'd felt, too, just beyond the womb's entrance, the hard, rounded shape of the baby's skull. Head down, at least, and facing its mother's spine. A small mercy, she thought.

Very small.

"My lady?" Dera's voice made her look round. Do you think the child will come by morning, then?" She was between pains, but her tone was suddenly panicky, as though whatever she'd seen in Isolde's look had made her afraid.

Instantly, Isolde smoothed all expression from her face and said, with practiced, reassuring calm, "By morning at the latest. Likely even before. The second babe nearly always comes faster—though the pains may feel harder than with your little boy."

The fear ebbed out of Dera's eyes and she nodded, her breath going out in a sigh. "By morning. That's all right, then. Reckon I can stand anything that long."

Isolde started to speak, but stopped herself and asked instead, "Can you walk a bit, do you think? That will help bring the child's head down."

ISOLDE HELD A CLAY JAR OF wine to the woman Dera's lips, wiped the liquid that dribbled down her chin. They had walked an hour or more, circling the tiny space Isolde had managed to screen off, Dera leaning heavily on her and stopping to pant and sometimes moan when one of the pains came on. Then, when the pains grew too strong for her to stand, Isolde had helped her to lie back on the straw.

Hedda had sent Gwyn from the kitchens, a plump, red-haired serving girl with crooked front teeth and thickly lashed hazel eyes. Gwyn had offered to keep watch, as well, but Isolde had told her to get what rest she could.

"I may have need of another pair of hands once the babe is born," she had said. "But you can sleep until then. I'll wake you if there's need."

The girl was asleep now, curled in the straw a little distance away beyond the curtains beside a family of four. And Isolde sat, watching the laboring woman and occasionally wiping her brow, telling story after story in a low undertone. Whether Dera followed the tales, Isolde wasn't sure, but she occasionally opened her eyes and smiled at the words. And so Isolde went on, re-membering a time when she would have been glad of something to think on besides the ever-tightening clutch of pain.

And the familiar cadence of the stories stopped her from thinking too much now, as well.

"Lady?"

Isolde looked down to find that Dera's eyes were open.

"I'm here. Do you want more wine?"

Dera shook her head, teeth sunk in her lower lip as she fought for breath. Then: "Not called labor for nothing, is it?"

Isolde was silent, as another memory—another one she'd never been able to lock away—rose in her. Of walking the floor through the night with the midwives, stopping to pant and bend double with the pain. Of the midwife's hands on her belly, her voice in her ear. *Push. Push with me, now.*

Isolde shook her head and wiped Dera's face with a damp rag as another contraction struck. The pains were getting steadily longer, as well as closer together and increasingly strong.

Dera groaned as the pain peaked, then lay back, gasping and panting. "It's certain sure God must be a man. If 'e weren't 'e'd have thought more on the way babes are born and come up wi' a better way."

In spite of herself, Isolde smiled. "I know. And yet you'd never want to change—be born a man yourself."

Dera had slumped back in exhaustion, but at that she looked up, one eyebrow slightly raised. "So you say, my lady. There's times when I'd give a good bit to be able to take a piss on the road wi'out getting my skirts all wet."

She sank back again, her eyes sliding closed. "But then it gives you patience to bear most things that come your way—and a mother needs enough of that, the good Lord knows."

Dera grimaced and shifted restlessly, trying to find a comfortable position in the straw. "There's days when you'd give a king's ransom to cram 'em back inside you again, just for the sake o' knowing they'd not be causing trouble yet awhile. But then other times . . ."

Dera's mouth curved in fleeting echo of the smile Isolde had seen the day before, and, without opening her eyes, she lifted one hand gropingly to rest on the tightening mass that held the child. "Other times, you watch them while they're sleeping and all of a sudden you're crying like a babe yourself, though you don't know just why."

Isolde's own smile faded. "Dera—" she began. But Dera had caught her breath sharply, though not, this time, at the onset of a pain. Her eyes had flared wide, and she was staring over Isolde's shoulder, her sweat-streaked face blanched. Isolde turned to follow the look, then froze, as well.

The guardsman Hunno stood in the entrance to the blanketed-off square, his battle-scarred face stony, his eyes shadowed and dark in the lantern's flare. Isolde stared at him a moment in silence. Later, she thought, later I'll likely be frightened of him. If I let myself think about how and why he's come here. Now, though, she was too angry for fear.

"Get out," she said. "This is no place for a man of your kind."

Hunno's gaze didn't falter, and he remained where he was, feet planted solidly, straddling the makeshift doorway. "Lord Marche's orders. I'm to serve as your guard until you can attend my lord Marche in the king's rooms."

Behind her, Dera whimpered briefly, though whether from fear or pain Isolde couldn't tell. The next moment, though, Isolde heard the other woman give a low, urgent grunt she recognized at once.

Isolde turned swiftly, and was in time to see Dera's body convulse in a fierce spasm, her legs drawn up, her body curled tight around the child within. A sudden gush of fluid from between her legs soaked her gown and the straw on the floor and steamed in the loft's chill air. Dera gave a wild, heaving cry, one hand flying out, palm up, the fingers splayed.

"It's all right." Isolde held the groping hand tight. "Your water's broken, that's all. You must be nearly there."

She waited until the contraction had passed, then turned back to Hunno and said, her voice low and furious, "All right. If you're to stay, you can lend us aid. Give me the sheep tallow from my scrip—there, on the floor. She's going to need to push, soon, and her opening will have to be eased as the babe's head crowns if she's not to tear."

It might almost, Isolde thought, have been funny to watch Hunno's face. Beside her, Dera gave another deep, urgent grunt, and then her body convulsed again, her mouth open and gasping, her face purpling with the strain. The guardsman had drawn back a pace, his blunt features rigid with distaste.

Then, abruptly, he turned to Isolde and said, his voice harsh, "I'll be outside. If you want to waste your time on a whore's bastard brat, go ahead. But you get your own salve. That's women's work, not mine."

He turned and was gone, letting the curtain fall behind him. Probably, Isolde thought, he would sooner face a battle line of enemy Saxons than watch a single woman birth her child.

The flash of bitter amusement faded, though, almost at once as she looked down at Dera's flushed, sweating face. Soon, she thought. Soon the child will be born, and then she'll know. And I don't know even now whether I did right in not telling her before.

Isolde dipped the cloth into the water jar one more time, wrung it out, then laid it on Dera's brow.

"It's all right," she repeated. She took Dera's hand. "Push when you need to. It won't be long now."

Chapter Fourteen

THE CHILD WAS BORN JUST as the loft was beginning to lighten with the first gleamings of the dawn. Born in a rush of brown fluid and blood and one final, straining groan of effort from Dera. Isolde lifted the hot little body, slippery with mucus and blood, turned the child over to thump its back with the heel of her hand, even put her own mouth over the child's and breathed softly into its lungs. It was no use, though. She'd known that from the first. Through it all, the child lay utterly limp and still, tiny legs and arms dangling, and beneath the smears of blood and the muck of birth, the babe's skin was neither blue nor red, but waxen pale.

Dera was struggling to sit up, her eyes terrified beneath the strands of sweat-soaked dark hair. She'd given birth before. She'd know what it meant that she'd not heard a cry. Dera's eyes moved from Isolde's face to the child's tiny, motionless form, and she gave a little whimpering moan.

Isolde eased the afterbirth free, pressed on Dera's belly to expel the last of the blood. She wiped Dera's face, tucked the woolen shawl about her shoulders, and held another vial to her lips. Mistletoe and bayberry, this time, to help stop the bleeding and prevent the hemorrhaging that could end a woman's life. Through it all, Dera lay unmoving, eyes fixed and dull.

Isolde lifted the child again. It was like handling a flower, or a fledgling bird. The joints of legs and arms felt as light and fragile as a sparrow's bones beneath the nearly transparent skin. With the same slow care, Isolde wiped the little body clean of the blood and mucus of birth, then swaddled the child tight, as though it had indeed been alive and crying for the warmth of the womb like other newborn babes.

Dera had still neither spoken nor moved, but when Isolde made to lay the child on her breast, she jerked violently away, turning her face into the blankets. Gently, though, Isolde forced the little bundle into her arms.

"Take her. You'll be sorry afterwards if you don't."

At first Dera kept her face averted, her lips pressed tight together. But then, slowly, she turned her head to look down at the child. Its eyes were closed, the faint fringe of lashes dark against the waxen cheeks, the small mouth curved like a bow. Slowly, almost unwillingly, Dera's hand lifted, smoothing the wisps of damp hair from the small rounded skull.

"I was right, then," she said. " 'T'were a girl."

And then her voice broke, her face twisted, and a great, shuddering sob tore free of her throat.

Isolde held her while the racking sobs ran their course, and at last Dera stopped crying and lay with her eyes closed, her breath coming in wet, snuffling gulps.

"Maybe . . . maybe it's for the best, after all." Her voice was unsteady, but she raised her free hand to scrub furiously at her dripping nose and swollen eyes. "Don't know how I'd have managed with two young 'uns, living on the road as we do."

Isolde was silent a moment. Then she said, "I can give you something to make you sleep, if you like."

Wordlessly, Dera nodded, and Isolde drew the little vial of

poppy syrup from her scrip. She waited until Dera had swallowed the dose and lain back in the straw once more.

"When your milk comes in, in a day or two, put your little boy to the breast. He's young enough to suckle, still—and it will help keep milk fever away."

Dera's eyes had been closed, but at that she looked up, gulped, then nodded dumbly. Isolde was silent, eyes on the tiny bundle in Dera's arms. Then: "And when you're able, listen to the pain. It will never go away. But listen to it, and it dulls enough that you can keep living, after a time."

"GWYN." ISOLDE BENT OVER THE SLEEPING girl and touched her lightly on the arm.

Scarcely any of the other travelers in the loft had so much as looked up when Isolde had pushed aside the screen of blankets and gone to wake the kitchen maid. It's times like these, Isolde thought, that set men and women the most alone. Too exhausted—or too full of their own cares—to spare a thought for anyone else, and wary of sparing even a glance for one in need, for fear they might be called on for aid.

Gwyn sat up with a start, blinking, her eyes bleared and puffy with sleep, black hair tousled and littered with bits of straw. Her gaze moved to where Dera lay with the child beside her, a fold of cloth now covering the tiny face.

Gwyn sucked in her breath. "Dead, then, my lady?"

Isolde nodded. "Dead. Go, now, and tell Father Nenian that the child will need burial." She stopped. "Tell him the child was born alive, and that I baptized it with the vial of holy water he gave me to use at such times."

The girl Gwyn, her brow furrowing, looked slowly from the bundled form to Isolde, and Isolde saw the shadow of doubt flicker across the clear hazel eyes. "Must have died almost as soon as it was born," Gwyn said. "I never even heard it cry."

Isolde nodded. "You were sleeping very soundly," she said calmly. The babe . . ." Isolde hesitated briefly. "The babe bled to death when I cut the cord. But you can tell Father Nenian that the child has been baptized as a true Christian, in the name of the Father, the Son, and the Holy Ghost. He need not fear to bury her in consecrated ground."

When Gwyn had gone, Isolde went back to Dera's side and sank down beside her in the straw. The other woman's eyes were closed and her lids looked puckered in the lantern's flickering light, her lips still bloodied where she'd bitten them during the pangs. Isolde didn't know if she would care whether or not the child was buried with other Christians. But it was worth the lie, if it gave her any comfort at all.

Isolde rubbed the knotted muscles at the nape of her neck and closed her eyes. The story she'd told of the child's death meant, too, that there would be another spate of rumor—another tale of the Witch Queen's ill magic to be whispered about the servants' hall. But all she felt for now was the ache of exhaustion as her body relaxed, and she could only think that, for now, at least, she need not move.

When Isolde opened her eyes she found Dera, whom she'd thought asleep, looking at her. Dera's eyes were dazed and tired, but aware.

"Is the pain too bad for you to sleep?" Isolde asked.

Dera's head moved in faint negation. "Not so bad." She was silent a moment, dark eyes straying listlessly to the timbered roof above, then coming back to Isolde. "He were a good man, your husband the king," she said suddenly. "I were sorry to hear he'd been killed."

The words caught Isolde by surprise, but she nodded. "Thank you."

"Kind, too. Not that he ever came to me for his pleasures," she added quickly. "You needn't fear for that."

Isolde bent and slowly smoothed the blanket, drawing it up and tucking it more tightly around Dera's shoulders. "I wouldn't have minded."

Dera's tongue touched one of the torn places on her lip. "But they say you're wedded again now, lady. To Lord Marche that was."

Isolde watched the play of shadow over the loft's walls. "Yes."

Dera swallowed. "Take care, then lady." Her words were beginning to slur, with the poppy and her own fatigue. "He's mean, that one."

A spreading cold traveled through Isolde's veins. "You know Lord Marche?"

"Paid me for a week's service a while back. Couldn't believe my luck, at first. Usually you're lucky to get an hour, never mind a night. But—"

Dera shook her head. "Ran away from him the second day. He'd have killed me for it, if he'd caught me. And there's few in the army that would even bother to spit on the body of one more dead whore—let alone stop him from cutting my throat. But—"

She broke off, fumbling clumsily at the neck of her gown. When she had untied the laces, she drew the sweat-dampened woolen fabric aside to bare one breast. "You see that there?"

The flickering lamplight showed a pair of puckered scars crisscrossing one another in the soft, pale flesh. "I was lucky, though. Heard afterwards from another girl what happens if he can't manage with you at all."

Her eyes were starting to lose focus, and her tone was drowsy, remote and almost unconcerned. "I saw a stallion, once. Gone lame in one leg—couldn't mount the mares. So he'd savage them. Bite their necks till they bled."

Dera stopped again, a shadow of a frown flickering across her brow with the effort of going on, her eyes already starting to slide shut. "There's men that hurt you because they're born rough and don't know no better," she said. "And there's men that hurt you because they've not had a woman in weeks. And then . . . then there's men that hurt you just for the joy of seeing if they can make you cry. Lord Marche—he's one of those."

Isolde waited until the woman's breathing had deepened and slowed, then bowed her head and rested her forehead on her hands, fighting the fear that was crawling through her. A mercy, she thought, in a way, that she'd been summoned to Dera's side as she had. The immediate urgency of the job before her, and the rhythm of familiar tasks, had kept her, for the most part, from thought of anything else. Now, though—

As though from a long way off, Isolde heard in the loft's rustling stillness the echo of her own words, spoken to Marche not even three days before.

Try it. I swear on my husband's soul I'll put a knife through my heart before I wed you or any other man.

The edge of the cross-shaped scar was still visible above the low neckline of Dera's gown, rising and falling with the steady rhythm of her breathing. *Down and up. Up and down.*

Isolde realized abruptly that she was scrubbing her hand across her mouth again and again. Listen to the pain, she'd told Dera. She'd learned that four years ago, lying in bed, her skin tight and burning with the fever, while Father Nenian muttered his prayers and anointed her with his holy oils.

But this was different. She'd felt, then, achingly empty, like a throbbing shell. Now she felt as though she'd shattered like glass, and try as she would she couldn't fit the pieces back together.

And Hunno, she thought, is waiting below. Waiting to take me back—

The wind outside must have shifted, for the voice came suddenly, blocking out all else from Isolde's ears.

I'VE HEARD MY LADIES SPEAK OF childbed, but I didn't know it would be like this. Mine must be harder than most. It must. I cried at first, but I'm too tired for tears now. If I died, I wouldn't mind. Women do die in childbirth. Why not me?

Another pain comes on, and I hold on tight to Morgan's hand, hearing her grunt in discomfort as my fingers clench on hers.

"Help me," I say. "Please. Make it stop."

She wipes my face, holds a cup of wine to my mouth. I can see her biting back impatience—though she's sorry for me, too, I know.

"It will be over soon. You're nearly there."

Another pain hits, and all at once something bursts inside me and there's a rush of water, hot and wet, on my thighs. Someone is screaming—I suppose it must be me.

My body is tearing, bursting open with a burning like fire, and I'm screaming . . . screaming. And then something hot and solid and slimy slithers onto my legs. At last—blessedly—the pain is gone.

Morgan's voice comes from a long way away. "You have a daughter."

Slowly, I open my eyes. With quick, practiced hands, Morgan is untangling the baby from the pulsing cord, lifting her, thumping her on the back. The baby's face is red, her eyes tight closed, her mouth open in an angry cry as she waves tiny fists. Morgan puts her on my chest.

A child. A daughter. My daughter. But she doesn't feel like mine. I look at her and feel . . . nothing at all.

I prayed for a child, every day, from the time I was fourteen and sent by my father to wed Arthur the King. Prayed on my knees I might give him an heir. Shared his bed and looked the other way while he bedded every fair-faced lady, every giggling serving maid. And now—

"Does it ever seem to you, Morgan, that our God must be a cruel one?"

"Yes." Morgan's voice is hard, without expression. "Yes, it does."

The baby stops crying at last and opens her eyes. Wide and gray, like the sea. I stare into the little face. My daughter. Mine and Modred's.

"Isolde. Her name is Isolde." And then I lift a hand and trace the fine swirl of dark hair on the baby's skull. "Poor little girl."

FOR A MOMENT AFTER THE VOICE faded, Isolde was still, the echo of her mother's voice still in her ears. Strange, she thought, that I know it was hers. Gwynefar had fled to take the holy woman's veil almost as soon as Isolde was born. She, at least, could have no part in the memories Isolde had locked away. Isolde drew in her breath, making ready to move.

And then she stopped, as her eye fell on the trapdoor in the loft's wooden floor. The trapdoor used by the stable boys to fork straw down to the horses below.

ISOLDE STOOD AT THE REAR ENTRANCE to the stables, rubbing the fingernail that had torn when she'd pulled the trapdoor open. She'd bruised one shoulder in the fall into the straw below, but she was now at the door that led to the brew house and the armorer's shed. And those areas, she thought, would be safe, deserted for several hours to come.

She eased the door open, then froze, heart lurching at the sight of a man seated on an upturned barrel in front of the armorer's lean-to, his back to where she stood. She held her breath, not daring to move. But the creak of the door hinges had already been enough to make him turn.

Ector the armorer swore violently, his heavy gray brows drawing together as he recognized Isolde. "Sweet bleeding wounds of Christ! Haven't you got anything better to do than to come hunting me down the moment I get free of your infernal poking and jabbing?"

The relief that washed through Isolde was so intense she felt momentarily sick. With all her strength, though, she willed every trace either of relief or of fear from her face, willed her voice to be steady and calm.

"How did you get out here? You oughtn't even to be up from bed, much less out in the cold this way."

The old man wore only a pair of leather breeches, worn shiny with age, and a threadbare tunic. He seemed, though, to feel no trace of cold, despite the chill sharp enough to raise gooseflesh on Isolde's arms.

"How?" Ector jerked his head at a wooden crutch that lay on the ground at his feet. "Walked, didn't I? Thought I might get a bit of peace after listening to half a hundred men moaning and groaning and farting in their sleep all night long. Might have known it was too good to last."

Isolde swallowed. "I'd better have a look at your foot. See how the wound is coming on."

Ector scowled and gave a short, irritable grunt, but he didn't resist when Isolde knelt on the cobblestones before him and began to unwrap the bindings on his foot.

"This is beginning to look better," she said after a moment. "How do you feel?"

"Feel?" Ector snorted violently. "Still got a great dirty hole in my foot, haven't I? Not to mention rheumatics from lying day in and day out on a cold stone floor—and I still want to heave my guts up every time I think about them filthy maggots you put in. Not that there's much to heave, what with a week of eating the pig-swill that passes for food in that infirmary of yours."

Isolde started to rewrap the bandages. Her hands were gradually regaining their steadiness, and her voice, when she glanced up at Ector, was nearly her own. "But apart from that, you feel well, do you?"

There was a brief silence, and then, for the second time since she'd known him, she saw a gleam of reluctant humor appeared in Ector's rheumy dark eyes. One side of his mouth twitched.

"Oh, yes. Apart from that, I'm ready to fight the Saxon army myself with one arm tied behind."

He broke off as quick booted footsteps sounded on the stones of the passage behind Isolde. Isolde felt herself go hot, then cold. There was no time to try to flee. No time even for a word to Ector, though she doubted whether that would have done good in any case. It was sheer instinct that made her duck behind Ector into the armorer's shed—instinct, rather than any hope she might escape discovery that way. If the man approaching was Hunno, Ector would tell him where she was. He had no reason not to speak—and every reason to stay in favor with Marche and his guards.

The interior of the shed was dark, the central brazier silent and cold. The walls were hung with the hammers and sharpening tools of Ector's trade. Isolde stood near the entrance and heard the man's voice, just outside.

"My lord King Marche's orders. We're to find the lady Isolde. You see any sign of her out here?"

Not Hunno, but another guard. Hunno must have discovered her absence and alerted some of his fellows. The silence before Ector replied seemed to go on for an eternity. Isolde waited, and was distantly surprised, now that the moment of discovery had come, to find that she wasn't afraid. If she felt anything, it was anger that all she'd done had gone for nothing.

Through a chink in the shed's rough slatted walls, she could see Ector turn his head slightly, frowning, rubbing his ear with one big, callused hand before he spoke.

"The lady Isolde?" he repeated. Slowly, he shook his head. "No, not a sign of her—nor anyone else till you came along."

"You sure? You've seen no one at all?"

Ector grunted, thin shoulders twitching irritably. "Last I checked I wasn't blind. There's been no one. And what would the lady Isolde be doing out here at this time of day, anyway?"

The guard didn't answer that. Instead he asked, his voice edged with sudden suspicion, "And just what are you doing out here yourself at this hour?"

Ector snorted, and Isolde could picture his scowl. "Think I was appointed king's armorer because I know how to whistle? There's a sight to be done with this new threat from the Saxons they're talking of. Came out here to work. Which I'll do, if you'll let me get on with it in peace."

When the roaring in her ears subsided, Isolde was still standing pressed up against the shed's outer wall, and Ector was in the doorway, his bent, wiry frame outlined against the pale morning light outside.

"You can come out now. He's gone."

Slowly, Isolde followed him out of the shed, Ector leaning heavily on the wooden crutch, hopping to keep the injured foot off the ground and swearing under his breath when toe or heel brushed against the cobblestones. With another grunt, he lowered himself back onto the barrel and sat, arms folded across his chest, head tipped slightly back and the injured foot extended. Reaction had begun to set in, and Isolde couldn't, at first, have spoken. Then she drew in her breath and met Ector's dark gaze.

"Thank you," she said quietly.

Ector was silent a long moment, his eyes steady on hers. His face looked in this early gray light like an image carved in one of the weathered god-stones that stood on the moor. Then he shook his head. "Whatever chance it is I've just given you, lass," he said, "I hope you'll put it to good use."

BOOK 11

Chapter Fifteen

I T WAS THE FLARE OF light that woke her. The light, and the
man's hand, heavy and hard, clamped over her mouth. The
hand was rough, smelling of onions and dirt and sweat, and
Isolde's stomach clenched in panic even before she opened her
eyes, even before memory swept back and she remembered fully
why she should be afraid. Instinctively, she twisted, struggling to
break free of the man's grasp, kicking, trying to lash out, but she
found she couldn't move. Her hands and feet were tied, knotted
together with something stiff and hard that cut into her skin.

One hand still over her mouth, her captor held her at arm's
length, so that she saw his face for the first time, and, strangely,
her first thought was one of almost dizzying relief. *Not Marche.*

Not even one of Marche's guards. This man was fair-haired,
broad-built and tall and unmistakably Saxon. Nor did he look
hostile. His eyes, fringed with thick, pale lashes and showing
pale blue in the glow of the campfire behind him looked curious—and, oddly, a little nervous—but nothing more. Isolde's
eyes moved from him to the fire, and she saw that there was a
figure crouched beside the fire's circle of light. A boy of ten, or

eleven, maybe, whose black hair and small, wiry frame marked
him a Briton as surely as his companion's build identified him
as Saxon-born.

Struggling to quiet the frantic beating of her heart, Isolde
looked from the boy to the man, as the memory of the past several hours returned. First standing in the little yard at Tintagel,
dazed with shock at what Ector had done. And Ector saying, "If
all you're going to do is stand there, I might as well give a shout
and call back the guard." Then cautiously making her way to an
arched gateway from which she could look in at the great court.
And, finally, drawing the hood of her cloak over her head and
slipping into a crowd of refugees shuffling out of the stables to
take to the road again.

The back of her neck had prickled as she passed out of Tintagel's gates, under the eyes of Marche's guard. But no one had
stopped her—or even spared her more than a passing glance.
And so she'd walked. First as part of the group, and then alone,
along the track that led away from Tintagel, across the grassy
headland and finally onto the windswept, barren moor.

Toward sunset, she'd found a cluster of trees growing in the
shelter of an ancient road-metal quarry. Their branches were
bare at this time of year, but they offered some cover, at least,
and a shelter from the bitterly penetrating wind. She'd wrapped
her cloak around her and been asleep almost at once, too exhausted even to try to eat any of the food she carried.

It was still night, now. The sky was black, without even a
hint of the dawn, the stars and faint silvery crescent of a moon
still bright.

The man who held her gave a short, wordless grunt, coupled
with a jerk of the head, and at the sound the boy rose from where
he'd been crouched by the fire and came forward. He was thin
and small, his chest slight, almost hollow, beneath a dirty tunic
made of what looked like rabbit skins stitched together with

rawhide. His face, too, was thin, sharp and cunning, the bones prominent beneath sun-browned skin, the dark eyes darting from side to side, as though scanning for danger. They flashed over Isolde in a quick, sly look before moving to the man.

The Saxon gestured with one hand, the other still clamped tight over Isolde's mouth, and the boy nodded. He turned back to Isolde, his eyes darting over her face.

"He says he'll take his hand away if you promise not to scream."

He raised one hand to scratch at his head, and Isolde saw that his scalp was covered in scabs, with tufts of fine dark hair growing up in uneven patches in between.

Isolde nodded. An easy enough promise. There was no one to hear her if she did scream. Unless some of Marche's guards were still out on the roads hunting her, and were somewhere near.

The Saxon took his hand away, at the same time shifting her weight effortlessly to set her down on the ground near the fire. Clumsily, Isolde raised her bound hands to push the tangles of hair out of her eyes, then looked up at the man and boy, trying to judge whether it would be safer to keep silent or to speak. The man was gesturing again. His hands were big, the palms callused and work-roughened, the nails dirty and torn, but all the same the movements were quick and even graceful, now that he had both hands free. The boy watched, then after a moment nodded and turned to Isolde once more.

"He says not to be frightened. He doesn't mean you any harm. He just wants your help, is all."

"My help," Isolde repeated. Her throat felt dry with the long day's walk over dusty roads, and her voice sounded a little hoarse. She shifted, studying the Saxon man. His clothing, like the boy's, had been stitched together from skins—leather breeches, a roughly made leather tunic, and a cloak of what looked like wolf's-pelt, the silvery fur matted and dirty with wear. He wore, too, a yellowed, pointed tooth—a wolf's, Isolde thought, or maybe a dog's—pierced and strung on a leather thong about his neck.

Not a soldier, then—though she might have guessed that already. She'd seen a beggar, once, robbed of hearing, who used his hands to speak in a little of the same way as this man. The man was watching her, now, his blue eyes still anxious.

Isolde drew in her breath, forcing both shock and fear back, letting them drain away until she could speak with careful calm. Then she turned back to the boy. "Ask him why he's tied me up this way if he wants my help."

The boy raised a hand to scratch at his scalp again. "You can ask him yourself—he's not deaf. His tongue's been cut out, is all." The boy's eyes darted sideways and back and he added, in an undertone, "left him a bit simple-like. But he can hear the same as you or me."

"Left him—?"

Isolde looked up at the big Saxon with a moment's shock, and saw what she'd not before. Beneath fine, straight blond hair clubbed back with another narrow strip of leather, his face was broad and strong, with heavy-boned features and a blunt, firm jaw. A proud, imposing face—or rather, it ought to have been. Now that she looked, Isolde could see that the blue eyes held a slightly blank, vacant look. As though, she thought, the soul behind them had passed through something beyond enduring and had retreated back, back to a safe, secure inner sanctum.

He was gesturing again, his eyes still anxious, still on Isolde.

"He says you wouldn't have listened to him if he'd just woken you up and asked you. He had to tie you up to keep you from running away."

Isolde's fear had all but evaporated by now, and she nodded, slowly, speaking to the Saxon for the first time. "I suppose that's true. But I won't run away now. Untie me, and then you can tell me what it is you want."

The big man seemed to hesitate a moment, but then he knelt a little awkwardly at her feet, the big, callused hands clumsy as they fumbled with the knots of the cord that bound her, with none of the grace they'd had in making the speaking-gestures. When she was free, Isolde rubbed her hands and feet, then stretched them out to the fire's glow, wincing as the movement and the warmth brought a return of feeling, and with it pain.

The Saxon man touched her arm, offering a half-filled wine-skin, and Isolde took it, gasping as the wine, thin and sour and tasting of goat, touched her parched throat. Swallowing with an effort, she handed the skin back and wiped her mouth.

"Thank you," she said, then asked again, "Now, what help is it you would ask of me?"

"We've need of a healer," the boy said, after the big man had gestured again. "And he's heard you're a rare fine one."

Fear swept back, tightening every nerve. If she'd been less tired, less dazed with weariness and sleep and lingering pain, she might have bitten the words back, but as it was they were out before she could stop them. "How do you know who I am?"

"Seen you out riding with the king." The boy paused, waiting for the Saxon man to finish. Then: "There's patrols—soldiers—out on the roads looking for you. But he says we won't hand you in if you agree to help us."

Soldiers—Marche's guardsman. Isolde had known already that they would be out searching, ordered to bring her back to Tintagel, but all the same, her body felt cold, despite the fire's warmth, her lips stiff as she replied. "All right. I agree."

The big Saxon studied her a moment, frowning, and then he made another quick sign.

"You word on it?" the boy asked.

Isolde nodded, more steadily, now. "Yes, if you wish it. You have my word."

The Saxon was silent once more, but then his face split in a slow, spreading smile, and he nodded. He got to his feet, made another quick series of gestures to the boy, then turned away and was gone, footsteps fading to silence as he passed beyond the circle of firelight.

"What did he say?" Isolde asked the boy.

The boy was standing a little distance away, idly fingering a worn knife he wore at his belt, and, from time to time, darting glances—half suspicious, half curious—at Isolde. At the question, he gave her another furtive glance, his dark eyes just touching her, then sliding away. He muttered, "He said he'd go and make sure there weren't any of the patrols still about."

"Should we put out the fire, then?"

The boy shook his head, and, still without meeting her eyes, said, "Nah. Not likely anyone's about. Ground's too rough for horses at night."

Isolde nodded. The night air was chill, with a biting wind, and she shivered, stretching her hands out to the fire and trying to think. She was sure—or nearly sure—she had no cause, for now, at least, to fear the Saxon man or the boy. But how far she could trust them, she didn't yet know. Marche would be sure to pay well anyone who could bring her back.

The thought of eating made her feel faintly sick, but all the same she unfastened the scrip from the girdle of her gown and drew out the parcel of food, forcing herself to take a few bites of one of the honey cakes Hedda had packed. A lifetime ago, that seemed. As she had hoped, the boy, after watching her a few moments, came to sit down beside her. He kept just more than an arm's reach away, but his eyes darted to the bundle of food in her lap with a look Isolde had she'd seen on countless faces of the men and women who came to Tintagel begging aid. At last he said, "You got any more of that?"

Isolde swallowed a bite of the cake, then nodded. "Yes, I've plenty. I'll give you some. If you'll answer some questions."

The boy gave her another suspicious, sidelong look, but he said, after a moment, "What do you want to know?"

"Your name, to start with. Yours and the man's."

The boy frowned, scratching absently at a scab on the back of one hand. His hands were chapped, reddened with cold, his wrists thin and fragile-looking as the smallest of the dry branches above. "Mine's Bran," he said at last. "And his is Hereric."

He held out his hand expectantly, and Isolde fished in her scrip, then gave him one of the smallest of the cakes.

"That all?" Bran looked down at his palm, his wariness for the moment forgotten. "One rotten cake?"

Isolde shrugged. "One is better than none, which is what you had before. And you only answered one question."

Bran eyed her, a gleam of calculation in his gaze. Then, after a moment, he pushed the cake into his mouth and, still chewing, said, "You want to ask more?"

Isolde nodded. Young as the boy was, his face held none of the softness she'd seen in other children his age. He had sharp, slanted cheekbones, and beneath the thatch of ragged hair his features had a hardened look, the mouth set in a wary, suspicious line. His eyes, dark under straight, dark brows, looked hard, as well, with the tautly watchful look of a horse that's been beaten or a dog that's been ill-used.

Isolde could see now, too, that there was a wide ring of skin, lighter in color than the rest, circling the thin neck. The mark left by a thrall-ring, the collar of iron fastened for life on those the Saxons bought and sold as slaves. This one must have been worn at least through summer, or the skin would have been tanned evenly by now. He'd been a slave at one time, then. Or still was?

"Do you belong to Hereric, then?"

"Belong?" A flush of anger warmed the sallow cheeks, and Bran's head jerked up, his eyes meeting hers directly for the first time. "Don't belong to anyone. Not anymore."

"I'm sorry." The boy's thin frame was stiff with resentment, and as a kind of peace offering, Isolde handed him another cake. Bran seemed to hesitate, but then he shrugged and accepted the cake, biting off and swallowing nearly the whole before he spoke again, his voice less wary, though muffled by the food.

"I was body-slave to Wuscfrea. One of King Octa's fighting men. But he was killed in the fighting up by Glevum. So I ran."

"The fighting near Glevum," Isolde repeated. "But that was last winter—the coldest months of the year. How did you keep from starving on your own like that?"

Bran pushed the last bite of cake into his mouth, settling himself more comfortably, his legs crossed. He shrugged again. "Lots of meat on a battlefield," he said indifferently. "Rotting, sometimes. But the cold mostly keeps it fresh. Only thing is you've got to get to it before the wolves."

"Rotting—"

With an effort, Isolde pushed away the image of the child scavenging over the field of battle, tearing meat from half-buried dead men's bones. The soldiers themselves were past caring. And that's probably, she thought, the most good that can come of one of these bloody wars. Food enough to keep one runaway slave alive.

She was silent a moment, then asked, "And who is it who needs a healer? You or Hereric?"

"Neither." Idly, Bran kicked at one of the fire-logs, sending up a shower of sparks. "It's Trystan."

His voice altered slightly as he spoke the name, and Isolde asked, "Trystan? Who is that?"

A curtain seemed to fall over the boy's face, leaving it hard and wary once more. He jerked his head dismissively and said, "Someone we know. He's with Kian. Not far."

He paused, and Isolde saw in his look wariness warring with the wish to say more. He hesitated a moment longer, then added, with a touch of pride, "I knew Trystan would need us. So I brought them here. Hereric and Kian. Found them and brought them here myself. We'd have gone after Trystan if he hadn't come himself first."

There were several questions, Isolde thought, that she might ask if she was to sort out the truth behind Bran's jumbled explanation. She wasn't sure, though, how much more the boy could be persuaded to tell her, and so, after a moment's pause, she reached into her scrip again and drew out a thick slab of salted mutton. She held it in her hand but made no move to offer it to the boy. "And after I've served Trystan as healer? What then?"

Bran's eyes were on the meat, but at the question he dragged his gaze away to meet her gaze. After a moment, he looked away, shifting uneasily. "Don't know."

He was still watching her slyly, though, the firelight gleaming on the whites visible beneath his slitted lids, and Isolde wondered whether he knew more than he said. No, she thought. *I can't trust either man or boy. Not for sure.*

Isolde's scrip lay on the ground between them, and in the silence that followed, Bran stretched out a hand, idly fingering the leather bindings. Then: "They say you're a witch."

Isolde nodded, her eyes on the leaping flames. "Yes," she said. "They do say so."

Bran transferred his gaze to the fire, stretched his legs out, and was silent. Then: "Is it true? Can you ill-wish someone and have them come to harm?"

Isolde lifted one shoulder slightly. "Don't know," she said. "But you'll find out if you don't put that purse of coppers back in my bag."

The boy's head came up with a jerk and he stiffened, as though poised for flight. Then, slowly, his muscles relaxed and, for the first time, the hard, wary look cleared from his eyes, making him seem suddenly younger than she'd guessed before. Nine, maybe, or ten—no more. He gave Isolde an unrepentant grin, showing a mouthful of crooked teeth.

"That was pretty good, that. Didn't think you were watching. You must have eyes like a hawk."

In spite of herself, Isolde smiled as well, and held out the slice of mutton. Bran drew the bag of coppers from the breast of his tunic, tossed it back into her scrip, and accepted the food. He tore off a chunk of the meat with his teeth, chewed, and then offered the slab companionably to Isolde. It was plainly meant as a gesture of friendship, and Isolde forced herself to take a bite before handing the mutton back. Bran took it, bit off another chunk, and chewed before saying, his mouth still half full, "Know any riddles?"

The question was so unexpected that Isolde looked up, startled. "Some," she said.

Bran nodded. "We tell them sometimes at night. Hereric and me—and sometimes Trystan, too. Helps—"

He stopped and shot a brief, uneasy glance into the darkness that surrounded them before turning back to Isolde. "Helps pass the time, like. Ever heard this one?" He swallowed the last of the meat, then licked the grease from his fingers, frowning in recollection. "I am within as white as snow. Without as green as herbs that grow. I am higher than a house, yet smaller than a mouse."

What riddles Isolde knew were from Myrddin. He'd used to tell them sometimes, along with the tales he sang in the banqueting hall on his rare visits to court. Isolde could still hear the echo of his voice, painfully clear in the empty night silence, the lilting cadences strong. *What is blacker than the raven? Death.*

What is swifter than wind? Thought. What is sharper than a sword? Understanding.

"A walnut on a tree?"

Bran nodded. "That's it." He moved his shoulders dismissively. "I guess that's an easy one."

Isolde glanced up at the night sky. Still no sign of dawn light, but the moon was beginning to sink lower toward the horizon.

"How long do you think Hereric will be?" she asked.

Bran shifted position and shrugged. "Not long, now. Unless he did meet up with some of the guard after all. But they wouldn't have caught him. He's simple, like—Kian says there may be a fire in the hearth, but it's only rarely someone's at home. But he knows enough to hide if he runs into a patrol." He paused. "You know any more riddles?"

As he spoke, though, his eyes were scanning the darkened moor, and Isolde wondered whether he was as unconcerned about his companion as he was trying to pretend. She'd seen one Saxon wanderer—a deserting soldier, maybe, or an escaping slave—hung at a crossroads, the sightless eyes pecked out by the birds, the body left to rot apart.

"Probably." Myrddin, she thought, with one of those quick, dull aches about her heart, had never repeated one, that she could remember. He'd seemed to draw them from some unending store.

Isolde shivered, remembering, too, the tales he'd told of the washer at the ford—a deathly pale ghost-woman who appeared at river crossings, washing the bloodstained clothing that was an omen of death. Or of the lakes haunted by spirits that demanded every seven years the payment of an animal or bird, or else they would take a human life instead.

She thought a moment, then said, "Here's one: Thousands lay up gold within this house, but no man made it. Spears past counting guard this house, but no man wards it. Do you know what it is?"

Bran shook his head, his brow already furrowed. He'd taken up a stray twig and now he scowled at the ground, jabbing at the earth as he thought. Isolde sat back to think, as well, her eyes sweeping the darkness around them. Whatever the man Hereric was, then, he was someone who would fear capture by Marche's guard. Though that might be only on account of his birth. A lone Saxon man risked imprisonment at the least, and likely far worse, if he were caught behind British lines.

"Got it!" Bran looked up suddenly, his brow clearing. "It's a beehive. That's—"

But then he broke off, his whole body going abruptly still as from out of the night there came a shrill, wild cry. Isolde stiffened, too, then relaxed as the cry was followed by a beating rush of wings and a small, sharp squeak.

"It's an owl—hunting mice or voles," she said. "That's all."

"I know that," Bran said quickly. "I wasn't afraid."

But a moment later, when the drawn-out howl of a wolf rent the night, he said, almost as though he'd read a part of Isolde's own thoughts, "I heard Kian sing a song, once. About a wild man who drove a pack of hounds through the sky. Hunting souls to carry into the land of the dead."

That made three times, now, that he'd spoken the name, and this time Isolde asked, "Kian? Who is that?"

Bran shrugged. "Another of us. He's with Trystan now." He frowned, biting his lower lip. "Trystan says there's no such thing as the wild hunt. That the dead are just dead, that's all. And there's another song Kian sings. About a man that passes an old battlefield and hears the ghosts of the men that died there screaming and fighting still." He shrugged again. "But I was at the battlefield after the fighting by Glevum, and I never heard anything like that. So I guess Trystan's right."

All the same, when the wolf's cry echoed across the moor again, he edged closer to Isolde, hunching his thin shoulders.

Bran's thin, cunning face and small frame could hardly have been more unlike the tall, sturdy boy Con had been. And yet a brief vision of Con rose before Isolde's eyes. Con, twelve years old and half sick with fear—though trying desperately to hide it—as he stood in her chambers and let her stitch up the cut on his brow.

"Do you know any stories, Bran?" Isolde asked.

"Stories?" Bran's eyes were still on the shadowed, rolling landscape of the moor beyond the circle of the fire, and he spoke as though he'd only half heard. Then he turned and nodded, suddenly interested. "Kian tells them at night sometimes, after the songs. There's one he told about a place not far from here. A pool, on the moor. And they say—" Bran frowned in an effort of remembrance. "They say that after the great battle—after Camlann—Arthur lay dying of a mortal sword wound."

The boy's voice, rough and uncultured as it was, had unconsciously slipped into the rhythm of a harper's song. He went on, "And he gave his great sword to his truest friend, Bedwyr, and begged him to throw it into the pool. And three times Bedwyr told the king that he had thrown the sword away as he asked. And three times he lied. But the forth time he did fling the sword away, to the center of the pool. And a white arm came up, up out of the waters and caught the sword. And drew it down beneath the surface of the pool. And—"

Bran broke off abruptly, looking up at Isolde, and said, his voice resuming its ordinary tone, "You ever hear that one?

Isolde stared out into the darkness at the shadowed shape of a boulder on the crest of a nearby swell of ground. Almost, she thought, it had the shape of a crouching hound.

"No," she said at last. "No, I hadn't heard that one." The fire blurred before her eyes, and she looked down at the boy. "I can tell you another, though. Do you know the story of the sea-maiden Morveren?"

Bran shook his head.

"Well, then." Isolde drew her cloak more tightly around her, and began. "This happened long, long ago, in a place not far from here—a place called Zennor, where the sea is both the beginning and the end for the folk who live there, where days are marked by the ebb and flow of the tide and the months and years by the herring runs."

She paused. Bran tossed the twig he'd been holding onto the fire, then yawned and edged slightly closer. "Kian's a rare good storyteller," he said. "But you've a nice voice for it, too. For a girl, I mean." He glanced up at her, then away, and added, with elaborate unconcern, "Pretty, sort of."

It was an oddly touching speech, and Isolde said, gravely, "Thank you." She took out the last of the honey cakes from her bag, breaking it in two and handing half to Bran. She took a bite of her own half of the cake, then went on with the tale of Morveren the sea-maiden, daughter of Llyr, the king who ruled the land beneath the sea. Of how Morveren had fallen in love with the voice of a mortal man as he sang about his work and had broken the laws of her people, covering her tail with a dress crusted with pearls and sea jade and coral and other ocean jewels to venture on land.

Isolde paused. Bran was yawning again and rubbing his eyes, but he looked up as soon as Isolde stopped. "And what happened?"

"For nearly a year, Morveren would venture up onto the land to hear the mortal man—Talan was his name—sing as he sat by the fire in his mother's house, tying fishing lines and mending his nets. But one night, Talan's singing was so lovely that Morveren could not keep back a sigh.

"It was just a little sigh, softer than the whisper of a wave.

But it was enough for Talan to hear, and he looked out the door from where he sat by the hearth and saw the sea-maiden. And he was struck silent by the look of her—and by his love for her. For these things will happen."

The story went on, of how Talan had vowed to go with Morveren to the land beneath the sea. Of how his kin had run in pursuit, trying to hold him back. And of how Morveren had thrown the ocean jewels from her dress so that the pursuers stopped to scrabble in the sand for them, allowing the sea-maiden and the fisher-lad to go free.

"And Talan and Morveren were never seen again. They had gone to live in the land of Llyr, in golden sandcastles built beneath the waves. But the people of Zennor heard Talan. For he sang to Morveren day and night, love songs and lullabies for the children she bore. And songs of the sea, soft and high if the day was to be fair, deep and low if Llyr would make the waters boil."

Isolde stopped and, glancing down, saw that Bran had fallen asleep. He lay curled on his side, one hand clenched tight beneath his cheek, the other flung out on the ground, his mouth open and relaxed, his breath coming in little snorting grunts. She watched him a moment, a memory rising in her of a face she hardly ever let herself see in her mind's eye, though neither could she lock it entirely away. A tiny face that had looked both like her and like Con, with a soft fuzz of gold-brown hair and lashes lying like fans against wax-pale cheeks.

She remembered, too, waking in the darkest watches of the night with a stray pain—the kind that came on without warning in the last weeks and meant the birth was drawing near. She'd thought of the births she'd attended—the women screaming and writhing as though their bodies were being torn in two. The weakest giving up and dying with the child yet unborn.

The child inside her had stirred at that, and she'd rested her hand on the place near her ribs where a tiny foot kicked with surprising strength, the small toes miraculously discernible beneath her own skin. Even toward the end, she'd not been able to tell whether the babe would be boy or girl, though she'd spoken to it often, simply as hers. Her own. And been almost frightened because already she loved the child so much it stole her breath. *Soon you'll be able to kick out in the open, under the sky. We'll go together up to the headland and listen to the wind and the sea. I won't give up before you can see the sky for yourself, I promise you.*

And then she'd turned over—awkwardly, because of her body's swelling bulk—and started whispering the opening words to one of the old fire-tales, the kind she was telling Bran now.

Isolde looked away, up into the darkened sky, then turned back to Bran's sleeping form. She'd already cried all the tears she could cry for the baby girl who'd stopped kicking the night before the first labor pang came, and who'd never drawn breath on being born. But all the same it was useless—dangerous, even—to let herself remember her now.

"And so," she finished softly, "from Talan's songs, the fishermen of Zennor knew when it was safe to put to sea, and when it was wise to anchor snug at home."

As she spoke the final words, a step behind her made her turn to find that Hereric had returned. The big man came forward to settle himself cross-legged within the circle of firelight, smiling at Isolde. He gave her a series of signs—slower than before—and nodded his head, as though in reassurance.

Without Bran to translate, Isolde couldn't be sure what he meant, but she thought he was telling her that they were safe—that he'd seen no one abroad. Hereric rummaged in a traveling pack on the ground and brought out a pair of dirty sheepskins, handing one to Isolde.

He had turned away, spreading his own sheepskin beside the dying remains of the fire, when the wolf's cry echoed again across the moor. Instantly, Hereric started, his hand moving as though unconsciously to the tooth strung about his neck. Isolde saw the big, dirt-streaked fingers move over the yellowed surface quickly, nervously, as he turned to look out across the moor. Whatever he saw seemed to reassure him, for he relaxed and settled himself on the makeshift bed. He seemed to fall asleep at once, rolling himself up in the skin and letting his head tip back, his hands folded protectively over the amulet on his chest and his legs stretched out flat across the ground.

Isolde spread her own sheepskin and lay down, too, pillowing her head on her arm. She could, she thought, escape now, if she chose. With both man and boy asleep and her hands and feet unbound, she could slip away easily and be gone before it was light enough for them to search.

The ground beneath her was hard, littered with twigs and small stones, and Isolde shifted position, watching the fire's glowing embers burn out. She'd given her word, though, that she'd not run away. And besides . . .

Besides, she thought, they have need of a healer. And it was a comfort, in a way, to have one of the splintered fragments of herself that she could hold on to for a time.

Chapter Sixteen

ISOLDE PUT A HAND OUT to steady herself as she picked her way carefully down the rocky slope toward the sea. She'd slept, at last, but had woken at dawn's first light, chilled and sore, every muscle stiff from the night on the cold ground, despite the sheepskin. She had, too, a fierce, throbbing headache behind her eyes. Bran and Hereric had been already awake, and they'd set out almost at once, after a breakfast of smoked fish and cheese and more of the thin, sour wine, keeping to the rough moorland country and avoiding the main roads.

They had met a few travelers—a boy herding goats, a tin-smith pushing his wares in a wooden cart—and passed a few settlements along the way where curls of smoke rose from the roofs and cows lowed contentedly in the fields. The countryside was still ravaged, though, from the recent fighting, and most of the farms they passed were either deserted or burned, pillaged and sacked by the Saxons as they'd made their final advance. Someday, maybe, Isolde thought, the families who'd fled would return to till the fields and dig up the valuables they'd buried beneath earthen floors. But not yet.

Now it was nearly evening, the sun sinking in the west in a blaze of fiery red, the shadows of dusk gathering as they descended toward what Isolde could see was a small cove on the shoreline below. One of the countless inlets that marked Cornwall's coast, this one too small or too shallow or too far from settlement for fisher-folk to use.

Bran had run on ahead, slithering and sliding down the rough, uneven slope, and Hereric turned to her and made a sign. *Nearly there,* Isolde guessed he meant. She followed Hereric to the bottom of the cliff path and saw that they stood on the pebble-strewn beach of a small bay, where a narrow stream ran steeply down another channel of rocky slope to meet the sea. A narrow jetty of stones jutted out from the shallows and served as a landing pier for a small painted fishing vessel. Its sails were furled, its bow bobbing gently in the steadily lapping waves.

Close by, Bran emerged from behind a goatskin curtain hung over a stretch of the cliff face, covering what appeared to be the mouth of a cave.

"Come on." He beckoned to them. "I've told them you're here."

The mouth of the cave was low enough that Hereric had to duck his head as he slipped inside, and as Isolde followed she found that they stood in a long, narrow chamber carved out of the surrounding rock, the walls tapering to a ceiling only a little higher than a man's head. A burning rush stuck in tallow cast a dim, flickering light, and the air was chill, damp and smoky and smelling of the sea.

Before her were two men, one half-lying toward the back of the cave on what looked like a rough pile of skins, his form in shadow, so that Isolde saw only his outline as he straightened, starting at their entrance. The second man had been sitting on a rough wooden camp stool at his companion's side, but as Isolde and Hereric stepped through into the cave, he, too, started, then rose.

"Kian, this is the healer-girl," Bran began.

The man laid a hand briefly on the boy's shoulder in acknowledgment, but stopped him before he could go on. An older man, Isolde saw. Past fifty, at least, barrel-chested, with squat, bandy legs and a thick shock of roughly cut grizzled hair. His face was harshly boned and square, with a thin, uncompromising slash of a mouth and black eyes set deep under heavy brows, the right eye dragged slightly askew and down by an ugly, puckered scar that ran from temple to jaw. His gaze, now, was angry, his brows drawn together in a frown, and he gave Isolde only the briefest glance before turning to Hereric.

"Have you gone out of your mind, bringing a woman here?" Kian said. "Healer or no, she—"

And then he stopped abruptly, turning to look at Isolde again. She saw shock—then recognition—dawn in the deep-set dark eyes, and knew that he, too, knew her now. His face darkened, and before she could react, before she even had time to see what he intended, he had seized her by the arm and dragged her forward, into the circle cast by the rushlight's flame.

"You!" His voice was a furious hiss. "Isn't it enough for you to trap the king with your dirty sorcerous ways without your going after a poor sodding fool like Hereric here?"

Isolde thought for a moment he would strike her, but before he could raise his hand, Hereric gave a high, wild cry, half human, half almost animal, and put a hand on Kian's arm.

Kian shook him off with barely a glance. "Don't try to stop me. She's bewitched you, you poor fool. Like her grandmother before her when she caught Arthur in her snares." His jaw hardened, and he said, eyes dark with fury on Isolde's, "It's women like you who bring evil to the world. Ygraine—Gwynefar—Morgan. Women like you who are at the bottom of all treason and misery and war. And now you come here—"

Isolde clenched her hands. It was a relief, in a way, to feel simple anger flooding her veins, after so many hours of feeling nothing but shame and exhaustion and fear.

"That's a lie."

Kian's grip on her arm tightened. "What did you say?"

"I said that's a lie." If she let herself stop to think, Isolde knew, she would be afraid. Afraid of the place and the band of strangers, and the man whose black-rimmed nails were now biting painfully into her arm. But for now, she was still too angry.

"Men may fight for their own gain—or revenge—or for their own stupid notions of honor and pride," she went on. "But no war in history has ever been fought for a woman's love. Anyone who blames Camlann on a woman—Ygraine or Gwynefar or Morgan or the Goddess herself—is as great a coward as the ones who first made up the tales."

A look of utter fury convulsed Kian's face, and then his eyes narrowed. He jerked her toward him again, his free hand moving to the hilt of the knife he wore at his belt. When he spoke again, his voice had gone very soft.

"She-devil. I'll cut your throat for that."

His scarred face was set. And his eyes—

Isolde felt a chill crawl down her spine. She had seen the eyes of a wounded wild boar, once, when she'd ridden out on a hunt with Con. The animal had taken a spear thrust to the shoulder, and was bloodied but not mortally harmed, and, churning the ground with its hooves, it had charged, small eyes glittering with a kind of mad, white-hot rage.

Kian's eyes, now, looked the same.

But before Kian could raise the knife, the second man, the man who lay in shadow at the back of the cave, spoke.

"Enough!"

Over Kian's shoulder, she saw him drag himself to his feet, as though the effort of moving cost him most of his strength. Trystan, he must be, then. The man in need of a healer's skill.

"Don't be a fool, Kian," he said.

Kian didn't move, though, didn't so much as respond to the other man's words any more than he'd reacted to Hereric's protesting cry. His eyes, hollowed by the flickering rushlight, remained fixed on Isolde, and his lips drew back, showing a row of broken teeth and bare, swollen gums.

"I'll cut your filthy witch's throat."

"Oh, for Christ's sweet sake!" With a painful, limping gait, dragging his left foot slightly behind, the man Trystan came forward, moving quickly despite the obvious effort it cost him, and jerked Kian away from Isolde. "Let her go—let go, I say. Now, look."

He reached out and, before Isolde could react, he had seized her left hand and pushed the sleeve of her gown back, revealing the heart-shaped birthmark on her inner wrist.

"If she's a witch, and this a true devil's brand, it won't bleed." In one swift motion he pulled his own knife from its scabbard and drew it across the patch of rose-colored skin. In the smoky light of the tallow flame, a thin, beaded line of red sprang up in the blade's wake.

"There—you see? Blood." He shook his head and added disgustedly, "Jesus, Kian."

Isolde stood frozen, stunned not by fear, nor even by pain, for the cut had been scarcely more than a scratch. She was staring at the man Trystan's hands. Strong, well-formed hands, with the muscled wrists of a swordsman. But on the left hand, two of the fingers were twisted, as though the bones had been crushed and never properly set, and the first joints on the middle and index fingers were gone.

Slowly, she raised her eyes to his face. He'd shaved his beard since she'd seen him last in Tintagel's prison cell. But it was unmistakably him—the man she'd known as Nifaran.

If he'd felt anything of the same shock at first seeing her, he'd had time to recover before he came forward, and now, as the blue eyes met hers, Isolde could read in them no trace of whatever he must think at finding her here.

Kian shifted uncomfortably. Then, slowly, "All right," he said. "Maybe you're right. Maybe. But witch or no, she can't stay here. Listen, the word on the road yesterday was that Marche's men were hunting her all about these parts. And offering a hefty payment to any that could bring them to her or tell them where she was. How—?" He broke off as Hereric gave another of those strange, half-animal cries, and rounded on the big Saxon. "Well, man? What is it this time?"

Hereric flinched back at the other man's tone, then started to make a few fumbling signs, but before he could go on, Isolde swallowed hard and found her voice once more. "He's trying," she said, "to tell you that he gave me his word I'd not be harmed if I came with him here. His oath that he'd see me safe from Marche's guard."

"His word?" Kian repeated. "Hereric gave you his word?" His voice was almost expressionless. Then slowly, deliberately, he hawked and spat at Isolde's feet. "That's what I think of a promise given to you."

He raised a hand, gesturing toward the twisted rope of scar on his cheek, his voice roughening in renewed rage. "You see this? This is the mark I carry of your father's treason." He paused for breath, his chest heaving, then went on, biting off each word, "I was a soldier, once. One of Agravaine's men. And when Agravaine chose to follow your cursed father into battle instead of Arthur, my lord king, I was sworn by the death-oath—to fight on the traitor's side and lose all with Agravaine and the rest who'd been fool enough to believe Modred would make the better king."

Isolde looked from Kian to the man she'd known as Nifaran and back again. "And so now you've decided to turn traitor in your turn? Betray all Britain and enter the pay of the Saxon kings?"

"You vile-mouthed, evil-tongued . . ." Kian's jaw worked, one of the gnarled, powerful hands clenching once more on the hilt of his knife. "If I didn't think you were worth something alive—"

"Kian!" It was Nifaran—Isolde stopped herself—Trystan.

Kian's head snapped round and he stood a moment, glaring at the younger man. Trystan's voice had been curt, but now as he looked at Kian his face relaxed, and the corners of his mouth twitched slightly.

"Christ, Kian, don't hold back. Tell us all what you really think of her."

He'd judged rightly, Isolde saw; the real moment of danger was gone. Kian's face was still set with anger, but the hand on his knife loosed its grip and he let out something between a grunt and a sigh.

Trystan nodded. "All right, then. Leave us, now, Kian. And you, Hereric and Bran. I want to talk to her alone."

"But Trys—"

"Leave us, I said."

Isolde saw Kian open his mouth, then, abruptly, close it again. And then, without a word, he turned on his heel and was gone, the curtain of skins at the cave's mouth swaying after he pushed past. Hereric seemed to hesitate a moment, brows drawn together in a worried frown. Then he turned to go, putting one hand on Bran's shoulder. Bran pulled away, though, and gave Isolde a quick glance. The suspicious, wary look was back in his eyes, and even in the midst of her fear Isolde felt a surprisingly sharp pang of loss—of loneliness, almost—that the small measure of trust she'd won from the boy had gone.

Bran looked quickly away again and said, lowering his voice,

"If she's going to try to trap you like Kian said, maybe we should stay."

Trystan cocked one eyebrow. "Think I'm too weak to defend myself against one girl? And her not even a witch?"

Bran's small, cunning face was momentarily transformed by what was, Isolde thought, one of the most adoring looks she'd ever seen in anyone, adult or child.

" 'Course not. But you said—" Bran drew himself straighter. "You said a fighting man's first duty was to guard his chief. That if he didn't, he wasn't worth the sweat off a tattooed Pict."

For a moment, lines of amusement fanned out around the corners of Trystan's eyes, and then he clapped one of the boy's bony shoulders. "Good man. I'll know you're guarding my back if ever there's need. But I'll be all right. Go on."

The fierce throbbing behind Isolde's eyes had returned, and she felt slightly dizzy with the cave's smoky airlessness. So she waited, struggling, in the silence that followed Bran's departure, to draw some fragments of courage about her for whatever she had to face now. When at last Trystan did speak, though, the words caught her off guard.

"I'm sorry for that."

Isolde looked down at the cut on her wrist, the trail of blood across the birthmark dried already to a beaded, blackening line. She was hearing, in the echoing silence of the cave, the hiss of Marche's whisper in her ear.

If what they say is true, you should be able to make my cock wither and wilt for daring to go where the devil's already been. We've time, now, to see, haven't we, just how much of a witch you really are.

The black wall in her mind must not have been built high enough. Or maybe there were only so many days that could be forgotten, so many memories put away. Isolde drew in an unsteady breath, then raised her eyes to Trystan's. Without the beard, his face was lean, the jaw square-cut, with a wide, flexible mouth.

She said, her voice cold and hard, "Sorry for what? If you mean the cut, it will heal. And if you mean what your companion Kian said, I've heard worse—and from worse men even than him."

Trystan rubbed a hand wearily along the length of his jaw, and Isolde saw that his tunic was stained on one sleeve with what looked like dried blood.

"I meant for what Kian said. I'm sorry for the cut, as well, but I thought you'd prefer it to being bound hand and foot and thrown into the ocean to see if you'd drown." He paused, then added, "He'd have killed you in another minute."

Isolde felt a chill ripple through her again, and she studied the man before her, trying to judge how far he might be trusted. His face was harder to read than Hereric's, but she remembered again that she'd liked him, despite his hostility, back in Tintagel's prison cell. And she remembered, too, the way Bran had looked at him. Any man who could inspire devotion like that could not be entirely corrupt.

Isolde let out her breath. Bran trusted Trystan, certainly. But that hardly meant she could do the same. She felt a pang of something like regret.

She would be desperately glad to be able to trust someone, believe in one man's honor enough to think he'd not do her harm. To rely on someone besides herself.

Isolde looked down again at the scratch on her wrist, then asked, abruptly, "How did you know the birthmark was there?"

Trystan was silent a moment. Then, with a brief, involuntary exhalation of breath, he dropped down once more onto the pile of skins. "Saw it when you were setting Cyn's wrists."

Isolde nodded, slowly. "And is Trystan your real name, then?"

He looked up at her, an expression she couldn't quite read

in the blue eyes, and seemed to hesitate before he said, "It's the name I was born with."

"And are you planning to do as Kian said?" she asked. "Turn me over for ransom to Marche's guard?"

Trystan shifted position, resting his arms across his upraised knees. Then he said, still watching her, "Any reason I shouldn't?"

"If it hadn't been for my giving you the knife, you'd still be a prisoner at Tintagel. That's how you escaped, isn't it? You couldn't have gotten free if you'd been unarmed."

He looked at her a moment, blank-faced. "Of all the—" Isolde saw his jaw tighten. "Yes, right. I should be eternally grateful to you for allowing me the privilege of cutting my own throat—for you can't tell me you expected I'd use the knife any other way. I should be grateful to you for deciding to grant your miserable little dribble of mercy only after I'd killed Cyn."

He stopped. His voice had risen, and now he burst out, with sudden violence, "Mother of God, Isa—"

He stopped abruptly, clenching his jaw and drawing a ragged breath, but before Isolde could speak he'd gone on. "Is there any reason you couldn't have given me that knife a day earlier? Cyn would be here—alive—instead of being a heap of ashes to be kicked and pissed on by Marche's guard?"

Isolde tried to call back the warming anger she'd felt when confronting Kian. But she seemed to see, in the curls of smoke that rose toward the cave's ceiling, a heap of smoldering ashes outside Tintagel's gate.

"You chose the day and the hour of Cyn's death," she said at last. "Not me."

Trystan was silent a long moment. Then he let out his breath. "True." Slowly, the anger died from his face, leaving it weary and suddenly bleak. Then: "And no. I'm not planning to turn you over to Marche."

"No?"

"No. For one thing, whether you believe me or no, I'd not ask Hereric to break his word. And for another—" he stopped and laughed, shortly. "For another, I can see Marche's face if I approached him to bargain for your ransom. I'd be back in his bloody prison cell before I could say two words."

And that, at least, Isolde thought, I can believe.

Trystan was still watching her, and he asked, abruptly, "Want to tell me why Marche's guard should be after you, as well?"

Isolde didn't answer, and after a moment he shrugged again. "All right. Doesn't make much difference, I suppose."

He shifted position, then sucked in a sharp breath, his mouth twisting in a spasm of pain. Isolde, watching him, felt again that brief tug of something like the Sight, but even as she reached for it, it slid away and was gone.

"Hereric said you'd need of a healer."

Trystan seemed to hesitate, then shook his head. "No. It's not bad. Hereric gets panicked at the sight of blood, that's all." He leaned back, flinching again as his shoulder touched the rock wall, and Isolde remembered the lash marks on his back. As though reading her thoughts, her jerked his shoulder. "Looks worse than it is. Though I'm bloody-damned sick of sitting straight and lying on my stomach."

Isolde's eyes moved from the bloodstain on the sleeve of his tunic to his face. Not, she thought again, an easy face to read. But she could see even in this dim, smoky light the lines of pain about the corners of his mouth, and the way he held his left leg stiffly out, immobile, against the cave's stone floor.

Even without the Sight, she thought, I'd have to be blind and feeble-witted both not to know he lies.

"Your leg—is it broken?"

Trystan let out an impatient breath. "I told you—"

But Isolde cut him off. "If Hereric made me a promise, I gave him one, as well. That I'd give you what aid I could."

Trystan started to speak, but she dropped to her knees beside him and ran her hands lightly along the injured leg, gently probing for a broken bone. At length she sat back.

"You're right. It's not broken. Just badly bruised. I'm afraid there's little I can do beyond telling you to keep off it as much as you can."

Isolde straightened, drawing back. It had been harder than she'd expected. Having to approach a man—any man. Touch him and smell the musky sweat on his skin. Nausea was rolling through her stomach, and she had to swallow before saying, "If you're not going to turn me over for ransom, and you've no need of me as a healer, am I free to go?"

There was another silence, longer than the first, while Trystan watched her. He was frowning, as though weighing alternatives. Then, at last, "No," he said again.

Isolde stiffened. "No?"

Trystan drew the knife from his belt and ran the thumb of his injured hand idly along the blade, the scars on the crooked fingers white and stark in the smoky light. "I can't let you go. Not yet, at any rate. Look"—he glanced up at her again—"you'll have seen the boat outside. But we can't sail it when the wind's from the west like this—we'd be blown straight back to shore. So until it shifts, we'll have to stay put."

Isolde worked to control her tone. "That may be. But why should that mean you need to keep me here, as well?"

Trystan's eyes were still on the knife blade. "Why. Yes, right," he muttered. Then he looked up, pushing a hand through his hair. "I said I'd not turn you over for ransom to Marche. But the guards will be looking for me, too. And if they find us here, I'll have need of a bargaining piece. Something I can offer Marche in exchange for letting us go free."

For a moment, Isolde felt nothing—nothing at all. And then a rush of feeling struck her. It was almost frightening in its intensity, and so overwhelming that it took a moment before she could give it a name. Anger.

Before she could stop herself she said, half choking on the words, "You dirty, bastard-born, cowardly traitor! And what if I refuse to stay? Or do you mean to tie me up as Hereric did? Keep me nicely trussed up till you can use me in your chicken-hearted bargaining?"

Trystan's face showed nothing of answering anger, or even surprise. Instead he rubbed a hand across the back of his neck and said in the same flat tone, "I doubt we've need to tie you up. Even if you escaped, you'd not get far before Hereric or Kian caught up with you and brought you back. They know the countryside around here a good deal better—and can cover ground a good bit faster—than you."

Isolde clenched her hands. "Fine, then," she spat. "So be it. Hide behind a woman's skirts if you've not the courage to face Marche's guard on your own."

Trystan watched her a long moment. Then: "If there are gods, they must be laughing themselves sick right now."

"What—?" Isolde began, but he cut her off.

"Never mind." He shook his head as though to clear it, then raised his voice slightly. "Hereric."

The big man must have been standing just outside the cave, for the skin curtain lifted at once and Hereric stepped through. Trystan spoke, using the Saxon tongue, so that Isolde caught only the rough meaning of the words, but she thought he was telling Hereric to take her outside, to see that she had food and a place to sleep for the night and that she was kept under close guard.

Hereric nodded understanding, then reached to put a hand on Isolde's arm. For a moment, Isolde stood still, her eyes on

Trystan. Then she turned abruptly and let Hereric guide her out through the mouth of the cave. The sun had nearly set. The sky was turning from azure to dusky gray, and the shadows were lengthening on the pebbled beach. The stiff sea breeze was salty and cool, and Isolde breathed deeply, trying to steady herself, still frightened by the rush of anger that had swept through her. And not only anger. A furious sense of betrayal, as well.

Though why I should feel betrayed I don't know, she thought. I could hardly have expected anything better from these men.

She raised her hands to rub her throbbing temples, then looked up as Hereric gave one of those strange, half-animal sounds deep in his throat. Frowning, he gestured to her wrists, and for a moment she thought Trystan must have told him to bind her hands again. But then Bran, appearing suddenly at the big Saxon's side, translated the gestures as before.

"He says he's sorry for tying you up last night. He hopes he didn't hurt you too much."

Isolde looked at the bruises that encircled her wrists. The purpling bruises were overlaid, now, with the chafed, reddened marks of the rope Hereric had used. Slowly, she shook her head and looked up to meet Hereric's gaze.

"No," she said. "You didn't hurt me. The bruises are . . . no fault of yours."

THE FIRE HAD BEEN BUILT FAR up on the beach, at a place where the cliffs jutted out and gave some natural shelter from the wind. An iron cook-pot hung by a cleft stick over the flames, and Kian was seated by the fire's edge. He held a crudely made harp on his lap and was singing—one of the songs of Macsen Wledig, hero who raised an army of Britons and conquered Rome itself in days long faded into the mists of time. Kian's voice was rough, rusty with age and the rasp of years of battle, but with a strange, haunting note that seemed somehow right for the surroundings: the empty, pebbled beach all around; the open, star-filled sky above; the ocean just below, its steady throb a counterpoint to the song.

Kian didn't look up as, at a gesture from Hereric, Isolde seated herself at a place opposite his, on the other side of the fire; nor did he so much as pause in his song. Isolde saw his face go hard, though, and knew that however much he might obey Trystan's orders, he was no more resigned to her presence than before.

Grateful for the fire's warmth, Isolde rubbed her hands over her arms. She took the bowl of rabbit stew Hereric ladled out and passed to her. The rabbit was tough, stringy, and the stew had little but the meat itself and a handful of wild onions, but she found she was hungry enough to finish the whole, dipping the food up with the slab of coarse brown bread that accompanied the meal.

When Bran had sopped up the last of the stew with his bread, he turned to her. "I told you Kian was a rare fine teller of stories." Kian had paused in his singing, and Bran looked across the fire at him. "Tell the one about Ambrosius and Vortigern, Kian."

Kian looked up from his harp. The scarred, carved-looking face was no less grim than before; nor did he answer Bran. But a moment later, he bent again to the harp and began the song of Ambrosius, betrayed as a child and driven into exile by the treacherous Vortigern, then riding out in triumph when he had grown to a man.

All about them, the dusk was drawing in. Twilight, the time of changing, when the selkies swam in from the ocean and shed their sealskins to become the fairest of men. And if a mortal fell in love with a selkie and wished him to return, she must go to the shore and cry seven tears into the sea.

The voice came without warning on a gust of wind. Morgan's voice again, from somewhere beyond the setting sun.

A MAN STANDS BESIDE ME. A *bent, ugly man, one shoulder crooked, one leg lame, dressed in the white robes and bull's-hide cloak of a druid-born.*

"You know as well as I that Britain will be laid to utter waste if this goes on, Morgan."

The festering hurt is there. I can no more keep from probing it than you can stop tonguing an aching tooth to see if it still gives pain.

"And you have come to act king's minion?"

Myrddin's brows lift. "That was unworthy of you, Morgan."

I let out my breath. "Do not blame me, my friend. I wonder, sometimes, whether I control what power I have. Or whether it rides me, instead, driving me where it will."

Myrddin is silent a moment, watching me. "An easy excuse. To blame the fates, and not ourselves."

"You say that? You who cast my son's fortune at birth and said he would grow to be his father's bane?"

The hurt is still there—scabbed over, maybe, by years, but still bitter as bile at the back of my throat. "You may tell my brother Arthur that he is reaping nothing but what he himself has sown."

AS THE VOICE DIED AWAY, ISOLDE became aware of Bran, speaking beside her, his eyes still on Kian as the older man continued the tale.

"Trystan's teaching me sword fighting," he said in an undertone. "Just with sticks, for now. But he says he'll let me try it with a real sword soon."

He paused a moment. Then, brows drawn together in a frown, he shot one of his quick, sidelong looks at Isolde. "So you're really not a witch, then?"

Isolde was silent, watching the fire's dancing flames as they leapt toward the darkening sky. The fire had been built with driftwood; there were shooting jets of blue and green amid the yellow and orange. And if Kian could know what I hear in the wind, she thought, he would think me a sorceress indeed—whether the mark on my arm bleeds or no.

"No," she said. "I'm really not a witch."

Bran was silent a moment, chewing. Then he shrugged. "Well, I guess you can still have this back." He held out his hand, palm up, and she saw that he was offering one of the bronze bracelets she'd brought from Tintagel.

Isolde took if from him. "Thank you," she said slowly. "But why?"

"Oh. Well." Bran frowned fiercely at the ground, scuffing one foot in the sand. "You know some good riddles, anyway." He turned abruptly away to Hereric, seated beside him. "Hereric, you ever heard this one? How did it go?" He stopped, his brow furrowed in the effort of remembrance. "Thousands lay up gold within this house, but no man made it. Spears . . ."

Isolde let her mind drift, too tired to think anymore. She'd fallen into a kind of half-waking doze, when she realized abruptly that Kian had stopped singing and had stiffened, his head turning from side to side like that of a war-hound scenting the air for danger.

"Bran." His voice was a low, curt bark of command, and he didn't turn as he spoke, but kept scanning the darkened beach around them and the cliffs above. "Go to Trystan. Tell him there's trouble. Now."

Bran had gone quiet as soon as Kian spoke his name, and now he moved instantly to obey, scrambling to his feet and darting toward the mouth of the cave. Beside her, Hereric drew the knife from his belt with one hand, while reaching with the other for the club at his feet. Kian had gone on with his song, of how the treacherous Vortigern ceded the land of Ceint to the warrior Hengist to secure his beautiful daughter Rowenna's hand. Isolde saw, though, that he, too, had drawn his knife, and that his eyes never left the cliffs, even as his lips shaped the words.

She sat, straining her ears, and then she heard what Kian must have done: above the song and the pounding of the surf, the high whicker of a horse.

Kian and Hereric exchanged a glance. Kian shook his head, breaking off singing to say, briefly, "Won't bring horses down here—too chancy on the slope of the cliff. Have to come on foot if at all."

It seemed to Isolde that the moments of waiting stretched out unendurably as they sat, both men's hands tight on the hilts of their swords. And then she heard a wordless shout from above, and the men came in a roaring, bellowing charge, down the cliff path to the beach.

Chapter Seventeen

THE MOONLIGHT SILVERED THE SHAFTS of their upraised swords and spears, but their bodies were at first only shadowy blanks, deeper darkness against the gray-black of the cliff. Then they drew nearer, and Isolde saw that they wore the leather tunics and helmets of soldiers, and that the shield the first man carried was marked by the crest of Cornwall's blue boar. Marche's guardsmen. Four of them.

Isolde had time to realize so much before Bran was beside her, tugging frantically at her arm.

"Here, now—with me. Trystan said I'm to see you out of the way."

As he spoke, he was pulling her away from the fire and into a shallow cleft in the cliff behind them. Isolde stood, back pressed against the rock, with Bran beside her. Hereric and Kian had both risen and now stood unflinching, braced for the attack, their eyes on the figures surging toward them across the sand. And then, from out of the shadows, Trystan joined them, armed like Kian with knife and sword, a leather jerkin hastily dragged on over breeches and tunic.

Isolde saw Kian give him a quick, disbelieving glance and open his mouth as though about to protest. But there was no time. Marche's guardsmen had stopped a few paces away, and for a long moment, the two groups of men stood stock-still, staring at each other across the open expanse of sand. Then, with a shout, Kian charged.

As though the cry had released a tightly wound spring, the men of Marche's guard charged, too, and all at once the beach was a nightmare of confused, frenzied movement, of men, grunting, swaying, slashing at one another with swords and spears, knife blades flashing wickedly. Kian had caught up a spear and was fending off two of the soldiers, his mouth set in a fierce, grim line, while Hereric wielded the heavy club against a third.

Isolde had lost sight of the fourth man, but then, all at once he was there, looming up out of the darkness before her and Bran, sword upraised. There was no time to move—no time even to scream. Isolde drew Bran tight against her side with one arm, the other flying up instinctively to protect her face from the slashing blade.

She felt the sword tip slash across the back of her wrist, opening a stinging cut, but even as the man struck, Trystan appeared suddenly at his back, seized him by the shoulder, and spun him round. The guardsman struck out again, at Trystan this time. Trystan raised his own weapon to block the blow, and the next moment he and the guardsman were locked in a furious struggle, muscles straining, chests heaving as they dodged and wove, blocked and slashed with their blades.

Trystan would have had the better of the other man. The guardsman was heavier-built, but Trystan was the better swordsman, his thrusts quicker, more keen to spot an opening in the other man's defenses. But Trystan was tiring; even in the firelight, Isolde could see that plainly. His face was streaked with sweat, and he still favored the injured left leg, leaving his movements off balance, slower that the guard's.

As well as the sword in his right hand, he fought with a dagger in his left hand—not the knife Isolde had given him, but a larger weapon, with a carved bone hilt and a long, deadly blade. The knife served to guard his weaker side and back up the work of the sword, but all the same, Isolde thought that his sword arm must have taken injury in his escape, as well. As the fight went on, his movements grew slower, his mouth tightening each time he swung the heavy blade.

And then it happened. The guardsman struck a blow at Trystan's left hand that knocked the dagger from his grasp and left him armed with sword alone. Then he aimed a kick at Trystan's injured leg. Trystan staggered, thrown off balance. He twisted, and in struggling to regain his footing, he lowered his sword. And as Isolde watched, every muscle frozen in place, she saw the guardsman's sword arm rise to strike.

She acted without hesitation, without even conscious thought. "Bran—your knife."

The boy only gaped at her, his face a blanched, frightened oval in the shadow of their niche. Isolde snatched the knife from his belt herself, turned back to where Trystan still faced the guard, and threw. The knife was a small one, more suited to cutting meat or gutting fish than fighting. She couldn't hope it would pierce the soldier's stiff leather tunic, and so she aimed instead for the exposed sword hand. The knife struck the guard's wrist—a glancing blow only, but enough. The man gave a sharp, startled cry, his head jerking round to see where the knife had come from, and then he went still, eyes on Isolde, his face a frozen mask.

That moment was enough for Trystan to regain his balance. His chest still heaved, and he was without a dagger. But he was able to raise his sword, block a fresh blow from the other man, and then twist away to continue the circling dance as they edged around each other, blades weaving, seeking an opening.

The guardsman was losing patience; as Isolde watched, his blows grew wilder, relying on sheer brutal force rather than subtlety or skill. Before the furious attack, Trystan fell back a pace, and his opponent raised his sword with a bellow of rage and slashed again. Trystan ducked just in time, and Isolde saw the blow aimed at his heart glance off his shoulder instead, ripping a jagged gash in his tunic. And then she felt Bran pull away from her side.

Isolde's heart gave a sickening lurch, but it was too late for her to hold him or even try to call him back. The boy ran across the sand and flung himself at Trystan's opponent, kicking, biting, screaming curses, flailing his thin arms against the guardsman's broad back. Trystan was still off balance from the blow, blood dripping from the cut in his shoulder, and before he could move, the other man had turned and lashed out automatically to meet Bran's attack. The sword flashed. Isolde saw Bran's face change, as he looked in wide-eyed astonishment down to where blood had begun to spurt from a wound in his own side.

For an instant, Bran stood, swaying, blood seeping between the fingers of the hand pressed to his wound, his small, thin face still a bewildered blank. Then, slowly, his knees buckled and he crumpled to the ground, face twisting. Isolde ran toward him, heedless of the fighting that was going on all around.

Trystan had managed to regain his dagger and was fighting Bran's attacker again, the knife in his left hand, the sword in his right, circling, thrusting, raising his own weapon to block the other man's savage blows. As Isolde dropped to her knees beside Bran, she was peripherally aware that Hereric had felled one of the other men and now, with a great bellow of rage, charged another, swinging the heavy wooden club in a wild arc above his head. And that Kian was locked in combat with the remaining guard. She scarcely noticed them, though, scarcely even heard the ringing clash of swords or the grunts and heavy panting of the men as they lurched to and fro on the rocky sand.

Bran lay in a crumpled heap, eyes still closed, the blood still flowing from the wound in his side, soaking the rabbit-skin tunic and pooling on the ground. His face, beneath streaks of dirt and ash, was white, and the breath came through his lips in a labored rattle. Quickly, Isolde fumbled beneath her skirt for the edge of her shift. The thin linen tore easily, and, with a quick jerk, she ripped a strip of fabric from the hem and held it, tightly wadded, against Bran's side. Almost at once, it was wet through, saturated with blood.

She glanced up to see that the three remaining guardsmen now lay on the sand—dead or unconscious, she couldn't tell— leaving the man Trystan fought the only guard still standing. The fighting had carried them closer to the fire, and she saw that, tall and heavily muscled though he was, this guard was younger than the others, with a full, soft-lipped mouth and the roundness of youth still about the shallow planes of his face. His nose looked broken, and blood dripped from his nostrils onto his chin and the leather tunic he wore.

He glanced from his fallen comrades to Trystan, still facing him with dagger and sword, and then to Hereric and Kian, now advancing toward him. For a moment, Isolde thought he would take them on single-handed. He stood, sweat pouring over his brow beneath the leather helmet, feet planted wide, braced to meet the onslaught. Then he wavered, turned, and a moment later was running back up the beach, toward the path leading to the top of the cliffs.

Kian and Trystan exchanged a look, and then, as though a command had been uttered or a decision made, Kian plunged after the fleeing man, sword at the ready. He vanished, as the guardsman had done, into the shadows of the cliffs, and Trystan turned and came to stand by Isolde, looking down at the boy.

Hereric was there already, crouching beside Isolde, his face twisted in anguished fury. He made a sign—a question, Isolde thought, echoed a moment later by Trystan.

"How bad is it?"

The stillness left by the end of the fighting was almost shocking, the sound of the wind and the waves all at once unnaturally loud. Isolde looked from Trystan to Hereric. Then, "It's bad," she said quietly. "I'm sorry."

She'd known, as soon as she heard the ugly, bubbling rasp of Bran's breathing, that he couldn't live. Already his closed eyes looked shadowed and sunken in their sockets, his lips bloodless, and when she felt for the pulse in his neck it was hectically fast, light and already uneven.

"How long?" Trystan asked.

Isolde took one of Bran's small, bony hands in hers. Men— and boys—died from the outside in, the life draining out of their bodies first from feet and hands, then legs and arms; then at last the beating heart would stop. The hand she held was icy cold, the fingers like a bundle of dry twigs.

"An hour, maybe. Not more."

Hereric gave an anguished cry, sounding like a wounded child himself, and Isolde raised her eyes to his.

"I'm sorry," she said again. "He won't suffer, though. I doubt he'll even wake."

But even as she spoke, the boy's lids fluttered, then flickered open. His gaze, dull and unfocused, passed over her and moved to Hereric, then away, and the thin face contorted in pain.

"Hurts . . . hurts . . ." The words ended in a whimper.

Isolde felt a twist of helpless anger, even as she pressed the hand she held more tightly. Unfair, she thought, laying her other hand across the boy's brow. A kind god would have let him just slip away instead of calling him back into consciousness now, to pain and fear. But though she'd never helped a child die of battle wounds, she'd sat this way beside countless men.

"I know," she whispered. "I know it hurts. But you'll be brave."

She doubted Bran took in the words; his eyes were still glazed with pain. But he might be comforted by her tone. She went on, holding his hand, the other hand stroking his brow. "You will be brave. Brave as Macsen Wledig. Brave as Ambrosius."

Bran stirred, his eyes moving slowly over them once again. And this time, when his gaze fell on Trystan, another spasm twisted his brow, and his gaze sharpened into groggy awareness.

"Trystan. Am I . . . going to die?" His voice was a reedy whisper, and as he spoke blood rose and bubbled between his lips. Gently, Isolde wiped it away with a fold of the cloth she'd held to the wound, afraid, for a moment, that Trystan would offer an empty platitude or soothing lie.

But Trystan met the boy's look without flinching, dropping to kneel on the sand beside him and laying a hand on Bran's shoulder.

"You die a hero, Bran. You will journey straight to Waelheall as all heroes do."

But another spasm—of fear, this time, Isolde thought—passed across the boy's face, and his eyes widened as though in panic.

"But you said—," he gasped. "You said . . . hunters . . . in the sky . . . You said the dead—"

Trystan stopped him with a gentle pressure of his hand. "I know what I said." He spoke steadily. "But I meant only the dead that had not been sent by fire to the gods. Heroes who die in battle journey to Waelheall, where they feast on boar and ale. And spend their days in training for battle with the beasts of the underworld. You must have heard the tales. Do you trust me?"

Bran's head moved, slightly, in a nod.

"Then listen to me, Bran." Trystan held the boy's gaze with his own. "You know I do not lie. We will build a fire for you, and it will send you straight to Waelheall, where all warriors who die bravely are sent. You have no need to fear. I promise you that you will live forever—and become as mighty a fighter as Arthur himself. Do you believe me?"

Bran's eyes—wide, the pupils dilated—moved once more over Trystan's face, and then the boy's breath went out, his head moving in a brief, feeble nod. Isolde saw the terror ebb out of his face, felt the frail, light body relax in her arms. Then, slowly, with a painful effort, Bran turned from Trystan and looked up at Isolde.

The slender throat contracted. His voice was fainter now, only the barest thread of sound, so that she only just made out the words above the noise of wind and sea.

"Voice . . . pretty . . . talk?" And then: "Please?"

Isolde saw Trystan's eyes flash to her face, but he didn't speak. Isolde drew in a shaking breath above a lump of ice lodged in her chest. She brushed Bran's cheek very lightly with her free hand, and the boy's mouth trembled slightly, but he made no sound, not even another whimper of pain. Like Con, Isolde thought again, all those years ago. Sick with fear, but still trying desperately to be brave.

"All right," she said softly. This, too, she had done many times before. She squeezed Bran's hand. "I'll tell you another story. The story of a great hero—one that has the same name you do, in fact. This is the tale of Bran the Blessed, King of Britain."

Bran was still watching her, and he smiled a little at that, before his lids drooped and then slid shut.

Isolde drew in her breath and began. "Bran the Blessed was king of the island of Britain, a mighty warrior, and a mighty king, brave and powerful and just. Now, it happened one afternoon that he and his fighting men were looking out to sea. And they saw thirteen ships come gliding over the rolling waves.

"'I can see ships out there,' said the king, 'making straight for us and coming in fast. Tell the men to arm themselves and find out what they seek on our shores.'"

Isolde paused. Bran's eyes opened, flickered shut, opened, then closed again. Already she thought she could see the grayness of death beginning to steal over his face, though the cook-fire they had sat around, what seemed an eternity ago, was beginning to die down, leaving only the light of moon and stars for her to see.

The story was one of the old legends, a long, rambling tale of battles lost and won, marriage alliances broken and made. Of talking birds and a magical cauldron and spears dipped in poison. At last, King Bran was fatally wounded in battle against the Irish king Matholwch.

"Nearly every fighting man in Ireland had perished in the war," Isolde went on. "And only seven of King Bran's own men had survived. They gathered round the deathbed of their dying king, with the tears running down their cheeks like rain. And King Bran spoke to them all."

Isolde paused again. The boy Bran's eyes were closed. His breathing was faint and labored, and she saw that bubbles of blood had formed between his lips once more. When she pressed his hand gently, she thought she felt a brief, answering press of his fingers against hers, but the pressure was so faint she might only have imagined it, wishing it there.

"'Do not grieve for me,' the king said. 'But though my body will lie here in Ireland where I laid down my life, take my head with you back to Britain. Carry it with you to London and bury it at the White Mount, with its face toward Gaul.'"

A slight sound made Isolde glance up. Trystan still knelt at Bran's side, while Hereric crouched at his head, as before. Now, though, she saw that Kian had returned and come to stand beside them, his scarred face a harsh, remorseless mask in the dying fire's light. He didn't speak, though, and after a moment she went on, telling of how King Bran's men found, on their way back to London, a fine feasting hall, where they paused to rest, and, charmed by the song of a flight of magical birds, they forgot all mortal misfortunes and their grief for their king and even their longing for home.

She couldn't tell whether Bran still heard her or not. He was breathing still, but the rise and fall of his chest was so slight as to be almost imperceptible, and when she squeezed his hand his fingers felt cold and lifeless, and she couldn't even imagine an answering press against her own.

"They stayed in the feasting hall for eighty long years, but the time passed so swiftly and merrily that it seemed to them no longer than a few short days. But one day, one of the seven companions opened a door in the hall, and there, in the distance, lay Cornwall. And at once, each one of the seven felt the weight of his loss and his grief for all those who had perished in Ireland. And more than anything, they grieved for their king. And so all that was left for them was to set out for London, to bury King Bran's head as he had asked."

Isolde stopped. The wind from off the water lifted the hair from her face. She felt the light, slender little body she held quiver slightly, the breath whistling painfully in Bran's throat. She bent to kiss the boy's brow, cool, now, as his hands, and clammy to the touch.

"At last they reached the White Mount, and they buried their king's head as Bran had asked. But such was the power of the mighty King Bran that in death he guards the land of Britain as ably even yet. And so as long as his head lies there at the White Mount, undisturbed, the land of Britain will be safe, protected by Bran the Blessed, Britain's king."

As Isolde spoke the last words, Bran's eyes opened. For a moment, his gaze met Isolde's, and she thought he smiled. And then his lids closed, another shudder shook him, and Isolde knew that what she held was an empty shell and nothing more. At first, no one moved. Then Trystan leaned forward and gently crossed the boy's arms over his breast. Isolde felt a hand fall heavily on her shoulder, and turned her head to see Hereric standing beside her.

The big man was weeping as openly and unashamedly as a child, tears streaming down his broad cheeks, and Isolde wished, for a moment, that she might cry, as well. The lump of ice was still lodged tight in her chest, but her own eyes were burning and dry as she looked down at Bran's face, the soft mouth and fringed lashes, the ragged patches of hair. He'd survived slavery, survived a winter of fighting wolves for battlefield carrion, only to die here, in her arms.

"I'm sorry," she said. "I should never have agreed to come here with you. I knew there was danger from Marche's guard."

Beside her, Trystan started to answer, then checked himself and turned instead to Kian. Isolde, watching him, had the impression of anger, tightly controlled beneath his deadly even tone. "The other one?"

Kian shook his head, face grim in the pale moonlight. "Got away. Had a horse waiting on top of the cliff. No chance of catching him up on foot." Kian stopped and jerked his head again, this time toward the bodies of the other guards that lay sprawled on the beach a short distance away. "But the rest are dead. I checked."

Trystan nodded and blew out a breath through his teeth. Then: "The one that got away will be back, though, once he's met with reinforcements." He glanced at the sky. "I doubt they'll risk another attack before morning, but we'll have to be gone by then. Hereric"—he turned to the big man, laying a hand on his shoulder—"you'd better gather as much wood as you can find." His mouth twisted. "We'll give Bran his fire, at least, before we move on."

Hereric dragged a blood-smeared fist across his eyes, leaving a trail of rusty red across his cheek and brow. Then he nodded and stumbled to his feet. His breath still came in ragged sobs, but he moved off down the beach, his body bent, his head lowered, scanning the sand for driftwood. Kian watched him a moment, then looked down at Bran's body, frowning.

"I thought Bran's people were Christian folk—the ones he had before he was taken slave, I mean. Never heard he believed in the Saxon gods and Waelhall and underworld battles."

Trystan shrugged. He wiped the blade of the knife he still held against his tunic and slipped it back into his belt. "It was that or tell him he'd spend eternity with Jesus in Heaven singing and playing a harp." His mouth twisted briefly. "Which would you rather if you were ten?"

Kian nodded, and Isolde thought the harsh planes of his face softened as he looked down at the slight frame she still held.

"Comforted the boy, anyway," he said gruffly. "He died well."

Trystan followed his gaze and was silent. "He did." Then he looked at Isolde. "Will you tell us, now, just why Marche should have his guard out after you?"

Isolde studied his face, thrown into a harsh relief by the light of the cook-fire beyond and the moonlight above. "Why should I tell you?" she asked at last.

"Why?" A muscle jumped in Trystan's jaw, and the fury she'd sensed in him before slipped briefly beyond his control. "Jesus, Mary, and Joseph, we've just been attacked and Bran killed. I've a right to know what for."

Isolde couldn't even summon up any answering anger. As he himself had said, he'd kept her here, planned to use her as a bargaining piece if the need arose. But the frightening rush of betrayal she'd felt had slipped away, leaving nothing behind but an aching, gray exhaustion. She shifted Bran's body gently, feeling the sharp bones of his shoulder blades press against her through the folds of her gown. Then, with her free hand, she reached to push the windblown hair from her eyes.

"All right," she said wearily. "I'll tell you the whole."

Trystan listened in silence, and when she had done, he said only, "That explains why Marche is so anxious to lay hands on you. If you did manage to get proof of what he plans, he'd be torn apart by the rest of the nobles and petty kings." He was silent a moment, frowning, his eyes on the pebbled sand, and when he spoke it seemed half to himself. "But I don't see how they could have known you were with us."

Kian, too, had been listening in silence, but now he cleared his throat and spoke for the first time since Isolde had begun. "Needn't have been her they came here for." He spoke half-unwillingly, as though reluctant to admit that the fault for the attack could have been other than Isolde's, but he went on, "Could have been you they were after, you know, Trys. You escaped the same time as she did—Marche would have told his guard to hunt for you, as well. And they thought you Saxon-born, from what you said. So they'd have been asking about a Saxon man, yes?"

Kian paused, rubbing his scar with the back of his thumb. "Well, Hereric's that, clear enough—might as well have 'Saxon' stamped on his forehead. And if anyone saw Hereric on the road and set the guardsmen on his track, it would be a stupider lot of men than Marche's guard that couldn't follow him here, the gods bless him and all poor—" He stopped. "And all like him." Kian shook his head. "He'll have left a trail like a herd of cattle over a field of new fallen snow."

Chapter Eighteen

ISOLDE WATCHED THE GREEN AND blue flames dance and lick at the still, small form that lay at their heart. It was a small fire; Hereric had been able to gather only a bare heap of driftwood. But it was enough. The figure in the center glowed orange, outlined by the flames.

Hereric, the tears still running down his broad face, had carried Bran's body to the pyre himself, had watched as Trystan knelt to kindle the blaze, then moved to stand and watch the fire do its work, his eyes reddened and dull.

Trystan had watched the flames in silence, but now he turned to Hereric and Kian. "We'd best be gone."

Kian, standing beside him, grunted agreement. "The boat, I suppose?"

Trystan's eyes strayed once more to the fire, then he looked away, lean face set. "You and Hereric go and make a quick pass around the top of the cliff and the road. Make sure things are quiet for now. And then we'll see the boat ready to sail."

Kian nodded, but Hereric seemed not to hear. He was still staring dazedly at Bran's pyre, his arms hanging slack at his sides, a trickle of blood from the fight running unheeded from the corner of his mouth.

Trystan let out his breath in a sigh, and then, still limping, he moved to Hereric's side and laid a hand on the big man's shoulder.

"We gave Bran a send-off any warrior would have been proud of. Nothing else we can do for him now."

Slowly, Hereric's head turned toward Trystan, and then his gaze seemed to clear. He stood blinking at the other man.

Trystan nodded. "Good man. Go with Kian, now. I want to be sure we're not going to be set on again before we start loading the boat. I'd go myself, but with this leg I doubt I'd make it halfway up the cliffs." He glanced down at Hereric's belt. "What happened to your knife? No, never mind"—this as the big man started to make a stumbling sign. "Here—take mine."

Isolde was silent as the two men turned and vanished into the surrounding dark. The little pyre had been built well; by the time the flames died, the little body within would be nothing but gray ash and charred bone. Her eyes were stinging from the smoke, and only when she raised a hand to rub at them did she realize she was shaking, shivering from head to foot.

She drew her cloak more tightly about her, then turned to Trystan. "And now that you know I can bring you nothing but further danger, am I free to go?"

Trystan didn't answer at once. In the fire's orange light, Isolde saw that he had a darkening bruise over one eye, and a narrow cut running the length of his jaw on the same side. At last he asked, "And if I did let you free? Where would you go?"

Isolde raised a hand again to rub the sting of the wood smoke from her eyes. She was, she realized, too tired to argue anymore, and so she said, "I'll go on—try to find the goldsmith Ulfin I spoke of. The one in Coel's employ, who carries knowledge of Marche's arrangement with the Saxons."

Trystan's slanted brows lifted. "Alone?"

"How else?"

"How——?" Trystan stopped. Then: "You'll go alone." He grimaced. "Yes, right. And if you happen to meet any wolves on your way, be sure to give them a good poke in the eye with a sharp stick, will you? You'd stand just about as much chance of surviving that as——"

And then he broke off abruptly, as, from somewhere above them there came a shout, followed by a high, wild scream.

Trystan swore under his breath and started for the upward path at a run, covering the ground more quickly that Isolde would have believed his injuries could allow. She followed, scrambling up the rocky incline in Trystan's wake. Her lungs burning, her heart pounding from the climb, she reached the top of the slope and saw Trystan standing a few paces away and staring at the man's crumpled body that lay in the scrub just ahead.

Kian was already starting to sit up, groaning a little and clutching his head when Trystan reached his side. The older man's scarred face was ghastly, bloodless lips drawn back in a grimace of pain, eyes unfocused and still half closed. As Trystan took hold of his arm, though, he shook his head, groaned again, and then struggled upright.

"Trystan." He spoke thickly, between raggedly drawn breaths. "Came at us . . . out of nowhere. Two of them . . . I . . . wasn't looking. Got me——" He grimaced. "Got me before I could even get a hand on my sword."

The line of Trystan's mouth tightened. "And Hereric?"

"Gone . . . took him . . . on horseback." Kian's face twisted again. "Saw that much before I fell."

Trystan swore violently again, then, as Kian flinched, shook his head. "I wasn't blaming you. On horseback, you say?"

Kian nodded. "Rode off at a gallop."

"Following the road?"

"Not as far as I could tell. Heading east." Kian gestured across the expanse of flat, open ground stretching away from the cliffs and the ocean's edge.

Trystan let out his breath. "No point in trying to follow, then. They'll be long gone. And in the dark, over rough, dry ground, we'd never pick up their track." He was silent, frowning in the direction Kian had pointed. Then: "Any idea who they were?"

Isolde could have gotten away. Slipped off into the darkness before either of the men knew she had gone. She stood in a deep patch of shadow cast by a boulder at the top of the track they'd ascended, and if Trystan knew she'd followed him up from the beach, he had entirely forgotten her presence by now. And Kian didn't even know she was there. What kept her there she didn't know, but all the same she stood silent, her back against the rough face of the rock, watching the two men.

Kian was shaking his head. "Didn't get a good enough look at them to tell whose colors they wore. Good fighters. That's all I can say for sure. And well mounted. Rode off from here like the wind."

Trystan nodded grimly. "Likely more of Marche's men, then. Must have taken Hereric for me—of all the bloody evil luck."

Kian frowned. "I'm surprised he'd bother—Marche, I mean. If the woman spoke true and he's planning—"

"Marche doesn't like losing." Trystan cut Kian off before he could finish. "And an escaped prisoner—whoever he is—is a loss."

Trystan was silent a moment, then seemed to rouse himself with an effort, for he shook his head and turned to the other man. "How badly are you hurt? Can you stand?"

Kian shifted, lips tightening to hold back a grunt of pain, but then nodded. "Reckon so. Just give me a hand up, will you?"

He was sweating and panting for breath by the time Trystan had raised him to his feet, and he swayed a moment, one hand braced against Trystan's arm, but he regained his footing and at last straightened his shoulders.

"All right, now."

Even in the moonlight, Isolde could see the swelling on Kian's temple, the flesh darkened and angry, trickling blood. Kian wiped at the blood with the edge of his sleeve. "We'll go after Hereric in the morning, then?"

Again Trystan was silent a space before replying, and Isolde saw indecision flicker across his face. Then he seemed to make up his mind. "No," he said. Kian opened his mouth to protest, but Trystan held up a hand. "No," he said again. "I'll go."

Kian had been gingerly flexing his muscles, testing for further injury, but at that his whole body went abruptly rigid.

"I want you to take the boat," Trystan went on. "You won't be able to manage open sea, not on your own. But you can work your way along the coast—follow the currents as much as you can."

A heavy line had appeared between Kian's brows, and now it deepened, dents of anger appearing at the corners of his mouth, as well. "You'd try to keep me out of battle—like some untried boy or squealing maid? When it was my fault Hereric was captured? If I'd been more on guard—"

"Stop." Trystan's voice was curt, but he laid a hand on the other man's arm. "And how do you think I feel, man? When I'm the one that sent him up here? When they likely took him for me?"

Kian stared at him a long moment, his face wooden. And then he pressed his lips tight together, a swallow rippling the corded muscles of his throat.

"I understand." Slowly, he unbuckled his sword belt, and offered it, sheathed weapon and all, to Trystan. "Take my sword, then, if you think I'm too old and unfit to wield it anymore."

Trystan let out an exasperated breath. "I think you're tough as old boot leather, and stubborn as a cross-grained mule." He squeezed Kian's shoulder briefly, then let his hand fall. "Keep your sword, you old fool. That's not why I said I'd go after Hereric alone."

Kian's face was still stony, but the hand holding out his sword belt slowly fell. "Why, then?"

Isolde, watching from her place of concealment, thought Trystan looked as though one more weight had been added to a load already difficult to bear. He shifted his weight, trying to ease the strain on his injured leg.

Trystan tugged a hand through his hair. "Because I'm the one Marche's men are after. They don't know you from King Arthur or Christ Himself. I went out as spy alone—and got captured for it. And if I hadn't, Bran would be alive and Hereric wouldn't be wherever he is now."

Kian's voice, when he spoke, was quieter, the rasp of anger gone, but Isolde saw that his look was as implacable as before. Not a man, she thought, to relinquish duty lightly. As he would have to have been, to have fought on her father's side at Camlann.

"That may be. But I don't remember swearing an oath to follow your orders. I'm my own man. And if I choose to go with you after Hereric, I will."

Trystan started to speak, then instead let out his breath in a long sigh. "You're right," he said. "I can't order you to let me go alone." He stopped and held the other man's gaze with his own. "I can ask you, though."

There was a silence. Kian shifted position, crossing his arms over his chest, his eyes narrowing.

"And you are asking?"

Trystan tipped his head in a wordless nod.

Kian eyed Trystan speculatively, his mouth still pressed into a hard, flat line. At last, "Why?" he asked again.

"For one thing, I'd rather you did me the favor of not getting yourself killed for my sake. And for another . . ."

"Well?"

Trystan's mouth twitched. "For another, the way our luck is running, leaving the boat is just begging to have it wrecked or stolen. And I'll be an old man before I can afford another."

Kian was silent a long moment, scarred face as grim as before. Then, though, his shoulders relaxed, and he gave a short, harsh bark of laughter. "True enough. All right, I'll take the boat."

Trystan relaxed, as well. He kept his tone steady, casual, even, but Isolde thought that he worked not to show sign of a powerful relief, and she wondered just what he planned that he needed Kian gone.

"Good. You go back to the boat now. Sail up the coast a ways, then turn and come back here. If all goes well, I'll join you in four—no, better make it five—days' time. And with luck, I'll have Hereric with me."

Kian nodded. "You coming back to the beach?"

"Not just yet. You go on."

"In five days, then."

Isolde watched them clasp each other's wrists, briefly, and was aware in the looks of both men how much in that parting was left unsaid. And then Kian turned toward the downward path, wincing as the movement jarred his head, but moving quickly and almost silently over the uneven ground. Isolde held her breath, but he didn't even glance in her direction and she stayed where she was, unseen.

Trystan still stood where Kian had left him. His back was half turned on her, and Isolde was wondering whether to keep still or try to slip away, when he spoke, though without turning his head.

"You may as well come out now."

Isolde's heart stumbled in her chest. But there was no point

in delay. He stood only a few paces distant; a few quick strides
and he could pull her out of the sheltering shadows himself. She
took a step forward.

"You knew I was here?"

He did turn, then, lifting one shoulder in a shrug, his face
a mask of light and shadow, like the Otherworld men in some
of the old tales. "I'd not have stayed alive this long if I couldn't
tell when someone was following close behind me—or waiting
somewhere near."

"And yet you said nothing until now?"

Even by moonlight she could see his mouth curve slightly.
"Yes, well, I couldn't have answered for Kian's reaction if you'd
come popping up at him out of the dark just as he was coming
round from a blow on the head. There's a limit to the number of
times in a night I can stop him from slitting your throat."

Then the smile faded, leaving his face bleak and exhausted
again. "There's something I'd say to you, though." He gestured
toward a nearby rock. "Sit down."

Isolde hesitated, eyeing him warily, and he let out an impatient breath. "Oh, for Christ's sake. Look"—he spread out
his hands—"even if I meant you harm, I'm unarmed. I gave
my knife to Hereric, remember? Here"—he moved back a few
steps—"I'll keep at least three paces away and you can get up
and bolt if I come any nearer. Agreed?"

It was a meaningless gesture, really, Isolde thought. In the
dark, across rough, unfamiliar ground, she'd not get far. Still,
she moved slowly to take her place on the rock Trystan had indicated. "Yes, well," she said. "I'd not have stayed alive this long
if I trusted strangers—let alone one who had me held hostage
barely two hours since."

She settled herself, drawing her cloak around her, then
turned to look up at him curiously. "How are you planning to
get Hereric back—and on your own?"

Trystan lowered himself gingerly onto a rock opposite hers and a little distance away, grimacing as the effort jarred his injuries. He settled himself, elbows resting on his knees. Then: "That's what I'd speak to you about. I haven't a hope of freeing Hereric on my own. I'll have to have help. Your help."

For a moment, Isolde looked at him blankly. Then she drew in her breath. "My help," she repeated.

Trystan's blue eyes were intent on hers. "What I'm offering is a bargain, a fair exchange. You want to find your man—this goldsmith you spoke of—true?"

Still wary, Isolde nodded.

"Castle Dore is on the southern coast. And the man you're looking for left Tintagel on foot not yet a week ago. At most, he'll have barely started on the return journey—that's if he's reached Castle Dore at all."

He paused, and Isolde nodded agreement again. "Yes, but what—?"

Trystan stopped her. "Right, then. There's a track, of sorts, across the moor. It would see you to Castle Dore in half the time of the main road. Help me get Hereric free. And in exchange I'll show you the shorter way. See you find your man—see you safely the whole way to Castle Dore, if need be."

"And can you tell me why I should want you as an escort? Or need your protection?"

Trystan's slanted brows lifted. "You want to risk running into a band of Marche's guardsmen on your own? After what you did to the one that killed Bran—the one that got away?"

"What I did . . ." Isolde frowned. "You mean throwing the knife?"

Trystan shifted position on the rock and laughed shortly. "Knife? By the time he gets back to his companions it will be an invisible elf-dart. Or a bolt of blue witch-fire shot straight from your hand." He stopped. "Jesus, Isa, if they catch you the only question will be whether they'll risk having their privates withered by a curse and rape you before they drag you back to Marche."

Isolde felt a wave of dizziness sweep through her, and a cold, throbbing mist seemed to rise before her eyes. From somewhere out of the chill haze, she heard Trystan say, "A good throw, too. Where did you learn—?"

And then he stopped.

Isolde rubbed her cheek. "Where did I learn to throw a knife? I don't know. Somewhere when I was young, I suppose."

She was forcing herself to breathe, in and out, but she felt Trystan's eyes on her, speculative and keen. He said only, though, "At any rate, I can't hope to tackle Marche's guard alone. So it will have to be by a bargain. You in exchange for Hereric."

Isolde's head came up and she stared at him. "What did you—?"

Trystan held up a hand. "Not actually. That's only how it's got to look to Marche's men. That they'll be getting you as a prisoner instead of Hereric. We'll just have to take the chance that they'll think you worth more to Marche than a stray Saxon. But I imagine they will."

Isolde had her breath back now, and she nodded, brows slightly raised. "Yes, I imagine they will."

Trystan seemed not to hear. Body still bent slightly forward, he was frowning down at his clasped hands. "The men who took Hereric don't know me—otherwise they wouldn't have taken Hereric in my place. So I'll be able to bargain with them without their realizing I'm the prisoner they were sent out to find. They'll know only that I'm part of a gang of masterless men who happened to capture the Witch Queen and are offering her as fair exchange for one of their own."

He paused, brows still drawn. "I'll give you my word that you'll not be actually taken by Marche's guard—and that I'll see you find your goldsmith." His head lifted, and his eyes met hers once more. "If in exchange you'll make a pretense of standing prisoner to be exchanged for Hereric."

Isolde's hands still felt slightly clammy, but the dizziness was gone. Slowly, she shook her head. "If Hereric has 'Saxon' stamped on his forehead, you must think I've got the word 'fool' stamped on mine. Barely two hours ago you were telling me you meant to use me as a bargaining piece if Marche's guard happened on us here. And now you expect me to accept your word that you'll not do exactly that as a means to get Hereric free? I might as well walk straight back to Tintagel and into Marche's prison on my own."

Trystan's jaw hardened, his eyes narrowing. "You think I'd—?" He stopped. "You don't trust me to keep a bargain? All right—here."

In a single violent burst of movement, he had risen to his feet and jerked a knife from the top of his boot. Another knife, Isolde noted automatically, for all he'd claimed to be unarmed.

He crossed the distance between them in two short strides and thrust the weapon, hilt first, into Isolde's hand. "Here—take it," he said. "If I break our agreement and let you come within reach of Marche's guard—or even leave you on your own before you've found your man—you can cut my throat. Or do it now, if you'd rather. Here—I'll make it easy for you."

With a quick, savage jerk, he tore open the neck of his tunic and raised his head, baring his throat. "Go ahead. If you think I'd betray you, here's your opportunity to see I never get the chance."

Isolde could see the thrumming pulse of blood at the base of his neck, the quick rise and fall of his chest as he drew breath, and she pulled back involuntarily, frightened by the force of his anger. Her fingers had closed automatically around the dagger; its hilt of carved bone was cool and smooth against her palm.

She said, with sudden certainty, "This is why you sent Kian away. So you could ask me for aid."

Trystan's jaw was still set, but he gave a short nod. "I wouldn't be answerable, either, for what he'd have said if I told him we'd got to ask your help in getting Hereric free." Then his mouth relaxed, slightly, in a brief twitch of a smile. "Especially not if you refused. As I said, there's a limit to the number of times I can stop him slitting your throat."

"And if I do refuse now?"

Trystan let his hand fall away from the neck of his tunic. "If you refuse then you can go—here and now, if that's what you choose," he said tiredly.

He must have seen the disbelief in her face, for he let out another exasperated breath. "In the last two days, I've been horse-whipped, beaten, stabbed, and slashed with a sword. You think I feel like chasing you on foot across open country if you try to run?" He shook his head. "I mean it. If you refuse, you're free to go on your way. Forget you ever saw any of us."

"And what will you do?"

"Me?" Trystan shrugged again, the blue eyes suddenly flat and hard. "I'll see what I can do for Hereric on my own. What else?"

Isolde, watching his face, found she believed him. He might lie about being unarmed, but he spoke true now. She wondered briefly whether it was usual to find honor of this kind among a band of mercenaries and masterless men. It might be rare—or it might be common, for all she knew, and she realized abruptly how little she did know of this country, for all she'd been High Queen these seven years.

But Trystan would go after Hereric without so much as a thought of turning aside. Admirable, she supposed. Though it almost certainly meant throwing his own life away along with Hereric's. Alone against Marche's guard, he'd not stand a chance. As he himself had said.

She looked out toward the curve of moonlit ocean visible past the edge of the cliffs to her right, then asked, "Who is Hereric, exactly?"

"What was he, you mean, before I knew him?" He shrugged. "I don't know. An escaped slave would be my guess. He's never said."

He stopped, and Isolde remembered Hereric's face, his broad, spreading smile as she agreed to accompany him here. Hereric, eyes wide with panic, clutching his pierced-tooth amulet to his chest. It must have been his scream they'd heard from the beach. She was scarcely aware that a decision had been made, but she heard herself say, "All right. I agree."

Chapter Nineteen

ISOLDE SAT ON A LICHEN-COVERED rock, listening to the soft trills of birdsong from the brush all around and watching a rose-colored ribbon grow along the eastern horizon as the day broke over the moor. They had followed the running stream up from the beach and made camp for the night near the water's edge. Now Trystan was sitting on the fern-lined bank, shaving with the edge of his knife.

Isolde rubbed her eyes, feeling dull and slow-witted with fatigue. She'd dozed off once or twice, lying on the sheepskin Trystan had given her, but she'd not dared let herself fall fully asleep. She might have agreed for Hereric's sake to what Trystan proposed. And maybe, she thought, for my own sake, as well.

The thought of meeting Marche's guard on her own still made a cold, hollow feeling settle in the pit of her stomach. But she still didn't entirely trust the man who now sat a short distance away, his face turned to look out toward the sea. There was nothing, after all, to stop him taking what coin and jewelry she still had and abandoning her here. Or simply tying her up and handing her over to Marche or his men.

Trystan had taken his tunic off to wash, and Isolde saw that he had a heavy, darkened bruise over his ribs and another one, fading to yellow about the edges, running almost the length of his right arm. He'd tied a makeshift bandage of torn cloth about the sword cut he'd gotten the night before. In the harsh morning light, the marks of the whip were still visible on the broad planes of his back, some still angry and red, others crusting with black. His every moment must be painful, though his face showed hardly any sign. He must, she thought, have cultivated iron self-control. Though perhaps slavery did that inevitably to a man.

Isolde thought of offering to see to his wounds. But there was almost nothing that she might do for him here, beyond what he himself had already done. The morning air was chill, and Isolde saw a ripple of gooseflesh along his arms before he picked up the tunic and quickly pulled it over his head. She waited until he'd returned and was rummaging in the travel bags before she asked instead, "How are you planning to find Hereric and Marche's men?"

Trystan took out a loaf of coarse brown bread from the pack. Isolde doubted he'd slept any more than she had. His eyes were reddened beneath a heavy bruise over one brow, and every time she'd glanced toward him the night before, she'd found him sitting slouched against a rock, arms folded across his chest, eyes on the glowing embers of their campfire.

Now he broke the loaf of bread in half, handed Isolde one part, and took a few quick, efficient bites of his own portion before he answered. "Not that many places they'll have headed with him. They'd either go to Tintagel or Castle Dore. And since Kian said they were headed east when they rode off, my guess would be Castle Dore. I doubt they rode far last night. With luck, they'll have made camp not far from here and we can catch them up before they've gone."

He swallowed the last of the bread. "You eat. I'll scout around a bit and see if I can pick up their trail. That will tell us for certain which way they've gone."

Isolde nodded and took a bite of her own portion of bread. The sleeve of her gown had fallen back from her wrist, and Trystan frowned, his eyes fastening on the exposed skin of her arm and the cut left by the guardsman's sword.

"You'd better tie that up. Here—" He took out another torn strip of cloth from his scrip and reached across, as though to take her arm.

"No!" Involuntarily, Isolde flinched away, pulling back before he could touch her. "No," she said again, though more steadily this time. "I'll see to it myself. It's not deep."

Before Trystan could answer, she had risen and crossed to kneel by the bubbling stream. She drew up a cupped handful of water and poured it over the cut, then used both hands to splash water on her face, as well. The water was icy and left her gasping and shivering, but it steadied her enough that she could tear a length of linen from the hem of her undershift and bind it around her arm.

And I wonder, she thought, whether I'll ever be able to so much as touch a man again and not feel instead Marche's hands. Smell his sweat on my skin.

She raised a hand and realized that there were tears on her cheeks. Furiously, she wiped them away. She closed her eyes, then slowly, deliberately, she finished washing, scrubbing the dirt and blood away from her hands and her face. She combed out her hair with her fingers, then replaited it into a single heavy braid, and when she turned back to the campsite, Trystan had gone.

"SOMEONE ON HORSEBACK CAME THIS WAY, at any rate." Trystan had dropped to his knees to examine a low scrub bush, fingering a broken branch and a patch of crushed leaves on one side. "You see?" He pointed to the mark of a horse's hoof, a little blurred around the edges, but still clear. "Nothing to show if it was the men who took Hereric. But a good mount—well bred. Nice curve to the hoof, and a good size."

He had returned to camp with the word that he'd picked up tracks still heading east, and they'd set out almost at once, crossing from the coast into the great, rolling stretch of wasteland that made up Cornwall's central moor. This stretch of country was all but barren, home to only a scattering of sheep farmers and goatherds, and so far they had met no one as they made their way past high cairns of tumbled stone and bramble-covered tors.

Now it was midafternoon, the sun high overhead as Trystan paused, whistling tunelessly under his breath. "All right, my beauty." His eyes swept the ground ahead for more marks of the horse's hooves. "Which way were you headed, eh?"

There was a patch of red, dark and wet, on the shoulder of his tunic, but if the reopened sword cut was paining him, he gave no sign. Four years ago, when Isolde had first started caring for the soldiers wounded in battle, an infantryman had come into the infirmary suffering from frostbite on his hands and feet, the flesh turned putrid, so that he lost a finger and two toes.

The man—Gavin, his name had been—had liked Isolde and had talked to her a good deal during the time he spent in her care. His troop had been caught, he said, in a blizzard that struck while they were returning from battle. He'd hung back to help a companion—a man with a sword cut to the leg—and in the blinding snow they'd somehow been separated from the rest of the troop and lost their way. And Gavin had walked for three days and three nights through the drifting snow—waist deep, in some places, he said—carrying his companion on his back.

Before they reached the shelter of a crofter's hut where they could beg for aid, they'd been attacked by a wolf. A lone hunter, separated from his pack by the storm as they themselves had been. And Gavin, with no chance to draw his sword, had broken the beast's neck with his bare hands.

He and his companion had survived—to be brought into Isolde's infirmary for care. And he'd grinned when Isolde, swabbing the deep slashes left in his forearm by the wolf's teeth and claws, had asked how he'd managed to kill the animal, weakened as he'd been.

"I'll tell you, lass," he'd said, grunting a bit at the sting as she cleansed the wounds. "I passed the time in walking through the snow by thinking on the meal I'd have when we got through the storm. The haunch of pork I'd cut myself . . . the size of the drinking horn of ale I'd swallow in one draft. And when we finally did reach shelter, I ate till I nearly puked and then slept the best part o' two days. But when the wolf came at us—jumped me out of nowhere—well . . ." He shook his head. "Doesn't matter if you're hungry or tired or half dead with cold—you just do what's got to be done, that's all."

She'd heard countless other stories like that since then. Men who'd run for hours on fractured ankles. Or fought through battles with broken ribs or arms. It was the same, Isolde thought, with Trystan now. Sooner or later, the reserves of strength that kept him going would run out. But for now, a slight stiffness in his gate and the reddened lids of his eyes were the only signs he gave of fatigue.

He brushed mud from the knees of his breeches and turned to go. "All right, let's move on. Not much we can do but keep following what tracks we can find—"

Then he broke off, his attention fixed by something in the distance. Isolde had his gaze to follow as a guide, but even so it was a moment before she saw it. A hut, its walls and roof built of the gray stones of the moor, so that at first glance it seemed only another cairn.

The hut stood at the foot of a gentle prominence of land on which rose one of the rings of god-stones that the Old Ones had raised for a purpose long since lost and that now, mute and often fallen, dotted the moor. A small brown mule was browsing in a paddock behind the hut. A small, walled-in garden had been dug to one side, the rows of furrowed earth turfed and bedded, now, for the autumn, the leaves of the remaining plants shriveled and beginning to fall. As they approached, Isolde saw that a man was bent over a blackening vine that climbed the far wall. Hearing their approach, he straightened.

He was, Isolde judged, somewhere between forty-five and fifty years of age, and, despite the dull black habit of a monk or priest he wore, he looked more like a soldier than a holy man. His body was squat and powerfully built; his arms were thick with muscle beneath the rolled sleeves of his robe. Beneath a head of wiry brown hair, his face, too, was blunt and square, with a pugnacious jaw, and a nose that had once been broken, though the effect was tempered by a pair of thoughtful brown eyes.

His eyes moved over them now in mild appraisal, taking in, Isolde saw, Trystan's bruised face and bleeding arm—and likely her own bloodstained gown and disheveled hair as well. Then he spoke, his voice slow and deep.

"Good day to you, friends. You've had some trouble, it seems."

He paused, as though inviting explanation. But it was an invitation only, Isolde thought, not a demand. There was only the gentlest of curiosity in the thoughtful gaze, nothing of either fear or surprise.

Trystan nodded. "Yes."

"Ah." The answer seemed sufficient, for the man asked nothing more, only tucked the pruning knife he'd been using into a rough sheath at his belt and asked, "And what can I do for you, then?"

Again it was Trystan who answered. "We're seeking a group of men—mounted men, who would have ridden past here either late last night or very early this morning. Have you seen any such?"

Again the considering brown eyes moved over them, and Isolde had again the sense of being appraised, weighed in some internal balance. Then the man seemed to come to a decision, for he nodded, dusting off his hands on the skirt of his woolen robe.

"You'd best come in. Columba is my name. Brother Columba. I've little here, but I can offer you some refreshment, at least, while we talk." He gestured toward a low stone bench that stood against the little garden's southern wall. "Be easy and I'll bring you a cup of wine."

He disappeared into the hut, returning a few moments later with an earthenware beaker and a pair of unglazed pottery cups. He poured out a pale, amber liquid into each cup and handed one to Trystan, the other to Isolde, nodding at Isolde's thanks.

"Honey wine. I keep a couple of hives up on the hill and occasionally persuade the bees to part with enough of the fruits of their labor to brew up a jar or two."

Isolde turned to look up at the hill behind the hut, her eyes moving from the round hives he'd indicated to the ring of standing god-stones, their square, jutting forms stark against the sky. Brother Columba must have seen the look, for he said, as though reading her thoughts, "You'll be thinking it's a strange place for a Christian brother to set up hermitage. But we've reached an understanding, the stones and I." He looked at the stone circle with something like affection. "They've been here far longer than I. Long enough not to begrudge an upstart like myself the space to live and to grow what's needed for food." He nodded, eyes still on the stones, his gaze distant, his head cocked, as though listening. "We bide each other company—and there's small enough of companionship out here on the moor to make it of value, however it comes. Now—"

He stopped and turned back to them, abruptly prosaic once more. "You wished to ask whether I'd seen a party of mounted men."

Trystan had let out his breath as he'd sunk down on the hard stone bench beside Isolde, and was now sitting slumped back, eyes closed. At Brother Columba's words, though, he roused himself with a visible effort.

"You've seen them, then?"

Brother Columba eyed him thoughtfully once again, and when he spoke it was not an answer to the question. "Your pardon, friend, but you look as though you'd be better in bed than seeking mounted men out here."

Trystan glanced up at the other man, a wry smile touching his mouth. "You'll get no argument from me." Then the smile faded, and he set down his cup of wine. "Unfortunately, though, we can't afford any delay."

Isolde wondered, briefly, whether Brother Columba would ask for further explanation, but he only nodded, as though Trystan's answer had given him all he needed to know.

"Then I'd best tell you what I know so that you can be on your way." He paused, then asked, "Will you let me tend to that wound on your shoulder while we talk? It's plainly causing you some grief, and I've some small knowledge of the herb-craft. It won't take long."

Trystan started to shake his head, then changed his mind and gave the monk another wry smile. "All right," he said, "I won't argue with that, either. If you've anything like a cure to offer, I'll take it with thanks."

Brother Columba smiled, too. "Well, not a cure, no. Christ may have healed the lepers, but I'm afraid my powers stop far short of His. As, of course, they should, humble sinner that I am. But I believe I can make you a bit easier before you go."

The sword cut in Trystan's shoulder was angry and red in the morning light, the flesh around it swollen. The bandage Brother Columba had cut away was stiff with blood, and had left raw, angry chafe marks where it had rubbed against the skin. Brother Columba shook his head over the injury and uncorked the bottle he'd brought out from the hut, pouring a little of the greenish fluid within over a linen pad and then pressing it to the wound.

"I'm afraid this may sting a bit."

Trystan sucked in his breath. "Jesus bloody Christ on a three-legged mule!" He gritted his jaw, then added, "Your pardon, Brother."

Lines of amusement had gathered about the corners of Brother Columba's eyes, but he said only, his voice mild, "Granted."

He went on with cleaning the wound, and Isolde, watching, felt a stab of guilt, sharp as a blade. Hereric had brought her to Trystan, had asked her aid as a healer. And *how long has it been*, she thought, *since I turned away from treating anyone—man or woman, Briton or Saxon-born—with an illness or wound? And yet this time I didn't even make the offer of aid. As though—*

"YOU'RE HURT, AREN'T YOU?"

He shook his head and tried to jerk away from the small hands that clung to his arm. He pressed his eyes closed. "I'm fine."

She said a word that made his eyes snap open: "Don't lie, Trys. Not to me."

He let out his breath. "I don't know why I bother."

"I don't know, either. You know I can always tell."

That made him smile a little, and he let her push him onto the wooden stool. The wide gray eyes filled with tears at the sight of the angry purpling bruises on his back, but then she threw her arms around him in one of her quick, impulsive gestures, hugging him fiercely.

"Never mind. When I'm Lady of Camelerd, I'll make you . . . I'll make you master of the royal stables."

In spite of himself, he laughed, and tugged the black braid of hair. "So that you can pester me to take you riding every day?"

"MISTRESS?"

Isolde came back to herself to find that Brother Columba had turned away from Trystan and was watching her, eyes anxious, a worried frown on the broad, heavy-boned brow.

"Mistress, are you all right? Perhaps I ought to have offered to let you rest inside. I know some ladies . . . the sight of blood . . ." His words trailed off.

The voice had been once more different from those that had come in the past. Closer. Seeming again to call like a selkie's song to the darkened space in her mind. And she could feel memories pressing back in response. Struggling, fighting to return, like floodwaters behind a rotting dike.

Isolde shook her head. "No, I'm all right. I'm used to wounds."

One foot in front of the other. Look forward, not back.

She picked up the bottle Brother Columba had set down on the bench and sniffed at the contents, the sharp, astringent odor clearing the last of haze from her sight, and she said, still trying to hold back the insistent press of the forgotten time, "Vinegar. And rosemary. And vervain?"

Brother Columba nodded. "I've found it keeps infection away." He gave her a keen glance from under his brows. "You know something of herb-cures yourself, then?"

Isolde caught herself up with a prickle of sudden unease along her spine. They were, she judged, about a half-day's ride from Tintagel, somewhere in the heart of Cornwall's central moor. She'd no idea whether stories of the Witch Queen would have spread to this remote spot. But recognition could only bring danger—both to Brother Columba and to her. She recorked the bottle and said, turning away, "A bit."

She could feel Brother Columba's gaze rest on her a moment more, but he nodded and turned back to Trystan, and began dabbing a yellow, greasy-looking salve over the wound.

"Well, as I was saying," he went on, and Isolde realized that she must have missed a part of what had gone before. "As I was saying, I didn't see the riders, so I can't say for sure even whether it was the group you seek. All I can tell you is that sometime before dawn I heard horses coming this way."

Trystan looked up sharply. "They didn't stop, though?"

Brother Columba shook his head. "That, also, I'm afraid I can't tell you." He drew out a strip of clean linen and began to wind it about Trystan's shoulder and upper arm. "Raiders or masterless men could hardly expect to find much worth stealing in a hermit's cell. But"—again the lines of humor gathered about his eyes—"I'm afraid I've a sad lack of faith in such men's willingness to listen to reason. So when riders come this way, I've gotten into the habit of . . . ah . . . removing temptation, so to speak, and slipping out and up onto the moor." The smile deepened a little. "As I say, it shows a sad lack of faith in my fellow man. But it saves robbers the sin of inflicting bodily harm on a man of God—and myself the sin of fighting back. So I've hopes the scales are more or less balanced."

Isolde looked from Brother Columba's broad, powerful shoulders and thickly muscled arms to the strong, pugnacious jaw and inexpertly set nose. And a man of God he may be now, she thought. But once he was a man of something else entirely.

Something that taught him of sword cuts and the treatment of wounds.

Brother Columba had finished wrapping the bandage around Trystan's shoulder and now began to carefully refold the extra strips of linen before tucking them away in one of his sleeves.

"So you see," he said, "I have little to offer you in the way of help. But I do know that the riders, whoever they were, came from the same direction you yourselves have done." He gestured.

Trystan moved his shoulder, testing the strappings, then slipped his arm back into his tunic and retied the laces at his neck. "Anything we can learn is a help." He got to his feet. "Thank you, Brother." He touched the bandaged shoulder. "And for this, as well."

Brother Columba waved the thanks away, then rose to his feet, looking from Trystan to Isolde. "If there's anything more I can do for you, remember that you can find me here."

As they moved away, Isolde glanced back and saw that the monk had returned to kneel in the earth at the foot of the climbing vine. The last sight she had of him, he had drawn out the pruning knife from its sheath and was carefully cutting away the dead branches and leaves once more.

"Is what he told us of any help?" Isolde asked, when they'd climbed the prominence behind Brother Columba's hut and now stood at its summit in the massive, brooding presence of the god-stones.

Trystan shrugged, shading his eyes with one hand as he scanned the rolling gray landscape spread out below.

"We know at least that if the men Brother Columba heard are the right ones, they were going at a gallop near dawn— which means they'd been riding hard all night. They'd need to rest the horses before they went much farther. We may find them yet."

He stopped, his face half turned away, so that Isolde could see again the oval scar on the side of his neck.

They'd likely all known slavery, then, at one time or another. Trystan, Hereric, and Bran. All except Kian, she thought, they've been slaves. And had come together, somehow, to scrape whatever living they could find fighting for the highest pay.

Isolde watched Trystan stoop, lift a crushed leaf to smell it, and then let it fall, and she wondered again where he himself had come from. His voice, now that he spoke to her in the British tongue, had a faint touch of an accent. Though that, she thought, might only be from years of living among Saxons.

She'd not forgotten, though, the way he'd fought the guardsman on the beach the night before. She'd seen enough sword practice and sparring between Con and his men to know that anyone weakened and injured as Trystan had been, but less skilled with a sword than he, would have been killed outright. Trained as a fighting man, she thought. And then somehow captured and branded a slave.

"Come on." Trystan eyed the sun, which was beginning to sink in the west. "We'll keep going till sunset, then camp for the night if we've not found them by then."

Chapter Twenty

ISOLDE CAME AWAKE WITH A jolt, her heart pounding, though she could not remember why. She pressed her hands against her eyes. But then, before she could clear away the last of whatever the dream had been, she was caught in a grip like iron. Something cold and sharp bit painfully into her throat and a harsh voice whispered low in her ear.

It was so much the same as when she'd been woken by Hereric that, for a moment, Isolde thought she must still be in the midst of a dream. But the voice this time was Trystan's, and the language was one she didn't recognize, the words guttural and strange. Then the blade of the knife dug once more into her skin and she knew it was no dream. He had her pinned—any attempt she made to struggle would plunge the knife into her throat.

Then, abruptly, he let her go and sprang back a pace, so that she was able to scramble to her feet and face him. The clouds had blown away, and the moonlight was bright and clear. She could see Trystan, crouched against the wall of rock at his back, knife at the ready. His face was streaked with sweat, frozen in a look of desperate horror or pain. But he didn't look at her. The blue eyes stared sightlessly ahead, unblinking and unfocused. He's not awake, Isolde thought with a sudden chill. He's dreaming.

She struggled to push away the last clinging remnants of sleep, struggled to remember what had happened before she'd fallen asleep. They'd walked for what seemed like hours before coming to this spot, where wind and weather had hollowed out a small place of shelter at the base of a granite-studded hill. She'd tried to stay awake. But she must have fallen asleep at last. And so must Trystan have done. He'd walked as far as she had that day, and fought Marche's guard besides. And the past two nights for him had been all but sleepless.

And now, Trystan still had the knife. But if she tried to wake him—if he was brought out of the dream suddenly—there was no way of telling what he would do. She'd seen men in the infirmary like this often enough when they were taken by a nightmare of battle—had seen them lash out, suddenly and violently, before they could be fully roused.

Isolde moistened her lips.

"Trystan."

Her voice was a murmur, barely audible above the sound of the wind as it whistled past the sheltering overhang of rock above their heads. Trystan didn't move—didn't even look in her direction. Isolde's throat felt dry, but she swallowed and tried again.

"Trystan."

This time his head turned slightly, the blank, bright eyes looking past her. Isolde willed herself to speak in a low, gentle murmur, as she had so often before when soothing a wounded man out of his dreams.

"It's all right. Put the knife down. It's all right."

Trystan's expression didn't change, but she thought the muscles of his shoulders relaxed slightly. Slowly, and with infinite caution, she began to creep toward him, still speaking softly.

At last she was within an arm's length of Trystan. He hadn't moved. Still in a crouched, fighting stance against the rock wall, he held the knife at the ready, but he hadn't spoken or cried out again.

Slowly . . . slowly . . . Isolde reached out a hand to touch his. As their fingers brushed, his arm jerked and her own heart leapt in response, but then he relaxed once more, and when she slid the knife from his grasp, he didn't resist. Holding her breath, she moved back, out of his reach, laying the weapon a little distance away on the ground. She'd let out a breath of relief and raised a hand to brush the tangled hair from her face when Trystan gave a ragged, wordless scream and leapt up.

Instinctively, Isolde sprang back, her hand pressed tight to her mouth to keep back a startled cry of her own. Trystan had gone abruptly still, his eyes still staring sightlessly at something beyond. Isolde stayed rigid. Unless he moved, he wouldn't be able to reach her. And he wouldn't notice her unless she somehow attracted his attention.

Then, his face still that stark, staring mask, Trystan's lips moved. "Holy God, kill me now." The words were a bare whisper, spoken as though they were wrenched from his chest. "Kill me now. Or else make me able to bear it."

He can't reach me, Isolde thought again. If I stay here—if I stay still—he won't even know I'm here. She could only imagine, though, what Trystan must be dreaming of, to bring that stark, empty look to his face. Or to make him pray for death. His head was thrown back, the muscles of his throat standing out like cords, and in the moonlight Isolde saw that his brow glittered with sweat and that his pupils were so dilated his eyes looked almost black.

She'd seen men in her infirmary trapped by nightmares— many of them. And back at Tintagel, she would never have left a man alone in the depths of such a dream.

Slowly, step by step, she began to make her way forward, until she could lay a hand lightly on Trystan's arm. She felt the muscles contract under her touch, and then her wrist was seized in a grip like iron, twisted painfully as Trystan dragged her toward him. Her heart jerked hard against her ribs, but she drew in her breath and spoke the first words that came to her lips.

"This is the tale of Trevelyan, the only man to escape when Lyonesse sank beneath the sea."

Lucky, she thought, that the tale was so familiar she scarcely needed to concentrate on the words. Her heart was still beating quickly, and her attention was fixed on Trystan's grip on her arm—and on the knife that still lay on the ground only a few paces away. He could, if he tried, break her wrist with one twist of his hand. But as she went on with the tale, Isolde felt Trystan's muscles gradually relax, and so she kept speaking in a soft, soothing murmur, telling the story of the ancient land that had vanished beneath the waves.

Isolde paused, tilting her head back so that she could see Trystan's face. He still held her tightly, his fingers digging painfully into her wrist, but she thought some of the starkness had faded from his eyes. And as she stopped speaking, the rhythm of his breathing changed again. He looked down at her, the blue eyes slowly focusing on her face, then shook his head as though to clear it.

"What—?"

Trystan stopped abruptly. He was still holding her, but now he released her, so abruptly Isolde fell back a pace. Then he half turned away to face the stone slope. He stayed there, motionless, still breathing hard, until at last the rise and fall of his chest slowed and steadied.

"What happened?" His voice was nearly back to normal, but he didn't turn, and she saw that the muscles of his neck were still rigid.

"You were dreaming," Isolde said. "You—" Her hand went involuntarily to her throat, where the blade of his knife had left a thin trail of blood. She didn't think he'd seen, but when he turned, his gaze flicked from her to the knife, still lying where she'd laid it on the ground.

"I see." His voice was expressionless as his eyes, flat as blue stones, traveled slowly from Isolde's face to the mark on her throat.

Isolde felt, all at once, the full weight of her own exhaustion. She sat down abruptly on the sheepskin she'd used for a bed. "It's happened before?"

Trystan, too, slid down to settle on the ground, started to lean back against the rock, then swore as his scored shoulders touched the granite wall. The angular planes of his face were silvered by the moonlight, slanted brows drawn together in a frown. Isolde hadn't expected him to be willing to explain, and was surprised when he said wearily, after a moment, "Not in a while."

He was still breathing deeply, and he tipped his head back, looking up at the night sky. "Scared living hell out of Kian a while back by trying to slit his throat while we were both on guard duty late one night. Though Kian can hold his own." He rubbed a hand the length of his jaw and gave a short laugh. "Damn near broke my wrist getting the knife away."

Isolde was silent. And then, for the third time since she'd first seen him, that strange, unnerving feeling of sameness swept over her. As though she'd lived—or dreamed—this all once before. Not a return of the Sight. And yet it left her feeling again slightly queasy, with a thrumming pain in her temples as though she'd indeed tried to call the Sight back.

"If I ask you a question," she said, "will you give me a true answer?"

She saw Trystan's brows draw together once again. "Another favor?"

"If I'd not thrown Bran's knife at the guard back on the beach you might have been killed."

"True."

Isolde waited, but Trystan said nothing more. "And . . . there's this." She touched the mark Trystan's own knife had left on her throat.

Trystan didn't move. His face was unreadable, his eyes flat and hard. But suddenly Isolde was chillingly aware as she'd been once before of how entirely alone they were, and of the strength of the hands that had just a moment ago held that knife. Then Trystan let out his breath, and the moment passed. He rubbed the space between his eyes. "All right. Ask."

"Who are you?"

Trystan let his hand fall and looked up. "That's no kind of question. What would you say if I asked you the same thing?"

"What would I say?" A feeling like broken shards seemed to scrape, briefly, inside Isolde's chest, and she shivered. "Then will you tell me what you were dreaming about?"

Trystan lifted one shoulder and half turned once more, his eyes on the darkened moor spread out beyond her. "What about? The past, I suppose."

"And that's no kind of answer."

Trystan sat motionless a moment. His eyes flicked to her, then away, and Isolde thought that this time he was going to refuse to reply. But then he said, in an expressionless voice, "I was sent to a flint mine. A slave camp. It was probably that I was dreaming of—it usually is. Crawling through some filthy tunnel in the dark and waiting for the air to give out or the rocks above me to cave in. That, or—"

He glanced as though involuntarily down at the mutilated left hand and stopped, abruptly, mouth tightening as though to keep back anything more.

After a moment Isolde asked, "How did you break free?"

"From the mining camp?" Trystan was still looking out into the night. "Killed one of the guards and made off." He gave another short laugh, mirthless, this time. "It was the dead of winter, too. Snow drifts as high as my head. Thought it was going to be the last truly stupid stunt I ever tried." He paused, and was silent, looking past Isolde at something beyond. Then: "That's when I met Hereric, though. Half dead and frozen, as well."

"How long ago was that?"

Trystan frowned. "Four years, maybe? No, five." He lifted his shoulder. "Anyway, he's been with me ever since."

"But he wasn't with you when you were captured?"

"Hereric? God, no." He spoke more easily now. He reached into his pack and drew out a horn flask of ale, working the stopper free with his teeth. "Lucky, too. He'd have stood as much chance as a worm in a hen yard with Marche's guard."

Trystan offered the flask first to Isolde, but she shook her head. She waited for him to swallow before asking, "And just what was your mission?"

Trystan lowered the flask and gave her a sharp glance from under drawn brows.

"You've a lot of questions, all at once."

Isolde didn't answer that, and Trystan was silent a moment, as though debating with himself. Then he seemed to make up his mind. "No reason you shouldn't know, I suppose. It's over now. Cewlin—he's one of Cerdic of Wessex's men—offered me pay to bring him whatever I could find out about the British army's defenses. I'd done jobs like that for him before."

"And Cyn?"

A shadow passed across Trystan's brow. "Cyn was Cewlin's man. Sent with me to be sure I didn't—" His mouth curved wryly. "Didn't lose my way on the return journey."

Isolde nodded. So he'd spoken the truth, then, back in Tintagel's cell when he'd said there was nothing but payment for service binding him to the Saxon side.

"Will Cewlin send someone else after you? Now that you've failed to return?"

Trystan took another swallow of the ale and shook his head. "I wouldn't think so. He'd only paid me half the agreed-on fee—the other half was for when I returned. Wasting any of his fighting men trying to find me would only be throwing good money after bad. Besides—" he broke off, a line appearing between his brows.

"Well?"

Trystan smiled without humor. "If what you told me is true, Cewlin won't have much need of what information I can offer now." He frowned again. "He must not have known of the alliance between Octa, Cerdic, and Marche when he made his bargain with me."

"Or the alliance hadn't yet been made."

"Could be, I suppose." Trystan was silent, brows still drawn, then went on, speaking half to himself. "I don't see, though, how what you said of a united Saxon invasion force can be true. I know what Octa and Cerdic think of each other. And I'd have said they'd as soon make alliance as walk onto a battlefield blindfolded, with a darning needle for a sword. Still—" He broke off and shook his head. "Never mind. Doesn't much matter what I think of it all."

He paused to take another draft from the flask, then wiped his mouth on the back of his hand. "Lucky for me Bran was able to escape and get to Hereric and Kian when the guard got me and Cyn."

Isolde looked up, surprised. "You had Bran with you then?"

Trystan's eyes were distant, and he answered without looking at Isolde, speaking almost more to himself than to her. "Bran always came along on jobs like that. He could pass unnoticed almost anywhere—slip into and out of an army camp without a hitch. And a fine hand at thieving food, if the hunting was poor. Could lift a hen or two or a wheel of cheese or what have you from a cotter's farm and be away before they even knew anything was gone."

Trystan paused, then laughed suddenly. "Once it was an entire ham. God, I'll never forget the sight of Bran dragging it into camp. It must have weighed as much as he did. He waited until we'd hacked it into pieces and started eating before he told us where he'd got it. Dragged it away from a den of wild dogs that had gotten it God knows how. Cyn and I were sitting there with the meat still in our mouths—and there's Bran telling us it hadn't got *much* dog shit on it and what there was he'd managed to wipe mostly away." He shook his head and laughed again. "I thought Cyn would heave his portion up onto his boots, but he finished the whole. He liked Bran."

Trystan broke off, the smile fading abruptly, his eyes focused still on something far off. Isolde imagined him picturing the two smoking funeral pyres, one for Bran and one for Cyn, and she wondered how much more he would answer.

"And what about Marche? I thought, from what you said to Kian last night, that you must have met Marche before—or at least known something of him."

But at that Trystan looked up sharply, and Isolde felt, all at once, that the distance between them was suddenly far greater than it had been a moment ago. He said, though, with no change in tone, "Not a wineskin deep enough to last me through the whole of what I know—and think—of Marche."

He stopped again, and studied her a moment, the look of half-curious speculation back in his gaze. "You've had your answers now. Do I get a question in return?"

Isolde frowned. "Do you want a question of me?"

Still watching Isolde, Trystan rubbed at the bandage on his

shoulder as if the wound were troubling him. Then: "What did you mean when you said two nights ago that you thought you'd learned to throw a knife when you were young? Don't you know?"

Isolde's brows lifted in surprise. "That's your question?"

Trystan shrugged. "Don't say, if you'd rather not. You didn't give me a promise to answer."

Isolde frowned again but the frightening press of memory she'd felt a moment ago had gone. Enough that it was safe to speak? She searched her mind, but found nothing. There was herself before and herself after Camlann, the two separated by the comforting, familiar wall.

"No," she said slowly. "It's all right. I suppose I don't mind."

It might have been simple fatigue that loosened her tongue. Or it might have been the feeling of isolation, the surrounding darkness, the lateness of the hour. Or perhaps her own fear of what lay ahead, making her understand why soldiers so often stayed awake, talking, the night before battle.

She'd never spoken of it before. But all the same, she found herself saying, almost before she realized, "You're at least as old as I am. Old enough to remember the plague year. Just around the time of Camlann. The sickness struck my father's fortress. It was . . ." She stopped. "There was no time, even to mourn them all. Every day there was another death—another one gone. The servants. The waiting woman. The other children. And . . . and my grandmother, as well."

She stopped, her eyes on a shadow of creeping vine on the granite wall at Trystan's back, the stem silvery in the light of the stars. "And then there was Camlann. And my father was killed, as well. I was thirteen then. And it was decided I should be married to Constantine." She moved her shoulders. "A good solution, I suppose. Modred's daughter and Arthur's heir. It brought the two factions together."

Isolde stopped again. Something had shivered and stirred beyond the black wall in her mind. After a moment she went on. "Dying of the plague is . . . a hard death. Not the worst. I've seen many others just as bad. But hard enough."

The night stillness seemed, all at once, almost a living thing, the darkened moor beyond a tangible presence, waiting. "I would dream of them—of my grandmother . . . my father . . . and all the others. Every night, I'd dream of them being alive. And then I'd wake—and remember—and cry for them all over again. Con was a year younger than I was, just past twelve when he was crowned. He was terrified of it all, really, but he tried so desperately to hide it. To live up to the position of High King. The great Arthur's chosen heir. And he had no one. No one but me."

She blinked as the image of that twelve-year-old Con rose before her. Set on the king's throne, dressed in ermine robes, and given Arthur's famous sword. She swallowed. Then: "There's an old tale. The story of Oisin and Tír na nÓg—the Land of Youth. Of how Niamh of the Golden Hair, daughter of the king of Tír na nÓg, fell in love with Oisin, son of the warrior Finn. And how she carried him off to the Land of Youth."

Isolde paused, remembering, then recited the words of the old tale.

"Delightful is the land beyond all dreams,
Fairer than anything your eyes have ever seen.
There all the year the fruit is on the tree,
And all the year the bloom is on the flower.
Nor pain nor sickness knows the dweller there,
Death and decay come near him never more."

She stopped and shook her head slightly. "The story goes that Oisin was happy in the Land of Youth, as husband to Niamh of the Golden Hair. But only so long as he didn't remember the life he'd left behind. One day he did remember—and he couldn't bear the longing for his father, his kinsmen, and his home. And so he begged Niamh to let him return, only for a short time. She agreed—and he went back."

Isolde looked out at the night sky. "Mounted on a white steed that moved over sea and land and sky as though they were all the same. But when he came again to the land of his home, he found that a hundred years had gone by. All those he loved were dead. And he himself was a bent, withered old man."

Isolde stopped. The wind outside their niche was rising, she thought, and there was a chill dampness creeping into the air. There would likely be rain by morning.

"After Con and I were crowned there was so much to be done. Rebuilding the army, restoring the patrols on the Saxon borders, negotiating alliances between the dukes and petty kings. Con wasn't old enough to understand it all. And I couldn't help him—or Britain—if I was still mourning everyone who had died. So I decided to forget—as Oisin should have forgotten, if he'd wanted to stay happy with Niamh. Forget all the time that had gone before."

She broke off, eyes still on the icy-pale stars. "It was hard, at first. But now . . . I'm not sure I could remember if I tried."

There was a moment's silence, and while it lasted her words seemed to hang suspended in the air.

Trystan shifted position. "Have you thought that even if you find your goldsmith and he does have proof of Marche's treason, you may still fail in what you've set out to do? That you may not be able to convince anyone of what Marche plans—or at least not in time to stop him from handing Britain over to the Saxons?"

"Of course I have. But it makes no difference."

"Though you're called the Witch Queen?"

The night air was cold, and Isolde folded her hands together under her cloak. "That's no fault of Britain's. If Marche and his Saxon allies succeed, thousands will die. Thousands of farmers and shepherds and hill-folk who likely have scarcely even heard of Marche or Octa—or of Isolde, daughter of Modred."

The wind had blown a fresh covering of cloud across the moon, making it too dark, now, to see Trystan's face plainly. He was a shadowed outline against the rocks, nothing more. Isolde could feel his eyes on her, though, and he said, after a moment, "And if you die for it?"

Isolde lifted her shoulders. "The stars will still shine tomorrow."

The silence seemed to stretch on longer this time, and Isolde shivered, feeling the familiar tug of remembrance the words always brought. This time, though—maybe because of all she'd spoken of for the first time in seven years—she felt a sudden sweep of desolation, wide and empty and bleak as the surrounding moors. Safer, maybe, she thought, to lock away the times when she'd laughed until her ribs ached or heard a voice she loved that didn't come on the wind. Safer not to recall the girl who thought she'd one day tell the fire-tales to her own child. Because this self—the one she was now—never would.

Safer, but lonely, as well.

When she looked up, Trystan was watching her, an expression she couldn't read at the back of his eyes. Then he looked away and said abruptly, "It's been a long day, and tomorrow will likely be longer still. You'd better get what rest you can."

He must have felt Isolde's hesitation, for he laughed and said, "You needn't worry. Here." He bent to pick up the knife and tossed it over to lie at Isolde's feet. "I won't sleep again, but you can have charge of this, all the same." He paused, then added, almost as though reading her thoughts, "You can trust me. I gave you my word I'd see you safe from Marche's guard."

He stopped. It was still too dark to see his face, but she could feel his faint smile. "And apart from anything else, my younger sister would skin me alive if I broke a promise I'd made."

Isolde was so surprised she stopped, midway to reaching for the knife, and looked up at him again, straining her eyes to see into the shadowed dark. "You have a sister?"

Trystan was silent a beat, then he said, "That's seven questions you've had, now, to my one. But yes. In a way, at least. A long time ago."

WHEN ISOLDE WOKE, TRYSTAN WAS GONE. Trystan was gone, and she was surrounded by men, helmeted and armed—and one and all of them bearing on their shields Cornwall's badge. Marche's men.

Isolde sat up, every muscle stiff from a night on the cold, hard ground. For a moment, she felt nothing—nothing at all. And then, as suddenly as before, anger filled her like wine poured into a drinking horn, so powerful that for a moment the world spun around her and bright specks darted before her eyes, the blood roaring in her ears.

Slowly, the world steadied, and her vision cleared. She'd been right about the rain. A chill, blowing mist was driving down, dampening the leather tunics and war helms of the men. None she knew by name, though one she recognized by his broken nose and bruised, battered face as the man who had fled the beach the night before last.

They were all staring at her, as though uncertain what their next move would be, and Isolde slowly sat up and straightened, the anger hissing through her veins.

And he'd gone to make his dirty bargain while she was asleep. That thought brought a fresh burst of anger. That Trystan hadn't even had the courage to betray her face-to-face.

The men were still watching her—five of them, she now saw, standing in a half circle about the entrance to the sheltered niche where she lay. Then one of them—a short, heavily built man with a draggled beard and pale, watery eyes—stepped forward.

"Get up." His voice was rough. "You're coming with us— now."

Trystan must then, she thought, have succeeded. Must have bargained for Hereric without revealing that he himself was the escaped Saxon prisoner they sought. Isolde drew herself up. The tide of anger was still breaking in furious waves against her ribs, and she didn't even pause for thought before she spoke.

"Very well," she said. "But first—the man who sent you here to find me."

The heavily built man had started to approach her, but at that he stopped, the watery eyes narrowing. "Man? What man?"

"He's the prisoner you were sent out to find. The Saxon who escaped from Tintagel. Marche will reward you richly for his capture. And he must still be in the area. He was wounded. He can't have gotten far."

For a long moment, the bearded guardsman stared at her, as though trying to judge whether or not she spoke true. Then, abruptly, he turned to the men behind him. "Gorlan, Mael," he barked. "Go and search."

The bearded man—the leader, he must be—watched the two soldiers depart, his back momentarily turned to Isolde. Isolde shifted position, and as she did her hand brushed against something hard. The hilt of the knife, she realized. Tossed to her by Trystan the night before and now lying hidden by the skirt of her gown.

With an effort like fighting free of the tide's pull, she forced the anger back and tried to think, her eyes moving over the three remaining men. Too many for her to stand a chance of escape.

Still, if she could get the knife secreted in her girdle, she would at least be armed.

"All right. Come on."

The bearded man had turned back to her and spoke with grating impatience. As well as being the leader, he was oldest of the group by ten or fifteen years—about forty, at a guess.

Quickly, Isolde grasped the knife through the fabric of her skirt and rose to her feet, holding the knife fast in the folds of cloth, out of sight. She pulled her traveling cloak close about her, and then, under its cover, slid the knife upward until it was free of the fabric and she could grip the hilt. She nearly dropped it, then, and her heart lurched as the smooth bone of the handle slipped on her sweat-dampened palm. But at last she managed to slide the knife into her girdle. And without any of the men seeing what she'd done.

The next moment, though, she thought the effort would prove vain, for the leader of the party turned to his two remaining men and said curtly, "Hold her. I'm going to search her. She may be armed."

The bearded man's hands were powerful, covered with thick black hair to the wrist, the fingernails long and rimmed with dirt. The thought of having those hands on her, moving over her body—

Then she looked up, meeting the guardsman's eyes, and saw in their look enough to make cold fear crawl through her as she remembered what Trystan had said on the beach. And where their leader goes, she thought, the rest will surely follow. Like wolves bringing down a sheep after the leader of the pack has leapt for the animal's throat.

But, as with wolves, if the leader of the pack was injured or frightened, the rest might turn tail and run.

In a flash, her eyes had swept over the older guardsman, taking in the swollen joints of his knuckles, the slight stiffness in his gait as he advanced toward her. Then she drew herself erect.

"Stop." The word came out like the crack of breaking ice, and the man drew up sharply, at first startled, then angry.

Isolde drew in a slow breath, hoping, as never before, that her guess was true. Then, "Touch me," she said, "and I'll make you pay for it in pain. You've an ache in your joints, haven't you, when the rain and damp come as they have today? The dampness gets into your bones so that some days you can scarce grasp the hilt of your sword or raise an arm above your head."

She stopped. The man had sucked in his breath and was staring at her, a flicker of fear beginning to show at the back of the pale, watery eyes, though it warred, for the moment, with disbelief. The men behind him—the younger ones—were beginning to look frightened as well, shifting their weight and muttering uneasily among themselves. Isolde met the first man's gaze without flinching.

"Touch me," she said again. "Lay one finger on me, and I'll make you writhe on the ground like a worm. Your bones will turn to fire within you and your joints will swell and pop like the fat on a roasting pig." She stopped, her eyes still on the bearded man's. Then she lowered her voice. "Touch me," she said, very softly, "and I'll make you wish you'd never been born."

BOOK III

Chapter Twenty-one

THE AIR OF THE PRISON cell was as damp and vile as before, the reek of filth and mold and decay strong enough to catch at the back of Isolde's throat and make it hard to draw breath. Something squeaked and rustled amid the straw at her feet. It was cold, too, and she locked her arms tight about herself, trying to stop shivering.

She'd had neither food nor water, and her stomach felt hollow, her head light with hunger, her throat achingly dry. But they'd left her a saucer lamp—a wick floated in a small dish of oil—and the feeble light it cast was enough, at least, to show her the dank walls around her and the muck-strewn floor. Isolde glanced down at the place where she'd hidden the knife, burying it beneath a heap of dirt-encrusted straw. She might have frightened the guardsmen who'd captured her out of a search, but she couldn't count on the next men she confronted being as easily driven away.

And, she thought, sooner or later—

Almost as though the thought had summoned him, the bolts outside were drawn back and the door swung open. Isolde froze.

Chilled and exhausted, dirty and aching, she felt as though she'd used up every last grain of her courage in facing down the guards.

Marche hadn't spoken, but was advancing slowly toward her, step by step. Isolde's chest felt suddenly tight, and she had to clench her hands and fight with all her will to keep from stepping back, from pressing herself against the far wall. At last they stood face-to-face. Marche wore the scarlet-and-ermine robes of the High King, a broad fillet of gold around his brow. His dark eyes locked with hers. And then, still without speaking, he raised his hand and struck her, hard, across the face.

Pain shot though her and her vision darkened, but she didn't lose consciousness. Isolde felt him hit her again, and then throw her to the ground, felt his hands fumble, then savagely rip at the bodice of her gown. She thought, It's going to happen again. And then, with a sick certainty, This time I'm not going to be able to bear it without crying out.

Isolde gritted her teeth, her eyes still tightly closed. But nothing happened. And then she felt Marche kick her, furiously, in the stomach, so that she rolled over and almost did cry out with the pain. She opened her eyes. And saw. And understood.

The blow had knocked the breath out of her, and as she struggled for air, blinking back tears, she seemed to hear Dera's voice, slow and drugged with the poppy syrup as it had been three nights before. I was lucky, though. *Heard afterwards from another girl what happens if he can't manage with you at all.*

Marche lashed out and struck her again, a savage blow to the head that made her vision blur again. Isolde gritted her teeth, bracing herself for another blow, knowing that there was absolutely nothing to stop him from treating her the same. And then—

A memory came unbidden into Isolde's mind. Marche, breath reeking of ale and drunken vomit, hands fumbling in the dark. And gasping out a name. *Modred.*

With an effort that left her dizzy and breathless, Isolde pulled herself straight. Her stomach still felt hollow, her throat clogged with fear, but she looked up at Marche and said, her lip curling, "Go ahead and beat me . . . if it makes you feel . . . more of a man. I'll enjoy . . . telling the men you place on guard . . . just what made you strike those blows."

Marche's face went red, then faded, abruptly, to the mottled white of utter fury. With a wordless grunt of rage, he seized Isolde with one hand, scooping up a handful of filthy straw from the floor with the other, then forced her lips apart and ground the muck savagely into her mouth.

Isolde choked, gagging, just as the figure of a guardsman appeared in the cell door way.

"My lord. There's a messenger come in for you. Rode in just a few moments ago. Says it's urgent and can't wait."

For a long moment, Marche didn't move but stood staring down at Isolde, his breath still coming fast and hard. Then he dropped his hold on Isolde's arm and stepped back, his jaw tight.

"You think I'd dirty myself on you in any case? You can stay here and rot, for all I care, until you face trial for witchcraft." Marche paused, his lips twisting in a small, tight smile. "The hearings will begin tomorrow morning in the king's council hall."

ISOLDE SANK DOWN ONTO THE STRAW, leaning her head back against the chill, moisture-slick wall and closing her eyes. Her lip was bleeding, and she could feel a swelling bruise on her cheek. The muscles of her stomach still burned, and her ribs felt as though they were on fire—though she judged that none, at least, were broken. The pain was worse if she tried to fill her lungs completely. So she sat without moving, trying to keep her breaths shallow and light.

A trial for witchcraft, she thought. I might as well have let Marche batter me to death here.

She opened her eyes and looked at the flickering saucer lamp. In this windowless underground cell, she had no way of knowing the hour or judging the passage of time, save by the burning of the oil. But morning couldn't be more than a few hours away. A few hours, then, and she would be tried, and condemned, and killed. Stoned to death. Or burned. For she had no doubt of the trial's purpose. It would serve as an excuse for Marche to kill her, that was all.

Isolde watched a curl of smoke rise, hover, then dissolve in the cold, dank air. She felt . . . nothing. Nothing at all. She shivered. Frighteningly numb.

In the end, she must have fallen into a half-waking doze, for when the sound of the bolts being drawn back came again, her head snapped up. If Marche had returned—

But it was not Marche who stood in the doorway. Isolde's heart had started to pound, and she shut her eyes and repeated the words, trying to steady herself. *Not Marche.*

"Father Nenian."

The priest stood uncertainly in the doorway an instant longer, then came forward, blinking as his eyes adjusted to the dark. His face looked drawn with distress.

"Lady Isolde. I'm more sorry than I can say to see you here. To see you—"

He broke off. With an effort, Isolde drew the torn edges of her gown together. Her swollen mouth made speaking painful, but she raised herself to meet the priest and said, "You shouldn't be here yourself, Father. If it's true I'm to be tried for a witch, there's danger for anyone seen to speak with me."

Father Nenian hesitated. He had held a loaf of bread, wrapped in cloth, and a jug of wine hugged tight to his body, and now he seemed to remember them, for he set them down on the floor before saying, "I thought, Lady Isolde, that you might wish the comfort of confession. Before . . . before tomorrow."

"The comfort of confession?" Isolde repeated. Her mouth twisted. "You mean in case I wish to confess to witchcraft, you can offer me absolution before I burn?"

Father Nenian drew back slightly at her tone. Then he said, quietly, "I have never thought or called you witch, Lady Isolde."

"I'm sorry, Father." The effort of moving stretched her bruised ribs, and Isolde sucked in a sharp breath, but she touched the priest's hand. "I'm sorry," she said softly again. "I know you have not. Though I've often wondered why."

Father Nenian's eyes met hers, their gaze clear and bright as the water of a spring pool. "I was given to the Church when I was five, raised by priests and holy men. I know little of the evils of the world. But I do know of good." He stopped, then said, simply, "I see goodness in you, Lady Isolde."

For a moment, Isolde's eyes stung with unexpected tears, and when she could speak, she said, "Thank you, Father. And thank you for the food, as well." She lifted the jug of wine and took a swallow, the liquid cool in her parched throat.

Father Nenian waved the thanks away, his face still anxious. "I only wish, my lady, that I could do something more for you."

Isolde wondered for a moment whether she ought to tell Father Nenian of Marche's betrayal. Whether he might be able to persuade the rest of the king's council that the High King had formed an alliance with the Saxon Kentish king. Far more likely, though, she thought, that they would say he'd been ensorcelled by the Witch Queen. Or that Marche would simply have him killed.

So in the end she shook her head. "You're a good man. And the people here will have need of good men in the days to come. Don't throw your life away along with mine."

Father Nenian was silent, then he said, a little uncertainly, "If you should wish the rite of confession, Lady Isolde—"

Isolde shook her head. "No," she said. "But I thank you again, Father. You were kind to come."

Chapter Twenty-two

MARCHE STOOD ON A HALF dais erected at the head of the room before the curtained doorway that led to the courtyard. He wore, still, the gold fillet about his brow, and his ermine-lined cloak was flung back from his shoulders; his arms were half raised. His voice echoed harshly in the silent, listening hall.

"We are gathered here to consider the charge of witchcraft and sorcery brought against the lady Isolde."

The words seemed to come at Isolde through a muffling fog. The emptiness, the frightening numbness, were still there. But as Marche spoke, she thought that if she had been able to feel anything at all, she would have felt a kind of savage satisfaction at seeing him avoid her gaze and keep his face turned away from the corner where she had been set to stand.

The king's council hall felt cold in the gray light of morning, the fire in the great central hearth unlit. The benches were as crowded as before, the faces as taut and watchful as when Isolde had last entered this same room. Not even a week ago, she thought. It seemed a lifetime.

After Father Nenian had gone, she'd not slept again, and so had been awake and at least braced when the guardsman had come to bring her here. She'd not been allowed water for washing, and she could smell the odor of the prison cell clinging about her gown and tangled hair. The bruise on her cheekbone ached, and her ribs still throbbed fiercely with every breath, but she forced herself to stand straight, to let her eyes move over the rows of dukes and petty kings, most of them surrounded by knots of their men-at-arms.

Owain of Powys sat in a place on Marche's right, near the head of the room, his pale, handsome face as smooth as always, though his finely arched brows were drawn together in a slight frown. Beside him, Huel, son of Coel, looked tired, his eyes puffy with lack of sleep—or it might have been with drink. But his mouth was set in an angry line, and he stared fixedly at Isolde, his neck rigid, his body lance-straight.

Beyond the layers of numbness and fatigue, Isolde felt a sense of dizzying unreality, as though she might wake at any moment and find all this simply a dream. It was a moment before she realized that Marche was speaking again.

"The first witness I give you to testify to the truth of the charge is Marcia, serving woman to the lady Isolde."

He seated himself, subsiding into a chair of heavily carved oak that Con had used in sessions of the council. There was a slight stir at the back of the room, and Isolde saw Marcia get to her feet. For a moment, Marcia's gaze fastened on Isolde, and a look of smoldering hatred crossed her thin, sharp-featured face. And then she swept on to stand facing the rest of the room.

Marcia, Isolde thought. Of course. She'd have fallen over herself in eagerness to testify. And I fairly placed every weapon she'll need straight into her hands.

Indeed, the maidservant's testimony was much what Isolde would have expected. She told of the scrying bowl Isolde kept in her rooms, with its black symbols and heathen charms. And, her voice sharp with malice, her small eyes alight, she told of how the lady Isolde, on the night before her marriage to Marche, had looked into the scrying waters, cursed all that was holy, and called on Satan, summoning him as her master and lord.

Marcia couldn't, though, resist improving on the story. When she had finished speaking of the summoning, she lowered her voice, her eyes sweeping over the rows of watching men. "And I . . . I saw him come, too. I opened the door after she thought I'd gone, and I saw the Dark One come and take her in his foul embrace. I felt the chill as he swept through the air, smelled sulfur and brimstone as he passed. And I heard his cloven hooves clatter on the stone floor."

Several of those listening from the rows of benches drew in sharp breaths at that, and the room buzzed with angry mutterings and stirrings even after Marcia had been dismissed and waved back to her place at the back of the hall. Isolde could feel the same hunger for bloodshed she had felt once before in this hall. Though this time the death-hunger was directed at her.

Marche rose to his feet again, his heavy face impassive, though there was a look of angry satisfaction in the set of his mouth. "The next witness I would offer the king's council is Lord Huel, who with myself witnessed how, with her evil arts, the lady Isolde did vilely murder his father, King Coel."

His angry, red-rimmed eyes still fixed on Isolde, Huel rose to his feet and faced the room. He didn't speak, though, and after a moment Marche said, "My lord Huel?"

Isolde saw Huel's throat contract as he swallowed. Then he nodded jerkily. "Yes. So she did."

Marche made an impatient movement with one hand, and the grave mask of his face cracked, briefly, as a spasm of irritation twisted his brow. Both movements were instantly controlled, though there was an edge to his tone as he said, "And will you tell us, then, what you saw?"

Isolde's mind had begun to drift again. Maybe it was thirst and hunger that made her head feel light, strangely disconnected to the rest of her body. Or maybe she had simply gone beyond fear. She scarcely heard Huel's reply, his testimony of how he had seen her take his father's hand and whisper spells under her breath. Huel's face is so like Coel's, she thought, and yet so unlike, as well. The courage was there, and the determination, but none of his father's intelligence or imagination. Or, for that matter, kindness.

Still as though from a long way off, Isolde heard again a ripple of movement and talk as Huel stepped down, and she saw several of the men turn to her with angry stares. And in none of the faces did she see a shadow of uncertainty or doubt. They condemned me long ago, she thought. From the moment I was crowned. This scene has been written, the verdict already decided these seven years.

She still felt nothing, though, and the men's anger hardly touched her. It was, she thought, as though she were still imprisoned. Trapped in a numbing fog—or in a tower of glass, like the Fisher King in the old tales.

Marche called others. Serving women to testify of the spells Isolde cast as she gathered herbs at the full moon. Of how she had enchanted Cabal, King Constantine's hunting hound, made him her familiar—a corporeal body for her master, Satan, to possess. Con, Isolde thought distantly, would have knocked the witness's teeth down her throat, woman or no, for that. Then— Isolde felt a distant flash of bitter amusement—the guardsmen who'd captured and brought her here took the stand, telling of how she'd threatened to see their leader blasted with writhing pain.

"And next I would call before you Gwyn, sometimes maid

in Tintagel's kitchens. Who did, five nights ago, help the lady
Isolde to deliver a child of a harlot in the stables here." Marche
paused. "And with her the lady Nest, who has in her charge the
woman herself. A slattern and a whore. And as guilty of witchcraft as the lady Isolde."

Isolde's heart contracted. Nest's harsh, blunt-featured face
was flushed with barely suppressed satisfaction. The girl Gwyn
followed on Nest's heels, looking frightened. And then there
was Dera, her arm held tight in Nest's grasp; she was ashen pale
beneath the wine-colored mark on her cheek, all the animation
gone from her face, leaving it slack and gray.

For a moment, Dera's eyes met Isolde's, but Isolde could read
in the look the other woman gave her nothing but exhaustion
and fear. Dera looked away almost at once, and as her eyes fell
on Marche, waiting at the head of the room, Isolde saw her jerk
instinctively back. Only a vicious tug from Nest brought her
forward the rest of the way, into the open space at the front of
the room.

Abruptly, the cold, numbing mists were swept away, the glass
walls about Isolde cracked and fell. She whirled in her place,
rounding on Marche and speaking for the first time since she'd
been brought into the hall.

"You—" She stopped, her hands clenched, fighting for
breath, unable to think of a name vile enough.

A tide of hot, furious color ran up Marche's throat as his eyes
met hers, and she saw his hands fasten, white-knuckled, on the
carved arms of the chair.

"Keep silent!"

Isolde drew in her breath. "Am I to be allowed no voice, then,
at my own trial?"

Marche's eyes narrowed, dents appearing at the corners of
his mouth. "If you think—" he began.

But before he could finish, Owain of Powys had interrupted

him, lifting a hand in a call for silence. "No." He turned to Isolde, and for a long moment the luminous hazel-green eyes were intent on hers. But before Isolde could read the expression in their gaze—or wonder why Owain should suddenly speak out on her behalf—he had turned back to Marche. "The lady Isolde must, in fairness, be allowed to speak. I propose we allow the girl— and the lady Nest—to say what they have to say. And then give Lady Isolde the chance to say whatever she wishes, as well."

Isolde was distantly surprised to hear a murmur of agreement from the rest of the room. She would have expected the council to side with Marche. But she had small attention to spare for Owain or any of the other men there. Her attention was fixed on Dera, standing in Nest's grasp and staring at Marche. She looked, Isolde thought, with a prickle along her spine, like a bird hypnotized by a snake, and Isolde saw her raise a hand to her breast, the fingers tracing the cross-shaped scar, hidden, now, by her gown.

Isolde heard little more of Gwyn's testimony than she had of all the rest. Prompted by Nest, the girl gave a stammering account of the birth of Dera's child. Of how she suspected Isolde had lied about how the child had died. Of how Isolde had tried to trick Father Nenian into burying an unbaptized child in consecrated ground.

And then Nest herself spoke. She wore a richly dyed gown of deep yellow, seeded with pearls, and her coarse black hair was held back by a pearl-studded net of golden-yellow thread. With a quick jerk, she forced Dera round to face the room. "You can see the witch-mark plain on the woman's face," she said. "And she's known among the whole of the army as one who tries to bait and entrap honest men. With the aid of the Witch Queen, she killed her own child. It must have been demon-spawned. And . . ."

There was more, but Isolde didn't hear it. Her hands

clenched on the folds of her gown, she waited until Nest had done, then drew in her breath and stepped a little forward, facing the room.

The hall went abruptly silent, and Isolde let her eyes move over the rows of hostile faces and watching eyes before she began.

"Every one of you here," she said, "was born of a woman. A woman who labored to bring you into the world, just as Dera, the woman before you, labored to birth her child four nights since." She stopped. Her voice was shaking slightly, but she steadied it and went on, her eyes once more sweeping up and down the benches that lined the walls.

"And if any of you," she said, "if any single man here, thinks that Dera wantonly killed her newborn babe, then you shame the woman who bore you and birthed you and gave you life."

She stopped. Another stir of movement and sound swept through the room, though the murmurs were different, somehow. For the first time, Isolde caught a faint uneasiness mingling with the charged tension of the crowd, and she thought, too, that some of the watching faces looked slightly uncertain. Marche must have felt it, too, for he rose to his feet, silencing the whispers and putting an end to all movement.

"I bring forward Madoc of Gwynedd. He, if any, has good cause to know the power of the queen's arts." Again he turned to Isolde, his eyes black and chill as stone. "The devil's whore has spread her thighs for Satan. And in return he has granted her the power to bring down and destroy honorable men."

There was a brief, expectant silence. And then, from the curtained doorway at the head of the room stepped Madoc of Gwynedd himself. Even as she caught her breath at the sight of him, Isolde thought, with another icy chill, that this final stroke had been masterfully executed. Carried out with the same calculation and skill that had won Marche countless fields of battle—and now won for him the High King's throne.

The burns that covered Madoc's face and hands had scarcely began to heal. His lashes and eyebrows were gone, and the skin of his face was red and angry, blistered and puffed. The wounds dragged his features askew, making his face like a travesty of a human head, a child's clumsy model in clay. Isolde could feel the waves of shock rippling through the hall, as Madoc's eyes, glittering dark and nearly lost in the pockets of blistered, oozing flesh, swept over the rows of his fellow petty kings. Then he spoke. His voice was cracked and hoarse, scarcely above a whisper, but it carried to every corner of the silent room.

"My lords. All of you saw how, in this very room, the traitor's daughter—the Witch Queen—threatened me for accusing her of being what she is." He stopped, throwing his head back so that the pale morning light fell full on his ghastly face. "Look at me. Look at what she has done in revenge. And then"—again the dark eyes went round the hall—"then, when you have gazed fully on what I now am, I challenge any man here to look me in the face and tell me she is not guilty as charged of sorcery and magic arts."

There was a burst of sound, beginning as a ripple of angry murmurs and then swelling to calls and shouts. Every eye in the room turned toward her, and Isolde saw several of the men surge up from their places, hands moving to clench the hilts of knives and swords, like wolves moving in for the kill.

Even in the midst of all else, Isolde's mouth twisted at the irony of it—that Marche should with one hand set up Madoc's ravaging injuries as a sign from God that he himself should be crowned High King. And with the other hand present those same burns as proof that she, as Satan's mistress, was capable of punishing any who incurred her anger or threatened her with harm.

Madoc of Gwynedd raised his arms for silence, and the room went abruptly still, the men frozen, half of them sitting, half already on their feet. And in the stillness, Madoc's voice rasped and crackled like autumn leaves, the word somehow more powerful, more carrying than a shout.

"I say the filthy she-devil should burn. Burn and go to her master in a fire like the one she set on me."

Dera's face had gone a shade paler; a sheen of sweat broken out on her brow. Most women in her place, four days after a birth, would be still in bed. And if she was condemned now, she would be thrown into the cell along with Isolde to await whatever sentence was decided here. And to be once again at the mercy of Marche, as well.

Isolde turned slowly away from Dera to meet Marche's dark gaze, and Isolde felt her stomach clench. And why, she thought, couldn't I have stayed numb?

There was only one path left her, though, one choice to be made. She forced herself not to break away from Marche's look.

"Let Dera go," she said, "and I'll confess to what you charge."

Chapter Twenty-three

I T WAS OVER EVEN FASTER than when the council had named
Marche High King. Dera was released, with the injunction
to leave Tintagel within the day. She passed out of the hall with
a quick, final look at Isolde, in which Isolde read—what? Relief?
Thankfulness? Fear on Isolde's behalf? Then she was gone. And
the Witch Queen was sentenced to die. To burn at the stake at
dawn the following day.

Even after the verdict had been spoken, the petty kings
and their men-at-arms continued to mutter angrily under their
breath, a few even surging forward toward Isolde, to be barely
held back by Marche's men, raising spears and shields. And
through it all Isolde stood, motionless and silent, and tried to
realize, fully, that her life was in fact to end the following day.
No chance, she thought, of another escape. *It's over. Marche
has won.*

She saw Owain of Powys turn to Marche and speak, though
the angry shouts and mutterings of the crowd covered the
words. Marche nodded abruptly, and then Owain threaded a
way through the crowd to Isolde's side.

"Lady Isolde." He sketched something almost like a bow. "I have offered to see you back to—" he stopped. Then, "To see you away from this place," he finished smoothly.

But just before they left the hall, Madoc of Gwynedd stepped into their path and stood, immovable, until the men-at-arms who had walked before Owain came to an uncertain halt. Madoc's eyes met Isolde's, and his jaw contracted, stretching the angry, blistered skin.

"Were it my choice," he said in a voice like metal rasping on stone, "you would die a worse death still."

Both hatred and fear Isolde had faced before, countless times in these seven years. And been herself sometimes angry and sometimes afraid. Now, though, meeting Madoc's black, lashless gaze, seeing fully the extent of the burns, she felt, all at once, nothing but pity—pity and a sense of waste.

She said steadily, "Your wounds must, I know, be causing you a great deal of pain, so I will forgive what you've just said. Maybe when you are healed you'll remember your fight with Marche—and be able to tell the difference between witchcraft and drug."

Then she turned away.

OWAIN KEPT SILENT UNTIL THEY HAD reached the block of prison cells. Only then, when the door to Isolde's own cell was open before them, did he turn to his men-at-arms and say, "Leave us."

The men bowed obedience and retreated to the far end of the corridor, out of earshot, though not out of sight, and Owain turned back to Isolde. "I'm sorry, my lady, to have to return you to such a place as this."

Isolde looked at him, uncertain what his intent had been in escorting her here—or in keeping her safe from the anger of his fellow councilmen. With Dera's release, though, the numbness, the empty indifference seemed to have settled over her once again, and she found that she couldn't rouse herself to care very much, one way or the other.

She lifted her shoulders. "It hardly matters. My residence here will be quite short. I'll be released permanently in another day."

Owain's hazel-green eyes were fixed on hers, and Isolde, out of habit more than anything else, tried automatically to read what lay behind their look. There was, she thought, a kind of speculative calculation in Owain's gaze, as though he were trying to judge whether to smile or to remain sober and grave. At last, though, he said, his voice still low, "A release—one of another kind—might be arranged instead, my lady."

"Arranged?" Isolde repeated.

Owain was quiet for a beat before he replied. He wore today a tunic of fine blue-dyed wool, the hem and sleeves shot with threads of silver, and the dagger at his belt was inlaid with garnets and seed pearls. He fingered the jeweled hilt idly before saying, "I admired your husband greatly, Lady Isolde. My lord King Constantine, I mean."

Isolde raised her brows slightly. "Did you?"

Owain looked slightly disconcerted, but he said, still toying with the jeweled knife, "Yes. Admired, and loved him, as well. I cannot think he would feel anything but sorrow if he could see you in this place."

Through the numbing mist, Isolde felt a stab of the old ache of grief. She tightened her hands. No, she thought. I'll never forgive myself if I give way to tears in front of this man—whatever he intends by this now.

Owain went on, "And so, as Constantine's loyal man, I feel it my duty to offer his widow the aid I know my lord king would have wished."

Isolde looked past him into the tiny, squalid prison cell, at the damp walls and piles of filthy straw. She seemed to hear Marche's voice, days ago, saying almost exactly those same words, offering her the same protection in the name of loyalty to Con. Then she'd been angry. That seemed impossibly long ago. But she was beginning to feel a galling impatience at Owain's presence—an overwhelming wish that she might be left on her own.

She turned, looking up into Owain's lean, classically beautiful face, and said, "Lord Owain, I am to die in the morning. I have, at this moment, little patience for listening to ambition parading itself as loyalty and goodwill. If you have anything to say to me, say it."

She thought there was a flash of anger in Owain's gaze, a brief tightening of the corners of his soft, finely molded mouth. He raised and lowered his shoulders, though, and said, "You do me an injustice, I think, Lady Isolde. But I will speak plainly, as you wish." He paused, his hazel-green eyes half veiled, and fingered the hilt of his dagger again. Then: "The men on the king's council condemned you to die, Lady Isolde, because they are afraid. Afraid of what a woman with the power of witchcraft might do. But I . . ."

Owain raised his eyes to hers and smiled. He stood close to her, leaning slightly forward, and she noticed for the first time that his teeth were slightly pointed, and that his smile was predatory. "I would not be afraid, Lady Isolde."

He paused, as though waiting for a response. When Isolde said nothing, he went on. "A woman skilled in witchcraft might be of high value to a man. You could tell who among your followers were loyal and who were likely to betray. Know in advance every detail of what your enemy planned." His jaw hardened. "Cut his throat and slaughter his men before ever he knew he was under attack."

Owain stopped again and seemed to come back to himself, his eyes losing their inward cast and focusing once more on

Isolde. Then: "Especially if, as well as a wife, she was also High Queen."

Isolde looked up into the refined, almost delicate, face of the man beside her. He was smiling, but his features seemed all at once sharper, edged with something unpleasant and hard. I did, she thought, ask for plain speaking. Though I wonder whether he can genuinely expect me to be flattered or pleased.

Owain had gone on, speaking more quickly now, his face eager, his hazel-green eyes alight. "What I propose, Lady Isolde, is a bargain—a bargain of advantage to us both. Help me to take Marche's place as High King, and I will both save your life and allow you to resume your place as Britain's High Queen."

Through the layers of numbness and fatigue, Isolde struggled to think. After all that had happened since she'd fled Tintagel— after being captured by Hereric and Bran, seeing Bran killed by Marche's guardsman, sleeping on the moor with Trystan under the stars—the world of betrayal and jockeying for power that surrounded the High Kingship seemed strangely unreal. To buy herself time, she asked, "And if I refuse?"

"Refuse?" Owain's gaze narrowed slightly, and a hard edge crept into the light, pleasant tone. "Death by burning is an unpleasant end, Lady Isolde." And then he stopped, and smiled again, showing the row of pointed teeth. He reached out a hand and ran his fingertips lightly down the length of her arm. "But I'm sure you're not going to refuse. I credit you with more intelligence than that."

Isolde slowly inclined her head, resisting the urge to jerk away from his touch. She wasn't afraid of Owain. He was weak— vicious—but she doubted he had the courage to do her bodily harm. This was her chance, though, if she chose to take it, to tell him what she knew of Marche's treason. She opened her mouth to speak, then stopped.

What made her hold her tongue she didn't know, unless

it was a slight uneasiness in Owain's manner, a caution in the hazel-green eyes, as though there were something he was trying to conceal, even as he worked to win her sympathy and trust. He might be willing to persuade the other petty kings to condemn Marche as a traitor. Or he might, she thought, simply make his own arrangements with the Saxons in Marche's place. His scruples—and his ambition—are about at the level of Marche's own.

Aloud, she said, "And how would you go about overthrowing Marche? Since you speak of wedding me, I assume you must intend to see him dead and not only dethroned."

She'd tried to make her voice neutral, but some slight edge must still have crept into her tone, for Owain's eyes narrowed once again, the soft mouth thinning.

"Don't tell me, Lady Isolde, that you would not rejoice to see Marche dead at your feet."

Would I? Isolde thought. She shivered.

Owain had gone on, speaking intently, his hands clasped behind his back. The hour could not be much past midday, but here in this underground corridor it might as well have been night. Torches burned at intervals along the walls, shadowing Owain's chiseled face and hollowing his eyes.

"The matter could, as I say, be arranged," he was saying. "The king's council is already in conflict with Marche. As you know, it had been decided that in the face of the threatened Saxon invasion, our forces would be spread out along Cornwall's border forts to meet the attack wherever it comes. But Marche is now urging that we mass our troops here, at Tintagel, and wait to move until we know more of where the Saxons plan to strike first. He's ridden out now with a battalion of his men on a scouting expedition, seeking to gain intelligence of the movements of the Saxon troops. And that means that the rest of the king's council and the troops still stationed here—"

But the rest of what Owain said was lost on Isolde. A sudden, blinding light of understanding had broken on her. She was remembering Trystan's disbelief in a united Saxon invasion force—how he had said that Octa would as soon ally with Cerdic as with a rabid dog. Of course, she thought. I should have seen it from the first. I doubted at the time the truth of the message Rhys brought the council, the night Marche was elected High King. I should have realized that no such united attack was planned. The story was a ruse to keep the king's council and their fighting men here. Marche's alliance must be with Octa and Octa alone.

Owain was still speaking, and Isolde broke off in her thoughts abruptly, her attention caught when he said, "Marche has appointed me leader of the troops stationed here at Tintagel in place of the man King Constantine made his commander in chief. And I—"

Isolde broke in. "You mean you've been appointed commander in Brychan's place?"

"Brychan?" A faint crease appeared between Owain's brows. "Yes, I think that was the man's name. Never mind him. He's no longer of any importance." He made a dismissive gesture. "What matters is that I now have control of the king's force that remains here."

He stopped and drew a step nearer, his voice softening, his hazel-green eyes turning liquid and warm. "Marche knows nothing of how to keep a wife content. But I"—he raised a hand and lightly traced with one finger the line from Isolde's cheekbone to her jaw—"I would serve you, Lady Isolde, and treasure you as my lord Constantine must have done."

It might have been the mention of Con—or the soft, insinuating touch—or the casual dismissal of Brychan. But all at once, Isolde's temper snapped, and she pushed Owain's hand violently away.

"I thank you, Lord Owain, for your offer. But I doubt you could fill Con's place—either on the throne or anywhere else you might try. And I've had enough of treason and betrayal and lies."

It was likely, she thought, that this was the first time he had ever been refused by a woman. The first time his easy charm had failed to gain him whatever he willed. For a moment, Owain's face was blank. Then a tide of angry color swept up from the embroidered collar of his tunic, turning his face an ugly red.

"You—" he began. His hands had balled themselves into fists, and for a moment Isolde thought she'd misjudged him and that he would strike her after all. But then he stopped, his eyes darting past Isolde and locking on something at the far end of the corridor. Isolde turned as well, then froze.

Trystan. He was on his feet, but just barely. His head hung limply to his chest, and his arms were stretched painfully between the soldiers that held him on either side. His tunic had been half ripped open, and the wound on his shoulder must have opened up again, for the sleeve was wet and red. His chest and what Isolde could see of his face were mottled with bruises.

Dragging Trystan between them, the two soldiers approached, and Isolde saw with a chill, hollow feeling that they were not part of Marche's guard, but instead two of Con's men. They made brief gestures of obeisance to Owain, and then the older of them, a dark man with thinning hair and a spare, narrow build, said, "My lord. This is the Saxon—the prisoner who escaped four nights ago."

For a moment, Owain was silent, his face still flushed, his eyes dark with anger. Then, abruptly, he seized Isolde's arm and gave her a sharp push that sent her through the doorway of the cell and nearly knocked her to the ground.

"Lock him up with the Witch Queen," he spat. "He can die with her tomorrow."

Chapter Twenty-four

ISOLDE STOOD STARING DOWN AT Trystan's still form. The flickering saucer lamp cast only a dim light over the cell, but it was enough to show that his injuries were even worse than she'd thought. His mouth was swollen, bloodied, and torn, and one eye was puffed and black, the lid smeared with blood. The torn fabric of his tunic gaped open at the throat, showing patchwork of purpling bruises, each one the size of Isolde's hand.

Isolde, staring at the bruises, thought, I've failed. Marche is still High King. There will still be an invasion. I will burn at the stake tomorrow. And now . . . Now Trystan will die, too.

As though the thought had somehow reached him, unconscious as he was, Trystan stirred slightly, a grimace of pain momentarily twisting his face, though his eyes remained closed.

Isolde felt guilt settle like a stone weight over her chest, and she thought, How could I have done it? How could I? I must have known what would happen, when I sent the guardsmen after him. Told them who he was.

She remembered again the blinding rush of fury that had filled her, but the memory seemed now impossibly distant, and as frighteningly incomprehensible as though it belonged to another lifetime. She'd trusted Trystan—warily, but trusted him all the same. Felt a kind of strangely matched alliance between them, the night they camped on the open moor and Trystan had spoken of Cyn and Bran. But to do what she had . . .

I might as well have gone mad, she thought. Whatever he did, however much he betrayed me, I wouldn't choose to be the one to condemn him to die.

That, though, was just what she had done.

Trystan stirred again, this time letting out a faint groan, and Isolde dropped to her knees beside him, drew in her breath, and began to take stock of his injuries. It was easier than she'd expected—easier than when she'd probed his leg for broken bones back in the shoreline cave. And having her hands occupied helped—a little—to keep her from thinking.

Though there was little she could do for him here—and without her store of medicines. And in any case, there was small point in dressing the wounds of a man sentenced to die at dawn. Still, she pressed lightly against Trystan's ribs, then gently flexed his fingers and the joints of his arms. No bones broken that she could tell, though the rest of his body was a virtual map of pain. She moved on, running her fingers gently over his skull, searching for swellings or breaks.

But even as she noted the hard knot of swollen flesh behind Trystan's ear—caused, she judged, by a club or maybe the toe of a booted foot—she was replaying in her mind the scene with Owain and castigating herself for losing her temper with him, as well. She thought, I ought to have pretended at least to consider his offer. Found a way to use him to get free of this place.

If what she suspected was true and the Saxon threat came from Octa alone, however much he was working in alliance with Marche . . .

In that case, she thought, our forces might stand a chance of winning the battle. If only they had warning in advance.

Isolde sat back on her heels, staring down at her clenched hands. Warned in advance, the army assembled here might be able to battle off another Saxon attack. But she could no more bring the king's council word of Marche's treason than she could heal Trystan's hurts. Or turn back time and unspeak the words that had brought him here.

Some slight sound or movement on Trystan's part made her look up to find that the unblackened eyelid had flickered open. The bruised eye was swollen shut, but the visible one was staring unseeingly straight ahead with something of the stark, frightening look Isolde had seen before. Then, abruptly, the look was gone, and the blue gaze cleared, focusing on her face.

For a long moment, Isolde's gaze met his, and she wondered what they could say to each other now—and whether he knew that he had her to blame for his capture, and the beating he'd gotten from Marche's guard.

At last, when the silence seemed to stretch on and on, Isolde said, "You're lucky. I don't think your ribs are broken. Only badly bruised."

Trystan had lifted his head slightly, but at that he sank back onto the dirt-caked straw, his eye slipping once more closed. He was all but motionless, though Isolde could feel him fighting for control.

"Lucky," he repeated. His voice sounded slightly hoarse. "Yes, right. A broken rib or two and I'd start to feel really sorry for myself."

The unblackened eye opened, and his gaze swept the windowless room. "Christ," he muttered. He shook his head. "The same bloody cell, even."

His gaze returned to Isolde and he watched her a moment in silence. Then he said, "That was quite a performance you gave

Marche's guard out on the moor. I thought the one that had to ride with you on his saddle would fall off the back of the horse trying to keep away."

Isolde had been brushing bits of straw from the skirt of her gown, but she stopped and looked up sharply. "You saw that?"

Trystan jerked his head in a brief nod. "From the copse of trees on the hill—just above where you were."

Isolde waited, but he said nothing more. No explanation, no excuse for what had happened. Though no angry recriminations, either, for her setting the guardsman on his trail—for all he must know, if he'd seen the whole of her confrontation with the guard.

Finally Isolde asked, breaking the taut silence that had settled between them once again, "Is Hereric free?"

Trystan's shoulders moved slightly and he said, without looking at her, "So far as I know."

Isolde waited again, but once more he was silent, his gaze fixed on the stones above their heads. She felt a brief twist of the old anger. "That's all you have to say to me?"

"No. But anything else would be a waste of breath."

Isolde frowned. "What do you mean?"

"Never mind." Trystan lay still another moment, as though gathering strength, then with another half-suppressed groan pulled himself to a sitting position, knees raised. His one open eye, flat, now, and hard, met hers, and he said, "Besides, I'd say the score is about even, wouldn't you?"

Isolde felt hollow sickness curl through her once again. It would have been cowardly to look away—but there was nothing, either, that she could say to him. And so she kept silent, her eyes on his.

After a long moment, Trystan nodded. "All right. We'd better think about how we're going to get free."

Isolde stared at him blankly. "Get free?"

"Yes, get free." Trystan's voice was edged with impatience. "I've no intention of sitting here with my hands folded, waiting to be killed. If I'm going to die I'd rather it was trying to escape." His torn mouth stretched in a grim smile. "If nothing else, it will likely be a faster death than whatever they'd have otherwise planned."

That, Isolde thought, is true enough. "But how—?"

Trystan shrugged again. "The same way I did before, I suppose. It will be easier with two of us. Though this time I'll have to try it without the knife."

Isolde's gaze moved from his bruised face to the sword cut on his arm and from there to the bruises on his chest and throat. She didn't know how he could hope to overpower a guard—or go more than ten paces without falling down.

It didn't matter, though. She thought, It's as he says. Better to die trying to get free than to wait here like sheep marked for slaughter. Slowly, she said, "I have a knife. The one you gave me."

ISOLDE STOOD STILL IN THE CENTER of the cell. They'd agreed to wait until nightfall, or as near as they could judge from the burning of the lamp, and the flame had flared and then died a few moments ago, just after she'd woken Trystan from a deep, exhausted sleep. Now the moist, chill darkness of the room seemed to clog Isolde's throat and press against her eyes, and her final exchange with Trystan rang in her ears.

"Scream," he'd told her. "As loud as you can."

"Is that what you did before?"

"Yelled, anyway. Loud enough that the guards opened the door to see what was wrong."

Now, staring unseeingly in the direction of the cell door, Isolde went over once more what—they had to hope—would happen. Hearing her scream, the guards would open the door, though probably one would remain stationed in the hall while his fellow stepped inside to investigate. And Trystan, standing to one side of the door, would jump the one that came through.

"We'll still have to face the other man," Trystan had said. "But he'll be expecting us to be unarmed. So we'll stand a chance, at least, of getting out of here."

And then he'd stopped. The next words were spoken under his breath, but Isolde had heard them all the same.

"Though if God knows what we're going to do after, I wish He'd tell us down here."

He'd not needed to spell out all the ways in which the plan could go wrong. Isolde could see them plainly for herself. If the guards didn't open the door. If one of them didn't step far enough into the room. If Trystan couldn't overpower him. And even if they managed to get free of the prison cell, they were still trapped within Tintagel's walls.

Isolde stopped herself and drew a long, slow breath.

Her scream rent the night silence like a bird's cry, high and wild. Nothing happened, and she screamed again—and again— before finally she heard the sound of the bar being lifted from the other side of the door. Isolde was momentarily dazzled by the sudden flare of light, and for what seemed an eternity she stood motionless, watching the guardsman who stood only a few paces away, peering this way and that into the darkness of the cell. Then, at long last, the guard took a cautious step forward into the room.

Isolde scarcely had time to see what happened next. In a flash, Trystan had stepped out from the corner and dealt the guard a vicious blow to the back of the neck. The guard sagged to his knees with a startled cry, and Trystan struck him again with the hilt of the knife. The man crumpled to the ground with a low moan, and Trystan straightened, knife at the ready, to meet the second guard, who had come to the door at his fellow's cry and now stood at the threshold, his own weapon raised.

There was another of those seemingly endless moments when time seemed to hang suspended. And then, with a lightning movement, Trystan bent, scraped up a fistful of straw from the floor, and flung it into the guardsman's face. Temporarily blinded, coughing and choking on the shreds of straw and dirt, the man jerked his hands instinctively to his face, trying to claw the filthy muck away from his eyes.

Trystan's second blow caught him in the pit of the stomach. His breath went out with a rush and a hard grunt; he doubled over, still coughing, and Trystan struck him again, across the back of the neck, as he had the first. The second guard, too, went down, and Trystan turned to where Isolde stood frozen in place, catching her by the arm and pushing her before him out into the corridor.

Once in the corridor, Trystan paused only long enough to swing the door shut and slide the bar into place, locking the guards inside.

"Come on. Quick, before anyone else comes."

They reached the end of the passage and took the stone stairs leading up to the courtyard two at a time. But when they reached the tower's exit, Trystan stopped just inside the doorway and turned again to Isolde.

"You know the layout of this place better than I." His voice was a barely audible murmur that carried less than a whisper would have done. "Which way is the fastest out?"

"The main gate is just ahead." She pointed into the inky darkness beyond the door. "But it's sure to be guarded, especially now. That leaves the western gate. It opens out onto the cliff path down to the sea. It's likely guarded, as well, but it's a more isolated spot and there won't be as many guards."

Trystan nodded and there was a moment's silence while

he stood scanning the courtyard outside. Then Isolde said, her voice, too, only the barest murmur of sound, "You didn't kill them—those two guards back there."

Trystan didn't turn. His body was still alert and poised for instant action or fight, but at last he said, with a faint, dismissive movement of his head, "The poor devils were only doing their duty."

He paused. Then: "Besides. Dead bodies would give away our escape just as much as live ones. And if we're not well away by the time they wake and sound an alarm, it's because we're already dead ourselves."

ISOLDE LEADING THE WAY, THEY FOLLOWED a path through the storage buildings and sheds, keeping to the darkest shadows and away from the torches that burned at intervals along the walls. A mist had rolled in from the sea, covering the light of moon and stars, and the night was damp and very dark, the biting air scented with salt from the sea below. They were within sight of the castle's looming outer wall when Isolde heard a shout from somewhere behind them and froze, the breath catching in her throat.

Three soldiers, their darkened figures blurred and half obscured by the mist, were advancing slowly on them, spears at the ready. Out of the corner of her eye, Isolde saw Trystan look from the soldiers to the outer wall and the arched gateway—just visible, now—as though gauging the distance.

Isolde thought, He's going to run. He knows—he must know—he can outdistance them. If he's on his own. If he leaves me behind. She waited for Trystan to break away, to run for the castle wall. But instead he turned his head, and his eyes, a bare gleam of light in his shadowed face, met Isolde's.

"Run. Get out of here."

She could only stare, and he said, furiously, "One of us can get free. Now go. Head south—there's a track along the coast. You'll be safe that way—the patrols never go there." Then, as Isolde continued to stand as though frozen and stare: "Run, I tell you!"

This time, he didn't wait for a reply. Instead of turning back toward the outer wall, he drew his knife and lunged toward the three soldiers, slashing viciously at the nearest of the men. For an instant, Isolde stood, still paralyzed. Then she turned and ran.

From behind her came the sounds of savage combat—the clash of metal on metal, grunts and muffled thuds—and it took all her will to keep from turning back. Ahead she could see the stone arch of the seaward side gate, lighted by twin torches, their flames glowing orbs of yellow orange against the drifting fog. And below stood a pair of soldiers stationed on guard, one on either side of the entrance. But they, too, had heard the fight going on behind her. They exchanged a brief word, then started forward, toward her, at a run.

Isolde drew back, pressing herself flat against the outer wall, heart thudding hard against her side, the stones of the wall, beaded with moisture, cold and slick against her palms. But neither man even glanced her way. Isolde risked one last look behind her, straining her eyes into the mist-filled dark, but she could see nothing. Only the vague, lurching shapes of the struggling men. Nothing to identify them. Nothing to show whether Trystan yet stood or had already been captured or killed.

Still, for the space of several heartbeats, Isolde stood motionless, hands clenched at her sides, drawing quick, shallow breaths, trying to force herself to turn away and yet unable to move. *What he did will be wasted if I stop or try to go back. There's nothing I can do for him. Not like this, on my own.*

She had started forward when a cold, wet press against her hand made her freeze, stomach clenching in fear. Then she sank back.

"Cabal," she breathed.

Even in the pale light cast by the torches at her back, she could see that the dog was thinner than he'd been a few days ago when she'd gone to Dera and left him behind in her rooms. His shoulder bones protruded sharply beneath the brindled fur. Isolde knelt, stretching out her hand, and Cabal snuffled into it, then thrust his nose against her face, whining softly.

Isolde sat back on her heels, staring at the big dog. I can't take him with me, she thought.

And yet she couldn't leave him, either. He would be starved. Or worse, she thought, remembering the testimony at the trial. One of Marche's men—or one of Nest's women—might well think to curry favor by killing the Witch Queen's demon-possessed hound.

Cabal gave another low whine and shifted his weight anxiously from side to side, his dark, liquid eyes on Isolde's face. Isolde straightened.

"Cabal, come on. Good dog. Quietly, now."

ISOLDE DRAGGED HERSELF UP FROM THE oblivion of sleep and lay a moment, disoriented, before memory returned. She sat up, pushing the tangled strands of hair from her eyes, then bent over, resting her head on her knees. She'd found the small rowboat that was kept for Tintagel's fishermen to bring the day's catch up from the sea, and had managed to row to the headland, with Cabal, huddled against the sea spray, in the prow. Her hands were blistered, and the fabric of her cloak and gown was stiff and chafing with the salt spray that had come at her over the rowboat's sides. At least, though, the clothes were now dry—dried along the way she'd come since she'd cast the boat adrift and scrambled ashore.

She had walked through the night, keeping to the narrow track that ran south along the headland shore as Trystan had said. She'd not dared let herself stop to think about what Trystan had done or why. But she'd gone the route he'd told her, running whenever she could, slowing to a walk only when her legs began to feel leaden with fatigue. And she'd met with no patrols. Only a stray pariah dog on the outskirts of one of the fishing villages she passed, that slunk away, tail between its legs, at Cabal's growl.

At the last, it had been sheer blind instinct that had kept her moving, putting one foot in front of the other. Instinct, and the pressure of Cabal's head against her leg or palm as he whined and butted at her every time she came to a halt. Finally, just as the first rosy light of dawn was breaking in the east, she'd found a sheltered place where a scrub of dry sea grass grew among the rocks. She had curled up to lie beside Cabal, and fallen almost instantly asleep.

Even now, her head swam as she sat up, tears of sheer exhaustion pressing behind her eyelids. She blinked them back, though, afraid if she let herself cry she'd never be able to stop. She'd been dreaming—a nightmare of endless narrow passages and suffocating walls—so that when the morning silence was broken by a man's drawn-out, agonized scream, she looked round, dazed, wondering whether the cry had been only a part of the dream. Then it came again, a harsh scream of terror or pain from beyond the jut of boulder and loose rock that screened the coast itself from her view. In a flash, Isolde was up, one hand on Cabal's bristling neck to keep him at her side.

The sun was beginning to set, turning the stretch of gray ocean at her back a fiery red; she must have slept through nearly the whole day. Slowly, keeping tight hold of Cabal's collar, Isolde rounded the screen of rock, then stopped short. Hereric lay prostrate on the ground, only an arm's distance away, with Kian standing over him, pinning him down.

Kian looked up, and his deep-set eyes flared wide in shock, then narrowed in recognition at the sight of Isolde.

"You." His voice was almost a growl. "What are you doing here? And where's Trystan?"

Still dazed with sleep and the shock of the meeting, Isolde said, stupidly, "He's at Tintagel. A prisoner."

"What?" Kian stared at her a moment, then, abruptly, seized Isolde by the shoulders, dragging her forward to face him. When Isolde didn't reply, he shook her, his face darkening. "Tell me! Now, do you hear?"

His scarred face was close enough that Isolde could see the individual bristles on his stubbled chin, smell the sourness of his breath.

Beside her, Cabal gave a low, rumbling growl, and Isolde said, automatically, "Hush, Cabal. It's all right."

She pressed her eyes briefly shut, trying to think. She couldn't hope to get free of Kian without telling him what had happened at Tintagel. The whole of the story, she thought. She knew instinctively that he'd wit enough to see through any half truth or lie.

And besides, there was Hereric, who now lay behind Kian on the ground, his broad chest heaving, his eyes wide open, fixed and glassy and staring up at the darkening sky. Plainly injured— or ill.

"Let go of me," Isolde said, "and I'll tell you."

Kian listened in silence, his face still a stony mask, his eyes hard and his mouth set. As Isolde finished, though, Hereric gave another of those harsh, terrible screams and struggled to his knees, trying to rise. Instantly, Kian whirled and dropped to the ground, seizing Hereric's shoulders and pinning him down again.

Hereric's face convulsed in sudden terror. His eyes widened and his lips twisted in another rending scream, so that Isolde caught a glimpse of the mutilated mouth within. He started upright once more, lashing out violently, so that Kian was nearly thrown to the ground in his efforts to restrain him.

Isolde moved toward them, and, hearing her approach, Kian glanced up, his face still angry and set. "Get away. Get back."

Isolde ignored him, dropping to kneel on the other side of Hereric.

She was able to think more clearly now, and Trystan's final words to her were echoing in her mind.

Head south—there's a track along the coast. You'll be safe that way—the patrols never go there.

It couldn't, though, be only chance that in following Trystan's direction she'd met with Kian and Hereric this way. Trystan, who would have known Hereric was injured. Who must have intended for her to find the other two men. And even apart from the look of appeal in Hereric's eyes, the leaden weight of what Trystan had done for her pressed slightly less heavily as she reached out to take Hereric's hand.

Isolde looked up at Kian again. "How long has he been like this?"

Kian was silent, but at last answered curtly, "Started last night. Fever. Got a sword cut in his side that's gone bad." Then, as Isolde reached to touch Hereric's brow: "Get back, I said! You think I'll—"

Another scream from Hereric cut him off, forcing Kian once more to turn and fight to keep Hereric on the ground. When the paroxysm had passed and Hereric lay still again, Kian was panting for breath, his brow beaded with perspiration. He turned to Isolde and said, his teeth gritted and the words spaced out and slow, "Get . . . back . . . now. You think I'm going to let you kill him?"

Isolde didn't move. "No. I think you're going to stand aside and let me treat his wound. Because unless it's tended to—and soon—you're going to watch him scream like this for hours— days, maybe—until he finally dies."

She reached out toward Hereric once more, then bit back a cry of her own as Kian seized her wrist.

"I said don't touch him," he barked. "I'll not let you catch either of us with your witch's ways."

Isolde's temper snapped. She turned to look up at Kian and said, between her teeth, "Don't tempt me. I've never stolen a man's soul or blasted his manhood before, but if you say one more word to keep me from helping Hereric, I may decide to try."

Kian's face went utterly blank, and for a long moment Isolde was uncertain whether he would strike her or cut her throat as once he'd threatened. But then, to Isolde's amazement, his eyes fell, and his fingers slowly loosed their hold on her arm.

"What do you say we should do, then?"

Isolde let out a long breath, then turned back to Hereric, laying her hand on his brow and then on his neck. In both places, the skin was burning hot and dry as parchment to her touch.

"We should get him under shelter first of all," she said. "Is there somewhere nearby?"

Kian was silent again, then said gruffly, "There's the boat."

He jerked his head toward the shore, and Isolde saw that the small painted sailboat was anchored a short distance away. Kian, following Trystan's instructions, must have sailed around the coast from where she'd first seen him and ended here.

"Can you carry him that far?"

Kian didn't answer, but he slipped his hands under Hereric's shoulders, hauling him half up, and seeing him struggle, Isolde moved to take the big man's feet. She expected an angry protest from Kian, but he only grunted and went on, his mouth tight and his shoulders rigidly set.

THE BOAT'S CABIN WAS A SMALL, square-built, windowless space smelling strongly of salt and fish. Baskets of supplies, dried meat and jars of ale, stood against one wall. Kian lowered Hereric with a thump onto a pile of skins in the corner, drawing a faint moan from Hereric before he lapsed into what looked like unconsciousness.

Cabal was at Isolde's side, whining and shifting his weight anxiously from side to side, but at a gesture from Isolde he subsided onto the floor, head resting on his paws. Isolde wiped the sweat from her forehead and looked round the cabin, shadowed, now, with the approach of night.

"Have you a lamp?"

Kian was silent a long moment, his face grim. Then he jerked his chin toward the figure on the pallet. "Why?"

Isolde didn't pretend to misunderstand. She turned, looking down at Hereric's ashen face, and gently tucked a woolen blanket around him. If she mentioned Trystan—thought of him, even—she'd be no help to Hereric.

"Because I've never in my life walked away from anyone sick or wounded. And I'm not going to start now."

Kian didn't reply, but studied her in silence a long moment more. Then, abruptly, he turned and, rummaging among the baskets, drew out a battered lantern, which he lighted and set beside Isolde.

The sword cut had, as Kian said, gone deep into the Saxon man's side. A deep, ugly wound, the skin around it crusted with blackened blood, inflamed and streaked with ominous tendrils of red. Isolde bit her lip, then turned back to Kian.

"Get some sea water. I'll use it to wash out the cut."

Kian's brow furrowed, an expression Isolde couldn't quite read on the scarred, weathered face, and then he spoke for the first time since she'd unwrapped the clumsy dressings that had bound Hereric's side.

"I've seen that done, sometimes. On battle wounds."

Isolde nodded. "Garlic would be better, but since I've no medicines here with me, it will have to do. And you'll have to hold him again," she added. "The salt will help clean the wound. But it's going to hurt him a good deal."

IT SEEMED TO ISOLDE THAT THAT night lasted an eternity, a nightmare of flickering lamplight and Hereric's searing screams, in which she labored over the wounded man with hands that grew almost numb with fatigue. Again and again she bathed the wound in Hereric's side, gritting her teeth when he thrashed and screamed at the touch of the salt water against his broken skin. She'd had to cause pain when she treated injuries or wounds often enough before, but having to hurt Hereric was somehow worse. Like torturing a child, she thought.

Toward dawn, she sat back after once more swabbing out the oozing wound. Hereric was sinking deeper into exhaustion, and he was no longer screaming, but groaning and sometimes whimpering pitifully like a wounded dog, his pale eyes fixed in mute supplication on Isolde's face. Isolde's hands shook as she pushed a lock of hair back from her brow, and sweat formed a cold trickle down her back, plastering the woolen gown to her skin.

She looked up to find Kian watching her, and to her surprise he said, breaking a silence between them that had lasted several hours, "Don't mind it, lass." His voice was gruff, but she thought the grim set of his mouth had softened slightly. "Let Hereric do the hurting. You just get on with the job."

Isolde drew a steadying breath and nodded. "We'd better change the wrappings again," she said. "They're nearly dry."

In an effort to bring down the fever, she had stripped Hereric to a loincloth and wrapped him in rags soaked with cold water likewise drawn up from the sea. He would shiver for a few moments after the cloths were wet, but so far his skin remained burning hot, the fever unbroken. At first he'd been able to take a few sips of ale from a skin Kian produced, but now, sunk in deep unconsciousness as he was, the liquid only dribbled uselessly down his chin when Isolde held the cup to his cracked lips.

They finished wrapping the freshly wet cloths around him, and Hereric's body convulsed with another violent fit of shuddering. Then, for the first time since they'd carried him aboard the boat, his eyes flickered open and fastened on Isolde's face, and his hand came out, grasping, fastening at last in a desperate grip on her wrist.

Isolde froze. For a moment, she was back in the great carved bed at Tintagel. The hand on her wrist was Marche's hand. But Hereric's eyes were fixed imploringly on her face, and so she stayed rigid, absolutely still, forcing herself to breathe, to slow the frantic drumming of her heart until memory receded, the sudden upwelling of terror and helpless rage subsiding. It's so much easier in tales, she thought. In tales, the story ends—is over, finished and done. But in life . . .

In life, she was left with a tale that seemed to repeat itself inside her, unceasingly, with every hour.

Hereric was still shivering, his teeth chattering, but he lifted one hand and made a series of feeble signs, eyes still on Isolde. Not wanting to break the moment of conscious contact, Isolde kept her eyes on his and took his other hand in her own. Without turning, she asked Kian, "What did he say?"

Kian cleared his throat before answering. Then: "He's asking if you'll tell a story for him. Like you did for Bran."

Isolde looked down into Hereric's bruised, sunken eyes, and seemed to see flashing before her the faces of all those others she'd watched die at Marche's hands. Con . . . Myrddin . . . Bran. She pressed her eyes closed a moment, and the flashing fragments of memory quivered and settled on a vision of Myrddin. Of the old man's sightless, sea-blue eyes looking up at her from above a blood-soaked white beard.

"THAT'S HER ANSWER? THAT I REAP only what I have sown?"

I watch as the king paces the length of the room, whirls, and paces again, the skirt of his ermine-lined robe billowing out behind. The marks of years—and of battle—on him are plain. A hardness about the jaw, a network of broken veins under the weathered skin.

And yet he looks not so different from the boy I saw crowned. Nearly twenty years ago.

"And is that," I ask, "so unjust a claim?"

Arthur's face twists. "Perhaps not." He gives a bark of angry laughter. "Maybe I should have listened more to the prating of the priests after all. I remember them saying something about the sins of the fathers."

And then he rounds on me, eyes suddenly narrowed. "You saw this, Myrddin. You told me that death was bred from such deeds as mine."

My brows lift. "I thought you had no faith in the Sight."

"I don't. I didn't. But—"

Arthur the King stops, an angry flush of rage running up his face. "Damn you, Myrddin, will you answer the question!"

I sigh. "Perhaps I did see. But only you can alter what will happen from this moment on."

Arthur's face works again. "You expect me to give way? Britain's High King made a common cuckold?"

All at once I feel tired. Tired and old. The calf muscles on my lame side ache with the long walk and the winter's chill.

Is fate what lies within a man? Or is his character written by his fate?

"No. I would not expect that."

A SHIVER RIPPLED THROUGH ISOLDE. MYRDDIN'S voice. She'd never heard him before. And did that mean that he yet lived somewhere beyond the western wind? Or only that he, too, was dead and gone with all the rest.

Hereric's hand still clutched at her wrist, his skin hot and dry on hers. And she could feel, still, the tiny threads of panic skittering through her blood, diminished, now, but still there. She thought of Trystan, imprisoned now at Tintagel. Or dead. The guards he'd taken on to let her escape would have small reason to leave him alive. She thought, too, of watching Brother Columba offer Trystan the healing she'd not been able to bring herself to give.

No, she told herself furiously. You're not going to let Marche take that, as well. Or claim yet another life.

She took Hereric's face between her hands, fixing her gaze on his.

"Hereric, listen to me. You're not going to die. Do you hear me? You're not going to die."

From behind her, she heard Kian make a wordless sound, as of faint protest, but she ignored him and went on, her fingers pressing into Hereric's temples, her eyes locked on Hereric's pale blue gaze, her voice fierce. "You're not going to die, because I won't let you. Do you understand?"

Hereric's fever-glazed eyes stared blankly up at her, but Isolde worked to keep her gaze steady on his, refusing to let any doubt—any fear—creep back in. For a long moment, all was silent. Then Hereric let out a shuddering sigh, his head moving in brief assent against the pile of skins.

Isolde let out her own breath and relaxed her grip, smoothing the hair gently back from Hereric's brow. "Good," she said. She took one of his hands in hers. "Now I'll tell you a tale."

She was silent a moment, hearing the faint, distant echo of that wind-carried voice. Then: "This is the story of Myrddin, whom men call the Enchanter. Myrddin, who prophesied for kings and set Arthur himself on the throne."

Hereric's mouth curved in a ghost of his usual slow, spreading smile, and Isolde wiped his forehead once more with a cold cloth, then began.

"Long ago, Vortigern, who was then Britain's High King, sought to build a tower at Dinas Emrys. But though every day his men would pile stones to build the tower's walls, every morning they would find the stones had crumbled to the ground. And King Vortigern's magicians told him that the tower would not stand until its foundations were sprinkled with the blood of a child born without a father."

Isolde paused. Hereric's lids had slid shut, and in spite of her fierce assurance a moment before, a chill ran through her as she watched the rise and fall of the big man's chest. His breathing was light and shallow, with a pause after each indrawn breath, as though his body tried to decide each time whether to stay alive yet awhile or yield.

She went on, though, telling of how Vortigern's men had found Myrddin—sired, so his mother claimed, by a spirit of air. And of how the boy Myrddin had saved his own life by proving to Vortigern that the fortress walls were shaken by the battles of two dragons in the earth below, one white, the other red.

Almost the words seemed to speak themselves through the mingled haze of her own fatigue and the hot smoke of the lamp, falling into the cabin's stillness, coiling like the chambers of a seashell, like links in a golden chain.

"And as the king and all his counselors looked on, the white dragon lashed out with teeth and terrible claws, so that all thought the red must surely be slain. But the red dragon rose up, fearsome once more. And when the battle was ended, the white dragon lay dead at the red dragon's feet. And so, Myrddin told the king, the future was foretold. The Saxons might hold sway over Britain for a time. But the red dragon of Britain would be victorious in the end."

The tale went on. Isolde's throat grew dry, and once Kian wordlessly handed her a cup of wine, but she took only a sip, then set it aside. She told all the tales she'd ever heard of Myrddin the Enchanter. Of the Pendragon and Lady Ygraine. Of Myrddin's sword test, by which Arthur, son of Uther, became Britain's High King.

Finally, Isolde stopped. The cabin was still, the boat beneath her rocking gently to and fro with the lapping waves. She was silent, remembering how, as she'd watched Myrddin walk away from her in the chapel at Tintagel, she'd felt as though she stood at the twilight of an age.

"Make up a story for me," Myrddin had said. "Make the one of the fair-folk who enchants me away a beautiful maid."

Hereric's eyes were still closed, and his face had a white, remote look that sent a fresh chill down Isolde's spine. As though he'd begun already to draw away. She swallowed hard.

"And so at last there came a time," she said, "when Myrddin's work in the world was done. And so one of the fair-folk came to carry him away. She was—"

Isolde's voice caught, and she swallowed once again. "She was beautiful. As beautiful as the spring. As beautiful as dawn. She might have taken any man to husband. But she chose Myrddin—Myrddin the wise—to dwell with her in a cave of clearest crystal deep in the heart of the hollow hills. And there are some—"

She paused, then said, her voice steady, "There are some who would say that the time for enchantments and magic in Britain was at an end. But Myrddin dwells in the hollow hills still, in a land of crystal and silver and gold. And plays his harp. And sings his songs. And those who listen may hear him yet, in the sound of the sea and the wind."

Isolde stopped and closed her eyes as the final words seemed to hang, echoing, in the air. She'd lost all sense of time as she spoke, and now the very walls of the cabin about her seemed insubstantial, shifting and strange, as though she'd crossed part of the way with Hereric along whatever path his spirit took as it drew toward realms beyond. All was silent, save for the rasp of the sick man's labored breath and the lap of the waves, and she tightened her grip on Hereric's hand as though with the touch she might keep him with them, draw him back toward life.

Then, a moment—or an hour—later, Kian touched her arm.

"He'll be all right now."

Isolde looked up, blinking.

"He'll be all right," Kian said again.

Slowly, Isolde rose. Her legs were stiff and cramped from hours of kneeling beside the bed. But when she bent over Hereric, she found Kian was right. His breathing was deep and even, and there was a glitter of sweat on his heavy brow. The fever had broken.

Isolde swayed a little, and would have fallen if Kian's hand hadn't shot out to catch her by the arm. His voice, when he spoke, was still gruff, but he steadied her and set her on her feet before taking his hand away.

"Best go get some rest. I can sit with him in case he wakes."

Isolde hesitated, but Kian had already drawn up a rough wooden stool to the side of Hereric's pallet of skins and was settling himself.

"Go on." He jerked his head at Isolde. And then he looked away and added, his voice still rough, "You've done a good night's work here."

Outside on deck, she found that Cabal had scrabbled a kind of nest for himself out of a pile of tattered sails, and Isolde lay down beside him, drawing a fold of the rough, salt-stiff fabric over them both. The dawn was just breaking, the eastern sky turning to gray. Isolde's every muscle throbbed with weariness, but all the same she lay a moment, listening to the waves lapping against the bow and staring up at the fading stars above.

The stars will still shine tomorrow.

She was thinking again, though, of Trystan sending her this way to meet with Hereric and Kian.

A verse she'd heard Father Nenian read floated through her mind. *An eye for an eye. A tooth for a tooth.*

And a life for a life? Does saving Hereric's life, she thought, do something to atone for what I did to Trystan?

Chapter Twenty-five

ISOLDE WOKE AND LAY A moment, disoriented, before she remembered where she was. Whatever she'd been dreaming of had gone—though it seemed to hang just out of reach. And as it hung there, she felt something stir behind the concealing wall in her mind.

Isolde sat up abruptly, pressing her hands to her eyes and shivering, once, convulsively. Then, when the last echoes had truly gone, she went to the cabin door and looked in. Hereric still lay on the pile of skins, Kian beside him. Both men were asleep. Hereric's mouth was slightly open, his head tipped back, while Kian sat with his chin sunk on his breast, lost in the sleep of deep physical exhaustion.

As soon as Isolde took a step toward him, though, the older man's eyes snapped open and he sat up, knife at the ready. Seeing Isolde, he relaxed, slipping the knife back into his belt.

"Soldier's habit," he said, nodding at the weapon. "Learn to sleep lightly, too—last to come awake usually means the first to die."

"Is Hereric all right?"

"Seems to be. Hasn't opened his eyes or stirred since you left him. Feels a bit cooler, though."

Isolde crossed to lay a hand on the big man's brow, then nodded. "You're right. The fever's gone."

Kian nodded. "Got some ale into him, too, a while ago." He rose with a grunt, arching and stretching his back, then shook his head. "I must be growing old. Never found it so hard to stay awake on sentry duty before."

He paused, then, with something of the gruff awkwardness of the night before, said, "Come and have something to eat. You must be half starved."

Isolde started to say she wasn't hungry, then realized that wasn't true. She was more than hungry. Her stomach felt hollow with lack of food. She hesitated, looking down at Hereric's sleeping face, the broad planes thrown into relief by the sunlight that slanted in through the cabin door. But there was little she could do for him, now. What his body most needed was rest and the simple healing power of sleep.

"All right," she said. "Thank you."

KILTING HER SKIRTS, ISOLDE WADED ASHORE to wash her face and hands in a tiny stream that ran down the beach into the sea, scrubbing the blood from her hands, combing out and rebraiding her hair. When she returned, she found that Kian had spread out a meal of bread, dried fish, hard white cheese, and ale on the deck. Cabal was beside him, and Kian was speaking to the dog in a low voice, Cabal responding with soft snuffling sounds and occasional thumps of his tail. Kian looked up as Isolde came to seat herself beside him against the rail.

"He's a good dog, this. A hunting dog, is he?"

Isolde nodded. "My husband's hunting dog—and war-hound, as well. That's how he comes by the scars on his back."

Kian's eyes went to Cabal's smoothly muscled coat, tracing the crisscrossed lines that marked the healed cuts of Saxon swords. Then he looked up.

"Heard the king your husband was a fine fighter, too. Good man on a horse, so they said."

Isolde held out her hand to Cabal, who came at once to sit beside her and press his wet nose against her palm. "Yes, he was."

They ate without speaking, the only sounds the steady beat of waves, the whine of the wind, and Cabal's contented gnawing on a bone. When Kian had done, he leaned back, fumbling for the knife at his belt, then took out a small chunk of driftwood and began to chip at it with the point of his blade. Isolde, watching, saw that it was the carved figure of a bird, the neck arched, the wings outstretched, seemingly just poised for flight.

"A seagull?" Isolde asked, breaking the long silence.

Kian nodded acknowledgment. With the tip of his knife, he started to make a series of tiny chips, creating the effect of feathers along the outstretched wings. "Can't stand the bloody creatures, really. Make the devil of the noise with their screaming—and they're forever dropping their filth all over the boat. Still . . ." He shrugged. "The wood seemed to want to take on that shape."

"It's very good," Isolde told him.

Kian shrugged again. "Picked up the habit on campaign. A good many hours to fill—not much to do between marches and battle."

"Were you in the army long?"

Kian was silent, frowning down at the little carving and flicking another chip off the unfinished wing before answering. "Enlisted as a boy. Some of the men in my unit were conscripted, but I chose to march. My father'd been an army man—fought for Agravain's father. Won his plot of land as reward for service." He stopped, lifting one shoulder slightly once more. "So I signed on to fight under the same banner."

He paused, and Isolde wondered whether he was remembering that she was, after all, still her father's child. But Kian only squinted hard at the beak of the little bird in his lap and went on.

"I fought—and I traveled. Must have marched the whole length and breadth of Britain twice over. Even crossed over to Gaul, once. When Arthur was called over there to fight for Rome."

He paused. This time the recollection of Modred's name could hardly be avoided, and there was a silence while the memory of that time and the ending at Camlann hung in the salt-scented air between them. Still, Kian didn't look angry—only thoughtful—and after a moment he went on, more to himself than to Isolde, the tip of the knife still flicking rhythmically at the carved wing.

"That's how I met Trystan—and Hereric. After Camlann, soldiering was the only trade I knew. I signed on as a mercenary to Gorlath, one of the petty chiefs in the north country. Almost Pict country—at the edge of the great Roman wall."

Isolde looked across at him, surprised. "Trystan was serving under Gorlath as well?"

Kian nodded. "Started out as a horse trainer. He's a good hand with the horses, Trystan is. He was a calvaryman, though, by the time I met him."

"How old is he?" Isolde asked. "Do you know?"

Kian frowned and shrugged. "Twenty-four? Twenty-five? He's never said. Young to be leading troops, but he's had a soldier's training, somewhere or other. And he's educated."

"Educated?"

Kian jerked his shoulder dismissively. "Can read and write and all."

"And you?"

"Me?" Kian looked surprised, but then he shook his head and said, with comfortable indifference, "Not a word. What use have I for all that? I can handle a sword and a knife and a bow and arrow, if I must. That's enough for me."

Isolde was silent, as once more remembrance—this time of where Trystan was now—hung between them in the salty air. Again, though, Kian remained silent, and after a moment she said, "Trystan has a mark of slavery, though, on his neck. Do you know how he came by that?"

Kian shook his head. "Never asked—and he's never said." He paused, beginning to carefully chip away again on the little seagull carving in his lap before going on. "We served Gorlath for some time, Trystan, Hereric, and me. But . . . well, it's not much of a life. Mostly fighting off cattle raiders and a lot of filthy tattooed Picts. Cut free after a time. And then . . . what Trystan proposed seemed as good a way of making a living as any. Fighting for whoever offered us the best pay, Saxon or Irishman or what have you." His brows drew together and he said, still speaking half to himself, "Suppose I'd a grudge against the kings of Britain, as well."

Isolde studied the weathered face opposite her, the puckered scar running like a seam down one side. "And now?" she asked after a moment. "What is it you want now?"

"What do I want?" Kian shifted positions, and seemed to consider, letting the knife blade rest idly against his thigh, eyes going distant as they looked out across the waves. "I want what I've not had these forty years and more. A settled home. A plot of land—just a few fields, enough to live on. Enough to stand on and say, 'This is mine.'"

Then he snorted and shook his head, seeming to come back to himself. "And what do I have instead? A third-part share in a leaky boat." He gestured, the movement taking in the listing mast, the slightly warped deck boards, and the ragged sails. "And about as much chance of owning my own farm as of finding a cow byre in the middle of the Irish Sea. Still . . ."

He stopped and took up the knife and the carving once more, bending again to chip at the seagull's feathered wings. "Still, I've no regrets. Trystan's a good partner. And a good friend."

The silence rested between them a beat, and then Isolde said, "Kian, I know you must blame me. For Bran's death. And now for what's happened to Trystan."

But Kian shook his head, squinting toward the line of cloud visible on the horizon. "Bran was a good lad," he said. "A good lad who deserved better than the end he got. But this is a war, in a way. And in a war there are always casualties. No point in asking why or thinking of blame. And Trystan?" He stopped again. Then, "No," he said slowly. "What's happened to Trystan is not your fault. Or rather, perhaps it is, but I don't blame you."

He glanced up at Isolde. "Suppose you acted as anyone would, thinking they'd been betrayed. But all the same, I don't believe it. I don't believe Trystan would have traded you to Marche's guard."

"Maybe not." Isolde watched a floating bit of driftwood as it was tossed by a wave, then carried to shore. "What does Hereric say?"

Kian grunted. "Precious little. He was half out of his head with fever by the time I saw him. Just said he'd been hurt getting away from the guard—and that Trystan had been the one to get him free." He paused, shifting position against the rail. "Not much you don't know, though, about a man when you've fought alongside of him a couple of years. Trystan would lie to God Almighty himself and rob Christ blind if that's what it took to live another day. But break his word? No. Still"—he paused and glanced up at Isolde before turning back to frown over his bird carving—"he made his choice to stay and let you get free. No point blaming yourself. He'd not want that."

Isolde didn't speak, but for the first time the silence between them was oddly restful. Kian nodded slowly, then looked up, answering the question she had not asked.

"I saw what you did with Hereric last night. And I'll not say you're not a sorceress yet. But maybe there's all kinds of witches in this world."

IN THE DEEPENING TWILIGHT, HERERIC'S FACE gleamed white as bone against the blanket of the makeshift carrying sledge, his eyes closed, his face twisted in a grimace of pain. Dropping back to walk beside him, Isolde laid a hand on the big man's brow, but the skin was dry and cool. At least the fever hadn't returned, though she wondered, looking down at him, how much other damage had been done by the day's long trek over rough ground.

Ahead, Cabal froze, the hair on the back of his neck rising as a black-robed figure emerged from the stone-built hut. The hut was just as Isolde remembered, nestling against the rising hill as though it had grown out of the bracken-covered slope. The small brown mule was still browsing in the paddock, the towering shapes of the standing stones rising behind, made secretive and shadowed, now, by the gathering dusk. Beside her, Kian shifted the burden of Hereric's sledge and came to a halt, frowning as he eyed the figure in the doorway.

"That's your holy man, then?"

Isolde nodded, and Kian rubbed his thumb along the length of his scar, from cheekbone to chin.

"And you're sure he'll not turn us—or Hereric—in to Marche's men?"

Isolde's muscles were aching with the long walk; her throat was dry. "No. I only think he won't. But we agreed that Hereric needs more help than I can give."

Kian hesitated, then jerked his head in unwilling agreement, though Isolde saw his hand move reflexively to the hilt of his knife. "Suppose we've no choice about it, then. Best get on."

Isolde started forward, but she heard him add, grimly, "I'll leave it to you to explain just who we are and why we're here."

But Brother Columba asked for no explanation, merely bid them welcome with the same incurious, tranquil calm he'd shown before, helping Kian to lift Hereric from the blanket sledge and carry him inside the hut. The lintel of the door was low, and both men had to stoop slightly to pass through. Isolde followed, Cabal padding along at her heels, then blinked as her eyes adjusted to the dimness within.

The hut was small, furnished with a low wooden bench that must serve as both seat and bed, a rough wooden table, and a cupboard, of sorts, that stood against the wall nearest the hearth. The rafters were hung with drying herbs, as in Isolde's workshop at Tintagel, and the air had the comfortingly familiar scent of lavender mingled with the more homely cooking smells of onions and beans. A little niche had been cut into one wall and a small altar stood within, draped with a fine white cloth and set with a pair of wax candles and a central wooden cross.

When he'd seen Hereric settled on the bench and covered with the single rough woolen blanket, Brother Columba reached for the small oil lamp that stood on the table.

"I seldom light it, unless I'm working over a preparation that needs to be tended through the night. It saves on oil. But now—"

He struck a spark and lit the wick, then set the lamp back in place and turned, his thoughtful brown eyes moving over Hereric before settling on the pad of bandages at the big man's ribs.

"Ah," he said. "Not just illness, then?"

Isolde had moved to kneel at Hereric's side and now began to peel back the cloth wrappings. The outer layers of bandage were dry, but the wound had bled again; the inner layers were wet and red. Out of the corner of her eye, she saw Kian shoot her a warning glance, but she nodded. No point, she thought, in lying when Brother Columba could recognize the truth well enough for himself.

"A sword cut," she said.

Brother Columba stood where he was, watching as she drew back the last layer of cloth, shaking his head as the ugly wound was revealed. Then he said briskly, "Tell me what you need, and I'll see whether I can find it for you. My store of medicines is small, but I think it will serve."

ISOLDE LAY CURLED BESIDE THE STONE-BUILT hearth, the echo of Brother Columba's voice, pitched in a low, musical chant, running continually through her mind. Hereric had woken while she was covering his wound with one of Brother Columba's salves, and had started up, wide-eyed and terrified at finding himself in a strange place. And Brother Columba had, with slow calm, seated himself beside the bed and begun to chant in a soft, soothing rhythm words Isolde recognized vaguely as one of the psalms Father Nenian read at Mass.

Reassured, Hereric had lain back down and had drifted off to sleep even before Isolde finished her work. He was still asleep now, as were Cabal and the two other men. Isolde could hear their soft breathing, punctuated by an occasional snuffle or whine from the dog who lay beside her, his powerful muscles relaxed. The fire in the hearth had died to embers, and she watched as a log turned slowly from glowing orange to gray to black, the edges crumbling into ash.

Isolde shifted position, then went abruptly still.

"DON'T GO, PLEASE. PROMISE ME." HER voice was almost unrecognizable.

"You know I can't."

He'd been bracing himself for anger, but instead her face went pale and all but blank with a look that was almost worse still. "This is only the beginning, you know."

"Have you . . . can you see something?" He hesitated as he asked, because she hardly ever spoke of how she sometimes knew what no human power could have shown.

She shook her head. "No. I'm afraid to try." Her face was still white and strained, and it came to him that he'd never before heard her admit to fear.

"I'm still afraid of what may happen," she said. She drew a shuddering breath and looked up at him, gray eyes bleak. "Trys, what if my father's army is beaten? What if you're killed?"

Say something, he ordered himself. Don't worry . . . it will be all right.

Any words he could think of sounded hollow in his own ears. Besides, he'd learned long ago that lying to her was wasted breath.

At last he put his arm around her, though it was scarcely ever he let himself touch her now.

"Then Arthur's armies will win the day at Camlann. And the stars will still shine tomorrow."

ISOLDE CAME BACK TO THE TINY hut and the light of the hearth and the warmth of Cabal at her side. The blood was drumming in

her ears and her throat felt swollen and painfully dry. The echoing words were gone, like all the rest, dying into the voice of
the wuthering moorland wind. But instead of vanishing entirely,
these echoes clung, sticky as cobwebs, and she felt once more
that terrifying press of memory from behind the shadowed wall
in her mind. As though the voice were there, part of the time
and the self that she'd lost, and now called her like the seal-men
in tales who lured maids into the sea.

All at once, the little, herb-scented room felt airless. Isolde
couldn't breathe—couldn't get free of the iron bands that had
suddenly fastened around her chest. Nor, suddenly, could she lie
there, still, before the hearth a moment more. She got to her feet
and was at the door and through it out into the night, stumbling
a little on the stones of the hut's flagged path. When she reached
the garden wall, a dark looming shape in the blackness of night,
she stopped and sat down, her chest still burning and tight.

At last her breathing steadied and her pulse slowed. Her taut
muscles were starting to relax, when a rustle close behind her
made her look round, expecting to find that Cabal had followed
her outside. But it was Brother Columba's black-robed figure
that stood there, outlined by the light of moon and stars.

"I was awake to sing the holy office," he said, "and I saw that
you were not inside."

He paused, his silence an invitation, though not a request or
demand that she explain. After a moment, Isolde said, "No. I
found I . . . couldn't sleep. I came out for some air."

Brother Columba stood studying her. The moon had risen,
its pale glow softening the rugged, square-jawed face and light-
ing the mild brown eyes. After a pause, he said, "I thought
perhaps you might like to join me. It's nearly the hour for the
midnight office."

"Join you?"

Brother Columba nodded. "I often go up to the stones for

the night prayers," he said. "It seems a fitting place for them, somehow."

Isolde was silent, and then, slowly, she rose to her feet, brushing crumbles of lichen from her gown. "Thank you," she said. "I'd like to come."

ISOLDE STOOD AMID THE TALL, SHADOWED god-stones, letting the sound of Brother Columba's voice wash past her.

"Sanctus Deus, sanctus fortis, sanctus immortalis, miserere nobis."

Holy God, holy and mighty, holy and immortal, have mercy on us.

There was a strange comfort in the words, as well as in being in the presence of something so old as the stones. Something that must have seen the sway of countless battles, the rise and fall of countless kings, and yet stood here, unchanged. Even the air felt strangely still, filled with a presence that seemed to wait, breath held. The presence seemed to her neither threatening nor beneficent, neither ominous nor kind. It simply was. Steady as a beating heart and with a voice as ancient as the moor and the hill and the earth itself.

"Behold, I was shapen in iniquity, and in sin did my mother conceive me. . . . Purge me with hyssop, and I shall be clean; wash me, and I shall be whiter than snow."

Brother Columba's voice seemed to mingle with the shadows and the beating stillness all about them, the low words settling into the darkness like folded wings.

"O Lord, open Thou my lips, and my mouth shall shew forth Thy praise."

Isolde had been watching the icy pale net of stars above, and it was a moment before she realized that Brother Columba had stopped chanting and was watching her, his thoughtful gaze on her face.

"You feel it, too," he said.

Isolde didn't have to ask what he meant. She nodded. "Yes."

Brother Columba turned his head, has gaze traveling over the looming stones that circled them round.

"I've often wondered," he said, "whether that's why the circle was built here. Whether this hill is a place of power. Or whether that only came later, with the stones themselves. Or," he added meditatively, as though speaking aloud something he'd gone over in thought many times before, "whether it's only that worship—worship of any kind—leaves a mark on a place that lasts long after the worshippers, and even their gods, are dead and gone."

"You think the old gods are dead, then?"

Brother Columba lifted his shoulders slightly. The moonlight carved deep shadows into the planes of his square-jawed face, making the once-broken nose look even more crooked than before.

"Dead . . . nonexistent . . . sleeping. It hardly matters. I believe in God the Father, God the Son, and God the Holy Ghost. Either I'm right or wrong. I'll find out when my days on earth are at an end. As will we all."

"I suppose that's one way of looking at it."

Brother Columba caught the dryness in Isolde's tone and smiled slightly. "In the meantime," he said, "I come here to sing the holy office. So, right or wrong, old gods or new, perhaps I'm safe either way."

In spite of herself, Isolde smiled as well. "Is there anything more left?"

"Only the hundred-and-twentieth Psalm."

Brother Columba drew in his breath, then in a low voice began the chant: "In my distress I cried unto the Lord, and he heard me."

The soft, rhythmic chant mingled and blended with the murmuring presence of the stones, and Isolde tilted her head back to look up at the vaulted night sky above.

The stars will still shine tomorrow, whatever—

Then she froze. The familiar words echoed in her mind, but in a different voice, this time. A voice she both did not know and knew.

And then, in a burst like the crack of a lightening bolt or the spark of two clashing swords, the wall of forgetfulness in her mind cracked, rumbled, and fell, and memory flooded in. For a moment, there was still herself before Camlann and herself after. But then the two halves joined, swam together, became one.

Balanced on the knife-edge moment of Trystan—a Trystan she knew as well as she knew her own self—speaking those words to her, years ago.

And then he'd gone to fight at Camlann and never returned.

It was some time before Isolde realized that Brother Columba had once more stopped chanting and was standing as though in prayer, hands clasped lightly before him, head slightly bowed.

Isolde looked from him up to the stone nearest her, tracing the line of a jagged, moonlit crack in one of the towering stone slabs, struggling to take in the recollection that had just burst upon her. She'd not chosen to remember, not sought the knowledge that now lay like a dull ache in her heart. Remembrance of who Trystan was. Why he'd not answered that question himself, that night camping on the moors.

But there's no going back, she thought. *I remember, now. I know.*

Brother Columba stirred and looked up, and Isolde drew in her breath.

"Thank you for bringing me here," she said.

Brother Columba's head dipped in brief acknowledgment,

and Isolde went on, "There is one thing more you could do for me, if you would."

"Of course, my lady. Anything in my power."

Isolde looked up at him quickly. "You know who I am?"

Silently, Brother Columba bowed his head again, and Isolde took another steadying breath.

"Good," she said. "That makes this easier, I suppose. I'd like to make my confession before . . . before I leave this place. Will you hear it?"

Brother Columba's brows drew together. "I have no claims to the priesthood, my lady. I have no authority to hear confessions—or offer absolution from sin."

Isolde made a brief, dismissive gesture. "That doesn't matter. I don't want absolution. Only for you to listen."

Brother Columba studied her a moment, and then a slight smile lightened his face.

"I can do that, my lady, of course." He gestured to one of the great stones that had fallen and now lay flat on the ground, tufts of grass growing round its sides. "Shall we sit? Unless you'd prefer to return to the hut?"

Isolde shook her head. "No. Here will do very well."

She settled herself beside him on the stone, drawing her cloak around her. There was a pool of moonlight at their feet, pale and almost liquid-looking amid the shadows cast by the stones.

"If you know who I am," she said after a moment, "then you know, also, who my father was. Modred—the traitor. Cause of King Arthur's death and seven years of land-bleeding civil war. I—"

Isolde stopped, shivering slightly, still dazed by the strangeness of remembering after having forgotten for so long—by the feeling of light and color and recollected sights and sounds where there had been only blackness. It was strange, as well, she thought, with an ache about her heart, to see her father's dark, secret, fine-boned face—so much a harsher, masculine version of her grandmother's—instead of only a name in a harper's tale.

"I scarcely saw my father," she went on. "He was nearly always away on campaign. And he was not the sort of man to concern himself overmuch with a daughter. Maybe if I'd been a boy—" She stopped, shaking her head. "But as it was, he left me for the most part with my grandmother, Morgan. People say she was a witch." Isolde moved her shoulders. "I don't know. Perhaps she was. She followed the old ways, and refused all dealings with the Christian priests. But she was a powerful healer. She used to say that if she could no longer be either maid or mother, she could still serve the Goddess as crone. She . . . taught me a great deal."

Isolde paused, for a moment feeling the rough bark of the twigs and branches Morgan had placed in her hands, looking down into the shimmering, oil-slick water in the scrying bowl. Watching her grandmother's own hands, white and small, digging plants from the ground with sure, firm plunges of a trowel. Hearing her grandmother's voice.

Beli the Great, the son of Manogan, had three sons, Lludd, and Caswallawn, and Nynyaw.

Still staring unseeingly into the darkness, Isolde went on. "I know she hated Arthur, her brother, because of—" she stopped. "But that hardly matters anymore. Any more than it matters now whether she was a witch or no. You know—all Britain knows—what happened in the end. The plague struck. And then my father died at Camlann. My grandmother and I were at the fortress there—the garrison my father had built to house his troops. My grandmother had wanted to be near him, in case—"

Isolde stopped again, her eyes on the silvery pool of moonlight at their feet. "Perhaps the Sight had shown her what was going to happen. She never said. But then, after Camlann, plague-sickness struck the garrison. It was—" Another shiver rippled through her as the newly recovered memory of that time bubbled and rose to the surface of her mind. "It was a ghastly time. The dead piled in the courtyard and burned because there were no men well enough to dig graves. The sick left to lie in their own filth because there was no one to tend them. I remember the stench of the place, still. It was said birds flying overhead would drop out of the air and die when they flew over the garrison walls. My grandmother and I did what we could, but there were only the two of us. And she was old by then. Old and tired, after Camlann. She'd lost her son and brother—and her place—all at one time."

Isolde broke off again, staring sightlessly out across the night-dark moor. "Marche . . . Marche had been given charge of the garrison by the king's council—the men of Arthur's force left alive. And he was appointed guardian to my grandmother and myself, as well. Prison warder, really," she said, her mouth twisting. "Though they didn't call it that, of course. But none of them trusted my grandmother—or me—even then."

From somewhere beyond the stone circle came the shrill cry of a night bird. Isolde shivered again. "When the plague struck, my grandmother asked Marche to let us leave the garrison. She . . . begged him, on her knees—not for herself, though. She wanted to see me safe—safe from the plague. And maybe from Marche as well. And Marche . . . refused."

Even now, a wave of bitter anger choked her at the memory, and Isolde clenched her hands on the folds of her gown before going on. "He refused, then rode off with his own men and left us there, walled in along with the sick and dying and dead. I suppose he—and probably all the rest of the king's council—hoped we'd fall ill of the plague sickness and die, as well. But—"

She stopped. Beside her, Brother Columba had neither moved nor spoken since she'd begun, but his attention was a

palpable force, his simple, undemanding silence oddly soothing. Isolde drew a steadying breath and then began again. "But
only my grandmother took ill. She was a healer, but she'd no
power to heal herself. I nursed her, but what I knew was more
a curse, I think, than a blessing. I kept her alive, for a time. But
it only made her suffering longer. She died. And it was said—
whispered everywhere—that all that had happened . . . the
plague . . . Camlann . . . all of it . . . was a punishment. A judgment from the Christ-God for her practicing sorcery and magic
arts. And if she'd been able to See the future, why hadn't she
done differently? Why make the land bleed with a seven-year
civil war? And all for nothing, in the end. For nothing."

Isolde stopped again, then went on, slowly, "I've thought
sometimes, you know, that we'd do better to worship the Satan
your holy books speak of. That he must be more powerful than
God or Christ, since there is so much more evil in the world
than good. But all the same . . . I gave up everything my grandmother had taught me. Gave up the Sight, as well."

"The Sight?" Brother Columba repeated.

Isolde moved her hand in brief dismissal. "Being able to see
things—know them before they happened. Or read thoughts.
Or watch events going on great distances away. Or hear the
voices trapped in the streams and trees and stones." She paused,
eyes on the shadowed stones. "My grandmother used to call it a
gift of the Old Ones. Passed through the blood to all the women
of our line. But all the same, it . . . wasn't hard to lose. One moment it was there, and the next it was gone. Just a kind of hollow
place where it had once come."

Still Brother Columba said nothing, and after a moment she
went on, "It did no good, though. We had a child—Con and I."
She paused, staring down at her clenched hands, the knuckles
white under the skin. Then: "It was a girl. Born dead. It seems
the God of the Christians is one to bear a grudge."

There was a brief silence, and then Brother Columba said, "Perhaps. Or perhaps He took a little angel into Heaven to sit beside Him. To escape a world of suffering and sin."

Isolde reached out and snapped off a few blades of the tough, springy grass that grew round the stone. "That's an easy answer."

Brother Columba seemed not at all discomposed. "A simple one, maybe. But so is faith. Not easy, but simple."

Isolde rolled the grass between her forefinger and thumb, the blades cool and slightly damp with the evening dew. "Perhaps." She was silent, remembering Con stumbling in, drunken and flushed with rage and striking her that single, furious blow. "Your fault," he'd shouted. "You and your cursed witch's blood." I can't, though, she thought, speak of that. It wouldn't be fair to Con. Especially when he'd dropped on his knees beside her afterwards, his face buried in the blankets, and cried, wide shoulders heaving with sobs.

Instead she went on, "I was ill for weeks afterwards with fever. It happens, sometimes, when the milk comes in and there's no babe to suckle. The midwife ... the physicians ... all thought I'd die. But then—" She broke off, seeming to smell the heavy oil and incense again, even in the clean moorland air. "Father Nenian came to read the last rites over me. To give me the sacrament, so that I might die in a state of grace and go to Heaven and the Christ."

She stopped again, her mouth twisting in a brief, bitter smile. "He probably saved my life. I didn't care, very much, whether I lived or died. But I wouldn't let myself go to the God who'd killed my daughter. So ... I lived. And I kept myself barren after that. I wasn't going to conceive another child for God and the Christ to kill."

She paused, then added softly, staring blindly into the dark, "Con never knew. It ... grieved him to think that should he fall in battle he would leave no heir to take the throne."

"And that is the sin you wish to confess?"

Isolde let her eyes travel once more round the enclosing circle of stones. She raised one hand, then let it fall. "I suppose so. Or . . . not confess, exactly. I just felt that . . . that I wanted someone to know the truth. In case I don't survive what happens when I leave here—whatever that may be."

Brother Columba shifted position, hands resting squarely on his knees. "Since I am not a priest, I cannot undertake to absolve sins. Nor even pass judgment on whether sin has been committed. I can only tell you that the moment we stretch out a hand for God's grace, it is there."

"Perhaps," Isolde said.

She could feel no real lightening of spirit, no lessening of the weight that had lain these years on her heart. But she found she was glad she had told Brother Columba, all the same.

She watched a ragged wisp of cloud drift across the face of the moon. "I'll not say you're not a sorceress," Kian had said. "But maybe there's all kinds of witches in the world." And I wish, Isolde thought, that he might be right. That I had even the smallest power to help me now—the slightest hope of defeating Marche.

The empty space within her blazed with sudden, flaring pain. And then, like a trickle of sweet, cool water, she felt something begin to flow inside. Her eyes were fixed on the patch of moonlight at her feet, and, very slowly, an image began to gather and take shape in the silvered circle of earth, just as, once before, an image of Con's war tent had gathered and formed in a fire's flames. Wavering at first, and blurred, like a reflection in water, then gradually steadying. A heavy man's dark-eyed, brutal face. Marche's face.

Chapter Twenty-six

MARCHE WAS SPEAKING. AT FIRST Isolde saw only his lips moving, and then slowly the sound grew, first blending with the soft night sounds of the moor, then rising and swelling until Marche's voice was all she heard.

You're a fool. If you'd shown any skill at all, the men would have followed you without question.

His head was thrown back, but Isolde had again the impression of nerves stretched almost to the breaking point. A boar, caught in a trap, lashing out at all who approached, be they friend or foe.

At first she couldn't see to whom Marche had spoken, but then the scene cast in the moonlit pool widened, spreading enough to show a second, younger man. Owain of Powys. Owain's handsome face looked sullen, his brows drawn together, the line of his mouth tight and turned down.

His jaw shot out in defiance. "And I suppose your men all stand square behind you in this?"

"My men know who they take their orders from," Marche said shortly. "And if there are any that disagree, they've sense

enough to hold their tongues. Besides, it's only the command-
ers that know. The rabble have only to follow where they
lead."

He stopped, eyeing Owain narrowly. Then: "You've not tried
to double-cross me, have you? Made a grab at the kingship for
yourself?"

"Of course not!" Owain's face flushed slightly, and his tone
was suddenly belligerent. "What do you take me for?"

Marche's lip curled. "I take you for a man who'd cut off his
own mother's tits if he thought it would win him an extra half
acre of land." He stopped again, then said, "You'd best not try
to betray me, though. The invasion is coming whether you keep
faith with me or no. The only difference will be what happens
to you after. The Saxons have special ways of dealing with their
captive kings." Marche's voice was soft, almost expressionless,
but some of the color ebbed out of Owain's face, and his throat
contracted as he swallowed.

"Of course not," Owain said again.

Marche studied him a moment more, then nodded, apparently satisfied. "Good. Then we'd best decide what we're to do."

Owain's brow furrowed. Then, "What about Brychan?" he
asked. "The king's men would follow him."

"Brychan?" Marche snorted. "Don't be more of a fool than
you can help."

"What do you mean? They'd trust his word, surely."

"I'm sure they would. And can you see Brychan standing up
and telling them that they were all to trot along and do our bidding like a lot of obedient little dogs?" Marche's control snapped
and he brought one fist down with a crash on a nearby table,
sending a chased golden goblet clattering to the floor. "God's
wounds, I'd have been better off making alliance with the village
whores!"

A hot tide of color—angry, this time—swept up Owain's

smooth cheeks, and his voice, when he answered, was tight. "You could make him do as you said, surely?"

Marche gave a harsh bark of laughter. "Of course I could. I expect I could make him cut off his own prick if I ordered him to it. But a leader that's been broken by torture's not likely to inspire much confidence in the men he commands, is he?"

"Well, at any rate, I don't see why the invasion's needed." Owain's tone was once more sullen. "Surely Octa—"

Marche drew a ragged breath, and said, teeth clenched, "I've told you. Octa has only enough of an army to fight the forces here. Not enough to squander on a second campaign. Now—"

And then, with a suddenness that made Isolde gasp, the scene was gone, burst like a bubble, and the pool of silver on the ground was only pale moonlight and nothing more. It was a long moment before she had her breath back, and longer before she realized that Brother Columba was likewise staring down at the place where the vision had appeared.

Brother Columba drew in his breath, like a swimmer surfacing, said in a low voice, without looking up, "I always wondered what it would be like, to be in the presence of a miracle."

Isolde shook her head slightly. "A miracle?" She looked across at Brother Columba, his eyes still focused on the ground. "You wouldn't call that witchcraft, then?"

She thought a slight smile touched Brother Columba's mouth. "Christ himself turned water into wine, healed the sick, brought back the dead. That might be called witchcraft, as well, by those who didn't believe." Then he raised his head and met her gaze, his brown eyes shadowed pools. "Magic or miracle— who can say? God gives power where—and when—he chooses. And He has promised to answer our every prayer—if not always in the manner we would wish."

Isolde shook her head. "I offered no prayer."

"No?" Brother Columba looked at her quizzically, his head

tilted slightly to one side. "But something brought you to the men with whom you now travel. Brought you to me. Brought you here, I think, to seek an answer."

"And now I've found it?" Isolde said. She was silent, her eyes once more on the pool of moonlight, now showing nothing more than the grass and the earth beneath it. Perhaps something *had* brought her to the shore the morning before. To meet with Hereric and save his life. It would be good to believe it. To believe that she herself was part of some larger pattern, as perfect and ordered as the tales she'd told.

And have I an answer now? she thought. Maybe. She could only guess at what the exchange between Marche and Owain meant. *But I do know, now, what I have to do.*

She looked up. "You realize that what happened—the vision—might have been granted by the power of the stones. By whatever was once worshipped here."

Brother Columba nodded equably. "It might, of course," he said. "But either way, it gives you a reason to hope, does it not?"

THEY SET OUT BEFORE DAWN, LEAVING Hereric still deeply asleep on the wooden bench, Brother Columba keeping watch by his side. There seemed, this morning, to be the sharp bite of winter in the air, with mist rising in curls off the gray, scrub-covered moor. Isolde kept her traveling cloak drawn close about her as she and Kian followed the track along which she and Trystan had come, Cabal padding along behind. When they reached the crest of a hill, Kian paused, squinting into the rising sun as he swallowed the last of the dry brown bread that had been their morning meal.

"Should reach Tintagel by night."

It was the first time he'd spoken since they'd left Brother Columba's hut.

Isolde nodded. "That's best, in any case. We'll stand a better chance of getting inside after dark."

She stood a moment, looking out over the stretch of moorland below, studded with marsh grass and still, glassy pools. However the vision she'd glimpsed last night had come, she somehow never doubted that what she'd seen in the moonlit circle of stones had been true.

Twice, now, she thought, I've run away. But I can't run away again.

If she was to stop Marche, it would have to be now, in the next few days. And that meant she would have to return to Tintagel, to make her case before the king's council, whether they believed her or no.

Isolde glanced at Kian, striding along beside her. For Trystan's sake, he'd agreed to accompany her, to help her get inside Tintagel's walls. For Trystan, Isolde thought, whom I have to try to set free, as well.

She wasn't sure, even remembering what she now had, whether Trystan was innocent or guilty of betraying her to Marche's guard. But she'd known since the night before that she couldn't leave him at Tintagel to die. Or maybe she'd known it from the moment Trystan had plunged into the darkness to take on Marche's guard. And that was why she'd avoided, until the night before, all thoughts of where her next steps must lead.

They had started down the steep incline, Isolde in the lead, Kian following behind, when it happened. Kian gave a sharp cry, as of pain or surprise. Isolde swung round, her blood running cold, expecting to see an oncoming patrol of Marche's guard. Kian, though, was lying sprawled on the ground, one foot still half wedged in a deep depression amid the scrubby grass.

Isolde ran to kneel beside him, and he gasped, face twisting, "Clumsy . . . fool. Stepped right into it. Rabbit hole . . . or some such."

His scarred face was beaded with sweat, and Isolde said, dropping to her knees and beginning to run her hand gently along his ankle and leg, "Have you broken something? Can you tell?"

Kian shook his head, eyes closed. "No. Not . . . my leg. It's . . . my shoulder." He spoke between harshly drawn breaths. "Goes . . . out of joint . . . now and again. Old . . . battle wound. Happened again when I fell."

Isolde's eyes went to his right arm, cradled protectively in the left, and she saw that the shoulder was twisted, set at an angle that must be agonizingly painful.

Hardly, she thought, an answer to prayer. Unless God meant to keep any besides her from dying in the attempt on Tintagel.

At her side, Cabal whined anxiously, and she put a hand on his head. Then she said, "I'll need help to get the joint back into place. I'm not strong enough to do it on my own."

She'd performed the operation before, on a few of the men with shoulders or hips dislocated in battle. Usually it took at least two, herself and Hedda working together, to pull the joint back into its socket. And despite his age, Kian's back and shoulders were as heavily muscled as any soldier's.

Kian's eyes opened at that and he scowled. "Help? And just where's that going to come from out here?"

Isolde knew his anger was for himself, not for her, and so she said, steadily, "I'll have to send Cabal back for Brother Columba, that's all."

Kian's brows rose in disbelief, but he was in too much pain to argue. Isolde turned to the big dog beside her and spoke in a low voice, holding his brindled head between her hands. Then, when Cabal had started off at a gallop, covering the ground in easy, loping bounds, she slipped the cloak from her shoulders and used it to blanket Kian, who had started to shiver convulsively.

Isolde, looking down at him, felt a prickle of fear slide down her spine. She was not at all certain, in fact, that Cabal would know what to do—or that Brother Columba would guess at what the dog's appearance meant and follow him back here.

How long they'd sat in silence she didn't know, when Kian spoke again. "Not much chance I'm going to help you get into Tintagel."

"No." Isolde looked out over the gray, barren landscape. "No. I'll have to go alone."

Kian's eyes snapped open. "Go alone? Have you gone out of your head?"

A series of memories flickered before Isolde, one by one, like shadows cast on a fire screen. Marche, chill and triumphant, accusing her of sorcery in the king's council hall. Marche, his face swollen and mottled with fury, standing over her in Tintagel's prison cell. Herself, lying in the great carved bed with its tapestried hangings—

She stopped herself, looking out at the smudge of rosy dawn on the horizon to clear the memory from her mind.

"Perhaps," she said finally. "But I don't see what other choice we have. I'll have Cabal with me. And if you give me your knife, I'll be armed, at least."

Kian's brows shot up again, but after a moment he fumbled with his good hand for the knife at his belt. "You know how to use this?" he asked as he handed it to Isolde.

Isolde grasped the hilt, and for answer sent it with a sharp flick of her wrist flying toward a tree that was growing out of a cleft in the rocks. It struck the gnarled trunk with a solid trunk and hung, quivering. She looked down, then in spite of herself smiled faintly at the look on Kian's face.

"I can juggle, too," she said. "Three balls at a time." Then she added quietly, her eyes steady on Kian's, "I'll get him back for you. If he's still alive."

There was a long moment where neither of them spoke, and then, slowly, Kian's tight mouth relaxed a fraction and he jerked his head.

Isolde helped Kian to lie back and did her best to stabilize his right arm with his leather belt so that the injured shoulder wouldn't be jarred during the wait. Gentle as she tried to be, Kian was unable to keep back a groan, and Isolde said, "It won't be long, now. We haven't come that far from Brother Columba's. He and Cabal should be here soon."

Kian grunted. "I'll do. No one's ever died of pain—you learn that much in battle."

Isolde fixed her eyes on the strip of windswept land that marked the route to Tintagel, bleak under a leaden sky. "And were you ever frightened?" she asked after a moment. "Before the battle began?"

"Frightened?" Kian gave a short laugh. "Every time. Trick is never to let it show. Convince the enemy you're not afraid, and you start to believe it yourself."

ISOLDE STOOD IN THE SHADOW OF a crag on the headland, looking across the causeway that led to the gates of Tintagel. Cabal had, after all, returned to them, with Brother Columba following as closely as he could behind. She'd left Kian in Brother Columba's care, with his face still gray and sweat-sheened, but with the shoulder pulled back into place, the arm strapped with linen bindings to his side.

Between her and the causeway lay the encampment of soldiers, the fighting men of the councilmen's armies that couldn't be housed within Tintagel's barracks. All was quiet, though here and there campfires burned among the shadowed war tents and from time to time the salty night wind carried a drift of laughter or a burst of song. The castle walls stood out, black and jagged as broken teeth against the black of the sky.

And Marche, so far as she knew, was somewhere inside.

Isolde started to take a step forward. And couldn't. Cold sweat was prickling on her neck, and she couldn't move so much as a muscle. She thought, I can't do it. The sun will come up and the soldiers in the encampment will waken, and I'll still be here. Because I can't take another step toward those walls.

And then, soft at first, then rising, she heard the voice.

I STAND AT THE KING'S BEDSIDE, looking down. He's still as death, though not yet quite gone. Soon, though. His skull is splintered, the gray tissue within laid bare.

I've thought of this moment for years. Whispered, again and again, what I would say to Arthur as I watched him die. But I feel . . . empty. A cruel trick of the gods, that when the gnawing canker of hurt is finally gone, there is a void left behind that aches as much as the wound.

The gray, puckered lids of the man before me flicker, then open, and eyes, black as my own, slowly focus on my face. A spasm crosses Arthur's brow, and his throat works.

"Morgan . . . for God's sake . . . I raised the boy. Loved him. Made him my heir. What more could I have done?"

For a moment, the furious hurt blazes again, burns bright as ever before. But then it dies to a heap of gray ash. "Nothing," I say, my voice flat. "There was nothing more."

FOR A LONG MOMENT AFTER THE final words died away, Isolde sat still, one hand clutched tight on Cabal's collar. She wondered briefly whether the voices of the past would always come to her this way. Morgan's voice again, though again the words were gone.

And yet she felt oddly steadied, all the same. Slowly, Isolde pushed the sweat-damp hair back from her brow and looked up, toward the towers of Tintagel, rising against the night sky and the moonlit sea. No other choice, she thought, but to go on.

ISOLDE LOOKED UP THROUGH THE DRIFTING mist at the castle's looming gate, at the wooden sentry boxes that dotted the battlements and the occasional guardsman passing on patrol along the top of the walls. If she had had only herself to consider, she might simply have walked openly up to the gates and demanded that the sentries take her to the council, come what might.

But I can't, she thought. Before all else, I'll have to try to find Trystan and get him free. That way, whether she succeeded or failed with the council, survived or faced the burning she'd escaped before, Trystan might have his own chance at escaping with his life.

Cabal stood at her side, head cocked, ears raised and alert. Isolde rested a hand briefly on the big dog's neck, then motioned him into position in front of the gate. Her palms were slick with sweat and her heart was beating hard, but she drew breath, scrubbed her hands across the folds of her cloak, then gave Cabal the signal he'd been taught to mean "alarm."

There was a brief moment's pause. And then Cabal threw back his head and howled, loud and long, the sound rending the night stillness, rising eerily above the sounds of the wind and the waves. He howled again . . . and then again. And then, slowly, the heavy wooden gate swung open and a man stepped out.

The sentry was one of Con's own men, though Isolde didn't

know his name. A younger man, with freckled skin and a shock of fire-red hair.

"It's the king's hound," Isolde heard him call back to companions still inside the walls. "There, now, good fellow," he said to Cabal. He held out a hand, palm up. "What are you doing out here, hey?"

Cabal, recognizing a friend, snuffled into the guardsman's outstretched hand, but he put back his ears and dug his paws into the ground when the soldier tried to pull him toward the gate.

"Come on, then. You don't want to be shut out here."

Cabal gave a low growl, and Isolde heard the guard let out an exasperated grunt. "Come out here and give me a hand with him, will you?" he called over his shoulder. "He won't budge."

Grumbling, a second guard moved through the gate. "The king's hound? What's he doing out there, then?"

"How do I know?" The first man was still bending over Cabal, trying to pull him by the collar. "Come on. We can tie him up inside and keep him with us for—"

The rest was lost to Isolde. She'd slipped through the half-open gate. Cabal would be safe. Though now, she thought, I'm entirely on my own.

Chapter Twenty-seven

H ER HEART POUNDING HARD ENOUGH to make her vision blur, Isolde reached the foot of the north tower's stone staircase and looked around a corner at the corridor that held the prison cells. Two guards were on duty, one on either side of the cell door, and a rush of relief swept through her. Trystan must be alive. He must be, she thought, or they'd not have posted a guard.

But she had still to get past that same guard. Slowly, Isolde retraced her steps, climbing to the top of the stair. Then, leaning against the cold stone wall, she pressed her eyes briefly closed. She had, somehow, to make the sentries leave their post, but her mind was a useless blank. She could scream, of course, as she had before to get free. But that wouldn't keep the guards away long enough. Then, from the stables to her right, came the soft whicker of one of the horses, clear in the night stillness, and Isolde opened her eyes.

Isolde pushed open the stable door, blinking as her eyes adjusted to the dark. The wooden gates at the ends of the stalls were closed, the stables silent, save for an occasional rustle of straw from shifting hooves, or a sleepy mutter from the travelers and poor folk asleep, as before, on the floor above. She moved softly along the row of stalls, then peered over the wooden gate at the animal within, one of Con's warhorses, a black stallion with a blaze of white on his brow.

She hesitated, feeling a moment's compunction. But the horse wouldn't be hurt, only frightened. And she could think of no other way. She set her teeth, took up the first of the clay ale pots she'd brought from brew house before coming here, and then hurled it against the base of the black stallion's stall.

Instantly, the great animal reared and whinnied, startled out of sleep by the splintering crash. Isolde bit her lip and threw another pot, then another. The stallion bucked and screamed, kicking out with its hind legs against the back wall, crashing against the stall's wooden sides as it stamped and tried to wheel round. The other horses were waking, and, infected by the black's angry fear, they began to buck and scream, too, kicking out and butting against the sides of their stalls.

Isolde heard startled shouts and muffled thuds as the noise woke the sleepers above, but she didn't wait. Heart pounding, she was out of the stables and pressed into the building's shadows, holding her breath as she watched the north tower door. All around the great court, soldiers were calling out, shouting, running toward the stables, but she stayed still, eyes still fixed on the tower entrance. It was possible—more than possible—that the prison guards might not respond to the alarm. But she'd done all she could. She could only wait.

After what seemed a lifetime, she saw the two guards emerge, exchange a brief word, then set off at a jog toward the stables, as well. Isolde didn't let herself stop to think. In an instant, she had slipped out from the shadows and was at the north tower's entrance, steadying herself on the wall to keep from falling as she ran down the stairs.

ISOLDE LIFTED THE CROSSBAR AND SWUNG the heavy cell door open. The smell hit her first. A sickening, sweet, smoky smell. Like charred meat. The rays of the torches from outside slanted through the open doorway and fell across the man, bound by heavy ropes to a rough wooden chair. Trystan's arms had been pinned behind him at an angle that made Isolde's stomach clench. His face was invisible, his head sunk on his breast. His tunic had been torn off him, and there was blood on his chest. And his shoulders—

Isolde shut her eyes briefly, then, drawing in her breath, forced herself to look again. The skin of his shoulders was raw with the raised marks of a whip, crisscrossing the half-healed scars of the earlier wounds. And interspersed with the bloody lash marks were what she knew to be burns, oozing and crusted all around with blackened skin.

She'd thought him unconscious, but at the sound of her involuntary gasp, Trystan's head lifted, and the blue eyes, dull and bleary, fixed on her face. His mouth was swollen and cut, and when he spoke his voice sounded hoarse, blurred, and almost drunken.

"Isa . . . what . . . ?"

"Quiet—there's no time."

She could still hear the frightened cries of the horses in the distance, and the shouts of men as they fought to get the animals under control, but she knew the guards wouldn't stay away long.

She knelt beside Trystan and drew out Kian's knife from the girdle of her gown. Her hands shook, so that it seemed to take an impossibly long time, but at last the ropes binding Trystan's legs slipped to the floor. Trystan's head had slumped to his chest again, and he took no notice as Isolde rose and went to work at the ropes about his wrists. Then, when his arms were free as well, Isolde took hold of his arm and shook it, hard.

"Get up. We've got to get away from here."

Slowly, Trystan's head lifted, and he blinked. Then, gradually, his gaze cleared and focused and he seemed fully to take in the fact of her presence.

"Not . . . a dream, then."

He shook his head as though to clear it. Then, more sharply, he said, "Jesus Christ, what are you doing here? You haven't been hiding in the grounds all this time?"

"No—I got away." Involuntarily, Isolde's eyes went to the burn marks on his shoulders, and Trystan's gaze followed her own. His mouth tightened.

"A branding iron," he said. "They wanted—Marche wanted—to know how you'd gotten free." His breathing was still unsteady, and his chest heaved briefly as he fought to control it. Then he went on, speaking between his teeth. "And where you'd gone. I couldn't tell them. And now it doesn't matter. Because you've returned."

His voice turned harsh with fury. "Mother of God, why come back? I told you to run—to get away."

The need for haste was a hard, constant pulse in Isolde's chest, and at that the control she'd been holding fast snapped and broke on a wave of answering anger. "And leave you here to die for me? Is that what *you* would have done?"

His eyes, hard and blue, met hers. "Obviously not."

The breath caught in Isolde's throat, but she said, shortly, "You make your choices, and I make mine. And I've chosen to come back here." She stopped. "Now, unless you want Marche to get to work on you again, get up. The guards will be back at any moment."

"Wait." Trystan swayed as he rose to his feet, his face ashen and his mouth tight with pain, but he caught hold of Isolde's arm, his grip hard and biting through the sleeve of her gown. "I want you to promise me something."

His face was beaded with sweat, and he drew a breath before going on. "Once before you gave me a knife—to use on myself as a way of escape. If we're caught—if there's even a chance we're going to be captured again—swear you'll do the same again. Leave me the knife—then run. Take whatever chance you have of getting yourself free."

Isolde's eyes moved once more over the lash wounds on his back, the oozing burns, the score marks of ridged flesh left on his wrists by the rope. She'd accomplished not even half of what she'd come to Tintagel to do, and she'd come too far to turn back or run away, whatever happened after this. But she nodded and drew Kian's knife once more from its sheath. She pressed the tip of one finger over the blade, then, with the bead of bright crimson that had sprung up, made the ancient mark of binding, first over Trystan's heart, then over her own.

"I give you my blood oath I'll leave you the knife."

A blessing, in a way, that he was so far gone in exhaustion and pain. Trystan seemed not to notice that she'd given him only half the promise he'd asked. For a long moment, their eyes met, and Isolde knew the unspoken thought was in both their minds. That these might well be the last words they spoke. Trystan started to speak, then stopped and raised a hand as though about to touch her. Instinctively, Isolde stiffened, and the moment was broken. Trystan drew in another ragged breath and turned toward the open doorway.

"All right. Let's be gone."

ISOLDE PUSHED OPEN THE HEAVY WOODEN door with a creak of hinges that sounded like a scream in the still, darkened corridor. She held her breath, but neither footsteps nor alarm came, and she pushed the door open entirely, so that a breath of the cool, faintly spicy scent of herbs washed over them from the darkness within.

"Wait a moment. I'll get a lamp lighted."

The room must not have been touched since she'd fled Tintagel. Isolde fumbled a moment in the darkness, but the small oil lamp was where she'd left it on the long wooden counter, flint and striker ready to hand. She lighted the wick, and the room sprang into view all around them. The hanging bunches of flowers and herbs, the stacks of clay dishes and neat rows of pots and jars.

She had bolted the prison cell behind them before leaving the north tower, and, miraculously, they'd met no one on the journey across the darkened courtyard and through the halls to her workroom. With luck, Trystan's escape would go undiscovered until morning, at least.

"Here—you'd better lie down." She gestured to the wooden bench that stood against one wall, covering it first with her traveling cloak before Trystan moved to obey, settling himself on his stomach with a tightly suppressed grunt of pain. Isolde, seeing his back fully for the first time, felt her stomach turn. She'd seen wounds far uglier on soldiers wounded in battle—many of them. But Trystan was right. Hurts inflicted deliberately, in cold blood, were worse by far.

Isolde moved to the cupboard and, after a moment's search, found a clay cup and a jar of wine. She poured a measure of wine into the cup, glanced at Trystan's back again, then added a measure more.

"Here. Drink this. It will help with the pain."

Trystan raised himself on one elbow to take the cup she offered, and he tilted his head enough to toss the entire draft back at one gulp. Isolde saw a brief shudder ripple through him before he sank back onto the wooden board. Silently, Isolde turned away, drawing out pots of salve and a jar of cleansing oil. Then she drew up a low stool beside the bench. Her eyes met Trystan's, and she said quietly, "I'm sorry."

Trystan moved one shoulder, his eyes sliding closed against the lamplight. "Not your fault."

Isolde gave him a painful twist of a smile. "Who else's?"

Trystan's shoulder moved again. "Mine. Marche's."

Isolde's eyes moved once more over the flayed marks on his shoulders, the burns and blackened skin. "Marche did this?"

Trystan's eyes were still closed, but his head jerked, briefly, in affirmation.

Isolde sat down on the stool, setting the pot of salve on the floor at her feet and unsealing the jar of oil. "Did he know, then, who you are?"

She saw Trystan's whole body stiffen, his head coming up so sharply that he grunted again in pain. His eyes were startlingly blue against the bruised skin.

Isolde nodded. "Yes," she said. "I've remembered it all."

For a long moment, Trystan neither moved nor spoke. Then he said, irrelevantly, "You used to tell stories then, too." Absently, he flexed the fingers of his left hand, the lamplight picking out the mutilated fingers and ridged white scars. Then he looked up again. "I slipped once or twice—called you Isa. Is that what made you remember?"

Isolde shook her head. "No. I—"

And then she broke off and froze, her heart contracting as though squeezed by a giant's hand. The hinges of the door had squealed again.

For the space of a heartbeat, Isolde didn't recognize her. Her heavy braid of hair was pinned tightly back, and she wore men's clothes. Breeches and a rough tunic, open at the throat. Then she shifted, and the rays of the lamp fell on her face, gilding the square, heavy planes of cheek and brow.

Hedda stood perfectly still, her tall, heavy form outlined in the door frame. The eyes, pale as winter ice, moved slowly from Isolde to Trystan and back again, and then she took a quick step forward into the room, shutting the door softly behind her.

It was the step—swift, almost catlike in its grace, and utterly unlike Hedda's usual deliberate, clumsy slowness—that made memory stir and then jolt with chilling clarity into place in Isolde's mind. The memory of another figure moving forward in just this way seemed to hang a moment, suspended, beside Hedda's advancing form. And then, like drifts of smoke pushed together by the wind, the two images merged and became one.

"It was you." Isolde's voice sounded strange, distant, and oddly detached, and her ears rang, as though with the steady drone of bees. "It was you I saw that night," she said again. "You killed Con."

Chapter Twenty-eight

HEDDA'S EYES MET ISOLDE'S, AND a slow smile spread over the broad, stolid face. It came to Isolde suddenly that, in all the years she'd known her, she'd never seen Hedda smile. It made her face suddenly a stranger's, and swept away any lingering doubts Isolde might have had.

"Yes." Hedda's voice was almost a whisper, the accustomed Saxon accent almost entirely gone. "I killed him. I stabbed the king through the heart. And felt nothing more than I would at wringing a chicken's neck or gutting a hog."

She stopped, pale eyes glowing, the smile frozen in place, and took a step toward Isolde. "Do you want to know how I did it? It was easy—so very easy. I knew the girl he'd summoned to his tent that night. Your fine husband the king would bed anything that moved after a battle, did you know that? We serving women used to say he'd take a goat to his tent if he couldn't get anything else. I only had to tell the girl he'd called for that night that he'd summoned me instead. And then—"

Hedda broke off. Her eyes had gone distant, but now they fastened on Isolde again. "And now you've returned here, to die as well. I'd hoped the guards I told where you'd gone would bring you back. But this will do."

Isolde saw that beside her, on the bench, Trystan had sunk back against the wooden boards. His face was hidden from her by shadow, and he didn't move, so that she couldn't tell whether he was conscious or no.

"You set Marche's men after me." Isolde was surprised to find that her voice, though still sounding strange, was quite steady. "So that's how they found me so quickly."

Hedda didn't answer, but her stranger's smile broadened.

Isolde thought, This is a dream—a nightmare. In a moment I'll wake up and realize none of it was true. She struggled to keep her voice steady.

"Why, Hedda? Why would you help me escape and then send men out to drag me back?"

Hedda's smile was gone in an instant. Her ice-pale eyes suddenly blazed, and she spat the next words. "Because I wanted you to know. I wanted you to know how it felt to be free one moment and a captive the next."

Isolde swallowed. "You must have hated me very much," she said.

"Hated you? Hated you?" Abruptly, Hedda threw back her head and laughed—a high, shrill crowing that echoed in the small room. Then she dropped her voice to a hiss. "Yes, I hated you. I hated you from the time you pleaded for my life and won me the right to be your slave." She stopped, taking a half step forward, her hands clenched and twisting before her. "Did you never think what it was like for me? I was a noble, once—a thane's daughter, with servants of my own. Did you never wonder how I felt? Dragged away from my life—my country—to be servant to you?"

Hedda's face worked, and her lips writhed, the usually still mask of her face utterly shattered.

"I'm sorry, Hedda," Isolde said. "You probably won't believe me, but yes, I did wonder. Though I never knew."

Isolde had set Kian's knife down beside the bench. She could see it out of the corner of her eye, from where she still sat on the stool; it was lying on the floor just out of reach.

Hedda was speaking again, her voice lowered again to a soft, implacable hiss. "I watched the king's soldiers raze my village to the ground. I watched my father, my brothers, spitted on their spears like joints of meat. I saw my sister's child—a little girl of seven—raped until she bled to death in the street. And I lived at your castle and brushed your hair and went with whatever man took a notion to poke his prick inside me because he'd beat me if I refused."

She stopped, her breast heaving, and Isolde forced stiff lips apart. "You should have told me."

"Told you?" Hedda laughed harshly again. "Add one more debt to owe you? One thing more I ought to be grateful to you for?"

Isolde hadn't taken her eyes from Hedda's face, but she felt Trystan stir slightly on the bench. "And is that why you killed Con?" she asked. "Because you hated me?"

Hedda's breathing slowed and steadied. "No. I killed your husband the king because it would set me free." She spread her hands over her belly, stretching the fabric of her tunic tight so that the slight bulge of an unborn child, three or maybe four months along, was plain. "Whose child do you think this is?"

Isolde had thought she was incapable of feeling any more horror, but at that, a slow chill slid through her stomach. "Not Con's."

Once more that slow, stranger's smile curved Hedda's mouth, but then she shook her head. "No. I'd like to make you think so. I'd like you to think I gave your husband the son you never could. But it's not. It's Marche's. And he's given me his word that he'll see that I and the child are made free. A trade. The life of the High King for my freedom."

Isolde forced the sickness in the pit of her stomach down and drew a steadying breath. "And how much do you think Marche's word is worth?" she asked. "A man who betrayed his own king so that he could be crowned?"

Hedda's face twisted angrily. "Quiet! You've returned, that's all that matters. And now I'm going to see you captured and burned—as you should have been before."

Isolde sensed once more a movement from Trystan, but she didn't take her eyes from Hedda's face. She shook her head and went on, regardless of the other girl's furious gaze and powerful, working hands.

"Has Marche kept his part of the bargain? Has he made any move to free you? It was all for nothing, Hedda. Can't you see that?"

"No!" The word was almost a scream. "Not for nothing! Do you hear me? Not for—"

Before Isolde could move, Hedda had sprung forward, her hands fastening like talons around Isolde's throat. Hedda's face was only inches from Isolde's own, and almost unrecognizable, distorted with hate.

"Not for nothing!"

Isolde jerked back, trying to break free, but Hedda was by far the stronger, and rage made her still stronger. Her fingers tightened. Isolde's vision darkened, but still she could hear the stream of curses and denials that poured from Hedda's lips, as though an infected wound had been lanced, allowing the poison to spew out.

As Hedda's hands tightened further, the blood roared in Isolde's ears. Her lungs felt as though they would burst. She shut her eyes, felt her lips move. Felt a flare of pain. And then—

All at once, the pressure on her throat was released. Air

rushed back into Isolde's lungs and her vision swam, then cleared. Hedda stood like a statue before her. She had taken a step back and her hands were flung up as though in self-defense. Her face, side-lit by the lamplight, had gone livid, her expression a frozen mask of horror, her pale eyes wide. She was staring, not at Isolde, but at something beyond. Her lips parted and a harsh rattle of air escaped, then changed to a high, terrified scream.

"No! You're dead! I killed you—you're dead!"

And then she moved—so quickly that Isolde had no time to react. She snatched up the knife from where Isolde had laid it on the floor and lunged forward, past Isolde, toward whatever she had seen. And at the same time, Trystan pulled himself half upright on the bench and caught hold of her as she came within reach. With a wordless cry, Hedda wrenched herself away, staggered, overbalanced, and fell, hard, against the stone floor. Isolde waited for her to move—to rise—but she lay utterly still, one hand curled beneath her, the other outflung.

Isolde's throat ached with the pressure of Hedda's hands, and she felt dizzy, still. But she rose slowly and went to kneel beside Hedda, taking hold of the Saxon girl's shoulder and rolling her onto her back. Hedda's tunic was wet with a dark, crimson stain that was spreading across her breast. She'd fallen on the knife, the force of her fall driving the blade cleanly into her heart.

For what seemed a long time, Isolde stood staring down at Hedda's lifeless body. At the slightly curled fingers, the splayed legs, the small bulge of the child. There was a trickle of blood at the corner of Hedda's mouth, but her face looked strangely peaceful. Peaceful, and younger, as well, the stolid control relaxed, the anger beneath it gone. And maybe, Isolde thought, her eyes on the still, softened face, Hedda is glad, too, that it ended this way.

Behind her, Trystan said, "I—"

And then he broke off, so abruptly that Isolde looked round

and saw that he had frozen in place, his whole body suddenly rigid, his head cocked, listening. And then she heard it, too. With the feeling of being plunged into nightmare once again, she heard voices from beyond the closed door, and the thud of booted feet in the corridor. Isolde looked from Trystan's taut face and scored, bloody shoulders to Hedda's motionless form. Then, in an instant, she had grasped the hilt of the knife and pulled it, with a grating feeling of metal against bone, from Hedda's breast. She was shuddering, but she pushed the knife into Trystan's hand.

"Here," she said. "I've kept my word. Give me yours that you'll use it only if you've no other choice left."

There was no time to wait for Trystan's reply. Isolde rose, willing her shaky hands to steady, scrubbing the tears from her cheeks. She swallowed several times, then straightened her back and faced the opening door.

Chapter Twenty-nine

M ADOC OF GWYNEDD STOOD MOTIONLESS in the doorway, backed by a handful of fighting men, and, Isolde saw, by Huel, son of Coel. For the space of several breaths, no one moved. And then, abruptly, Huel wheeled, as though to go in pursuit of help.

"No." Madoc's voice, still harsh and creaking as it had been at her trial, broke the silence, and he put out a hand, holding Huel in place. "No," he said again. "Wait."

He didn't go on, though, and neither did he move. Instead he remained in the doorway, his eyes fixed on Isolde's, scrutinizing her with an almost palpable intensity. It was Isolde who spoke at last.

"Well?" she said. "Are you going to summon the rest of the king's council? Lock me again in a prison cell?"

Slowly, Madoc shook his head. In the flickering lamplight, the burns on his face looked as angry and red as they had before, his features still twisted, dragged askew by the healing scars.

"No," he said. "At least, not yet." He stopped. Then he said, in the same painful, rasping tone, "I'll not act until you've had a chance to explain your words to me at the trial."

Isolde studied his distorted face, the eyes hard, the mouth set in a flat, angry line. She'd not looked in Trystan's direction since the entrance of the men, but she could feel his stillness behind her, feel him holding himself poised, ready—though for what, she couldn't be sure.

"Another trail, do you mean?" she said at last. "A private one, between us two?"

Madoc's shoulders jerked. "If you want to put it that way. I believe in justice, Lady Isolde, whatever I think of you myself. Therefore—"

He stopped.

"Therefore you'll grant me a chance to speak freely before you condemn me once more to be tied to a stake and burned for a witch?"

Madoc gave a short nod, though he didn't speak again. Isolde might have simply given up there and then. *For I can't imagine,* she thought, *that I've any real chance of success.* Still, somehow, in that moment on the headland when she'd heard Morgan's voice she'd put behind her all thought of surrendering or turning back. And so instead she drew in a slow breath, summoning up every last bit of courage—willing every scrap of strength into her tone. Then she looked up again at Madoc.

"Very well," she said. "A trial it shall be. Who will speak first, you or I?"

Huel had been silent up until now, but at that he stiffened. His narrow face, so like Coel's and yet so unlike, as well, still showed the ravages of grief, and his eyes were bloodshot, the lids swollen.

"Another trial? Madoc, are you mad? When you heard her confess with your own ears to her crimes?"

Isolde was about to answer, but before she could speak Ma-

doc had shaken his head. "In fairness," he said with careful de-
liberation, "she might have done that to save the life of that
woman—the whore . . . what was her name?"

"Dera," Isolde said, through gritted teeth.

Madoc nodded. "Yes, that was it," he continued, still speaking to Huel. "She might have confessed to save the woman Dera
from Marche's threat."

He paused, his dark gaze narrowing as he studied Isolde's
face. "But you also said at the trial that maybe one day I'd recognize the difference between witchery and drugs. What did you
mean?"

A man, Isolde thought, of strange contradictions. Who could
beat a child in anger, but refuse to allow a witch to be burned
without what he considered fair trail. Who could, when roused,
use language as foul as that of any foot soldier. And yet still go
daily to kneel in the chapel and hear the Mass sung.

Beside him, Huel was shifting impatiently, and Isolde saw
that the men-at-arms behind them were stirring, as well. She
kept her attention fixed on Madoc, though, willing all anger or
fear aside.

"I meant," she said, "that Marche isn't the man to leave the
outcome of a fight to chance—or to God, either. He drugged
your wine the night you fought. Surely you must remember the
way you felt after you'd drunk?"

Eyes still intent on her face, Madoc nodded slowly. "All
right," he said. "Perhaps. How do I know, though, that it wasn't
you that drugged the wine?"

"Me?" With an effort, Isolde kept the impatience from her
tone. "You can't have it both ways. Either I'm a witch and could
have no need to resort to drugs when sorcery would serve as
well, or I'm innocent of the charge. And what possible reason
could I have for wishing to see Marche crowned High King?"

"He made you High Queen as soon as he was crowned."

Isolde felt a twist of the now-familiar sickness rise. "Yes, and I ran from Tintagel before we'd been wedded even a single day."

"Enough of this!" Huel had been standing with one hand clenched on the hilt of his sword, and now he broke in angrily, his face contorting. "Do you deny you killed my father?"

"I do deny it, yes. Coel's murder, too, was carried out by Marche's hand."

"Marche?" Anger and disbelief warred on Huel's face. "Why should Marche have killed my father?"

Isolde looked at him, feeling, even in the midst of all else, a stab of pity for his loss. He was left, now, to rule in his father's place as king. And he must know well enough—as Con had known—that he'd not half the skills as leader to fill his father's place.

She said, her voice quiet, her gaze locked on his, "Listen. And I'll tell you."

SHE TOLD THEM ALL. EVERYTHING OF what Coel had discovered. What Marche himself had admitted before her and Brychan. And she told them of Con's murder, as well—though she said nothing of Seeing his death herself. Instead she steeled herself and gestured toward Hedda's lifeless body sprawled on the floor behind her and told the men what the Saxon girl had done at Marche's command.

When she had finished speaking, there was a long moment's silence. A little of the anger had ebbed out of Huel's face, though the disbelief remained, tinged now with something like bewilderment as he struggled to take in Isolde's story.

"I knew," he said at last. "I knew that my father mistrusted Marche. That he was worrying over something just before he died. That I knew. But . . ." He trailed off, gaze turning inward as though he sought to recall the details of that time.

For some time now, Isolde had sensed nothing from behind her, no movement from Trystan at all. She turned her head slightly, but could tell nothing in the shadows that flickered over that part of the room. Nothing except that he lay still, stretched out on the wooden bench.

Madoc was still watching her intently, and now he said, "It seems to me strange, Lady Isolde, that any witnesses you might call to lend credence to this story of yours are dead." He gestured toward Hedda. "The girl can hardly get up and confess to having killed my lord King Constantine. And we've only your word for what she said—and how she met her end."

Isolde looked down at Hedda's pale face, then forced her gaze back to Madoc. "Brychan—" she began.

Madoc cut her off. "Brychan, too, is dead. Killed this morning. Executed on a charge of treason by the king."

"Killed?" Huel's head came up, his attention caught by the word. He shook his head. "Hanged in the courtyard—a traitor's death. But we all saw the marks. His back had been flayed so that the skin was almost gone." Huel stopped and swallowed convulsively. "A lesson, Marche said. In what he would do to anyone that betrayed him."

Isolde stood frozen. She seemed to be separately aware of each part, each nerve of her body. The hiss of the blood through her veins. The harsh beat of her own heart. But there was after all, she discovered, a limit to how much horror you could feel. How much fear and how much sickness, as well.

But if she could feel nothing more of horror or fear, she could still feel rage.

"And this is the man," she said, her voice biting, her hands tight at her sides, "that you have chosen High King?"

Madoc's distorted mouth twisted still further at that, and he gestured toward the angry scars on his face. "If you remember, Lady Isolde, I had no wish to see Marche or anyone else crowned High King. Now, though . . . If what you say is true . . ." Isolde saw him struggling to make up his mind. To decide whether he believed her or no.

"And where is Marche now?" she asked.

Madoc and Huel exchanged a look. "Ridden out," Madoc said at last. "With his own army of men. He said he would return once he'd learned what he could of the movement of Saxon troops."

Isolde nodded. "Yes. I don't doubt he will return. With Octa and the Kentish army at his back."

Madoc gave her a sidelong glance. "So you say."

But Isolde could see both men wavering, could read the doubts about Marche flickering in their eyes. She looked from one to the other. "If Marche has ridden out, Owain of Powys is here at Tintagel still. Charge him with what I've said. Then see whether or not I've spoken true."

Madoc was silent a moment longer, watching her closely. Then, abruptly, he turned to the men at his back.

"Go," he barked out. "Go find Owain. Then summon the rest of the king's council to the council hall. This has gone too far to be settled here, among only ourselves."

When the men had gone, Madoc's eyes fastened on the bench behind Isolde, seeming to notice Trystan there for the first time.

"Who is this man?"

Isolde turned, dread rushing back in a wave. Trystan had not, after all, given her a promise that he'd not use the knife until all else failed. But to her astonishment, she saw that he'd fallen asleep, his hand still loosely curled about the hilt of the knife, his bruised face relaxed. At any rate, she thought, that makes this simpler.

She turned back to Madoc and Huel.

"A messenger," she said calmly. "From my own lands—from Camelerd. Marche's men took him on the road—tortured him, thinking he might know where I'd gone. But he must be released, whatever you decide about me. He was doing his duty, only. He has nothing to do with all that has happened here."

Madoc looked down at Trystan's sleeping face, a frown furrowing his brow. Then he shrugged.

"Well, whoever he is, he doesn't look as though he could be much danger to anyone, the shape he's in. I suppose he might as well stay here." Then he turned back to Isolde and studied her a long moment, his eyes still hostile, though the anger was now mingled with a look of intent valuation.

"You might have come before the king's council with what you've charged. Instead of fleeing—acting on your own. I fought beside your husband, as did my lord Huel. You might have trusted us with what you suspected or knew."

Isolde looked from Huel's narrow face to Madoc's burned one. "Yes," she said. "You did fight beside Constantine. And so did Marche and so did Owain. And would you call the climate of the king's council—now or at any other time—one of mutual trust?"

Madoc regarded her steadily a long moment more. Then, abruptly, he turned for the door, his shoulders twitching in impatience. "They'll be assembling in the council hall," he said. "You'll come?"

Isolde spared a final look at Trystan before turning to the door. That part, at least, of what she'd undertaken to accomplish was done, as far as she was able. "Yes," she said. "I'll come."

Chapter Thirty

A HASTY FIRE HAD BEEN kindled in the council hall's central hearth, but the room still felt damp and chill. Isolde shivered, and she saw more than a few of the men who were taking their places on the benches hunch their shoulders against the chill. Huel had taken his customary place, surrounded by a handful of his father's nobles and fighting men, but Madoc stood at the room's head. Above him was the ancient warrior's skull, grinning ivory in the raftered shadows.

Isolde, too, had seated herself in her usual place, the seat that had once been Con's. Madoc had ordered two of his own men to guard her, one on either side—which was lucky, perhaps. She saw several of those entering the hall go momentarily slack-faced with shock at the sight of her, then start toward her, stopping only when the guards, hands on their swords, motioned them back.

She was watching the door, and so saw when Owain came into the room. Madoc's men must have roused him from sleep, for his sleek hair was slightly ruffled, and the heavy gold brooch on his cloak was fastened askew. Isolde thought he might have been drinking, as well, for his eyelids looked reddened and slightly puffy.

The men who'd summoned him must have said nothing of the purpose of the night's gathering, for he appeared untroubled—faintly uneasy, maybe, as his hazel-green eyes swept the room, but nothing more. Seeing Isolde, he, too, started visibly, then, after a brief hesitation, moved to settle himself on the bench along the opposite wall.

Madoc waited until the benches were filled, the men all assembled, before he cleared his throat, drawing the eyes of everyone in the room. His burned face looked ghastly, and Isolde saw more than one of those around her flinch at the sight and look quickly away.

"My lords," he began. "When last we assembled here, it was to pass judgment on the lady Isolde." He spoke in short bursts, and Isolde, watching, wondered how he managed to stand at all, let alone hold himself erect and address the hall. He must be in nearly agonizing pain, though save for a tightness about his twisted mouth, he gave no sign. "We were asked," he went on, "to determine whether she was guilty of witchcraft or no."

A murmur, half angry, half uneasy, went around the room at that, but Madoc held up a hand and the noise stilled.

"But the reason I have called you here tonight has nothing to do with that charge. I ask you to set all question of witchcraft and sorcery aside." He stopped and directed a sharp glance at Isolde before adding, "As I do . . . for now."

There was still hostility in his gaze, and, Isolde thought, suspicion as well. But he turned back to the room at large and continued.

"Owain of Powys." His eyes found the other man. "This matter concerns you. I ask you to come forward before I go on."

Isolde saw a momentary flash of alarm in Owain's eyes, but it was quickly covered, and, with only a faint, puzzled smile,

Owain rose smoothly and came to stand near Madoc at the head of the room.

Madoc spoke slowly, his voice grating and dry, though that might only have been the effect of his injuries and the pain. He recounted the story Isolde had told, beginning with Con's murder and ending with the bargain between Octa, Owain, and Marche. He was careful, Isolde noticed, to give no hint of his own opinions, make no attempt to sway the council in one direction or another. Evidently he believed in justice, as he'd said—or at least as much justice as might be found among his listeners here.

As he spoke, Isolde saw several of the men present turn to stare hard, first at her, then at Owain, and heard low-voiced mutterings here and there around the room, but she couldn't tell whether they believed the tale or no. Owain himself, though, seemed to grow increasingly uneasy. He stood straight, head and shoulders thrown back in a stance of easy confidence, but as Madoc's slow, inexorable voice went on, Isolde saw the pose become just a little forced, saw Owain begin to shift his weight, slightly, from foot to foot.

Then, when Madoc's account had come to an end, Owain tipped back his head and gave an incredulous laugh. To Isolde, the laugh also seemed forced, a shrill note creeping in, but the frank, open look Owain gave the room was almost his own.

"And for this," he said, turning to Madoc, "you've routed us all out in the middle of the night? If you're so unlucky that you've no one to make staying in bed worthwhile, Madoc, you might at least have a care for those of us that have."

That won a burst of laughter and a few hoots and raucous shouts of agreement from the rest of the men, and, drawing confidence from the response, Owain went on. "You actually thought it worth calling a council meeting over the . . . the ravings of a known sorceress?" He shook his head. "I might be angry, Madoc—but that the charge is so absurd. I'll not trouble to deny it, that goes without saying. Still, I must object to the waste of my—of all of our—time. And to the insult of your making such a charge without a shred of proof."

As Owain was speaking, Isolde caught several murmurs of agreement from around the hall, and saw even Huel turn an angry glance at Madoc. They're going to side with Owain, she thought. Or at best, the council will be split again. Split and at odds, one with another, just when Marche's attack comes. She wondered briefly whether she would do any good by speaking or only make matters worse, but before she could open her lips to try, Madoc had once more held up a hand.

She would have expected an outburst of anger from him at Owain's words, but though his face darkened, he spoke still with judicial calm.

"I wouldn't say there's no proof. There are Marche's own actions, since he was crowned High King. You know"—Madoc turned from Owain to include the rest of the king's council in his glance—"we all know, that Marche insisted on our remaining here at Tintagel, and insisted on the majority of our forces remaining in the encampment here as well. And we all know, too, that at Tintagel we're surrounded by the sea on three sides out of four. If a sizable force did attack us here, we'd be speared like fish in a barrel."

Isolde saw Huel, and perhaps a few others, nod or at least seem to waver at that. But then Owain broke in, his voice low, almost gentle, his handsome face pitying as he turned toward Madoc.

"My lord of Gwynedd. None of us here would make light of the hurts you have suffered, and I doubt many of us could bear them as well as you have done. And I have no doubt that you've cause to feel a grievance against Marche, though you yourself joined in praying for a sign of guidance, and the answer we were given was no fault of the High King."

Another murmur of agreement went round the room, one or two of the men-at-arms thumping on their shields with the hilts of swords. Isolde saw Madoc's broad shoulders start to sag slightly with fatigue. He'd not be able to go on much longer. And it was more than possible that he'd not even have the wish to try. He'd called this meeting of the council so that Isolde's claims might have fair trial. He'd never said he himself believed that any part of her accusations was true.

Isolde closed her eyes. It would be helpful, she thought, if another flash of Vision might come to her now, with a hint as to whether she'd guessed rightly or no. There was nothing, though. Not even a flicker to aid her in what she had to do. She opened her eyes, drew in her breath, and prepared to bluff as never before.

She rose in her place, facing Owain across the room. "And I suppose, my lord Owain, that you know nothing of offering me marriage yourself? Nothing of trying to usurp the High King's place while Marche himself is gone?"

Owain had been half turned away, but at that he swung round, meeting her gaze across the heads of the other councilmen. And then, quite suddenly, the memory of what Trystan had said of Cerdic and Octa returned. They'd as soon trust each other as walk onto the battlefield with a darning needle for a sword.

Isolde kept her eyes on Owain. "There never was an alliance among the Saxon kings," she went on. "Cerdic of Wessex and Octa of Kent are enemies lifelong. They'd not trust each other— even to attack a common foe. The story was a lie. A ploy, only, to keep Britain's forces here. Marche's arrangement is with Octa alone."

Watching Owain closely, Isolde saw a faint tightening of

alarm about his mouth, but he recovered himself almost at once, turning to face the room.

"My lords, it's plain she would say anything to escape the punishment her crimes deserve. But we needn't sit here and listen to the poison tongue of a sorceress and witch. I propose we put an end—"

Isolde cut him off. "And do you also," she said evenly, "know nothing of a planned invasion of Camelerd?"

She'd been holding her breath, still uncertain whether she'd guessed the truth or not from the fragments she'd glimpsed inside the circle of god-stones. And if she'd not spent the past seven years in taking just such gambles and watching faces for just such signs, she might have missed the shock that flashed like lightning across Owain's handsome face.

"What? I don't—"

But Isolde interrupted him again, pushing the brief flare of relief and triumph aside so that she could go on. She took a step forward, toward Owain.

"Do you know nothing of an agreement between Marche and Octa, granting Octa Camelerd—and without the loss of any of his own men? Nothing of Marche ordering you to win the allegiance of Constantine's own army so that they might follow you to attack Camelerd? To defeat Drustan, who oversees the country in my place, so that the lands could be handed over to the Saxons—along with the lives of your fellow Britons here?"

She'd been moving slowly forward as she spoke, advancing until she and Owain were only a handsbreadth apart. From here, she could see the light sheen of sweat that had broken out on Owain's upper lip, and the nervous twitch of muscle about his eyes. He seemed about to step back; then, with an effort, he stood his ground, shaking his head. His face seemed to have changed, sharpening somehow as it had once before, his eyes darting from side to side like those of a rat trapped in a cage. The hall was utterly silent now, the murmur of voices and rustle of movement entirely stilled. Isolde drew in another breath.

"Do you know nothing," she went on, "of Marche accusing you of betraying him?" Isolde paused, then said, very quietly, "You asked Marche what kind of man he took you for. And Marche—Marche said, 'I take you for a man who would cut off his own mother's—'"

Owain broke. Abruptly and completely, though not in the way Isolde had anticipated he might. He made a quick, spasmodic movement of denial—and then he lunged for her, knife drawn. Isolde's advance had brought her well within his reach. She jerked back, but not in time. In an instant, Owain had caught hold of her and had twisted her around, one arm holding her flat against his chest, the other pressing the blade of the knife to her throat.

"Don't move!" Owain's voice was a ragged hiss. He cleared his throat, then went on. "Don't anyone move. One single twitch from anyone and she dies."

Madoc, standing the closest of any, had taken a half step forward, but at that he froze, his burned face blank with shock. In the moment of silence that followed Owain's command, Isolde saw identical looks of stunned disbelief on the faces of the men all along the benches. Time seemed to have slowed. The thud of her own heart seemed heavy and exaggerated, the pause between the beats unnaturally long.

Madoc was the first to recover himself. He took another step toward Owain. "Don't be—" he began.

"I said don't move! Don't move unless you want her dead at your feet."

Isolde had no doubt Owain was panicked enough to carry out the threat. He would cut her throat in a moment, whether it would aid in his escape or not.

Convince the enemy you're not afraid, Kian had said, and you start to believe it yourself.

Isolde swallowed, feeling the muscles of her throat ripple against the knife blade. "This is madness, Owain," she said. "You've no hope of getting away. Do you honestly think a single man here would let you go free for the sake of my life? Mine? You—"

"Quiet!" Isolde felt the blade bite into her skin, and a warm trickle of blood start down her throat. "Not another word!" She felt Owain's chest heave behind her as he drew a shaking breath. "Now," he went on, still breathing hard, "my own men—to me. The rest of you stand aside."

Owain must, Isolde thought, have been expecting trouble of some kind after all. As his men rose slowly to their feet, she saw that he'd brought with him a dozen or more fighting men—more by far than any of the other councilmen in the hall. They were young men, all of them, and their faces looked strained and set as they moved out of their places, hands on the hilts of their swords. Isolde wondered how much Owain had told them. Perhaps nothing at all. They'd all of them have given their blood-oath to follow him, though. To defend him to the death, if need be.

Isolde could feel the tension in the room, the lines of strain arcing the air, tight as the warp and weft of colored thread on a loom. Still with the feeling that time moved with an unnatural clarity, she watched as Owain's men approached, swords drawn. And then it happened. Huel lurched to his feet, drawing his own sword and lunging forward with a wordless cry of rage.

Whether he'd decided her life wasn't worth saving, or whether he'd simply lost his temper and acted without thinking at all, Isolde didn't know. In a flash, though, he had made a quick, sharp thrust with his sword and run the first of Owain's men through. The young man's mouth opened, his eyes widening with shock. Blood spurted from his chest as Huel jerked his blade free. And then the man crumpled to the floor with a dull, meaty thud.

Instantly, the lines of tension that had held the rest of the room still snapped and broke, the anger and hunger for violence that had simmered in the room from the first surging to the surface in a rush. All along the hall, men sprang to their feet, drawing their own weapons, even as the remainder of Owain's men leapt to their fellow's defense. In a moment, Owain's men had formed a tight circle about the fallen man, backs turned inward, hacking and slashing outward with their swords at any who approached. They were outnumbered, by far—but there were enough of them to make the fight likely to be a long and bloody one. The hall rang with the clash of swords, the furious shouts of fighting men, and high, angry screams as the wounded went down.

THEY SAY THAT WHEN YOU SET out on revenge, you dig two graves, one of them your own. Maybe that's true. For I'm dying now. My body's gone numb and cold, and there's a weight on my chest like stone.

Man and woman alike, we all come to a death. And so this, then, is mine. I wonder if all who come to this moment feel this way. As though what we'd died for wasn't worth death at all. As though we'd barter away our souls for just another day of life. Another hour. Another breath.

If all of us, men and women alike, are afraid.

A voice speaks, suddenly, beside me. Clear and sweet and low. For a moment, I can't make out the words. And then I can. A tale of Avalon, where nine priestesses tend the Goddess flame, and the grief

*of any wound can be healed. Where time is a curve, without begin-
ning or end.*

Almost, I can hear a distant chime, like silver bells.

ISOLDE WAS STILL, LISTENING TO THE echoing voice die away. And
then, with a start, she realized that Owain's arm about her had
gone slack as he watched the seething mass of fighting men, the
knife hand dropping slightly from her throat. Only slightly—
but it was enough. In a single quick movement she had ducked
under his hand and twisted free of his grasp.

"Stop!"

It was likely pure surprise that made the men stop fighting
momentarily and look up at her shout. Even Owain, reaching
for her, knife still drawn, froze in place. The pause was long
enough for Madoc, still standing close by, to come up behind
the other man and grasp him by the shoulders, jerking him
backwards and at the same time twisting one of Owain's arms
behind his back. Owain let out a sharp cry of mingled surprise
and pain, then was still.

Isolde looked over the hall, at the several men who lay already unmoving on the floor. And at those standing, panting as
they gripped their daggers and swords or pressed their hands to
bleeding wounds. She remembered Madoc accusing her, once,
of trying to cast a spell over the king's council, to trap them in a
net of pretty words.

Pitching her voice to carry to the far end of the hall, Isolde
said, "My lords, I spoke to you once before of the need to unite
in the face of a common foe. And if ever there was a time when
Britain needed such unity, surely it is now."

All about her, the men were starting to stir and shift uneasily.
Isolde raised her voice and quickly went on.

"Whatever you think of me—whatever hatred you bear me because of my father's treason—you can at least agree that it was war between my father and Arthur, Briton against Briton, that brought us to the state of siege we're in now."

She paused to draw breath. "The accusations I made against Owain and Marche are true—as Owain has just proved before you all. Marche and Octa will be upon us soon—may be moving toward us even now. If we let fighting take hold among ourselves, Britain will be blotted out entirely in the battle that is surely to come. Arthur's Britain is gone. But we can still salvage what remains—and raise a new nation on what we hold fast." She turned to Owain, still prisoned by Madoc's grasp. "Even you, Owain. You've gambled for power and lost. Do you truly want to see Britain fall entirely into Saxon hands, as well?"

For a long, breathless, silent moment, Owain's eyes held hers. It would, Isolde thought, have made for a good ending if she'd been able to read in his gaze any sign that he'd been changed— touched by what she said. But though she saw several emotions cross his face—fear . . . . frustration . . . anger at being thus found out and trapped—it was cold, hard calculation that settled in his gaze at last. Isolde could almost hear the thoughts passing through his mind, hear him deciding that his best chance of survival lay in trying to win back as much favor with the king's council as he could. And only then, slowly, did Owain shake his head.

Isolde felt suddenly exhausted, utterly spent. "Then call off your fighting men," she said. "And tell us what you know of Marche's plans."

ISOLDE SAT AS SHE HAD ONCE before, listening to the stillness of the now-empty hall, watching the fire gradually burn itself out in the great central hearth. It must, she thought, be nearly dawn. After the dead and wounded had been carried away, the council had sat for hours, first hearing Owain's testimony, then debating what measures both for attack and for defense ought to be taken in the days to come.

Now a step behind Isolde made her turn to find Madoc himself, his burned face looking as exhausted as she felt. He sat down beside her and they were both silent for a time. Then Madoc said, his mouth twisting slightly, his voice even more hoarse now with fatigue, "Strange. I won these scars in trying to prove the need for a High King was gone. And now I find that I am taking up the mantle myself."

It had been the council's final act before the meeting had broken up: the decision to choose Madoc as High King, to lead them through the current crisis and set a course as they prepared to face Octa and Marche.

And stranger still, Isolde thought, that she and Madoc should be sitting here together in the empty hall, speaking together like two survivors of a war. But Madoc seemed different, somehow. *As I am. As are we all.*

Isolde blinked the lingering glow of firelight from her eyes. "Maybe the man who makes the best king is one who would not have wished for the place at all."

Madoc frowned, but then nodded. "Maybe." He paused, then went on, still frowning, "It goes against the grain to have pardoned Owain. But I don't see that I had any other choice but to let him go."

Madoc's first act as High King had been to declare formally, with the agreement of the rest of the council, that the charge of witchcraft against Isolde was withdrawn. His second act had been to face Owain and, his mouth grim, offer him pardon, as well, in token of the council's gratitude for his having warned them of Marche's planned attack.

"You could have done nothing else," Isolde agreed. "Whatever he has done, he is still king of Powys—and we can ill afford to turn an entire kingdom against us just now. Do you think Owain's loyalty will hold this time?"

Madoc gave a short laugh. "Owain has all the loyalty of a snake. But I don't think he'll run off to join Marche and Octa, at least. I doubt he has the nerve. And besides, the rest of us will be watching him. We couldn't risk a formal execution for treason—but there are always such things as accidents. And stealth-killings, as well. He'll not dare betray us again."

Madoc was silent again, his eyes, too, on the fire. And then he turned to Isolde. "You never said, Lady Isolde, just how you knew of Owain's alliance with Marche. Or how you could quote Marche's exact words to him."

A memory rose in Isolde of the presence of the standing stones and the moonlight. "No," she said, after a moment. "I did not."

"And?"

Isolde met Madoc's gaze, and saw that the doubt and the slight, uneasy fear were still there. Diminished, maybe, but present nontheless. And she knew that he knew it, too. From outside the hall, she heard the thud of horses' hooves, the clink of bridles, and the murmurs of voices. The men were beginning to muster, preparing to ride out and meet the Saxon advance head on, as planned. In the stable yard, a rooster's crow heralded the coming dawn.

"And are you sure," she said, "that you want to ask me that now?"

There was another short silence while Madoc's eyes remained locked on her own. And then, abruptly, Madoc rose to his feet.

"Good night, Lady Isolde," he said. "Good night and thank you for all that you have done."

Chapter Thirty-one

I SOLDE WOKE IN THE GREAT carved bed in her own quarters to find pale gray morning light streaming in through the tapestried hangings. Her head was throbbing fiercely, almost as it had done after a coming of the Sight, and she had only the vaguest memory of making her way here from the council hall, and none at all of falling asleep. She'd not even undressed—she was still wearing the gown—now crumpled and filthy—in which she'd fled Tintagel, all those days ago.

Isolde pushed back the fur-lined blankets, then froze, transfixed by the sight of her own hand lying palm-down on the quilted coverlet. The knuckles were chapped and reddened, the nails still dirty and torn from her time outdoors. She moved her fingers, watching the fragile bones glide beneath the skin. She'd not thought, three nights ago, that she would live another day. And earlier, when she'd looked down at Con in his coffin, swearing that Marche would not take the throne, she'd even—if she were honest—half hoped that the fight might cost her her life.

And yet here she was. Alive. Alive, she thought. And sleeping in the queen's quarters once more.

Slowly, she turned her hand over and stared at a faint pink line across her palm, the mark of an old scar. Then she rose, going to the washbasin to bathe the several days' worth of dust and dirt from her face and hands, then shaking out a clean overtunic and gown from where Hedda had folded them away. There would be time, now, to grieve. Time to mourn for Hedda—and for Con—and Brychan and Myrddin and all the rest. And for Morgan, as well.

And time, too, to put the memories that had come back to her somewhere she could bear to keep them from now on. The memories of Marche—and the memories of all that she'd locked away those seven years ago, as well. She'd not chosen to remember. And yet, somehow, she wouldn't choose to forget again. Fragments, she thought, all of them. And for the first time since she'd fled Tintagel, she felt as though those fragments were reshaping themselves into a whole—different, maybe, but complete.

Isolde looked from the overtunic and gown in her hands to the bronze scrying bowl, still in its accustomed place by the hearth. Despite the throbbing pain in her temples, she could feel nothing now in the space where the Sight had once come—no more than she had in the council hall the night before. And yet . . .

And yet she remembered that moment in her workroom, when Hedda's hands had fastened round her throat. Her lips had moved in words she thought she'd forgotten, and she'd felt that brief, blazing flare of pain. And then—

Isolde's hands moved to her throat, touching the bruises left by Hedda's grasp. She'd not seen, herself, whatever Hedda had. But she remembered the Saxon girl's scream. *No—you're dead. I killed you.*

And maybe that, Isolde thought, is a reason to hope, as well.

ISOLDE STEPPED INSIDE HER WORKROOM, DIM and shadowed in the gray light of early morning. Her eyes went at once to the bench where she'd left Trystan asleep the night before, but the man she found there wasn't Trystan. Ector was seated with his head tipped back against the wall, hands folded across his middle, narrow chin sunk on his chest. He looked up sharply as Isolde entered, his wizened face as forbidding as ever, his mouth grim. The bandages, Isolde saw, were gone from his foot, and he wore now a pair of cracked leather boots of incredible dirtiness and age.

"Did you want me to look at your foot?" she asked him, after she'd bidden him good morning.

Ector scowled. "No, I don't," he snapped. "I'll thank you to just leave my foot alone. Wound's healed. You've no excuse to go poking and prying at it anymore."

Isolde smiled faintly. "And that's why you're here? To tell me that?"

Ector looked away at that, shifting uneasily, and made an awkward, uncomfortable noise in his throat. "Mmmph. Well." He stopped, then looked round the workroom, at the rows of salves and ointments, tinctures and pills, at the ceiling strung with drying herbs.

"Got a good bit in the way of medicines in here, haven't you?" he said abruptly.

Isolde's eyes, too, went round the room, surveying the carefully prepared herbs and cures. "Some," she said. "But not enough. There's a battle coming. A bad one—perhaps the worst since Camlann. There'll be wounded—many of them—here before long."

Ector was silent, his gaze on the floor. When he spoke, his voice was gruff, and Isolde thought there was a faint tinge of color in the wizened cheeks. "Well," he said, "they might do worse than land in your care."

Isolde smiled again. "Thank you," she said. She paused. "And you're welcome, as well."

Ector's eyes remained fixed firmly on the toe of his right boot, but the grizzled head jerked in the briefest of nods. "Mmmph," he said again.

Isolde hesitated, then asked, "Ector, did you see a man here when you came in? A tall man—badly burned about the back and arms?"

Ector grunted and looked up. "If you mean the man who was asleep on this here bench when I came in, he's gone."

Isolde stared. "Gone? What do you mean?"

Ector's face had settled into its usual dour lines, and he moved his shoulders irritably. "Gone's gone, isn't it? He woke when I came in. Asked me did I know the way to the stables. I told him, and he left. Said he was—"

But already Isolde had turned and was gone, passing through the door into the great courtyard and crossing toward the stable yard.

SHE FOUND HIM AT THE FAR end of the stables, checking the bridle on a dappled gray mare that was used by the army as a pack animal. A clean tunic covered the burns on his shoulders and back, but the bruises stood out on his face, livid patches of purple and black. Isolde approached quietly, but all the same he looked up when she was still at least ten paces away. He didn't speak, though, and after a moment Isolde said, "How did you get them to give you the horse?"

Trystan shrugged, his face expressionless. "Told them it was on your orders. The stable hands have other things to worry about just now than what happens to a lone pack mare."

"I suppose they do."

Trystan turned away, slipping the bit into the horse's mouth, rubbing the dappled neck with a practiced hand when the mare tossed her head and tried to protest. There was a moment's silence, and then he said, without looking up, "So the king's council's decided you're not a witch after all?"

Isolde crossed the remaining distance between them, smoothing a stray lock of hair, still slightly damp from the washing with lavender water she'd given it before dressing in her rooms. It still felt strange to be clean after so many days of sleeping outdoors—to be dressed in a gown not stiff with sand and dried mud.

"No," she said. "But they're willing to pretend not to believe it—for now. As you said, there are other things to worry about. More important than deciding whether I'm guilty of sorcery or no."

Trystan nodded, but he didn't speak. His head was bent to the task of harnessing the horse, and Isolde studied his face again: the sharply defined curve of his cheek and jaw—stubbled, now, with several days' growth of gold-brown beard—the slanted brows and clear blue eyes, the left one still with a fading bruise.

He looked, she thought, terribly tired. Hardly surprising, after what he'd endured these last few days. She tried to trace in his features the echo of the boy she'd known, all those years ago. Tried to fit the two images together, the boy she remembered and the man standing before her. He'd be—how old, now? Twenty-two, Isolde thought. If I'm twenty.

The silence stretched out, and then Isolde said, "You were just going to slip away? Leave without a word?"

Trystan's shoulders lifted again, and he turned, heaving the saddle up onto the horse's back in a single, fluid movement.

"What was there to say?"

"What was there—?" Isolde forced herself to sound calm—brittlely so, but still calm. "For one thing, you might tell me how it was you left me out on the moor."

Trystan did glance up, briefly, at that. "I thought you'd made up your mind already what I'd done."

Abruptly, Isolde felt the control she'd been hoarding slip from her grasp. All at once, she was as angry with him as she'd ever been.

"And do you think I should have trusted you?" she demanded. "When you didn't even trust me enough to tell me who you really were?"

And then she stopped, drawing a steadying breath. "I didn't remember you," she said, more quietly. "I've told you why. But I did remember what you told me, all those years ago."

Trystan turned away abruptly, jerking the saddle girth into place. He gave a harsh, angry laugh. "That the stars will still shine tomorrow?" He stopped and straightened, pushing the hair back from his brow. He looked at her a moment, and then shook his head. "Maybe not so much has changed as I thought. I'd no real help to offer you then, either."

"And that's why you're leaving?" Trystan didn't answer, and Isolde, said slowly, "No. It's because of him, isn't it? Because of Marche."

She saw Trystan's mouth tighten, but she was too angry to keep from going on.

"I was right," she said, "when I guessed that your mother was Saxon and your father Briton-born. Your mother was Saxon. A Saxon princess—sent to strengthen the alliance my father had made with Cerdic. And married to Marche. Your father."

She stopped, her eyes moving to the bruises on his face, the brand marks on his neck and shoulders, just visible above the collar of his tunic. She said softly, "You can't keep running away from him, you know."

Trystan swung round. "You think that's what happened seven years ago? That I ran away?"

Isolde shook her head. "No. Not then. I remember—"

She saw a muscle tighten in Trystan's jaw, but when he spoke his voice was once more taut and dangerously controlled. "What do you remember?"

Isolde closed her eyes briefly in an effort of remembrance. Those days were still a blur of fragmented memories, a jumbled haze of grief.

"It was just before Camlann," she said at last. "You left to fight, and never returned. We all thought you were among those dead—or captured."

She stopped. Even now, she felt an ache in her chest at the remembrance. When her father was dead, and Morgan taken ill, and the plague tightening its grip on the land. And then the word had come back at last that Trystan, too, was among those lost in the final battle between Arthur and his son.

Trystan's eyes were flat and opaque as blue stones, and his mouth was pulled into a humorless smile. "Captured? Yes, I suppose you could say that."

But before he could go on, the stable door beside him opened, and Hereric ducked his head to step inside. The big man's face was still pinched and gray-looking, and his steps were slightly unsteady, but the slow, spreading smile he gave Isolde was as broad as before.

Trystan drew in a breath. Then: "Rode in this morning with Kian," he said curtly, in answer to Isolde's look.

Hereric touched Trystan's shoulder to attract his attention, then made a rapid series of signs. It was a long moment before

Trystan turned back to Isolde. His eyes, weary and startlingly blue against the bruised skin, met hers.

"Hereric says he's well again," he said. "And that you saved his life."

Isolde let out a breath. For Hereric's sake—for Hereric, who was standing at Trystan's side, watching her, his broad face a little anxious—she smiled.

"I'm glad you're better, Hereric."

Hereric made another sign.

"He says—" Trystan began.

"I know what that one means." Isolde squeezed Hereric's hand and said, "You're welcome, Hereric. And a blessing go with you, when you leave here."

Then, slowly, she turned back to Trystan. Silence stretched between them once more, and something in Trystan's face made Isolde remember those echoing flashes that had come to her since first she'd seen him again. That had brought back her past, called until at last she'd had no choice but to listen and hear. Fragments . . . memories . . . of her and Trystan—years ago, she thought they'd been. Of Trystan—

She frowned, trying to call the lingering echoes back. But no. Whatever the flashes had shown her was gone, vanished as completely as the words themselves.

She had her own memories, though. Of Trystan mending a broken toy cart for her when she was small. Of taking her out fishing with him in the boat he'd made himself. Of bullying him into letting her doctor the hurts he'd show to no one else—the lash marks and bruises he'd gotten at his father's hands.

"You were—"

Isolde stopped. What had Trystan been? Her companion? The brother she'd never had? Her only friend?

She looked up into his face again, her eyes on his. "You were the only person I've ever counted on, Trys, besides my grand-

mother and myself. I won't part from you in anger now. A blessing go with you, as well."

Unconsciously, she had reached out to touch Trystan's hand
as she had Hereric's, but as her fingers brushed his, Trystan
jerked back as though burned.

Of course, Isolde thought, her eyes moving again to the
lashes of the whip, the marks of the branding iron on his skin.
He must hate me now.

And then she shivered, shocked—and frightened, as well—
by how much that realization hurt. She turned quickly away and
forced herself not to look back. She'd lost him seven years ago,
when she was thirteen, and grieved with all her heart, because
he'd been her childhood companion, her protector, her only
friend—all that and more besides. In the seven years since, he'd
changed. They both had. And she'd not expected that losing
him now, again, would be a grief almost as sharp.

She'd gone halfway across the great courtyard when a touch
on her arm made her turn.

"Kian!"

Kian's scarred face looked tight with weariness, and he held
himself stiffly, his right arm still bound to his chest by the strappings she'd tied the morning before.

"I saw Hereric with Trystan," Isolde said. "How did you get
in, the two of you?"

Kian's shoulder on the uninjured side lifted. "Easy enough.
Borrowed Brother Columba's mule and waited at the gates here
with all the others come to beg aid."

"Didn't you trust me to get Trystan free?"

At that, one side of Kian's mouth tilted in a brief, unexpected
smile, and it occurred to Isolde how much had changed between
them, too, since their first encounter in the dank sea cave, when
Trystan had only just stopped him from going after her with the
knife.

"Well, I thought maybe you'd need a bit of help, at any rate."
He paused, then said, his face again grave, "You saved Trystan. And
Hereric, as well. If it hadn't been for you, they'd neither of them be
alive now. And so I wanted to say thank you. And that I—"

Kian stopped, as though having trouble speaking the next
words. "I was unfair to you," he finished at last. He straightened
his shoulders, meeting her look squarely. "I can't take back the
things I said, when first Hereric brought you into the camp. I
can only say that I'm sorry for them. And ask your pardon."

"You have it. It is—it already was—yours." Isolde paused,
then said, her eyes on Kian's, "I can't change the past, either. Or
erase what my father did. I can only do what I can to see that the
same wrongs aren't committed again."

Kian studied her. "You mean to take a hand in it, then? In
getting ready for the war that's on its way?"

Isolde's gaze traveled slowly around them, her eyes moving
over the gray stone walls and towers of Tintagel, shrouded by
mist and echoing like harp strings with all that had gone before. With Uther's love for Ygraine, and Arthur's birth. With
Myrddin's prophesies and Modred's betrayal and war. And now
with Brychan's death, and all the others who'd died at Marche's
hands. And with her memories of Con, who'd fought to hold on
to Arthur's victories. To raise the Pendragon banner in triumph
once again.

All about them, soldiers were passing to and fro, making
ready to march out to meet the coming assault. Madoc and
Huel, their differences forgotten, at least temporarily, in the
face of a common foe, were drilling their men in formation.
Though how long the alliances established in the council hall
last night would last, Isolde didn't know. And in a corner of the
courtyard, Father Nenian stood handing out bread and mead to
the exhausted-looking travelers come to beg for aid. As Isolde
watched, a small, dirty boy wriggled out of his mother's grasp

and ran, shrieking with delight, toward the soldiers lined up with spears and swords.

The time was ended, she knew, when she could think simply of stitching one wound, setting one bone. And she was remembering, too, that moment of paralysis on the headland the night before—and been utterly unable, for that space of time, to move or go on. She'd told Trystan, just now, that he couldn't keep running away. And I'm going to have to face Marche as well, she thought. Sooner or later. It won't be ended for me until I do.

And so she nodded in response to Kian's questioning look. "I've won a voice on the king's council—for now. So, yes. I mean to do what I can."

Kian, one eyebrow raised, looked at her. "You think there's much chance of success? Of holding out against the Saxons again?"

Isolde lifted her shoulders. "There's always a chance. And we've the lady Nest—Marche's kinswoman—as hostage. Marche may be willing to come to terms in exchange for her."

Privately, Isolde doubted Marche would care enough, even about Nest, to bargain for her freedom or life, and she was silent, recalling the scene in the council chamber the night before. Nest, roused from her bed and flushed with sleep, had been brought in by a pair of Madoc's men, and had faced the council angrily when she'd learned what was to be done. But it had been Isolde her eyes had fixed on at last, her thin mouth twisting.

"It's a low, filthy trick," she'd spat. "Using a woman as hostage and bargaining piece in war."

And Isolde had nodded. "Yes. It is. And so was trying to have Dera burned for witchcraft along with me."

Isolde came back to the present to realize that Kian was speaking, though she caught only the last of what he said.

"Reckon you can do with every able-bodied fighting man.

Though it will be a day or two before my shoulder's fit for raising a sword."

For a moment, Isolde could only stare, unable to quite believe what she'd heard. Then she asked, "Kian, are you sure?"

Kian gave short nod. "Sure enough."

"Trystan—"

"Told Trystan the same. He's not best pleased, but he'll not
try to stop me."

Isolde looked into the weathered face of the man beside her,
at the scar he'd won on the battlefield at Camlann. Camlann was
over. Arthur and Modred, Myrddin and Morgan and Gwynefar
lingering now only as names in the bards' tales and, perhaps, as
voices in the wind. One age is ended, she thought. And another,
perhaps, begun.

"You needn't, you know," she said at last. "I'd grant you a
holding on my own lands—in thanks for what you've done.
You'd have your land and your farm."

Kian was silent a beat, but then he shook his head. "Farm's
not much good if the Saxons come and burn it to the ground,
is it? No. I fought for Britain once before—I reckon I can do
it again. Besides—" He stopped, and that small, unaccustomed
smile tugged at his mouth again. "Probably I'd be bored to tears
after a week of plowing and hoeing and scattering corn for hens.
Do me a favor if you'll take me on to fight."

Isolde hadn't cried last night—hadn't even cried at bidding
Trystan goodbye. But now, all at once, she felt tears stinging her
eyes.

Before she could speak, though, a powerful white-and-
brown-spotted form galloped toward her from across the great
courtyard, and jumped at her, half knocking her to the ground.
Kian smiled again as Cabal whined, thrusting his nose into
Isolde's palm.

"Looks like there's another here who'd not be forgotten."

Isolde bent, briefly, over the big dog's head, hiding her face in his bristling fur until the tears were gone. Then she straightened.

"If you're sure, then you can join and welcome," she told Kian. "We've need of every man if Britain is to survive this coming storm."

Historical Note

BOTH THE TRYSTAN AND ISOLDE legend and the King Arthur
legend of which it is a part are steeped in magic. The world
of the tales is filled with the voices of prophesy, with enchanted
swords and Otherworld women and the magical Isle of Avalon,
where Arthur lies in eternal sleep, waiting to ride once more to
Britain's aid.

In fact, if a historical Arthur existed, he was probably a
Celtic warlord of the mid-sixth century, a warrior who led a triumphant stand against the Saxon incursions onto British shores.
Tristan was likely a roughly contemporaneous warrior, possibly
the son of a Cornish petty king, whose cycle of tales was eventually absorbed into the legends growing up around Arthur and
his war band.

The Arthurian legend as we know it today is a result of
roughly fourteen hundred years of revisions, retellings, and
graftings onto the story's original frame. The version that forms
the backdrop for *Twilight of Avalon* is one of the earliest tellings
of the Arthur story: that recounted by Geoffrey of Monmouth
in his *History of the Kings of Britain*, written in the mid-twelfth

century. In this version, the now-famous Guinevere-Lancelot-
Arthur love triangle does not exist; in fact, Lancelot is not yet
even present as one of Arthur's fighting men. Instead, it is Modred, Arthur's nephew and heir, who betrays the king by seizing
both Guinevere and the throne.

Likewise, I have taken the earliest reference to the historical
figures of Tristan and Marche as the basis for the characters in
my story; this is a memorial stone in Cornwall with the inscrip-
tion *Drustans hic iacet Cunomori filius,* which means "Drustanus
lies here, the son of Cunomorus." Many scholars have plausibly suggested that the characters referred to are the Tristan and
King Mark of later medieval tales, Drustanus being a recognized variant of the name Tristan (or Trystan) and Cunomorus
being the Latinized version of the name Cynvawr, identified by
the ninth-century historian Nennius with King Mark.

Beyond that single reference, though, almost nothing is
known of the historical figures who inspired the later tales of
romance centering on the love triangle between Tristan, Isolde,
and King Mark, tales now widely known through poetry, paint-
ing, opera, and even popular film. I have given the characters a
story which, beyond names and a few basic structural points,
bears small resemblance to these tales, but which I felt might
plausibly—or at least conceivably—have formed the foundation
on which the later stories were laid.

The other characters in *Twilight of Avalon* are entirely fic-
tional, barring Madoc of Gwynedd, who is loosely based on
Maelgwn Gwynedd, the sixth-century king of what is now
North Wales, and Myrddin, who may indeed have been a famed
Welsh bard. Apart from these, though, *Twilight of Avalon*'s Britain is a blending of legend and truth, an attempt to portray the
historical world of sixth-century Cornwall while still honoring
the legends that are, after centuries of telling and retelling, as
real as historical fact.

Acknowledgments

THE AUTHOR WOULD LIKE TO thank the following:
    My daughter, Isabella, who was born halfway through the first draft of this book, for being such an incredibly good sleeper and all-around great kid—without your kind cooperation, I could never have gotten through several more drafts and found both an agent and a publisher all before your first birthday. My husband, Nathan, who has provided peerless technical support and every other kind of support imaginable for the last ten years—but then, you always knew marrying an English major would pay off, didn't you? My mom and dad, who have been my own personal editors, cheerleaders, babysitters, chauffeurs, and fashion consultants ever since this journey began. Sarah, my writing partner and personal encyclopedia of all things historical. Cindy and baby Michael, for wardrobe and technical assistance. David Nash Ford, whose excellent website www.earlybritishkingdoms.com was of tremendous help in creating a plausible geography for Britain in the mid sixth century. My superb agent Jacques de Spoelberch, who offered incredibly keen and helpful editorial advice, guided me through every step of the submission and publication process, and every time we spoke made me feel like I was his only client, though of course

he has many, many more. And last, but by no means least, my wonderful editor Danielle Friedman, whose insights and enthusiasm were an invaluable guide, and without whom I would never have uncovered the book I'd intended to write all along.

Thank you all.

Twilight of Avalon

For Discussion

1.   In the prologue Morgan says, "If a soul lives with each mention of its name, I will be forever young and beautiful as the Morgan in tales" (page 5). How can storytelling keep a person alive?

2.   Throughout the novel various men offer Isolde protection. What protection can a man offer her physically? Politically? Do you think she needs a man to protect her?

3.   The story takes place during the early years of Christianity in Europe. How did this affect the action of the story? Where do you think Isolde stands in terms of religious beliefs? How do you think the emerging Christianity contributed to the fear that she was a witch?

4.   From the moment Con dies all of the men begin treating Isolde differently. Does her role as queen offer her any protection? At what times does her life seem to have worth? When does she seem disposable?

5.   The phrase "The stars will still shine tomorrow, whatever happens to me here" is repeated throughout the story. How did this phrase help Isolde find hope? What do you think it means? How did learning who originally said it to her change it's meaning for you?

6. Isolde says that "No man is evil to himself, he will always find reason enough to justify his acts, at least in his own mind" (page 136). How did men in this novel seem to justify their acts? Do you agree with Isolde's statement above?

7. After Dera loses her baby Isolde recommends that she "listen to the pain. It will never go away. But listen to it, and it dulls enough that you can keep living, after a time" (page 197). How could Isolde benefit from taking her own advice? Have you found that paying attention to emotional pain helps to diminish it? What result can come from masking or ignoring the pain?

8. Isolde is widely believed to be a sorceress and has even been dubbed the "Witch Queen." Does she use the speculation to her advantage? Kian says "Maybe there's all kinds of witches in this world" (page 355). What kind of witch do you consider Isolde?

9. During a conversation with Arthur, Myrddin wonders, "is fate what lies within a man? Or is his character written by his fate?" (page 344). How do you think the various characters in *Twilight of Avalon* would answer this question?

A Conversation with Anna Elliott

Stories of Trystan and Isolde have been told for generations. What was your first experience with these characters? What made you want to create your own story for them?
I first encountered the both the Trystan and Isolde legends and the Arthurian legends of which they are a part in college. I was studying medieval literature, and completely fell in love with everything about the Arthurian world. But it was a bit of an accident that I ended up weaving the two legends together in the way I did.

Twilight of Avalon was inspired by a very vivid dream in which I told my mother that I was going to write a book about Modred's daughter. When I woke up, the idea just wouldn't let me go. Then in the very early stages of outlining, when I was just beginning to get an idea of the shape of the story, I was looking at Celtic names for my protagonist. The name Isolde caught my eye and I thought, hmm . . . and began to realize how many aspects of my story already fitted with the Trystan and Isolde legend. So blending the two together just felt completely natural from then on.

Why did you decide to tell the story from Isolde's point of view? How might the story have read differently from one of the male characters viewpoints? Do you consider Isolde a feminist?

As I mentioned above, the idea of writing a book about Modred's daughter was inspired by a dream, and then once I started to think about the story it just came to life in my head as Isolde's own very personal journey. Because of that and because of being so bound up in Isolde's character as I was writing, it's hard for me to even imagine how the story would read from anyone else's point of view. Although the next book in the trilogy, *Dark Moon of Avalon,* alternates between Isolde and Trystan's perspectives, and it was great fun for me to step outside of Isolde's character and see her through someone else's eyes.

To me, a feminist means someone who fights for the right of *choice* for women: someone who believes that women should be allowed the freedom to make the choices that determine the course of their lives. I would consider Isolde a feminist of her time.

Each chapter features a small drawing of a harp as a recurring symbol. Why did you want us to remember this harp throughout the novel?

To me, the harp was a symbol of storytelling, which was one of the major themes of the book, from the voices of the past that come to Isolde, to the stories that Isolde herself tells, to the Trystan and Isolde legend itself. Both the Arthur legends and the Trystan and Isolde stories had their roots in Celtic bard's songs, which would have been orally transmitted for perhaps hundreds of years before finally being written down. I found that to be one of the most poignant aspects of retelling the legends: the sense that I was catching just a faint echo of a real, human voice from a world that now existed only within the tales themselves.

Like all great historical novels, *Twilight of Avalon* blends well-known legend with original fiction. How did you try to stay true to the characters of Trystan and Isolde established in the centuries-old legends? What about your story is completely unique and original?

Obviously, my version of the Trystan and Isolde story is very different from, say, the version popularized by Wagner's opera. The legend as we know it today is very much a product of the courtly medieval style of literature, very much grounded in and shaped by chivalry and knightly honor and that sort of thing. The story really reflects a twelfth or thirteenth century world and sensibility, which doesn't work so well when you try to drop it into sixth century Britain, which is when the real Arthur, the real Marche and Trystan (if any of them actually were real) would have lived. So that was really why I wound up being fairly free in my adaptation of the legend: to make it belong better to the world of dark age Britain I was uncovering—and falling in love with—in my research. I did, though, try to be faithful to what seemed to me the most important plot elements of the original stories: Isolde's skill as a healer, Trystan's role as a mercenary soldier, Isolde's marriage to Marche, etc.

Why did you choose to title the novel *Twilight of Avalon*? What does the location Avalon mean for Arthurian legend?

In Arthurian legend, the dying King Arthur is ferried away to be healed of his wounds on the magical, mist-shrouded Isle of Avalon, and for me, Avalon symbolizes the unique magic that lies at the heart of the Arthurian tales. I chose the title *Twilight of Avalon*, because it captured my sense of Trystan and Isolde's

Britain: a place in which Arthur has been killed at Camlann, and the magic of his world is fading from the land. I liked the double meaning of the title, too. On the one hand, it could seem a bit sad: the end of an era, a farewell to all that has gone before. But though we in America usually think of twilight as the end of today, there are many cultures around the world in which evening is seen instead as the beginning of tomorrow.

What can we expect in the next installment of the series?
At the time of writing, I've completed *Dark Moon of Avalon*, the second book of the series, and am currently at work on *Sunrise of Avalon*, the third and final volume of my Trystan and Isolde trilogy. In *Dark Moon of Avalon*, Isolde is sent on a dangerous journey as emissary to one of her father Modred's former allies in a desperate bid to gain support for Britain's forces. The book alternates between Trystan and Isolde's viewpoints, so expect to see them deepen and develop their relationship as Isolde begins to truly heal from the events of *Twilight of Avalon*.

Enhance Your Book Club

1.   Read more about the enduring legend of Trystan and Isolde: http://en.wikipedia.org/wiki/Tristan_and_Iseult

2.   Visit www.EarlyBritishKingdoms.com for a more well-rounded understanding of the setting for the novel. The author credits the site in her Acknowledgments section!

3.   Have a movie night with your book club and watch the 2006 film *Tristan and Isolde*. Which actors would you cast to play Trystan and Isolde if *Twilight of Avalon* were made into a film?

4.   Isolde is skilled at using herbs to help treat the sick and injured. Do you know of any home remedies or natural cures you can share with the group?

Continue the romance in

The Dark Moon of Avalon,

coming in Spring 2010.

 **TOUCHSTONE**
A Division of Simon & Schuster
A CBS COMPANY